MW00939106

The Butcher's Cleaver

The Butcher's Cleaver

✦

(A Tale of the Confederate Secret Services.)

W. Patrick Lang

iUniverse, Inc.

New York Lincoln Shanghai

The Butcher's Cleaver
(A Tale of the Confederate Secret Services.)

Copyright © 2007 by Walter Patrick Lang

All rights reserved. No part of this book may be used or reproduced by any means, graphic, electronic, or mechanical, including photocopying, recording, taping or by any information storage retrieval system without the written permission of the publisher except in the case of brief quotations embodied in critical articles and reviews.

iUniverse books may be ordered through booksellers or by contacting:

iUniverse
2021 Pine Lake Road, Suite 100
Lincoln, NE 68512
www.iuniverse.com
1-800-Authors (1-800-288-4677)

Because of the dynamic nature of the Internet, any Web addresses or links contained in this book may have changed since publication and may no longer be valid.

Certain characters in this work are historical figures, and certain events portrayed did take place. However, this is a work of fiction. All of the other characters, names, and events as well as all places, incidents, organizations, and dialogue in this novel are either the products of the author's imagination or are used fictitiously.

ISBN: 978-0-595-47476-9 (pbk)
ISBN: 978-0-595-71185-7 (cloth)
ISBN: 978-0-595-91747-1 (ebk)

Printed in the United States of America

For

Judah Philip Benjamin

A Most Remarkable Man

Ole Missus married Will de weever.
Will'um was a gay deceiver.
Look away, look away, look away
    Dixie Land.
He allus' said he meant to please'er, but he had a face like a butcher's cleaver.
Look away, look away, look away,
    Dixie Land.

    Dan Emmet.

Foreword

At the beginning of 1863, the Great War known in the North as "The Rebellion" and in the South as the "Second Revolution" was in equilibrium. Armies had been formed, great battles had been fought, but the North had not yet been able to translate its massive strength into effective military power, power that could crush all before it. The South had surprised and shaken the world with the ferocity of its resistance to invasion and the fighting quality of its smaller forces.

The outcome hung in the balance. Both sides were conditioned by the wisdom of the age to seek decision in a climactic battle of annihilation. The combatants were only slowly coming to the conclusion that the numbers of men available for slaughter and the sheer scale of the murderous combats would decide the issue by attrition. This was not a conclusion that either group really wanted.

No one had expected a war like this.

The Southern states had assumed that "reasonable" men would accept their right to leave the Union. They reasoned that they had joined voluntarily, and had been careful not to allow anything to be placed in the Constitution of 1789 which would keep them from leaving. They did not believe that the basic issue between them and the North was African slavery. They thought the North and especially, New England to be inhabited by an alien people bent on ruling them. They regretted bitterly an earlier generation's decision to enter such a union.

The North was only slowly taking up the cause of Abolitionism. The war was making this emblem of New England pietism into something needed by the masses to sustain faith in the worthiness of a struggle to master the South. The "butcher's bills" were so high. Surely there must be some higher meaning in this sacrifice.

Lincoln's election in 1861 as a minority president caused a panic in the South. The belief was widespread that the North would simply suppress and dominate the South. Now they were locked in a struggle to the death. Who could know the outcome? Perhaps there was some key to a secret door that, in opening, would bring an end.

Perhaps there was not.

16 April, 1853
(An Affair of Honor)

Mist drifted in slow moving clouds over the water's surface as the river flowed to the sea, brushing as it went against the land with an easy and familiar sound.

It was a peaceful moment. There was laziness in the cool air. It brought the kind of feeling that made you never want to emerge from under the bedclothes, a moment that made you want to burrow deeper and deeper into the safety and warmth, dreaming, dreaming. It was the moment in which the night begins to leave the earth. It was the instant, frozen in time, when insect life is hushed and birds have not yet stirred from their rest. The dark was lifting just a little, so that a Moslem might have said that a white thread could almost be distinguished from a black and that the day might begin.

At this moment of expectation, a group of men were gathered around a fire on the Potomac's bank. They laughed and passed a flask among them and someone who did not know better would have thought from watching them that this was the end of a night's hunting or fishing. He would have thought them neighbors from nearby Alexandria who had come together for a night of sport and now were waiting to share the Spring glory of a Virginia sunrise. He would not have guessed at the anger that was in the hearts of the men who stood by the crackling warmth. In the dimness of the false dawn, the four rubbed their hands above the glow. The flask passed among them, glinting in the flames' orange light with the glint of old silver. Laughter rippled around the ring, but it was the old habit of courtesy which brought it. In their hearts was emptiness, a hollow space that ached from the pain of the cause of their meeting.

A few feet from the fire, a doctor sat in silent, disapproving expectation. His Negro coachman had placed a folding chair beside the buggy in which they had come. Surgical instruments covered a white cloth on a camp table by the doctor's elbow.

Pale light came slowly into the small clearing. The animals of the day looked at them with passing interest as they woke. Birds stirred in the hardwood trees. By the fire one of the men found his watch, and peering at its face remarked, "They should be here by now. Do you suppose they will arrive together?" A look of wonderment at the thought crossed his face.

"Hah!" whooped a darkly elegant man. He pointed with a silver headed cane away through the woods in the direction of Mount Vernon. "If I know Claude Crozet Devereux, he's sittin' by the road up there waitin' for your man to show up, and will follow him down here. Always polite Claude is, always, almost to a fault. Doctor, will you have a drink? I've been savin' this for a special occasion. It is ten year old Montebello apple brandy, your genuine Virginia Calvados."

The black coachman came for the flask.

The owner of the brandy squinted across the fire at the other three figures. All were turned out in the tall hats, tail coats and patterned waistcoats thought necessary by the custom of the day. This display of wealth and taste contrasted strongly with the doctor's severe black and the simple clothing of the several servants who stood nearby.

"How did this happen?" one of the others asked morosely. Anger was half hidden in the edges of his voice.

The owner of the flask glanced at him, then smiled. "Well, now, there are some things that everybody knows, but just aren't for sayin'. George Daingerfield knows that. All you Daingerfields know that … That's how we play the game, is it not? You two gentlemen are aware of the insult. You would not be here to act for your cousin if you were not.." He continued to smile across the flames.

The Daingerfield to whom he had spoken said nothing. He turned and spat into the river, seeming to find something worthy of attention in the green Maryland hills beyond.

"What does your father say about this, Patrick? What does Charles Devereux say?" the second Dangerfield across the fire asked. He spoke to the fourth man in this party of "friends." "You are Claude's brother," he continued. "Can you not stop him?"

Patrick Henry Devereux was by far the youngest of the group. He seemed almost a child beside the others. Tall, pale and black haired, he stood silently beside his cousin, Richard Mayo, the owner of the flask. After a moment's thought, he turned away, unresponsive.

"My uncle is deeply disapprovin' of this meetin'," the cousin replied for him, still smiling. "As, usual he finds fault with his first born son, but that is an old, old story. Claude is much like old Richard, his grandfather, my great-uncle by marriage. You knew him? Married my grandfather's sister he did, Elizabeth Mayo, fine woman, a great beauty in her day. You may have heard of her. She was often hostess for my uncle Joseph Mayo, the mayor of Richmond?" Still smiling, he pulled himself back with effort to the business at hand. The black looks across the fire had turned him from a further discussion of family. With a shrug he laughed aloud. "What man can live in comfort with his own father's judgment on him starin' from his son's face?"

"I did not ask you that, Mayo!" one of the Daingerfields snarled.

"No, but I did answer you, and you must be content with the answer. You will get no other." The smile appeared to have become permanent.

The Daingerfield who had been absorbed in looking at the Maryland shore across the river turned back to Patrick. "And Madame Devereux, your mother, what does she say?"

The black haired youth faced him with anger in his expression. "Our mother knows nothing of this! And she will not! Do we agree?" The ferocity which shone from his pale eyes took the other man aback.

"Yes, yes, of course, Patrick. I only thought to ask."

At that moment, in a rumble of iron wheels, two more buggies rolled down a dirt track and into the clearing. They went to opposite ends of the grassy space and stopped.

A big, beefy, blonde man climbed down from one. He held a wooden box under one arm. His seconds went to him.

Claude Devereux stepped down from the other vehicle to consider the scene. He was black haired like his brother with skin so white that you could see blue veins beating in the side of his throat. Of medium build and medium height, he would not have stood out in a crowd. He would also not have been thought handsome in the usual sense of the word, but women had never seemed to notice. Today, he wore a white shirt with its sleeves rolled above the elbow, had his hat in one hand, and his coat in the crook of an arm. When he was a boy, a neighbor, Colonel Samuel Cooper, had once told Claude's grandfather that the boy would be a leader, that he had seen many men, and that Claude had the mark on him. The mark showed on him now. There was something in his posture and the tilt of his head that made him suddenly the center of the group. Even George Daingerfield could look at no one else.

His younger brother Patrick and the Mayo cousin walked to join him. He took a swig of the apple brandy, blinking at the bite of it. "So, you must still be hunting with that old Dutchman in Strasburg?" he asked Richard Mayo.

Mayo looked surprised. "Rutz? Yes, of course. What would we do without Fred Rutz and his excellent apple orchard? What would occasions like this be without his panther piss? Claude, they won't take it back. We tried. It's no use."

Patrick nodded in agreement.

The duelist shook his head. "Well, that's it then," he said. "Too bad, too bad." He shuddered slightly. Perhaps it was the early morning chill. "So be it. Bill, you come with us," he said to a mulatto servant who stood with the three white men. This man had driven the buggy into the clearing. He nodded, took the coat, from

Devereux, folded it and placed it on the seat. The four then walked to the center of the clearing to meet the other side.

The principals stood three feet apart to hear their seconds discuss the circumstances of the quarrel, and the challenge.

Claude Devereux looked his opponent in the face. *Christ, George, please don't make me do this*, he thought. *You didn't mean it. Just take it back. We all know that what you said was true, but we can't have it said. Take it back here and now. We'll shake hands. I'll pour you a drink of the apple poison. We'll forget it.* He did not want to fight this man. They had grown up together, been at school together. He could not comprehend the blindly destructive drunken urge which had made George Daingerfield say what he had, had made him persevere when sober in the injury he had offered Devereux's family, and its position in the community. He tried to engage the other man's eyes.

Daingerfield avoided looking at him.

Aunt Betsy says you've always been jealous of Bill, even when we were boys. If that is so, give me a chance to make it right for you. I can't let stand what you said about my grandfather, about.. Devereux became aware that the seconds had asked him something. "What?"

The open blue velvet box held a pair of flintlock pistols in fitted pockets. *Ebony grips, silver chased. English*, he thought.

"It is your choice, Claude," one of Daingerfield's cousins said.

He inclined his head. "Bill, pick one."

The mulatto reached into the box, grasping a pistol.

Daingerfield's hand grasped Bill White by the wrist. "Keep your nigger's hands off my weapons, Claude," he rasped.

Devereux grabbed him by the shirt front pulling him forward. "George, you haven't learned anything yet," he hissed, his eyes glowing. "We don't have to do this with pistols. That was your choice. I am quite willing to change to shotguns, or knives unless you think you might have been a little hasty in what you said."

Daingerfield pulled free. With the remaining pistol in his right hand he turned and walked to a line scratched in the sod. Devereux joined him, escorted by Bill White, who still held the flintlock. They stood back to back, looking a little strange because of the difference in their size, but otherwise alike in white shirts and black trousers. The mulatto glanced around, to see how close all the others stood. "Mister Devereux, you don't have to do this," White whispered. "None of us expect it. My daddy, he doesn't expect it, doesn't want it. Don't do it. Please."

Daingerfield turned his head slightly to listen.

With a sick feeling in his gut, Devereux shook his head. "No. It has gone too far."

White moved back as the seconds began to count and the two men stepped away from each other.

Devereux turned at the number twenty to face his enemy. He was an excellent shot, his skill honed by many years of devotion to the hunt. Daingerfield's shirt looked as big as a barn door.

They stood with pistols raised at an angle.

"Fire at will," Mayo called.

The ball hummed by his ear, followed by the report. At first he thought it had missed altogether, but then he felt the wet on his shirt. He could feel the steady stream of warm blood falling on his shoulder. The spreading stain grew larger by the second as blood dripped from a mangled earlobe. *He tried to shoot me in the head. The bastard tried to kill me.* "George, a last chance," he called across the distance.

Daingerfield threw the gun away. "Damn you. Claude! Damn your false friendship! Damn your nigger loving grandfather! Damn you all! Damn you all! Damn your nigger.."

The bullet hit him squarely in the middle of the chest, clipping the bottom of the breastbone on its way to the spine. He sprang back in a wildly spread eagled position, his spasm driven by damage to the spinal cord. The body lay on the grass. Its heels drummed against the soil for a moment, and then were still.

The doctor came over to look at the ear. He waved absentmindedly in the direction of the corpse. "Looks like another hunting accident. I'm going to have to sew this up, Claude." Devereux nodded and the surgeon went to work with a needle.

Daingerfield's servants picked up the body to take it away." We're sorry Claude, even if he wasn't," one of the seconds cried from beside the corpse.

"It's all right, Henry. It's over," he replied.

1

The Return

21 January 1863
(Richmond, Virginia. Ten Years Have Passed)

The meeting President Davis had asked for was held after dinner. It was decently timed to avoid unwanted curiosity on the part of the other guests without offending them because they had not been asked to attend. Such niceties of social life were not much observed in Richmond in the circumstance of 1863. People were too busy trying to survive to worry very much about wounded feelings. Jefferson Davis' house was still an island of good taste, but it was notable as an exception. Dinner parties were unusual as well. Because of the Union naval blockade it was too difficult to find the supplies necessary to set a respectable table.

The President of the Confederate States of America could have had whatever he needed. War and Navy Department contractors and speculators stood ready to fill the larder of the White House. Davis was not the man to allow such a thing. He was more inclined to aggravate the decline of his health by insisting on eating army rations. His wife, Varina, would not, in any case, have accepted luxuries for her pantry while so many citizens were going hungry.

In spite of these difficulties, the four friends waited until the others had left and then retired to the study for the desired talk.

Every old soldier knows that wartime winters are inevitably among the coldest on record. This January, the weather was exceptionally severe. Varina Davis heard the wind under the eaves as she watched the three men settle before the grate in the library fireplace. The crimson velvet draperies stirred within the confines of their golden cords. The light from the gasolier chandelier flickered on the wallpaper. She liked the effect created by the golden light on the flocked, wine red paper. The grey haired Negro butler poured coffee for the two guests and the Davises. The silent figure looked to her for instruction and closed the doors behind him as he left.

General Lee had brought the coffee with him from his army's headquarters. He had come by train today and would return to Fredericksburg tomorrow. The coffee had been traded for tobacco across the picket line. Union Army soldiers always wanted Virginia tobacco.

Varina settled herself into the small chair beside her husband. She was much younger than he and the difference in age had begun to seem even greater as his health worsened. She caught a glimpse of herself in the mirror above the mantelpiece while crossing the room. *I hope he did not marry me for my looks*, she thought. *He grows more distinguished and I become more matronly.*

The fourth person in the room sat back in a corner. The edge of the fireplace cast a shadow which all but hid his face. The man's small, well-shod feet were planted firmly on the carpet. A flowered silk vest covered his round little belly. All you could really see of his face was the warmth of his smile. His name was Judah Benjamin. He was Secretary of State.

Varina's eyes met his across the space formed by the circle of friends. She returned the smile. *What would we do without you, Judah? How could my dear husband carry his burdens? It is strange,* she thought, *how much these three have come to trust and rely on each other. They know each other so well and it has been so short a time, really.*

President Davis began to speak. "General Lee, I don't like to call you away from your Department, but Judah and I have continued our prior discussion concerning our political and military prospects and I wish to hear your views with regard to our present thinking. It does not seem that our friends at the North are ready to back away as yet, does it?"

Lee put down his cup and straightened his back in the chair. A slight twist of one side of the mouth made Varina think he might have a touch of the neuralgia that had come on him of late. *He is too old for this nonsense of living in tents in all kinds of weather, too old.*

"They continue to grow stronger on the front facing my Department," Lee said. "The prisoners we receive are a mixed lot. Some are veterans. Many are newly recruited, from new regiments. There are also many recent immigrants from Europe. There is a new factor as well.."

Davis gestured to show his desire that the general should continue.

"Some of the captured officers are saying that efforts are under way to create a large force of Negroes to employ against us."

Benjamin shook his head. "The fools will cause an embitterment of relations between the races that will never end!"

Lee agreed. "That is undoubtedly true, and I fear for my ability to control the actions of our men against such troops.."

The President shifted his attention back and forth between them. "And what of our strength?" he asked. Impatience at bad news showed in his face. "Where are our opportunities? You are not a man to dwell excessively on our disabilities."

While the general thought of his response and waited for the chief executive to compose himself, the woman thought about him. Robert E. Lee never seemed to Varina to be wholly human. His serene beauty and gentle manner enfolded him in armor so complete that the genuine personality within could only rarely be seen. The popular image of him as soldier-saint competed with that of the engineer intellectual, the "King of Spades." She had known him in circumstances in which the pressures of a degenerating military situation had been such as to grind most men to dust. He had never changed. He was always the same, calm, deliberate, kindly, considerate, and inhuman. Varina knew the General's married life had long been unhappy. She had heard of the violent, sudden rages which his staff sometimes suffered. Most of all she had been told of the fierce joy which animated him on a battlefield. She often thought of the "tic" in his face and wondered at the price he might be paying for the restraint and self discipline which ruled him. *These Virginians are strange people,* she thought. *I wish I understood them better.*

Lee began softly, slowly, anxious not to add to Davis' worries. "I fear, Mister President, that we have reached the practical limits of our strength. We now have in our forces very nearly the largest number of men possible given the size of our white, male population. We can bring into service each year a newly matured group of our youth, but if losses are what we have seen thus far ..."

Davis shook his massive head. "Yes, yes, I know. We will grow weaker and weaker while they grow stronger. The Secretary of War tells me the same thing. How can we halt this game while we are still seen as possible victors?"

Lee showed no sign of irritation at the thought that he had been required to travel 80 miles to answer questions for which Davis said he already knew the answers. "Mister President," he said. "I continue to think that we must once again carry the war into the enemy's home country. There we must bring him to battle and break his will to go on."

Davis raised his voice in agitation. "Break his will! Yes! That is what we must do! But how? It would be most fortunate if you or Bragg could destroy a major army and cause a political revulsion against the Republicans, but can we stake all our hopes on that? We are the weaker party in this struggle. I have great faith in you. I pray to God, our Father, each night that his Providence will be revealed to us, but I think we must look beyond that possibility. Too much is at risk to wager it all on the hope of a victory of annihilation. No. We need to investigate carefully the chance that there may be some combination of political or commercial influences which could be used to divert history from the path that we fear it is now following."

Lee listened to the heat and desperation in the president's voice in the courteous, deferential way that all who knew him expected. He knew he must not show how little hope he had in Braxton Bragg. Bragg was Davis' friend and the commander of the South's army in Tennessee. Lee knew how little chance there was that Bragg would accomplish any such thing. His facial coloring changed slightly, growing redder in a flush that spread from the collar up.

He is not happy, Varina reflected.

The General spoke. "This would appear to be State Department business." All present knew that the Confederate State Department's main business lay in the field of intelligence. A country without foreign recognition had little need of diplomats.

Davis agreed. "Yes, except that we, I, would like to combine an attempt to influence events in the North with the campaign of invasion which you have proposed to me previously."

Varina knew that everyone in the room was sure that Robert E. Lee would agree to almost anything to obtain approval of his plans for the summer campaign.

"And how shall this be done, sir?".

"I believe we should send a secret emissary to the North to study this question and make recommendations to us as to the greatest vulnerabilities of our enemies."

Lee seemed puzzled at this proposal, leaning forward in his chair, cup in hand. "Sir, we have many informants and scouts in Washington City and other places in the United States."

The President shook his head. He coughed in impatience. "Not the same thing, not at all. Tell General Lee what we have in mind, Varina."

It was not the custom of the day for women to intrude themselves into such discussions, but all present knew that the custom of the day was nonsense in a society at war for survival. This society needed the help of the best minds available and Varina Davis had never been known as a woman afraid to offer her opinions.

She began. "We need to send a man of proven ability, intellect, and courage. He must be a man of action who possesses a background which will allow him to move freely in the right circles. He should be someone in whom you all place confidence," Varina paused, not looking at Judah Benjamin, waiting.

The Secretary of State murmured, "I think I have found such a man. We have been looking at him for some time and he has been given the chance to prove himself suitable, a chance he has made admirable use of.."

The general considered this statement and the meeting itself for a moment. "Do I understand correctly that this person is a member of my command?" he asked. Displeasure showed once again in the pinkness of his neck and ears.

Benjamin inclined his head.

Lee went on, "And you wish my agreement so that there might be no insuperable difficulty with the Secretary of War?"

"Just so," smiled Judah Benjamin.

"Who is this officer?"

"Captain Claude Crozet Devereux."

Lee smiled a little in recognition of the name. "Ah, yes. I know the family well. We are fellow townsmen.. No. I think not. He will not want it. If circumstance had been slightly different, he would be much senior to his present rank. He might be yet. I did not wish to allow his detachment from the Army last winter for this foolishness in France." He realized he might have gone too far and looked around before going on. "He should have his own regiment. He has fought like a lion on every field since the first Manassas, has been three times wounded, I believe." He looked both thoughtful and slightly guilty. "I should have done something about a regimental command for him earlier." Turning to Davis, Lee said, "I do not wish to give him up to this. I need him. You know I place little reliance on Secret Service devices."

The President grew visibly paler. The lines about his mouth tightened.

Lee watched him for a few seconds. Anger that a good combat soldier would be wasted struggled within him against his deep-seated conviction that the legitimate civil government must be obeyed. *At least he will go home to that lovely woman who has been so unhappy with him. Perhaps they can work it out. That would be something of value,* he thought. He bowed his beautiful grey head. "We are, as always, at your disposal, Mister President."

Wednesday, 2:00 A.M., 4 March 1863 (At Sea Off Wilmington, N.C.)

The sea heaved with a motion which brought to mind the restlessness of a man unhappy in his sleep.

The ship lay quietly in the dark, moving with the sea, stirring rhythmically in the fog, almost invisible in the trough of the waves and appearing to be nothing more than an exceptionally dark patch of night on the crests. Her engine whispered softly to the sea, turning slowly, waiting for a sign, waiting for welcome to shine out from the fort ahead.

In the surrounding blackness, the hunters lay quiet, filled with the certainty that such a night would bring their prey. How many hunters there might be could not be known until the ship made her run for the entrance to the river behind the fort.

In the ship, the master knew the hunters waited. He knew this from the trouble of his past voyages to this place and from the odd sounds which came to him through the protecting mist.

Officers grouped on the quarterdeck looked almost relaxed, leaning on the rail, seeming somewhat distracted, perhaps lost in a memory of the land. Some faced shoreward, others stood with hands in pockets or with arms folded, looked in directions from which they could only hope to see with the ear's eye. None of them could have said what it was specifically that made them certain they were not alone on the water. Occasionally, one or another would turn his head toward some almost heard echo of man's presence.

Suddenly, off the port bow the lights of Christmas appeared, arching high into the sky, burning green and red with a fuzzy, half lit space between them. A collective sigh of unjustifiable surprise and relief circled the deck.

The helmsman turned.

The master nodded at the gap between the lights. "There you go, helm!" he called. "That's the Cape Fear!"

Officers spoke at tubes, and went forward to supervise the run for the river's mouth.

All those on board felt the ship gather itself up. The ever present vibration of the massive walking beam steam plant shifted in frequency, shaking the inner complacency which had gathered in the wait. Water hissed in passage down her iron flanks.

From his position by the after rail, the only passenger on the quarterdeck noticed the ship's ensign filling as she gathered way. It matched in national identity the company burgee at the head of the single stumpy mast, "*Let Her Rip*" was her name. Liverpool was her home port.

Above the rising sound of the accelerating ship, the passenger began to be conscious of stirrings in the fog, of the distant but unmistakable cries of voices. These were followed by bugle calls in an arc from the port beam to almost dead astern.

A ship's officer beside him calmly remarked, "They can't possibly see us in this. They will run for the channel close in and hope to keep us from the estuary."

The passenger thought for a moment of his reason for travel and reflected on the embarrassing contents of his baggage. "Will they succeed?" he asked. He did not want his bags searched by a Navy boarding party.

The Englishman hooted at the thought. "You needn't worry, Mister Devereux. This ship will walk away from anything the U.S. Navy has within 500 miles."

Claude Devereux's silent moment of confidence was ruined when the British officer continued, "Unless we strike some damned bar that has shifted since the last time."

"And when was that?"

In place of a direct answer the mate reflected on the excellence of his company's vessels in this trade. "You see, sir, we were built just for this, low silhouette, shallow draft, interior construction with the largest holds she will contain. That is why your stateroom is so small. Four months it has been, sir," he finally said to answer the question.

Lights could now be seen to port.

I can't be taken like this! Devereux thought. *Not like this. Think! If they board, I'll throw my official papers over the side in a pillow slip. Better weight it first.. Then I'll look for another Yale man, or maybe one of Hope's navy relatives. There are so many that there must be one out there somewhere. Unfortunately they have probably all heard that she isn't pleased with me.."*

Astern, distant engine noise was followed by the awesome creak and rumble of deck guns being run out.

"Let Her Rip" surged forward with a following sea lifting her periodically in a way that threatened the interior peace of landsmen aboard.

The red and green lights grew in brilliance as the batteries to either side of the estuary continued to fire rockets. The aurora around them swelled and made them stars descended from an impossibly colored sky.

The ship to port fired a warning shot.

Devereux judged the fall of shot to be so far off as not to be a worry. He watched the lights which had appeared to the left and behind. They actually seemed smaller.

The captain began to laugh. "The damned Yanks are sloughing off. They must all be down in Port Royal Sound and Beaufort chasing the colored girls."

The slackening of tension among the ship's officers was clear as the blockade runner gained ground in her race for life. Backslapping and mutual congratulation ran around the quarterdeck.

God damn it! I hope these people know what they are doing. Devereux thought. *A Yankee prison I don't want! How would I explain to one of Hope's cousins? I see it now. Well, Captain, my wife is the most delectable creature on earth, but she can't stand me, don't you see, because I'm not you.. Or perhaps, see here Captain! Your cousin loves us all very much at home and wishes to save us from what we are.. Maybe not.*

Suddenly, the sky ran red and white with rocket trails off the bow. The mate was puzzled. "Why would Fort Fisher fire rockets?" he muttered. "If they don't stop, they will expose our position." He was speaking of the giant Confederate earthen fort which guarded the mouth of the Cape Fear River. Upriver lay Wilmington, North Carolina, their destination.

The master stepped to the rail and went up into the rigging. "Masthead! What do ye' see?" he cried to the lookout above.

"Gunboat sor!" came the reply. "Smaller than we, off the fort and in the channel!"

Fort Fisher roared its anger. The trajectories of red-hot shot and the trailing sparks of shell fuses were unmistakable across the shrinking distance.

Devereux joined the officers standing on the rail. He clung to a piece of standing rigging to keep his balance. He would have been surprised to know how impressive he looked at that moment. His black hair was shot through with grey and the years had honed the flesh of his face to a hawk's profile. It was a face that properly belonged to a predator. Salt spray wet his cheeks. Now he could see what lay ahead. Light from the rockets and star shells cast a horrible multicolored glow on the scene before him. A Union Navy gunboat stood off the fort. She seemed a pitifully small object. She was not more than half a mile from the batteries, and fearfully exposed to their fires. Clearly, the small ship was positioned there to halt the passage of blockade runners in the channel at night, but she had somehow gone too close to the fort, and the scheduled approach of the blockade runner had caused her discovery.

As Devereux watched, the little ship turned to starboard, presenting her stern to the guns, hoping to steam away into the darkness. She seemed a tiny thing, a side wheeler with one smoke stack and two little deck guns.

With a rushing sound and roar, a salvo from a mortar battery fell vertically and straddled the gunboat.

She seemed untouched.

The sound of a cannon firing from astern the blockade runner turned heads on the quarterdeck.

"Let Her Rip"'s crew and passengers cringed from the howl of an incoming shell. It split the sea 100 yards to port.

Devereux gripped the stay, wondering if there might be a safer place somewhere on the ship. He had just decided that there was not and that he might as well try to look unconcerned when a noise like a clap of thunder almost made him lose his hold on the rigging.

Those about him turned together as the horizon glowed yellow forward. The sound of massive detonations rolled over the quarterdeck like water.

"Captain! The gunboat!" the masthead watch screamed out.

Before their eyes the black outline of the little vessel was hidden by a billowing flower of flame.

"Sweet Jesus!", swore the master, "There she goes!"

A direct hit had torn the little ship in half.

"The magazine?", Devereux wondered aloud.

The mate nodded silently.

"Let Her Rip" closed on the wreck.

The captain paced his deck and peered fearfully at the fort ahead. "Hoist our recognition signal. Let's see if they are going to do the same for us," he said.

Colored lights rose in the rigging.

The U.S. gunboat lay broken and burning abeam.

"Colors!" cried the master. The Red Ensign dipped to half staff. Officers and men lined the rail.

They'll all drown, Devereux thought until he saw boats putting out from the fort to pick up survivors.

This scene came unhinged with resumption of the fire of Fort Fisher's batteries. The men on "Let Her Rip"s decks pulled their heads in as the projectiles passed overhead with a roar.

"Not to worry boys!" yelled the captain. "They are holding off our pursuers."

The deck heaved in the eerie light of the rockets. It rose again.

Devereux looked inquiringly at the British officers.

They looked concerned. "The bar. Now we will see," said one.

A shudder shook the ship, a dragging sensation followed, then a feeling of lightness and speed.

Laughter swept around the group. "We are in the Cape Fear River, Mister Devereux," the mate told him. "You are in your own country now."

The thought moved him, but the knowledge of the cargo of war materiel which the ship carried toward Wilmington, cargo he had bought in France, gave him satisfaction.

10:00 A.M. 4 March
(Wilmington, North Carolina)

Young men can sometimes be quite old. The white early springtime sunshine pouring through the many paned window made the young officer's red-brown hair into something strangely like a halo. He gripped his pen clumsily above the papers on the desk in front of him, staring at them with baffled wariness.

Eight feet away, across a landscape of threadbare Turkey carpet, Claude Devereux watched him fret and judged him. *Red cuffs, two collar stars, a lieutenant colonel of artillery, perhaps 30 years old, perhaps.*

The young colonel was the Provost Marshal of Wilmington. He was the Confederate officer responsible for the good order which had to be maintained in this essential blockade runner's port. The weight of this task in wartime would have made any man impatient and irritable but in this man there were complications. The most important of these was that he hated his job. This began to show immediately, for as he sat contemplating the man and the papers before him, the young colonel commenced to glow with anger from within. You could see it in the changing tones of ruddiness in his neck and the set of his eyes.

Devereux waited. *He is going to work me over,* he thought *He hates people who are what I seem to be. Careful.*

The provost marshal studied the human object before him. Resentment was strong in him. Resentment against those who hid abroad, those who sought profit from the holocaust of fire that he had known, and would not know again. "Have you traveled extensively in Europe, sir?" he asked.

"Before the war I was in the Paris office of Devereux and Wheatley, our family business."

Smug certainty spread over the officer's features. "And this would be what sort of business?"

"Bank."

"Ah, yes, a Virginia bank I suppose."

"Alexandria."

"Still in business?"

"My father and brother are trying to keep the bank alive."

The glow deepened. The red cuffs wrestled with each other. "Well, sir," the young man spat out. "I imagine that there are a lot of Yankee payrolls and contracts which would make that possible."

Devereux considered a reply, but then thought about the cane leaning against the wall, about the white scar that ran down the other man's face, out of the hair, and into the collar. He also thought of his mother who felt so imprisoned in occupied Alexandria. He thought of his own pain, thought of the mornings when his often broken and badly healed bones screamed for mercy. The pistol ball still lodged beneath his ribs hurt him now when he moved on the chair. *Say nothing! Hell,* he thought, *I'd hate me too if I were he.* In the end, he decided that he would not defend himself, that nothing could be said. "The papers before you, colonel," he began evenly, "state that I have been abroad on the business of our government."

"The State Department?"

Surprise filled Devereux's face. "No, the War Department."

"Are you an official of the War Department?" the provost marshal asked.

Reluctance to reveal much of himself struggled in Devereux with the desire not to be held in contempt by one of his own. "No," he finally said, surrendering to his humanity. "I'm an army officer, detailed to purchasing mission duties for the last four months."

The atmosphere altered slightly.

"Rank?"

"Captain."

"Regiment?"

"17th Virginia Infantry."

The eyes at last began to look at him. "You were at Manassas?"

Devereux nodded. "I was in both of them."

"Were you hit?"

Devereux nodded. *Was I hit? Do you want to see the mess the canister made of my right leg?* "I haven't lost a lot of bone as you have."

The artilleryman looked at the table top.

"But, then, my naked hide will never be very beautiful again!" He laughed aloud and the colonel smiled, joined to him in the gallows humor of the front line veteran.

"What's the situation now?" Devereux asked.

The red sleeves ceased their inspection of the desk. One of them produced a paper from the interior of the piece. The colonel scanned the contents while speaking, half to himself. "The main front is stabilized in Virginia along the Rappahannock River on either side of Fredericksburg. There are some interesting and nasty little pockets held by the Yankees here on the coast." He held out the sheet of paper. "You will be interested in this."

The telegram had been sent to await him. It summoned Devereux to a meeting in the capital "at his earliest convenience." *What the hell is this?* It was signed by the wrong man, by a man for whom he did not work. "I do not have the pleasure of the Secretary of State's acquaintance," he said.

"Captain," the provost-marshal murmured, "I was with Stonewall in the Valley when he went several rounds with Mister Benjamin over interference with plans. I am sure you recall that Mister Benjamin was briefly Secretary of War. You will find him an obscure conversationalist, but then Jews often are."

"I will need transportation to Richmond."

The scarred man grappled with his regret for what he had earlier said. "You will, I hope, realize that I must be vigilant here. Wilmington crawls with clever, grasping men who feed on our need. I am sick of them!" He looked up to see if his words were accepted.

Devereux bowed his head slightly.

The other officer appeared relieved. "The cars still run along the tracks, if slowly," he commented with a wry grin. "We will see you on your way. A lot of odd, doubtful people come through this port."

5:50 P.M. Sunday 8 March

Peace time Richmond had been a city which seemed content with itself and its role as capital of the Commonwealth of Virginia. It had never been very large, but there had always been a certain reserved vitality in its preoccupation with the management of the political and business affairs of the state. Virginia had one foot in the agrarian South, another in the boom country of the Ohio valley and a third in the emergence of the industrialized power of steam, coal and iron.

Devereux smiled to himself. *Perhaps that was our biggest problem. One could say that we were called on to be too many things. In the end we had to choose. It was inevitable, really.*

The mayor's conversation resonated in the room. That was not surprising. This was his house and Claude was both his nephew and houseguest.

This had always seemed a sheltering house. Devereux's childhood memories were filled with visits. It still echoed with the sound of his mother's laughter. His father was a major figure in these memories, as in all others of his youth. He was always there, protecting, correcting, teaching, reproving.

The street made itself felt through the big windows. Across the way there was a noise of hammering. Traffic passed. A bird looked in.

He began to listen, suddenly concerned that he might have missed something requiring a response.

Joseph Mayo loved his own voice. The lucid, soft sound had been the key to his long tenure in public office. On the stump he was close to being irresistible. In his youth that voice and his florid handsomeness had made him a bachelor both feared and coveted by mothers with available daughters.

The mayor rambled on. "My boy, you will weep to see poor old Richmond and the state to which she is reduced. One can't walk the streets these days without tripping over the worst sort of people who ever lived. Whores and contractors, the town is full of them. The government seems powerless to prevent the looting of our public funds by scoundrels bent on nothing but gain!"

Devereux looked askance at the other man. "Surely you are not this upset by the presence of 'the ladies of the evening'! Soldiers must have their diversions."

"No! No! You know what I mean. Don't practice your famous wit on me! The worst feature of this invasion of profiteers and office seekers is that there isn't a hotel room to be had anywhere for a price honest men can pay. Irony of ironies! The last people able to find accommodation in Richmond are the soldiers sworn to defend us! I really must force the council into action on this." Devereux did not wish to believe that old Joe was fishing for thanks but realized that prudence would provide it. "I am, as always, in your debt, uncle," he said. "This time it is for saving me from the street itself." With satisfaction the younger man watched the older twitch in irritation.

"Enough!" Mayo protested. "Now that you have a night's rest, what news is there from abroad?"

"I was there to help the purchasing agents on the continent." Devereux replied. "I'm not really the right man to talk to on diplomatic issues." Joe Mayo was not truly Claude Devereux's uncle. Devereux's father had several times explained the degree of kinship exactly. It was something like cousin, twice removed. "Uncle, do you know Judah Benjamin?"

"What business do you have with Mister Benjamin?"

"None that I know of. A telegram was sent to me in North Carolina which indicates that I am to meet with him and the Secretary of War, Seddon."

"When?"

"I presumed to have your man Michael carry messages to their offices this morning. A War Department clerk showed up with this just before you came home." He showed his uncle a note.

Mayo smiled, "Seven in the evening. That is certainly Benjamin! He seems incapable of ending work before midnight." Mayo looked ruminative for a moment. "Judah Benjamin is a fine man and a great patriot," he said. "Much misunderstood by his inferiors, especially by those who wish to think evil of any Hebrew. He bears their abuse well, without flinching. I think he is the most able man in the civil government, except for the President, of course."

"This is his third cabinet office."

"Nothing should be made of that," the mayor responded, waving a hand dismissively. In black broadcloth and immaculate linen he looked every inch the gentleman Devereux knew him to be. "The screeches of his enemies are happily ignored by that good man, Jefferson Davis. In any event, Varina likes him, Benjamin, that is."

"You mean Mrs. Davis?"

His uncle inclined his large, white fringed head. "They are fast friends."

"And Seddon?"

His uncle held up one hand to his forehead in a histrionic gesture of surprise. "Of course! I forget! You went to France when George Randolph was still with us as Secretary of War."

"He sent me, Uncle. I liked him."

"Yes, yes, you would. In the event, it developed that he was Thomas Jefferson's grandson to the core and he proved to be unbiddable by Mister Davis of Mississippi. Randolph recognized that he must leave the cabinet. I would not have you repeat that. His health was a convenient way out. He is consumptive. Seddon is a useful man for the President, efficient, dutiful but not excessively independent. You will see them both? Be certain that they know you are my kinsman.

Christ, what have I gotten into, Devereux mused. *Randolph was someone I could talk sense to.*

"And now tell me of your mother's people, you visited them in that little town in Champagne, didn't you?"

7:40 P.M., Monday 9 March

The Mechanics Building did not seem an auspicious symbol of the prospects for permanence of the Confederate States of America. This large, rather shabby wooden construction somehow was the home of both the War and Navy departments. Claude Devereux waited for an hour in an ante room on the third floor for his audience with the Secretary of War. One of his hobbies was architecture and the construction trades. He had often taken part in the erection of buildings belonging to his kin and had become a keen critic of the work. The moldings in this place amused him. He slowly ran his eye over them taking note of the poor joinery and lack of detail. His meditation on the Mechanics' Building was interrupted at one point by the entrance of two army officers who nodded briefly, then sat in the corner discussing what must have been their common business.

Devereux thought this rude but was grateful that he did not have to listen to more talk about the hardships of Richmond wartime life.

Anger and impatience built within him as time passed. He considered this wait to be bordering on insult. Who was this James Seddon to keep him waiting? Devereux cast back across the wide circle of his acquaintance but could not readily bring the man to mind. *Is this what we are fighting for,* he thought, *that citizens should wait like hirelings for an audience? I ought to just leave. To hell with them!* He wished desperately to be allowed to return to his men. He closed his eyes for a second and tried to summon them.

> He usually could remember them best on the road, in one of those interminable, grinding marches that ate up the miles and shoe leather alike. After he was commissioned, it had taken him months to absorb the hard lesson that his men's feet were his personal charge. In the end, he had understood. At halts on the march, he made them change their socks and walked down the line looking at their bare feet, checking for blisters. Suspicious looking feet, the kind with blotches of bluish skin, he massaged. The regiment was always under strength. He had to be sure that every man possible would stand in the line of battle when needed. In any event, they were his men.
>
> The greatest march of all came to mind, the bone crushing endurance race that Longstreet's First Corps had run from below Culpeper, going up to the west of the Bull Run Mountains. It had gone on for days in the burning heat of August. The long lines of pack mules in the division's supply trains kicked up vast amounts of dust and all seemed to have an instinctive desire to urinate in every body of water they found along the way.
>
> Food had given out on the third day in a way they had come to expect. The march went on with empty stomachs, the brown dust caked on faces until men and uniforms were indistinguishable.
>
> They turned east at Salem, heading for Thoroughfare Gap, spurred on by the knowledge that Stonewall's Corps stood alone beyond the mountain, alone against all of John Pope's army. They smashed a Yankee cavalry brigade which tried to halt them in the gap, tearing it to bits and throwing aside the pieces like chaff into the wind.
>
> The Corps closed on Jackson's right flank, forming a right angle to his line. In that position they watched Pope's foolish massed attacks on Jackson's men, watched until late in the afternoon.
>
> The Yankees did not seem to comprehend that Longstreet now stood on their flank.
>
> At last the order to advance had come. He took his place at the right of the company. His brother Jake stood beside him, his old friend Fred Kennedy just behind.
>
> The skirmish line was out in front. His troops pushed through the woods at a trot, bayonetted rifles at the trail. Pope's flank hung open before them.
>
> The sun was too low.

You could hear the high pitched, keening roar start over on the left of the advancing line.

All of Dutch Longstreet's Corps, in line of battle, was swinging forward as a giant gate, rolling up Pope's flank, folding it in upon Jackson's defense along the railway. It was a huge trap, like driving game.

His company line broke out of the forest. To left and right as far as you could see, they were all there, 30,000 odd screaming scarecrows driving before them the best army the United States possessed.

Dear God, he had prayed. We need another hour of your light to finish it. Don't let this be for nothing! Not for me! Not for ...

Devereux opened his eyes and focused on the two officers. "Does either of you gentlemen know where Montgomery Corse's brigade is at the moment?"

They seemed startled by his question. The Engineer major and Signal Corps lieutenant looked at each other for indications of intention. The major was the taller of the two. His skinny body and aquiline features gave him the profile of a large wading bird. This fancy was reinforced by coppery red hair.

Rather like the bird's crest, Devereux thought.

The lieutenant was short, stocky, squat really. His eyes were the most memorable thing about his person. Pale blue, almost grey, they gave his face a strange look, like one of those pale eyed dogs that are seen occasionally. The major said that General Pickett's Division had marched through the city going south on 17 February. More than that, he said, he knew not.

"Devereux is the name," Claude offered. "Are you going in with me?"

"Yes. I'm Harry Jenkins," the major replied. "I've been reading what reports you have been able to send from Europe. This is Franklin Bowie. As you can see, he is from Signal."

"You must be from the Secret Service Bureau, Major," Devereux said quietly. "I have been their property these last months."

"The Adjutant General's office, actually," Jenkins corrected. We don't ordinarily talk about it much but since you are 'one of us' and we are here to meet with you.." Jenkins shrugged expressively. "There has been a hell of a row over you," he went on. "The War and State departments, or rather their chiefs, have been going at it for days."

Devereux's mind nagged him about the lieutenant. "I don't wish to be unpleasant," he said, "but what does the Signal Corps have to do with this meeting or my trip to Europe?"

Lieutenant Bowie flushed at the implied challenge to his presence. He thought for an instant. "I thought your file said that you had done some work for Major Jenkins' group last winter in Alexandria, Captain," he finally replied.

"Yes."

"How did you get there?" asked Bowie.

The major shook his head. "He went in through the outpost line by himself, Frank. He doesn't know yet about the luxuries of your touring and freight service."

Well I'll be damned! "Are you suggesting," demanded Devereux, "that I really didn't have to skulk about over half of northern Virginia, in the dark, in the snow, trying to keep a horse quiet, in order to 'get there'?"

Bowie was clearly satisfied at the image. "We hadn't really got well started then," Bowie said. He still looked as though he liked the idea of Devereux's trip to Alexandria.

Jenkins searched for something acceptable to say. "I knew your brother Patrick at school," he offered.

"Ah, the Virginia Military Institute," Devereux responded. You are, then, another of Stonewall's chicks, hatched out by the great man himself."

The major nodded. "I had the misfortune of attempting to study 'Natural and Experimental Philosophy' under 'Old Jack'."

"Wasn't much of a teacher was he?" Devereux remarked. "Pat says he doesn't think Jackson is quite right in the head."

"I was terribly sorry about Patrick's injury," the major said, changing the subject.

*Ah! You don't want to talk about th*at, *do you! Nothing like the old school tie..* "Yes, well, my brother is one of the few men I've heard of who has managed to have a horse fall on him, kick him unmercifully and then bite into the bargain. A passerby shot the beast to keep him from dragging Pat off down the road. When he came to, my beloved brother railed for days against the 'horse murderer'." *Maybe Jackson isn't so unusual among you children of the VMI..*

Secretary Seddon emerged from his room, looked expectantly around, beckoned, and disappeared to await them.

Devereux entered the inner office imagining that he would see Seddon sitting grandly alone at his table. That was not so. Judah Benjamin was instantly recognizable from the newspapers. He sat in a barrel backed chair at the corner of Seddon's desk.

He must have come in a back door. That's why we waited so long. They have been discussing us.

In the oil lamplight the two men were intriguing. Seddon looked tense, reserved. He appeared to be avoiding looking at the man sitting three feet away to his right. Benjamin was improbable in appearance. Small, plump, somewhat dandified in dress, he wore a cherubic smile of welcome. Seddon waved them to chairs. "We are happy to have you back, sir!" he said. "I trust the journey was not too difficult?" The voice was pure Richmond.

"Blockade runners are not the thing for a holiday, but I have no complaints," Devereux replied.

Benjamin spoke. "At least the yellow fever has disappeared from the Wilmington area. Do the authorities think it will return?"

"A quarantine is planned beginning next month," Devereux said. "It is thought that this will prevent a recurrence. *Let's get to it!* 'I was unprepared for receipt of your telegram, Mister Secretary," he said.

Benjamin was unrepentant. "My eagerness for news sometimes gets ahead of proper system, Mister Devereux. Fortunately, James is not one to hold it against me. Our two departments have shared interests in what news you bring, and indeed in your future."

Seddon looked in the dim light, as though he might have been carved and not born. Devereux tried to remember why Seddon's face was familiar. The image of the man in his mind showed Seddon seated in his father's office in Alexandria. *I'll have to look in the records, but I think we hold a mortgage on your farm, Mister Secretary of War,* he thought.

Judah Benjamin's enunciation was perfect. His voice had the quality expected in a musical instrument. Harmonious and deep, it was full of the Carolina low country and New Orleans.

Seddon cleared his throat and spoke again. "Since you went to Europe during the service of my predecessor I would benefit from hearing of your mission in its entirety. Could you do that, Captain?"

Certain that the Secretary of War wished, as much as possible, to be master in his own house, Devereux spoke directly to him. "General Randolph issued instructions last fall for me to be detached from Corse's brigade for a period of six months. I was sent to France under orders from Major Jenkins' superior, General Cooper. I arrived in late October."

"Why you, Captain?"

Devereux began to work his way through the probable future course of this conversation. He saw how unlikely a return to the Army of Northern Virginia might be. *Better be careful. Don't give them anything they can use to keep you away from the company. Sit up straight! They will not know that the ribs are not really right anymore.* "My mother is French by birth," he said. "I was born in Paris and have both Confederate and French nationality. We have a lot of family in French government circles, mostly army."

"The implication is that you speak French."

"Yes." *Sans aucune doute.*

Jenkins stirred.

Attendance at many meetings had made Seddon familiar with the signals. "Yes, Jenkins?" he asked. "Tell us."

"I am informed that Captain Devereux's speech is indistinguishable from that of a Frenchman," the red headed officer stated firmly.

"An exaggeration," Devereux interjected. *Actually, a Champenois.*

"John Slidell tells me the same thing," added Benjamin. "Slidell's French is impeccable. He writes that you were the most effective member of his mission." The smile seemed beatific.

"Ambassador Slidell is kind. The truth is that my mission was not much of a success." *Except with one or two charming ladies..*

"Let us take up the tale again," Seddon urged. "You arrived in October."

"Yes, sir."

Seddon seemed impatient with the conversation.

Perhaps he can be persuaded to let me out of this, whatever it is, Devereux thought. He went on with his report. "The fable we announced to Parisian society," he said, "was that I had come as a member of the purchasing team. I told everyone that I worked for General Gorgas in the Ordnance Bureau. I did help as best I could with business contacts, banks, and so forth. I also tried to keep out of the path of the United States authorities in the city."

Seddon peered through the gloom at Jenkins. "And what was he really there for?" he asked.

"We knew of Captain Devereux's many qualities and truly surprising connections from Mayor Mayo.."

Damn you, Joe!

"Secretary Randolph thought him a perfect man to study for us the true state of mind of the French establishment on the issues of recognition and intervention." Jenkins glanced at Claude. "His modesty presumably is not going to allow him to mention the branch of his family's bank which is found in Paris nor the many officers of the Emperor's army who are his cousins."

Jenkins' thoroughness deserved respect, but Lieutenant Bowie's face showed that he was enjoying the show far too much. Devereux resolved to extract a suitable payment for the entertainment.

The Secretary of State spoke. "Captain Devereux, I believe you were also to attempt to move your French friends in our direction. I have always found the French to be a people susceptible to rational argument."

Devereux shook his head. "That isn't possible in the present circumstance for many of the same reasons which make the French populace hesitant to buy our bonds."

The cherub face slipped for just a second.

In that moment, Devereux saw someone else in the Secretary of State's chair, someone hungry, fearful, looking to be attacked. Devereux had not expected that Benjamin would be so tender on the subject of his favorite project.

"A great disappointment," Benjamin murmured. "I had hoped that Baron Erlanger would be more successful in his financial efforts on our part. In your view, why is it not possible for the French to face up to their preference for our side?"

"The Emperor, general staff, the Empress Eugenie, the Quai d'Orsay and nearly all the officer corps wish to see us become independent but they are afraid of the plunge."

"Why?" persisted Benjamin.

Devereux hesitated for a second then decided to hope that making himself offensive might cause them to send him back to his regiment. "They are unconvinced that we will defeat our enemy if left to our own resources."

"Damn it! That's why we want their help!"

All eyes turned in unison to Lieutenant Franklin Bowie.

"Well put, young man!" Seddon said. "Please continue, Captain."

The comment made Seddon more interesting than Devereux had expected. *I can't do anything for you,* he thought, *will you let me tell you that?* He plunged on. "My French friends are often accused of having the souls of bankers." The irony of this appealed to him. It showed in a slight upturning of the corners of his mouth. "Like a bank they do not wish to do anything important for us if we really need it."

Benjamin rocked silently back and forth, enjoying the joke.

Devereux watched him while finishing this thought. "We must win big somewhere."

Seddon seemed depressed. "Fredericksburg was not big enough?"

Devereux smiled. "It seemed big enough at the time, but then there was Sharpsburg beforehand which is difficult to call a victory and there has been a string of disappointments in the West."

"And the loss of New Orleans surely counts for something against us," Benjamin whispered. "Surely something. What else?"

"The slavery question." *Why did I say that? Not a good idea, not good at all!*

"Yes?" Benjamin actually leaned toward him.

"The French masses," Devereux went on, "are thought to be resolutely against us since Lincoln's proclamation on this subject. The workers, farmers and petty bourgeoisie all believe our social structure an anachronism which should be altered."

"Damn! Your pious foreigners should try to live with some of these niggers!" Bowie looked surprised at his own boldness.

Seddon stared in the direction of the signal officer.

Major Jenkins held up a hand, manifestly hoping that Bowie would stop.

Benjamin's eyes never left Devereux's face. It made you feel curiously naked. "And you think so too, don't you, Mister Devereux?" he asked. The cherub's eyes demanded an answer.

Devereux felt strangely compelled to tell the truth. There was something at once so vulnerable and so intelligent about the man that a glib answer was impossible. "I think," he began, "that independence is more important than our servants, whom we will have to give up in any event. Truly, the time is past. We should move on." For a second, he and Benjamin were locked together in recognition. He had always tried to avoid thinking these things through to their ultimate ends. He had never quite succeeded. In Benjamin's face he saw someone who would need his help.

The other two officers were hushed, waiting for the storm.

The Secretary of War glanced from Devereux to Benjamin and back. "There are many throughout our government who think you are right on the slavery question, Captain," he said calmly. "I am not one of them. I pray that it will not come to that." James Seddon was not a man to lead policy in so risky an area as this.

"What are your plans, Captain Devereux?" the Secretary of State asked politely. Benjamin really had no right to ask an army officer such a question.

Devereux looked at Secretary Seddon for a sign.

A small nod turned him back to Benjamin. "I wish to return to my regiment," he declared.

The Secretary of War looked at his hands, folded in his lap, then at him. "We have something you must do first," he said. "The Secretary of State and I must require you to go to Washington City."

Devereux's loneliness, his deep hunger to be with those who loved and needed him welled up. The thought that he would be forced to live alone, that he would again be deprived of the society of his friends and kinsmen overwhelmed him and he could not hold back. "I **must** insist, sir," he told Seddon. "I really do want to be returned to regimental duties. I did not join the army for secret service work. The 17th regiment is a gathering of my neighbors. They were recruited, at the beginning, before secession, in Alexandria. I came back from France to be with them. I was with them all last year, from Manassas to Sharpsburg. My company.." Something in their faces stopped him. *That was too much. You must not let them see you! They could be allowed to see the limp in the damp times, but not this!* He knew he had gone too far. Now they knew his weakness. Now they would have their way.

The Secretary of State smiled. "And so you shall, Captain. We all know of your previous service with that grand body of men! We also know that your father and yourself are substantial citizens of the Commonwealth, not to be dealt with arbitrarily."

Seddon blinked at that. People of Devereux's class never referred to their position. If advantage was taken, it was done behind the scenes, discretely. He watched the exchange with impassive amusement. The community of culture which he shared with the banker made him feel what must be hidden behind the inexpressive face.

Devereux focused on the Secretary of War. "May I have one of the men from my regiment to employ in this affair, sir?"

"You may have whomever you want, Captain," Seddon replied, smiling broadly.

Devereux turned to smile at the Louisiana cherub. "How may I help you, sir?" he asked.

6:00 A.M. Thursday, 12 March, 1863

Thursday started early for Devereux. He had dreamed a terrible dream. George Daingerfield had come to him in the night, dressed in the same blood soaked white shirt in which he had died. He came with increasing frequency since the war had begun. At times Devereux saw him in waking hours as well, saw him in the faces of soldiers. His father and grandfather had come in the dream with the man he had killed. His father had embraced Daingerfield, walking away with him into the dark. His grandfather stood alone with Claude, watching the others go. The old man then turned and told him something wonderful, something he had always known must be true, but which had never been made clear. They shook hands, and Richard Devereux walked away. Just as his grandfather disappeared from view he realized with despair that he could not remember what it was that had been said.

He woke all at once in the way that had become instinct. A year and a half of marching, waiting, watching and fighting had sharpened the primordial skills of the hunter. Only slowly did he recall enough of the dream to become really unhappy.

Lying in the shuttered, darkened room, he felt that night must still prevail in the street. He began to realize this could not be so. *There was so much noise! Why was there so much noise?*

Uncle Joe creaked and wheezed down the stairs and out onto the brick veranda. His loud voice penetrated Devereux's attempts to return to sleep. "What are you men at with this soldier? Let him be! You dare to raise your hand to me? Damn you!"

Devereux reached the front door while in the act of wrapping a dressing gown around himself.

Three men in the street had a firm grip on a bedraggled, bleeding human object, a Confederate soldier. His slouch hat lay in the gutter. An assortment of rough clothes in variegated shades of brown covered his bony frame. The shirt sleeves had fade marks where a sergeant's chevrons had once been sewn. Faded, dirty blue braid showed him to be an infantryman.

One of the captors advanced up the front steps and stood with a clenched fist before the mayor. "Get in your house, old man!" he shouted.

Devereux stepped past Mayo and interposed himself directly. "Do you have any notion who you are yelling at?" he asked. *My God, my knee hurts! Don't give in to it now!*

"I don't care if it's Jeff Davis hisself!" the man bellowed. "He's interferin' with our lawful duties. Get out of my way or take your medicine with'em."

"This is the mayor of Richmond, Joseph Mayo." Devereux informed him.

The shabby, sullen figure moved back into the street. "No offense, sir," he muttered over a shoulder. "We're after this deserter. That's all."

The criminal under discussion looked a great deal like all the other Rebel infantrymen in Devereux's experience. "Who do you belong to?" he called out.

"Kemper's Brigade," the man said, lifting his head. His face was bearded and bloody. The nose looked broken.

The 17th Virginia had been, for a time, in Kemper's Brigade. Devereux walked down onto the cobbles, up close to the prisoner.

They looked at each other.

"I'm an officer, why do they want you?" he asked. In this man, he saw someone he could help, someone who would need him.

The soldier's eyes suddenly held hope. "Get me out of this, sir!" he said. "These bast'uds will kill me. I just took a couple of weeks off. There's been nothin' much happenin'. A man needs time off, some time with a woman. I want to go back before the Spring campaign starts up. I was tryin' to get on a boat to City Point when Winder's men caught me."

During this little speech, Claude glimpsed two familiar figures approaching on horseback.

Lieutenant Bowie led a spare horse.

Jenkins halted his mount before them. "Morning, Devereux," he said, "found some new friends?"

"Major," Devereux pled, "these ruffians belong to General Winder, the city commandant. They have beaten this soldier and threatened the mayor."

Jenkins greeted Mayo respectfully.

"Do we have to accept such behavior?" Claude asked. The question was entirely in character for him. He did not believe that free men should ever submit to government abuse.

Jenkins handed the senior detective a document. The man in civilian clothes read it through and looked up. "We want no trouble with your office, Jenkins, but we have orders to carry out. This malingering bum has been hiding out in a whore house full of high yellah gals for a week!"

"General Winder does not intend that you detectives should terrorize the streets," Jenkins shot back. "Take your prisoner and go."

"No!", interjected Claude. "We'll take him back to his unit. We're on our way to City Point. Pickett's division is there. His commander can punish him for the offence."

"That's right" the rifleman chimed in. "My colonel will skin me good!"

The boss detective rounded on Devereux, "And where are **your** papers?"

It was not a good thing to say to Claude Devereux. He shared with many of his people a taste for personal combat. The courtesy habitually practiced among them was an antidote for an inclination to mayhem. The war had given him a chance to know how good mayhem could feel. Now, a sense of isolation from those closest to him added to this weakness. His sense of social responsibility, and his dignity would normally keep these emotions in check, but would not necessarily prevail against provocation like this. With him, discourtesy could shred the restraints. Rage began to shadow the scene, darkening his vision. He began to feel the sweet, hot ecstasy of battle. The possibility of once more stilling his pain, his loneliness, of drowning it in this repulsive creature's blood consumed his being. He started toward the man who had spoken to him.

The detective backed away.

Jenkins intervened, putting his horse between the two. "They are both in my custody. I will answer for it to General Winder. Leave now!"

"You can't do that!"

Bowie barked from nearby. "Move along now! Move along, or we will come back with those who will move you.."

The provost detectives moved off down the street.

"You are a lot of trouble, Claude, a lot of trouble," Jenkins observed, while watching them go. "But, I am sure you will prove worth it, won't you?"

Devereux stared at his opponents as they slowly drew away. *I could tell him, tell them how badly damaged I really am, but then no one would let me do anything at all. I could sit at home with Patrick, and father..* Regret struggled with relief in his heart. The red tide receded. "How long have they been acting like this?" he asked of no one in particular.

"This is the worst I have seen," remarked the mayor.

Bowie spoke up. "Jeb Stuart was in town and out visiting last month. A bunch of them jumped him and his staff. It was almost the end of some folks." He seemed to enjoy the thought.

The mayor remembered his manners. "Come in the house all of you. Michael will make us some breakfast, such as we have."

Jenkins dismounted. "Thank you, sir, and then we'll be off. A launch is waiting for us at the government pier. You can carry this man on that plow horse, can't you, Frank?"

2

The Regiment

6:00 P.M.

Mud. Red mud. It was the very substance of the road. Virginia creeper surrounded them, festooning trees just strong enough to bear their parasitic burden. The season was so young that the forest stood naked, forked, clawing at the overcast with bark scabbed fingers.

Devereux was of a tradition which assumed that life would be filled with animals; dogs, the odd cat, game animals, but above all horses. The dun colored gelding that he rode was uncertain about him. The animal's clay colored face swiveled, one eye visible in the dimming light, slyly peering at the human over his massive shoulder as the chance came. Man and horse were both alert to the possibilities. Devereux promised himself that the creature would not get a chance to roll on him. "Lieutenant, this must be your horse," he said.

Bowie cloaked himself in injured innocence. "Why would you say that, sir?" he asked.

"Because he is looking for an opening for some crude and hurtful enterprise."

Jenkins saw a cue. "Why, Claude, if he injures you, maybe we'll just let you go back to the infantry." He looked up at the darkening, dismal sky. "It's late. Your friend, Private Thacker was more trouble than I expected."

On the left, a wintry field was under cultivation in preparation for the growing season. Ten black men and women worked at clearing obstacles on the edge of the improved area. They seemed to be preparing to end a long day. Off to one side, a horse drawn plow waited. Standing with the team were two more black men, one much older than the other. Jenkins asked if they knew where the turnoff might be for General Corse's camp. The older man removed his hat and walked to the road so as not to shout. He stopped at the side of Jenkins' mount. "Good day, Cap'n. We don't know who they is but a big bunch of so'jers be in the woods by the run over there."

The picket post was on a logging road fifty yards inside the tree line. They rode into it without noticing the motley brown and grey figures in the shadows.

"Halt! State your business," came the challenge.

Jenkins produced his documents.

The sergeant in charge inspected them, looking at the horsemen in the twilight the while. His attention wandered among them, finally settling on Claude. "Captain Devereux?" he asked.

"Yes, it's me, Fred," Claude answered.

"Good to see you back," the dim figure replied. "Your brother is in our company area about half a mile down there. He'll be glad to see you, talks about it all the time. Will you stay?"

Devereux got a good, firm grip on the mask. "Where is General Corse?" he asked.

One of the soldiers walked them to the brigade headquarters area.

Jenkins looked thoughtful. "You know the sergeant back there?"

"Frederick Kennedy, lives on West Street, runs a stable. We once were apprehended by the parish priest while playing tag in St. Mary's Cemetery." Looking at the private walking beside them Devereux said, "You're new."

Startled, the man looked up, a boy really. "Yes, Cap'n, I was conscripted this winter. I'm from Lynchburg. You're a famous man here. They all want you back." Suddenly embarrassed, he looked at the ground, his face hidden from them.

The evening chill of the air, the faint smells of leaf mold, wood smoke and horse all began to soak in. He could hear the men in the woods all about them, laughing and chopping firewood. The aroma of camp cooking merged with the rest. His heart ached with the desire to stay, to be allowed to sink back into the brotherhood he had always sought.

They arrived at brigade headquarters. The group of tents was just off the logging trail, hard by the creek. Lanterns hung from branches or stood on camp tables. Somewhere around you could hear the headquarters' animals, restless at the arrival of strange, foreign horses.

Brigadier General Montgomery Corse came out of his tent with several familiar faces behind him. "At last!" he cried out. "We had a message from Richmond. We've waited all day for you, Claude. Come in, come in. Who are these gentlemen with you?"

10:00 P.M.

Lieutenant Colonel Arthur Herbert, commanding the 17th Virginia Infantry Regiment, slid and squelched his way along the path in front of the three led horses. "This is the darkest night yet," he laughed. "We've been in this wood for a week. It rains every day, and I still can't find my way around at night without running into trees! I may get shot by a sentinel yet. How long do you think you'll be gone this time?" Devereux had the yellow-brown gelding on a short lead, expecting the worst of his teeth in the dark. "I expect to be back in a couple of months.." He listened for comment from Major Jenkins behind him but none came. Devereux had known Arthur Herbert for so many years that he knew what the other man sounded like in various situations. He often thought of Herbert at Frazier's Farm in the Peninsula, where he had half dragged, half-carried Devereux out of the forest, away from the muck he had fallen in.

The regiment's bayonet attack in the darkened wood had disintegrated into a swirling mass of company combats and individual fights. He was a lieutenant then. His company commander had died that night in a chance meeting with a battalion of Union infantry. The 17th had blindly charged into the enemy troops without any real comprehension of their numbers, driven on by the brigade commander's order to clear the wood before dawn. Devereux took charge in the dim chaos as soon as he realized that the captain's voice was gone. He had managed to drag "H" Company back from the edge of eternity, physically manhandling men as necessary to force their withdrawal, but a 12-pounder Napoleon gun firing blindly in the dark had filled his leg with the little lead balls called canister. Corse gave him "H" Company as a reward. Devereux still had the scars from the artillery fragments in his leg. He could feel them tonight, walking through the wood behind Herbert. Without Herbert, he was sure that he would still be lying under the pines in Frazier's wood lot. From the dark outline of Herbert's back there now emanated the wheezing and throat clearing that showed intense embarrassment and discomfort. "I had to give 'H' company to Bill Fowle," he finally said. "We didn't know when you'd be back and I had to have a permanent company commander. I'm sorry."

It had the force of a physical blow. He tried to gather up the fragments of his dream. He took refuge in the behavior expected of him. "In your place I would have done the same thing," he said "Bill is a trained soldier. My brother knew him at the Military Institute. He has been in the company since the beginning. What else could you do?"

"Thank you, Claude," Herbert replied. "You know, of course, that as soon as you finish this mission we will want you back. You heard what General Corse said. He wants you for brigade staff. I'm afraid there won't be a lack of employment for any of us before we're through. Are you going home?"

"Yes." The sick thought that this was true settled into his bones. He tried to bring forward his mother's image, tried not to think of his incomprehensibly, permanently hostile father, of his unhappy wife.

Herbert sighed, then laughed, "I never thought I would be so glad to think of a business competitor running loose in my marketplace without me. Do me a favor. Come back and tell Corse and me how the banks are doing. There has to be a strangely humorous providence which has caused this regiment to contain so many bankers."

Devereux smiled invisibly. "We are the leading citizens of the town."

"I suppose that must be so," Herbert answered. Certainly your father would have to be described that way. In any case, it would be nice to know if any of us are going to have somewhere to go when this is over. Here we are. I'll leave you. God Speed!"

His hand tingling from Herbert's grip, Devereux led his big, ugly mount into the circle of light under the trees, in front of the tent.

There were half a dozen men in the clearing, sitting on camp chairs, boxes, logs, or the ground. The fire was big and bright against the March night. Overcoats and heavy jackets were in general use. A general commotion followed, filled with the welcome of soldiers for their own. Devereux made a special point of telling Bill Fowle that he was pleased the company was in good hands. Fowle looked grateful. He glanced away in embarrassment and spied figures emerging from the darkened wood. "Here come your brother and Bill," he said. "They had begun to think you weren't really going to arrive today."

The newcomers walked in out of the dark, summoned by the noise. The two silent figures stood frozen in the flickering light cast by the company fire. Side by side they stared at Claude. In the dimness their butternut clad bodies were hard to distinguish against the forest background. Devereux reached their side of the clearing without consciously moving his feet. He seized the shorter of the two men in his arms. *Now, I know you are alive*, he thought. *Now, I can face mother.* Behind his brother's back he held out a hand. The second man shook it vigorously.

An hour later, Lieutenant Joachim Murat Devereux, known to his friends as Jake, stared across the fire with disbelief at his admired older brother. "You're going to leave again?"

Claude waved at the two intelligence officers with his tin cup, scattering the dregs of his coffee into the fire where it hissed in little drops, dancing on the red logs. "It doesn't appear that I have a choice. My guardians are both protective and insistent." Claude had always delighted in the company of his youngest brother. Six more months of service in the field had not noticeably coarsened the young man's manner. He still seemed the classics student that secession had wrenched from his place at the university.

Captain Fowle had not said much during this family reunion. Nevertheless, his slender, blanket wrapped presence was clearly the axis around which activity in the clearing revolved. Devereux could not help but feel strongly mixed emotions as he watched.

"To what are you detached, Claude?" Fowle asked.

"Signal Corps," injected Franklin Bowie.

Major Jenkins coughed in irritation at the unnecessarily volunteered information.

Jake Devereux grinned in satisfied discovery.

"Secret Service," ran the whisper around the circle of unavoidable presences in the outer darkness of the clearing.

"I wonder if you all are as beaten up as I am by our wanderings," Jenkins said, earnestly hoping that someone would help him stop this public discussion.

Bowie peered about. "There must be some nice soft ground without tree roots around here somewhere."

Fowle spoke up. "We still have the best cooks in the brigade. Corse is always trying to get Snake Davis and Jim Smith to move to his mess, but you're not going, are you boys? We'd starve here without you." An unseen listener answered. "I don't know Cap'n, maybe the pay is better and the wagon seats softer with Gen'ral Corse." The laughter which emerged from the darkness seemed to accompany an old and well liked joke. "Don't you worry none, honey! Breakf'st will be special tomorrow," the voice concluded the conversation.

7:00 A.M., 13 March

"Life is good!" Bowie announced to the forest clearing. "This is the best ham I've had since I don't know when, and, it's not rainin' any more!" Bowie sat astride a log, tin plate in hand, sopping up the remnants of his meal with a biscuit. Finishing up, he reached down for the infusion of odds and ends that served as a substitute for coffee.

Two black company cooks were busy with late comers who wandered into the clearing, received their ration and disappeared again into the dripping woods. The soldiers, the cooks, the officers, all were weathered in the way that men who have lived outside for months are weathered. Their rough clothing was the variegated proof of the inadequacy of the supply system and the independence of their spirit. Clearly no one cared which possible assortment of uniform pieces each man chose to wear. Serviceable, and durable, it was practical but hardly uniform.

Bowie sat quietly for a minute, thinking about the food and looking at the cooks. "Are you boys here on your own," he finally asked them, "or did the government impress you out of a home or farm? And where did you get this stuff? I know the commissary department didn't come up with that meat." Snake Davis, the senior cook, responded. Suspicion crinkled the skin around his eyes. *Why is this strange white man asking*, he thought? "We both free. We come with the boys from town when we all left, long time ago. I used to be cook to Mister Mills, but when he died I was free. Same thing with Jim, diff'rent family is all. Cap'n Herbert axed us to cook for the comp'ny back then and we still do'in it." As an afterthought Snake added, "We don't have no slaves with this comp'ny."

Captain Fowle had listened. "In this regiment," he said, "we've got about 65 or 70 Negro cooks, teamsters and pioneers with us. It isn't policy, but it works out right now that mostly they are free. They like it better that way as you can see. Bill White over there," he pointed at the meeting going on at the far side of the clearing, "with your major and the Devereuxs is chief teamster in this regiment. The other regiments in the brigade have a mixture of slaves and free. Why do you ask?"

Bowie saw that he had trapped himself into the necessity of an explanation. "I farm 800 acres in the Northern Neck," he said. "King George County is where it is. My father has another farm in the same place. We do wheat and tobacco most of the time. Last month the commonwealth government seized 20 of my hands and 15 of my daddy's for work on the Virginia Central. I guess I'm more than a little sensitive to this issue. These boys don't cause trouble, being free and all?" Bowie was surprised to see that he had become the object of close inspection by the other officer. Captain Fowle cleared his throat and turned to the cooks who were listening. "Where did you get the ham?" he asked Snake Davis. Jim Smith jumped at the chance to explain. Directing his speech first to Fowle and then Bowie he began. "Did you see that wuk gang in de feel up by the genr'l's camp? Dat old black man, he's de overseer o'dem folks. He say he runnin' de place while de masta's gone. Dey need some t'ings like nails, a wagon wheel, t'ings. Me and Snake we traded fo' hams out o'dat ol' man's own smokehouse. He makes good hams." Jim turned to the other Negro, looking a little frightened.

Snake spoke. "That's how we come to have hams, Lootenant. Didn't you think the breakf'est was good? We need some real coffee but we have to wait on that for the next fight when we'll get some Yankee coffee. It comes in five pound bags with sugar already in it. We got a lot of it a while back, but we're out now."

At the other side of the clearing, Claude Devereux, Jenkins, Jake Devereux and Bill White were sitting on two rubber ground sheets, deep in conference. This talk was already half an hour old and building to a climax. Jenkins decided he should show his control of the discussion. "So, as you can see, Captain Devereux has some confidential business for the army at the North. He will be absent for several months." Jake raised his head. He did not believe the intelligence officer and looked at him in search of clues to his character. Jenkins continued, "He will then come back to this command. Bill, he wants you to accompany him. General Corse and Colonel Herbert agree that you are a contract teamster and can go where you wish. If you do agree to go with the captain, my bureau will begin to pay you during this period." The Devereuxs and Bill White glanced at each other behind their immobile faces. Jenkins felt that he was somehow the butt of a family joke. As he inspected them, he noticed how familiar and easy they looked with each other. Bent together in a circle, the two white faces and the pale brown one seemed to belong in the same picture.

The elder Devereux spoke. "Bill, the major is waiting for some indication of what you will do." White was taken aback at that. "I'm sorry, Mister Claude," he said. "It didn't come to me. I will go, Sir," he said to Jenkins.

Jake sat back and looked at his brother. "And that leaves me here. Well, at least I have the prospect of an active campaign season. It looks like somewhere down in Tidewater for us in the next week or so. You will bring back news of mother and Aunt Betsy of course, and you needn't worry, Claude, I will be the best file closer for Fowle that he ever dreamed of."

Claude peered at his brother. "What does an outstanding scholar like you have to do with such military things?"

Jake's blue eyes twinkled above the chestnut beard. "I sing of arms and men!"

Claude said. "I am jealous. What does your muse sing of the division commander? We all know he hasn't the brains of a chicken. Rumor has it that he is now in love with a schoolgirl who lives in Richmond."

Jake smiled, relishing the thought. "General Pickett's faults are not such as to earn him serious disapprobation here," he said, "but we are grateful that Longstreet keeps track of what George might decide to do."

"I think that is not something we should discuss in this setting," Jenkins interjected. He looked embarrassed at this talk of senior officer personalities.

They walked out of the shade into the newly emerged sunshine.

Jake grabbed his brother's sleeve. In a voice only Claude could hear, he whispered, "Be nice to Hope, she deserves better than you've been to her. It isn't her fault. We are different! Mother will make her accept us. Be patient."

Bowie scrambled for the horses.

"Time to go," said Jenkins.

Jake watched them disappear, down the road to the landing, four men on three horses. The red mud clung to the horses' legs and flanks.

3

Ashland

8:35 A.M., 15 March

The solarium was a neatly constructed example of nineteenth century architectural folly. Entirely glass, it could be thought of as resembling an oversized Eskimo ice house which magically had become transparent. Alternatively, one could imagine that it was a Brobdingnagian cheese board, complete with a crystal dome.

Bill White found himself wondering how small boys with slingshots were kept from the place. He noticed two cracked panes close together three feet from the ground and smiled to himself. He sat to one side in the strange little building, half listening to Jenkins, Devereux and Bowie talk. He watched Devereux, imagining that he must be seeing the place through the sardonic prisms of thought in which White had long ago learned to delight. He was correct. Devereux's meditation on the glasswork had resolved itself in favor of the cheeseboard. Surrounding the solarium was a vast expanse of lawn. It had been a long time since White had done much with lawns. This one was enormous, reaching into the distance, right up to the veranda of the brick hotel.

Bill started listening closely when he heard the change in tone of voice which signaled the start of real discussion. "What *is* this place?" Devereux asked. "I am unaccustomed to the methods of your *metier*, Major. It still is strange to me to travel at night in the caboose of a freight train, stop on a siding and complete my journey in a closed carriage. I gather we are somewhere north of Richmond."

"Ashland, we're at Ashland," Jenkins answered. "The hotel is a resort. The Richmond, Fredericksburg and Potomac owns it. We have the use of the wing you slept in. We find this to be a convenient location for instruction, as well as a place to house visitors who should not receive a great deal of attention from the general public. We have friends from abroad who will help prepare you. In addition, an officer will come from General Lee's staff to insure your understanding of his needs."

"And the onward travel?" asked Devereux.

The Signal Corps officer entered the discussion. "I'll take care of that," he said. "Don't bother yourself with it. We'll talk about it later." Bowie appeared very confident of the competence of his own function in this project. He looked at Devereux silently for several seconds, making up his mind about something. "We don't want this Negro to be at these meetings," he said. Jenkins must have agreed. He added nothing.

Devereux stared at the two men, his eyes unblinking. "I want him included in what we do here," he said. "I am going to require the help of someone I trust to cover my back."

Jenkins shook his head, cleared his throat and spoke. "That, evidently, is a distinction which few achieve, Captain. Why do you have such confidence in this man? He is, after all, black, and free or not, his loyalty to the Confederate States must be examined." Harry Jenkins' gaze was fixed on Devereux's face. He did not look at White.

Devereux stared back. With rising emotion at the indignity of the scene he glared across the table. "I will take whom I wish, Jenkins, or you can go yourself! We will then see how convincing the sound of your Southside voice is to the Union Army."

The Engineer officer grew whiter around the edges of his face. Mastering himself, he said, "We all know that I can't do this and that you have some chance. I would appreciate it if you would respond more calmly. I meant no offense." Bowie watched this exchange with growing annoyance. "Come on, Devereux!" he said. "Play the game! We have no reason to trust this man. Tell us why we should."

"Ask him yourself."

Growing steadily paler, Jenkins turned his head to White without taking his eyes from the white man. "Bill," he asked, "why are you with us?"

White had not thought this interrogation would affect him emotionally. He had expected some such thing to happen, expected to be challenged by these strangers, had known that his reserves of self-control would easily deal with the situation. He now found this to be untrue. Rage welled up inside him. Images and jumbled words poured through his mind.

> *How can you ask me that?* he thought. *What else must I do for you to believe? Maybe you would not ask if you had seen me and the other drivers dragging the regiment's shot and maimed out of the firing line in the Peninsula. It went on for almost a week, day after goddamned day! If you had seen their blood on us and heard the teams screaming in fear of the death whirring about them. Maybe if you had seen General Corse tell me not to stand so close to him at Sharpsburg. He said that only fools like him had to do this. He never moved and I never moved. If you had seen this, maybe then you would let me be.*

The eyes were unreadable, but the smile was warm. "Why Sir, my home is in Alexandria and I do believe you will win the war."

"That's all?" asked Bowie.

"Isn't that enough?" snapped Devereux.

Jenkins began to look at White even as he answered. "No. I don't believe it is anything like the whole truth, but it will do, Claude. It will suffice. Your instruction will start after lunch, both of you, if you wish."

At two o'clock they began. The two Englishmen had spent a great deal of time in the solarium. You could see it in the comfortable sprawl of the huge one and the automatic reach with which the small, rabbity one placed his teacup almost exactly on the stain in the wooden table top. Their entry was accompanied by hearty expressions of solicitude for anyone dragged to this isolated spot as well as sentiments of wonder for the beauty of the rather unremarkable countryside. They claimed to be recent immigrants, newly embarked on patriotic volunteer work for "the cause." The big, fat one was named Philip Hare and the little one wished to be known as Henry Rocklin. The fat man beamed at Devereux. "Understand you speak French, lovely language, lovely folk, lovely women!" He began a rambling discourse on the marvels of Gallic civilization in a French which Devereux heard with growing amusement. It was perfectly fluent, but appeared to have been learned on the Marseilles' docks. Claude smiled at the thought of the embarrassment which his mother would experience to hear the vulgarity of some of the idioms.

White was in his seat in the corner, just behind Devereux. The black man found himself fascinated by the Englishmen, particularly Hare. His enormous bulk was surprisingly hard. It did not shake much during his convulsive bouts of laughter. Bill thought himself a good judge of people. This fat man's jocularity and good humor were not genuine. The little man was very odd. One eye was larger than the other. His wavy, thin hair hung in wispy locks on his forehead. The clothing looked expensive but inappropriate. A linen suit was too light for the season. They said they had served together in the Indian Police, gradually working their way over the years into the management of confidential informants as a trade.

Devereux was a good listener. Voices had special meaning for him. The two were upper class in their diction. *Britishers of their origins do not serve in the colonial police.* The little one had something of the British army officer about him. Devereux shared the prejudice of many Americans of his time against the British. The possibility of their support against the United States might make cooperation necessary, but the memory of parliamentary oppression and two wars was yet strong. Nevertheless, he rose to the occasion and remarked that it was certainly fortunate for the South that they were available to help with their experience in these things.

Rocklin rubbed his too large eye. "Colonel, it is colonel, I believe?" Claude thought about this. *How intriguing? These foreigners are clearly establishment types. They have been given a less than complete knowledge of his task by Jenkins. This must mean that these two wanderers are with us, but not of us. Jenkins must believe that these two would restrict their conversation to that which was immediately at hand. How surprisingly naive! How unlike him..* "Yes, lieutenant colonel in fact," he said.

The rabbit beamed, delighted to know that he might get more from this talk than a chance to impart his hard won skills. "We are informed that your mission will take you into the capital city.

"You mean Washington City?" Claude replied evenly.

The rabbit smiled again, but the teeth looked bigger this time. "Quite so, quite so, not Richmond. It is likely that you will find it advantageous to get the private assistance of persons who already have the information that is wanted."

Claude did not disagree.

"Tell me, Colonel, how do you think one does this?" the rabbit asked.

After some thought, Claude began, "I imagine that it would be profitable to think of this as a form of seduction. The desired person is cultivated, flattered, feted. Attention is showered. Identification is sought between the goal and that which the intended victim thinks he or she wishes to do. At some point a gradual acquiescence and action are obtained." He stopped.

Hare looked out at the lawn.

Rocklin grinned. "You have done this before."

Claude thought of the circle he had built in Alexandria the previous winter. He thought of his friends and the necessity of protecting them from these men. "No, not in this work," he lied, "but I have the usual knowledge of seduction and the process must be a lot like tying up a bargain in international commerce. That, I know a lot about."

The big man stopped smiling and nodding at the lawn. Hare turned to focus on Devereux, looking unconvinced. "Colonel, most of what you say is correct, but you have failed to describe the most difficult step." The big, square head continued to speak, the jaw opening and closing impressively. "We have found that only by rare chance and in odd circumstance is it possible to 'seduce' someone who does not wish it." Seeing that he had Devereux's undivided attention, he went on. "What must be done is to make an appreciation of the approximate locale in which the right man or woman might be found and then one must spread wide the net."

"And," Rocklin added, "one listens, and looks and feels, waiting for the moment when a sensitive soul discovers in another, a secret hunger which must be satisfied."

"Does it matter what the hunger craves?" Devereux was whispering now. There was something about this discussion that was darkly disquieting.

The big head spoke. "Very little, actually. As a general thing, almost any hunger is of use. It matters not how praiseworthy or despicable that hunger might be."

Rocklin recommenced. "One dreams, of course, of discovering a cabinet minister who harbors an overpowering desire to associate himself with one's cause from political conviction, but alas, a desire for vengeance or simple lust is more common."

"And after this hungering soul is discovered and diagnosed, I should apply my ideas of seduction?" Devereux found this line of talk deeply absorbing. Something in it gripped his mind, forbidding the indulgence in other paths of thought so common to him in talks like this. For some reason he suddenly thought of his grandfather as he looked in dreams.

The rabbit grew enthusiastic. "Gradually, gradually, being careful not to frighten the quarry. Slowly you must associate the hunger with your task in the mind of the victim, slowly becoming more demanding in return for your apparent efforts to slake the need."

With shattering suddenness, Devereux knew he was hearing his own vulnerability described. *If this how it is done, who better than me to do it?* He eyed the smaller man. "I didn't know they had cabinet ministers in India," he said.

The big one rumbled, deep in the chest. "Well done! After your return I reckon we'll have a good idea of the strength of Hooker's army?"

The pathetic obviousness of the attempt to fish for the details of his task aroused his contempt. "Perhaps so, I intend to look around in the British embassy for possible friends. Do you know anyone there?"

The bait lay on the table, nearly visible it was so obvious.

The little fellow spoke. "Not really. The only man we know there is the assistant military attaché, Major Neville. He might be someone to discuss things with, if the chance arose."

Surely Jenkins must know this! He must know these Limey bastards are playing their own game. "I'll remember," he said.

"Why don't we stop for tea?" Hare asked pleasantly. "You and your chap take a stroll in this lovely park and then come back. We want to talk to you about hidden communication with informants and ways to deal with the police, if they are pesky."

6:00 P.M.

The solarium didn't feel like such a friendly and secure place after the sun went down. It was extremely dark outside. White could occasionally glimpse a sentry walking a post which took him all the way around the building. He couldn't be seen until his silhouette interrupted your view of the hotel, then he was obvious.

They were discussing the possibility of food when a maid arrived from the hotel with a big tray.

"Who are those English people?" asked White while they were eating.

"Some part of their government which is helping but doesn't want credit," Claude replied "The British are like everyone else. They are waiting to see if we make it on our own before they get committed. I asked Jenkins if he knew what they really wanted. He said I had passed a test." They laughed together at that.

More silhouettes crossed the light from the hotel windows. Voices approached. The sentinel challenged. The glass door swung inward. Jenkins and two men they had not met before in this adventure entered. Their breath steamed in the lamp light. The first of the newcomers had a familiar face for Devereux. Looking at him, he had a vision of a dinner party somewhere. The man was a virtual fashion plate by Confederate Army standards. The trousers of his uniform actually matched his overcoat in shade. Such a thing was almost unseen except among the highest ranking of officers. Claude thought he resembled one of the pictures in the uniform regulations. He looked a little worn, but nevertheless elegant. The man smiled as he crossed the floor. "Captain Devereux, so glad to see you again, sir! I remember well our conversation at my cousin's house in Culpeper. It must have been in '56. Yes. No. '55. Long ago now!"

"Ah yes, Charles Venable isn't it?"

"Absolutely! I'm flattered you remember." Still standing in the middle of the floor in his overcoat, Venable suddenly turned to include the other newcomer. "Forgive me! This is Lieutenant Morgan of the 43rd Cavalry Battalion."

"Mosby's Rangers," Jenkins offered in clarification.

"I believe I knew that, Harry," responded Devereux. The sarcasm was deliberate. Devereux was not a man to accept the position of student to which Jenkins had reduced him. This pawn had teeth.

The cavalry lieutenant gave him his hand. While locked in the grip of the big, hard hand, Devereux considered its owner. In a room filled with medium sized men, this one was a giant. He was six foot two or three, with black hair, and deep blue, almost violet eyes set deep in a heavily tanned face. His posture was slightly hunched with one shoulder a little higher than the other. Venable might be a model of military appearance but this man represented a different school of thought concerning dress for 'the field.' He wore blue trousers tucked into soft black boots, and a short grey jacket edged in faded cavalry yellow braid. A red and black flannel shirt showed under the jacket. Devereux took note of the two collar bars of a first lieutenant. The whole display was surmounted by a black felt hat which looked somewhat like a bowler equipped with a larger brim. The effect was an amalgam of circus rider, jockey and soldier. "How do!" he smiled, exposing a lot of white teeth and pumping the hand up and down. As this handshake ran its course, Major Venable stood to one side in his overcoat, hat in hand, still savoring the flavor of Devereux's response to Jenkins. Officiousness was not appreciated in the circles in which both he and Devereux lived. You could see his enjoyment of the rebuke in the corners of the eyes mainly. There were small laughter wrinkles which were beyond the control gripping the rest of his face. "I suppose it's warm enough in here to take this off," he said at last, throwing back the half cape and reaching for the buttons.

Bill White appeared at Venable's elbow, expecting to help with the bulky coat.

Sensing the unexpected presence, Venable shifted his attention while continuing to undo the many buttons of the double breasted garment. "And who might you be?" he asked.

"He's a teamster with our city's regiment, and a member of my father's household," Claude answered. "Montgomery Corse lent him to me for this trip."

Venable listened, then turned back to White and addressed him directly. "You have been working for the army by your own wish?"

Bill nodded.

Venable handed him the coat and inspected the dark skinned man before him. White and he were of a size. Bill wore butternut brown pants and jacket, rough in texture and closed with plain buttons. The jacket was piped in the pale blue of the infantry.

Venable laid a hand on Bill's sleeve. "We thank you for your service. Why don't you put that somewhere and go for a walk? I must speak with Captain Devereux of matters that should not be heard by many."

Lieutenant Morgan watched White close the door behind himself.

Bill felt the man's observation, knew the watchful eyes were on him. He walked out of the circle of light to stand beside the sentinel. The soldier halted, waiting for him, glad of someone to visit with in the cold and wind.

The group in the solarium sat to discuss their business. "Yes," Venable said after a few minutes, "I've been with General Lee's staff now for some time, handling odds and ends as an assistant adjutant general. Among my tasks is a responsibility for the adequacy of our relations with the War Department in secret matters. I make arrangements for Mosby to support War Department informants, as we are doing here."

"As I recall," Devereux commented, "Major Mosby's battalion belongs to Stuart's cavalry."

Venable agreed pleasantly. "That's right. They are Stuart's property but we give him direction as to what to do with them."

Devereux recognized in this man someone of his own class. He felt comfortable with Venable, felt that he could be relied on to do the sensible thing, to take action proportionate to reality. "You want me to detect Hooker's intentions for a spring campaign?" he asked.

"That was our thought a few weeks ago. We still want that, but a new mystery has arisen."

Devereux waited.

The staff officer continued. "We have always been fortunate in the inability of the U.S. command to form an accurate opinion of our real strength in the field. McClellan didn't want to know how many of us there were in front of him. It suited his strange mind to wish to oppose more of us than could possibly have existed. It gave him an excuse for inaction, a state which he apparently preferred. To that end he obtained the services of the Pinkerton detective agency which by some odd process supplied him with the absurd accounting which he used. Pope and Burnside did nothing to improve this when they took over for short periods of time." He smiled, enjoying the memory of these two victims of Lee's army.

"And now this blessed state of affairs has changed?"

Venable raised his eyebrows and looked to Major Jenkins who picked up the account.

Jenkins' face was still red with embarrassment at having been thought gauche by these representatives of his society's ruling class. "Two weeks ago Stonewall Jackson's corps, east of Fredericksburg, picked up a Union deserter," he said. "He was a Canadian who had decided that war against us was not as enjoyable or glorious as he had thought it might be. He was an officer's orderly from the artillery reserve of the Army of the Potomac. You know, Hunt's men. Jackson and Stapleton Crutchfield, his artillery chief, talked to this Canadian. To their annoyance, he knew our total strength to within 5,000 men. He told them he had overheard the number in the conversation of two officers. We find this worrisome."

Devereux was intrigued. "What could have happened?"

Jenkins went on, "Whatever it is, it does not appear to have affected other fronts. Prisoners in Mississippi and Tennessee don't seem to know any more than they ever did and our friends and agents in Washington and Chicago know of no big change in the way of calculating our strength. We conclude that the headquarters of the Army of the Potomac itself is the heart of this mystery. They may, I stress may, be doing something there which is exceedingly dangerous to us. We want to know what it is.

Claude thought a moment, then asked, "This means Hooker himself is responsible?"

"One cannot discount the possibility," said Jenkins. "The man is renowned as an administrator. His personal life is disreputable but we do not doubt his ability."

Devereux looked quizzically to Venable who seemed faintly exasperated. "Harry," Venable spluttered, "not even General Lee cares who Hooker may be sleeping with nor how much he drinks. We hope he drinks a lot! Devereux, please do what you can about this as well as the question of Hooker's intentions. We have about 65,000 men available to turn back the offensive which is inevitable later this Spring. General Lee has found it necessary to send substantial detachments away, notably to the Suffolk area in southeastern Virginia. Information on enemy plans will help us immensely in positioning ourselves to deal with them. We think that the Union Army will begin to move around the end of April. This doesn't give you much time." He glanced at Morgan. "We would like you to have a means of sending messages to the Army of Northern Virginia directly, as well as by the facility the Signal Corps will provide. To that end, Mosby's cavalry will give you the services of an experienced soldier whom I suggest you somehow make a part of your household. He will be your man for the period of this effort and will carry messages for you to Mosby. From Mosby the messages will be couriered and telegraphed to me at army headquarters which is now near Fredericksburg. Lieutenant, why don't you go on with the rest of this?"

Devereux interrupted. "Is Pickett's division part of the force which will go to the Suffolk area?"

Venable was willing to be informative. "That is your division isn't it? Yes. I thought so. You're right. They are going to seek to pen up the Union garrison of Norfolk while supplies are brought in from the area." Venable gestured for Morgan to begin.

The big man was slow to start.

Watching him gather his energies, Devereux realized that Morgan's massive presence concealed a shyness which reflected itself in a flush that spread under the tan.

"I'm from Company B of the 43rd Battalion," he began. "We are mostly Fauquier County men in that company. We have a man named Isaac Smoot, a sergeant, who we think can be of help to you. He was a deputy sheriff before the war. He's from Haymarket, near the Bull Run Mountains." He looked up at Devereux to know if that meant something.

A nod started him again.

"He knows Washington City well, as well as Fairfax County and Alexandria. His work often took him there before the war, prisoners and runaway slaves, you know. We are sure he can cross the lines pretty much at will."

"Why do you believe this?" Devereux asked, remembering how difficult doing this had been the previous winter.

Morgan appeared amused at the question. "He does it often. He crosses into Maryland and into Yankee held territory on our side of the river. He was a scout for the raid on Fairfax Court House."

Devereux looked blank. "I've been out of touch," he said at last when no one explained.

Jenkins spoke. "Mosby went into Fairfax at night last week and pulled a drunken brigadier general out of his bed. We have the prisoner now in Richmond. Smoot was in that. He comes highly recommended."

"What's he like, Lieutenant?" Devereux probed, wanting to be certain that they were not saddling him with someone they wished to be rid of.

Morgan scratched the side of his nose nervously, looked out the glass side of the building at Bill White and the sentry.

They were deep in conversation.

"Isaac Smoot is a poor man," he began. "He has a wife and two small children, all in Haymarket. His family is from over in the Shenandoah Valley. The father moved to Fauquier when Isaac was little. The father never seemed able to do anything right. Every job he ever had ended in failure. His son, Isaac, just naturally took to being a sheriff and then a soldier. He is a disciplined man, in his own way. He was out with Turner Ashby's cavalry in '61 and did well, but then Stuart decided to make them over into regular troops and Isaac ended up in the 11th Virginia. He didn't like that. He especially didn't like some of the West Point officers that were brought in. So, when John Mosby was looking for good cavalrymen to serve on their own ground, Smoot was a logical choice." Morgan suddenly was a little defiant and resentful. "We have never had reason to regret our decision to take him in."

Devereux began to understand Smoot through Morgan's willingness to defend him. "Are you from Haymarket, Lieutenant?" asked Devereux. Morgan nodded. "Just outside."

"Does he fight?"

The lieutenant laughed aloud with such force that White and the sentinel started for the building, stopping when they received a wave off from Jenkins. "I'm sorry, Captain," Morgan said. "Your problem will be to keep him from fighting at the wrong time. He will obey orders, but you should expect him to want to take someone's head off."

"Is he a slaveholder?"

Morgan frowned. "No! No money! I said. I thought I had said that. The only thing he ever did with blacks is chase them for other people."

Devereux digested the information, then asked, "How will you get him established in the Washington City area."

Morgan relaxed. "That's easy. We will have him ride into Fairfax Court House, turn himself in to the Provost Marshal as a civilian refugee and take the oath of allegiance to the Union. He will then report to you in Alexandria. Simple."

Devereux sat back and considered each of the three men in turn. Major Venable's well-bred features refused to look disapproving, seeming to acknowledge the inevitability of treachery and deceit in such matters. Morgan clearly was unconcerned with the ethical niceties involved in false oaths given to an enemy. Only Harry Jenkins was badly discomfited by the idea. Jenkins finally spoke. "It works, damn it, Claude! The Yanks are so eager to think we are falling apart that they readily accept all sorts of line crossers. To them we are all still U.S. citizens who have temporarily gone astray."

"I suppose it is no worse than killing their men on the battlefield." Devereux muttered. "This must be what you have in mind for me as well."

Jenkins shook his head. "You will have to decide for yourself once you arrive. Another possibility would be for you to employ your French nationality."

"I'll think it over."

Lieutenant Morgan erupted with resentment, rising from his chair. "Do I understand that you think it below you to do what one of our men will do?"

Devereux shook his head. "You don't have it exactly right. I think it beneath both of us, Smoot and me, but that doesn't mean I won't do it.." He turned back to Jenkins. "I suppose the Yanks won't bother to question Bill's loyalty to 'Mistuh Linkum'?"

"They never do," Jenkins said. "We find it useful in the matter of couriers."

"Anything else?" Devereux asked. He was more than a little tired of the three of them. He would do what they wanted, but there was no joy in it, no relish at all. He thought of the Englishmen and their description of his vulnerability. He wondered what his wife would say when she knew what he had done.

"No. The two of you and Bowie will leave for the Potomac tomorrow morning," said Jenkins.

Venable expressed his "sincere best wishes" and those of General Lee. Lieutenant Morgan shook hands slowly, his eyes guarded. He said nothing at all. Claude wondered what Sergeant Isaac Smoot would hear of this meeting.

The glass door closed behind him. The cold night air felt wonderful. Bill White lifted a hand in farewell to the ghostly figure of the sentry and walked to join him on the way to the hotel. He could hear Morgan's angry voice behind him in the solarium.

11:32 P.M.

Trees stood guard on the periphery of the lawn. A three quarter moon in a cloudless sky lit the scene in ghostly silver. The sentry trees encircled the open space, the advanced party of an army which crowded against them, pressing them toward the hotel. The forest seemed endless. Claude knew that could not be, but the visual effect was overwhelming. He stood at his bedroom window, listening to Bill's regular breathing on the divan in the sitting room. He wanted to think through the events of the day. He felt deeply grateful for Bill's willingness to accompany him on this trip. Claude hated isolation, feared it more than death or wounds. He had felt that way as long as he could remember.

His mother had always been there for him. His brothers were his greatest friends and the White family was part of the life which he cherished. Nevertheless, there had been something missing. There was an inability to be content with himself, an incapacity to satisfy many of those around him. It was curious. School had been easy, any school, Washington College, Yale. His father had insisted on Yale. Many Southerners sent their sons there. He suspected that his father had hoped that the difficulty of the place would challenge him. It had not. Schools were not difficult, merely tedious. Business was not for him the challenge that so engaged many of his colleagues. Somehow, none of this mattered. The people who most doubted him were among those he cherished most. His wife, his father, they were among the foremost critics of Claude Devereux.

His body felt a cessation of movement in the hallway outside the bedroom door. The perception of this negative sensation spread upward from his stockinged feet. By the time it reached the knees, he was moving toward the wall beyond the door hinges. Leaning back against the wall, he listened for sounds which might reveal the number of his visitors. A very slight tapping vibrated the door. Claude wondered if he could have heard this sound from the window. With his right hand he reached across the door and unlocked the key. Standing next to the hinges, he saw the handle rotate in the moonlight. The door swung in. No one entered.

"Yes?" he asked.

"May I come in?" a low voice responded.

"Of course you may, friend. Just step into the room where we can see you."

A man's figure came forward holding its hands in front of the torso, careful to move deliberately.

Devereux shut the door and locked it. He walked to the night table by his bed and lit the lamp. The feeble yellow light shone on the face of the manager of the hotel, John Wood.

Wood did not appear to be concerned with Devereux. His attention was fixed farther away. Across the room in the arch of the parlor door, Bill White covered the visitor with a sawed off double barreled shotgun. "No need for that!" Wood wheezed. "I am here on State Department business. May I sit down in my own hotel?" he asked. They took seats around a small table in the adjoining parlor. Wood was middle aged, officious, overweight and overbearing. Devereux had noted him in an earlier incident in the lobby when he had attempted to reduce the level of accommodation provided to Jenkins' party. Lieutenant Bowie had spoken to the man in a corner. The manager had returned to his counter flushed and angry, but acquiescent.

Devereux's peripheral vision was excellent. While inspecting Wood for signs of his purpose he watched White take up a position from which he could both block the door to the suite and hear their conversation.

The frightened man moved restlessly in his chair. "Don't you care why I came to speak to you?" he asked hopefully.

"You are going to tell me or you wouldn't be here."

This reply and the meeting thus far were not proceeding as the hotelier had anticipated and did not fit his image of his own position in the world. He grew visibly upset. "Judah Benjamin sent me to talk to you before you go to the North."

"Why?" Claude asked. "We parted on such good terms when last we met."

Wood began to see that Devereux was yet another of the high bred gentlemen who everlastingly dealt with him on the basis of amused, ironic, condescension. For Wood, life had begun on the Baltimore waterfront. He had struggled all his life to make men like Devereux behave toward him as a peer, someone of stature. He began to feel lightheaded with humiliation. His anger centered on the man before him. "Smart people listen when Mister Benjamin speaks!" he rasped. "Do you want to hear what I am to say?"

Many of Claude Devereux's peers would have been concerned to see that they had seriously wounded Wood's self esteem. They would have sought to make amends, sincerely wishing to repair any damage to their relations with this stranger. Devereux cared nothing for Wood, thought him contemptible, but saw what had to be done. "Mister Wood, you must forgive me for the informality of your welcome," he said. "I was not expecting you. I very much want to hear what news you have from Secretary Benjamin."

Wood seethed in his seat, torn between a desire to lash out and an unavoidable need to do business with Devereux. Prudence triumphed. "The Secretary is charged by President Davis with general supervision of the activities of the various secret services. You may not know, but he now controls all moneys so employed." Wood was still glaring.

To help him along Devereux registered an acceptable degree of astonishment at this information.

Wood felt better. "This facility is operated by the War Department, but the secretary has asked me to act as his personal representative at Ashland."

Devereux marveled. *Benjamin has planted this worm in the apple?* "Do you expect to be here long, Mister Wood?"

The man swelled with self-important confidence. "Soon the Secretary will be given direct control of all the secret services. Yes, I will someday direct this establishment!" Sure that the proper tone had been established, Wood spoke again. "Mister Benjamin wishes you to be reminded of the request he made you and to state that he and the President consider it to be the more significant of your tasks."

He and the President, Devereux wondered if Jefferson Davis would find that amusing, or perhaps a surprise.

"The Secretary also wished me to tell you that when you return from this mission he personally will see that you are returned to your regiment in accordance with your expressed wish. He said to pass on to you that he would prefer for you to remain in a senior position in the State Department or secret services, but that it will be your choice."

My choice! A cruel joke. "Please give the secretary my greetings." Devereux answered. "He need not fear. I will return with the best judgement that I can muster."

Wood was immensely pleased at the prospect of relaying such a positive response. He thought of leaving, then remembered the rest of his message. "One more thing. We, of the State Department have a number of friends in Washington. If you need help, you should call upon Mister Thomas Green, an attorney who resides by the City Canal at 17th Street. He will be instructed to expect you. He will do whatever he thinks wise to assist you."

"Should I go to him in difficulty only?"

"No! No! I have tried to explain it to you. This mission of yours is essentially our business in the State Department. Mister Benjamin desires you to make contact with Green as soon as practicable. The Secretary will communicate with you through Green."

The gross figure slipped into the darkened hallway.

White saw him off, watching him disappear around a corner. Locking the door, he propped a chair against the latch.

Devereux waved him to the chair in which the visitor had sat.

The chair was unpleasantly warm from the man's body.

White sat with the weapon across his lap. "Why don't you tell me, Claude? It's the only way, if I'm to help you."

Devereux smiled. "Thank you Bill. Did you recognize Charles Venable?"

4

The River

3:00 P.M., 16 March
(A Signal Corps camp on the lower Potomac)

Bowie watched the two men from his seat by the cook's hut. They had sat by the river bank for more than an hour. Fifty yards separated them. Bowie increasingly felt that there was less space than that between them. Neither of these men was comprehensible to Bowie. The black man's carefully cultivated air of subordination hid something. Bowie was sure it was something dramatic. The white man was an infuriating mixture of charm, aristocratic haughtiness, intellect and the detachment which comes with old money. Bowie had never had much dealing with Catholics. He knew there were many in places like Alexandria and Richmond and that the army was full of Irish. Some units had Catholic chaplains. If Devereux was an example of the breed, Bowie judged that he would prefer to continue to deal with Protestants. In addition to everything else, the man's reputation as a combat leader demanded respect. You couldn't ignore the fact that this son of privilege had returned from Europe to join the army as a private soldier and had risen to commissioned rank through performance on a half dozen murderous battlefields.

The priest in Alexandria that Bowie had visited in search of information to help in choosing the man for this mission had said that Devereux's relationship with his father was "a minor crucifixion." What did that mean?

The camp on the Potomac was a makeshift collection of huts and tents. There were several like it along the big river. The Signal Corps used these camps and the men and boats located at them to carry men and secret mail across the river. The headquarters of this camp was housed in the small frame house which had sheltered the farmer owner in the days before the river had become an international border. Devereux had added to Bowie's discomfort by asking why the crossing would be here, opposite Port Tobacco on the Maryland shore. "Why here, he had asked, where the river is so wide." "Why? Why?" Did the man never accept anything? After worrying over this question for a while, Bowie had asked Lieutenant Howard Cawood, the officer in charge of the station, why the crossing site was at this point on the river. Cawood had laughed and told him that he wanted to move it but could not without approval from Richmond.

The sun shone brilliantly on the river. The wind gusted erratically, driving sheets of tiny, shimmering waves before it. It was cold. The wind felt like a knife.

Bowie sat far enough back from the bank to be safe from observation by river traffic. Two U.S. Navy gunboats had passed in the last hour. They were converted river steamers. Each had small deck guns and improvised armor along the rail on the weather deck. They hugged the far shore, seeming convinced that a daylight approach to the Virginia side would be hazardous. The thought pleased Bowie, but there was still some chance that a sharp eyed officer with a glass might spot something. He wondered if it would be possible to persuade Devereux to sit in some place less exposed, probably not.

After watching his two charges a few minutes more, Bowie decided it was time to see what could be learned from Devereux's pet. He climbed to his feet, and limping from a sleeping leg, he approached White. "I want to talk to you, Bill," he said taking a seat beside the black man.

Bill looked up. The eyes held Bowie, "Yes, sir?"

"Are you clear on what we are going to do tonight?"

White scrutinized him for a minute, wondering what this was about, then recited as expected. "You and Lieutenant Cawood are going to take us by boat to Maryland. From the way everyone is acting this must be something they do all the time."

Bowie nodded in agreement.

White resumed. "We will go into Port Tobacco, in Charles County, Maryland, which is over there somewhere. He waved a hand at the far shore. The postmaster, who is a friend, will provide a wagon. We will go to Baltimore with you. I guess Lieutenant Cawood will not go to Baltimore?"

"That's right Bill he needs to come back with the boat. You don't talk like nigras do, Bill. Why is that?"

"I've lived with white folks all my life, sir. Madame Devereux, Mister Claude's mother, is a French lady, as you may know, sir. She has never accepted the existing law against the education of my race, against teaching us to read. She taught me and my brothers to read and write, and other things."

Bowie marveled at the perfect impassivity of the face and the absolute neutrality of the voice. Considering White, he had the insight to realize that a life in which he had worried continuously about white reactions would have made him much the same. "How long have you been free, Bill?"

"Mister Charles Devereux, Captain Devereux's father, freed my parents when his daddy died. I was born after that. I have always been free."

"Mister Charles Devereux has a reputation as a stern man. Is that true, Bill? Is he a hard man?"

"He's a good man, sir. He is a lot like the folks I saw in Connecticut when I was there with Mister Claude at Yale University before the war. He believes in hard work. He doesn't hold with fooling around or going fishing too much." Bill frowned. "He thinks white and black folks should be good to each other but not too close."

"But you grew up in his house, Bill, he allowed that."

"That's work, and responsibility and churchgoing and such things as that."

"The Devereuxs. Have they been good to you, Bill? Are you married?"

White considered the white officer carefully, remembering the tenor of many of his previous comments and suspicious of the direction this talk was taking. "My family and the Devereuxs have been together for a long time now. Yes, I'm married. I have a daughter. My wife is in Alexandria."

"Is she free too?"

White's unease began to break through to the surface of his face, displaying itself in a slight tick in the corner of his mouth. A reply was unavoidable. "No, sir. She is my property. I borrowed the money from Mister Charles to buy her. I still owe him some. I was planning to free her when I paid off the money. Mister Charles was going to help me with the lawyers, but then the war came.." Bill came to a ragged end in embarrassment.

"You and Captain Devereux have been together a lot."

"Oh, yes! Mister Claude, Mister Jake, and me, we always went fishing, hunting too, mostly deer, in the Blue Ridge."

"And what did Mister Charles think of it?"

"Not much. He gave the young gentlemen hell about it, mostly Captain Devereux. Jake, he was the baby and was safe from disapprobation and such." White was laying it on a bit thick now playing the faithful darky instinctively to avoid further inquiry from Bowie. *Ease off*, he told himself, *he isn't that stupid.* "Mister Patrick, he was always the best thought of. Mister Claude caught it, but he caught it about everything."

"Why? Was he not trustworthy?"

"No! No Sir! It was because Mister Claude was too much like the grandfather! He's full of spirit and life and wanted to have fun. My father says he is the spit of the old man. Mister Charles, he sees his father.." Bill fell silent. "I can't say more, sir. It's a family matter." *Don't tell him. Don't tell him. He should see.*

"That's all right, Bill. I believe I understand now. Get some sleep. This should be a long trip." Bowie strolled away to the house to digest what he had heard and reflect.

Not a bad man, White thought watching him walk away. *Not bad at all really, just limited. I wonder what he would think of all the lectures I heard at Yale, sitting in the corners of the rooms while Claude sat up in front..*

At the end of a long day of waiting, sunset brought the darkness they needed to be safe. Several hours later, they carried the boat down to the water. There were eight men altogether; four Signal Corps oarsmen, Lieutenant Cawood acting as helmsman, and the three passengers.

White saw Devereux take out his watch and open it as they passed the cook's fire with the boat. Claude told him the time, 11:00 P.M. Six of them carried the boat. It was about twenty feet long and of the type long used for smuggling on the Maryland coast. It was built to lighter cargo ashore, with a high freeboard and ship lines to her hull. Bill somehow had been assigned the task of carrying the rudder and tiller until they got the boat into the river.

There was a three quarter moon which lit up the river dangerously in an unpredictable way. The sky was alive with puffy clouds pursuing each other from west to east. There wasn't much ground level wind but Bill White thought it must really be blowing up above for the clouds to be moving that fast. The ever changing sky made the visibility vary every few minutes.

Bill wore a new set of clothes which Cawood had brought from somewhere that day. They had no labels. Bill wondered what sort of impression that would make if he had to explain, but had decided it wasn't worth talking about. A lot of clothes had no labels. The Signal Corps soldiers had all made a great show of their wonderment of "how fine" he appeared in his new clothes. He was careful not to tell them that his closet at home had several suits in it that were considerably better than this one. "Hand me downs" from the Devereux closets were, after all, from the best tailors in New York and London.

Ahead of them, the river bank appeared out of the night. The bow of the boat inclined down. There was a small wet noise, followed by dimly seen bobbing at that end of the craft. Two soldiers held the stern to the bank while oars were shipped, rudder mounted and passengers seated. The last two men ashore shoved hard and were pulled over the side. They floated free, drifting from the riverbank.

Bill sat in the bottom of the boat next to Devereux. Lieutenant Bowie took his place on the first thwart forward of the helmsman's seat. He faced aft, chatting with Cawood. It was easy to see that these two men were old friends. Muffled laughter welled up from their vicinity. Bill caught a reference to some distantly connected female relative of Cawood's. Bowie whispered that he was going to visit the lady "come what may." One of the oarsmen ventured the opinion that he should bring someone with him for protection or assistance when he did. The soldiers chuckled and nodded in agreement. Serious rowing commenced. The bow swung around to point diagonally upstream at the far shore. The oars moaned in the rowlocks.

The moon came and went, peering from behind the clouds.

Devereux leaned toward Bill. "What did Bowie want this afternoon?"

"Nothing. He's just trying to figure us all out."

The other man nodded. *Well, good luck to him! Many have tried,* he thought.

Half way came and went. The pace flagged a little as fatigue crept into the rowers. The night was cool but they all began to sweat. You could smell them. A smell of men, wood smoke and inadequately washed clothing hung in the air. They stopped talking for a time and then suddenly Bowie rotated his head to the left and sat upright in the stern, motionless. After listening for a moment, he pointed in that direction. Lieutenant Cawood turned to face downstream. Together, they peered through the moon dappled night, listening.. "Pull!" rasped Cawood. "There's something coming! There isn't supposed to be another patrol for an hour!"

The river was almost two miles wide at this point. They had crossed the greatest part.

Downstream, lights crawled into view, marching around a headland. One, two, three, four.

Bill's guts contracted. *This has to be a patrol.*

The sound of the gunboat's steam engine reached them. They watched the lights rotate to track across their stern.

"Pray for cloud," Bowie muttered.

The oarsmen pulled, pulled hard. Bill could see that the bow was pointed into a little inlet which grew as he watched. *Jesus! If I can see the shore, then they can see us!* he thought.

The night grew steadily brighter.

Looking up, Bill watched the moon drift out from the gauze wrapping of the racing clouds. *This had to be,* he thought. *It hasn't been this bright the whole time, or maybe it just seems that way.*

A steam whistle sounded on the patrol boat. Her bow swung away from the previous course.

"They see us, damn them!" Devereux cried. He stared at the gunboat's lights, making them into a pattern in his head, a pattern that outline the silhouette of the small ship. *My God, it is just like that poor little thing at Wilmington. What is this, some sort of revenge?*

Bowie cried out, "Get your backs into it, or we'll all be in Fort Warren prison for the duration!"

"I thought this was routine," Devereux commented. The fear of further mutilation was strong in him now.

Bowie stared at him, then turned back to watch the oncoming naval vessel. She was gaining on the rowboat.

The inlet was very, very close.

A deck gun banged. The shot shrieked in, splashing into the river nearby.

The gun banged again.

Not very large caliber, Bill thought, *if it makes that sound.*

The projectile ripped into the trees on one of the headlands of the little inlet. You could hear the ball smashing and tearing as it caromed about in the woods.

We're in the bay, Bill thought. *This should be all right. We will have to run from the boat into the forest.* The deck gun fired a third time. The three inch cast iron ball came aboard the boat in a descending arc. Crossing the stern from starboard it severed Lieutenant Bowie's right arm just below the elbow. Continuing on its path it struck the soldier rowing on the port side just behind Bowie. It entered his chest on the right side and came out his back killing him instantly. The boat itself was untouched and the ball went into the water.

Bill was facing forward, willing the boat up onto the bank when he heard the solid shot hit.

The dead man fell into the bottom on Devereux.

White jumped for the oar, trying to prevent a loss of momentum. You could hear the gunboat behind them, its engine noise growing in detail and menace.

Bowie sat stunned. He looked in amazement at the upraised, mutilated remnant of his arm.

Devereux pulled the belt from the dead man's body and wrapped it around Bowie's upper arm.

The boat ran up on the little gravel beach that had been their goal. The crew leaped for the side, dragging the passengers, their dead comrade and Bowie behind them. Devereux and Cawood half-carried Bowie toward the tree line.

The little cannon fired once more. The shot went high, into the branches of the trees. The fugitives could hear leaves and branches falling from the damage done to the trees.

Bill prayed that the gunboat would not switch to canister, would not spray them with the multitude of lead balls that would surely find them. Looking back as he entered the trees, he could see her She was hove to, broadside, just beyond the two headlands. He could see the gun crew grouped around the deck gun on the bow that had been firing at them. *They're loading. Run!* he thought.

The little party struggled rapidly inland in the darkened forest, smashing through the underbrush, trampling saplings and marsh plants.

Bowie began to moan. The sound was soft now, but Bill knew he would probably be screaming soon as the pain killing effect of shock wore off.

The group stopped.

"How far to help?" Devereux demanded.

"About a mile and a half to Port Tobacco, sir," Cawood answered. "There are several who will help us there, including a doctor."

"I don't think we should drag the lieutenant farther while he is in this state," Devereux said. "I suggest we cover him with our extra clothes to keep him warm and leave him with Bill. These men will guard against a landing party while you and I go for help." His commanding presence and obvious experience in dealing with wounds left no room for argument.

The two officers disappeared in one direction while the other soldiers slipped back into the woods to watch for further attentions from the patrol boat.

Bill sat on the forest floor with Bowie's head in his lap, he had wrapped the wounded man in the extra clothes, but he kept pulling them off to look at his arm. The officer stopped moving after a while and lay hugging his stump to his chest. He was trying not to make noise, knowing the danger of the situation, and the continuing closeness of the gunboat. He periodically held the wreckage of his arm out to look at it.

Bill wished he had some whiskey for him.

Bowie's eyes cleared of pain obsession. He smiled at Bill. His face began to take on a familiar, increasingly blank expression.

White grabbed his hair, yanking the head around to make the eyes see him. "Don't die, damn it!" he growled. "Nobody said you could die! Think about that great time you wanted back in the boat! Think about Cawood's cousin! Think about anything, damn you!"

The eyes focused. "Bill, I can see it now. It has come to me. I see who you are. You really are one of us. Why are you with us?"

Anger rose like bile to the back of Bill's throat. *Careful!* he thought. *This man is going. Don't say something you will regret forever.* "I made my choice, Lieutenant," he murmured. "I will win or lose with you. I can't help it if you don't treat us right. I can only hope for better, but whether you like it or not, I am one of you! You won't be able to deny it after the war. This is my country. The Devereuxs are my people." Bill held his breath for a moment. He knew quite suddenly that he was talking to a corpse. With his left hand he closed the eyes and sat rocking in the dark, clutching the dead soldier to his bosom.

7:35 P.M., 17 March, St. Patrick's Day (Baltimore)

Lieutenant Cawood looked reasonably convincing in civilian clothes. His blond good looks and spare, athletic body attracted more attention than might have been desirable, but he carried himself with apparent unconcern as he smiled and nodded his way through the railroad station buffet. The only truly incongruous thing about him was the depth of his tan. He had the bone deep bronze look that is arrived at only through months of life out of doors. Arriving at Devereux's table, he sat and took up the coffee that had been ordered for him. They were seated in an isolated corner of the room. Devereux's back was to the crowd The mirrors which covered the walls were helpful.

"Where's Bill?" Cawood asked over the rim of his cup.

"He's in the colored's room the other side of the bar." Devereux accompanied the information with an inclination of the head.

Cawood could see across the buffet to an open door at the far side of the room. A stand up bar filled the other room. It was crowded with Union army officers and a few men in civilian dress. Beyond the bar another door led into the room Devereux spoke of. The buffet itself was a plain but clean dining room dominated by what looked like walnut wainscoting below mirrors which made the place seem larger than it was. A long table, furnished in reasonable linen and plate carried the repast for which the room was named.

Cawood surveyed the other diners as he sipped his coffee. *Travelers. All travelers,* he thought. They were a mixture of business people and military men. There were a few women in the room. One of the most notable was three tables away. Cawood made an effort not to stare at her, in part from courtesy, but also because he did not want to establish eye to eye contact with anyone in the room. People tended to remember you much better if that happened. Nevertheless, she was memorable and the lieutenant absorbed her image in little parcels, sweeping his eyes over her each time he looked around the room.

"I've been drinking her in myself," Devereux whispered. "What do you think? Is it the hair or the skin that is so striking?"

"The rest of her looks awfully good to an affection starved soldier from the backwoods," commented Cawood.

"The navy Commander who is sitting with her is rather protective," Devereux said. "Actually, I would say jealous. He looks around the room every few minutes in the hope of catching someone mooning over her. He has looked at us twice since you sat down. Who do you suppose those other people are?"

Cawood surreptitiously studied the companions of the handsome woman and her escort. The two elderly women were well dressed in a style which might come back into vogue some day. *Sisters*, he thought. The conversation between them and the naval officer seemed to consist of pleasantries which hugely amused the three women.

"Your train will be along shortly," Cawood said, turning back to Devereux. "Let me run through things to make sure we are in accord. I have your tickets, yours in the parlor car and Bill's in the ordinary cars. The tickets show you both as passengers from New York. Your story is that you got off the early train about 2:00 P.M. to conduct some business in the harbor district, a bank, of course." He looked at Claude to make sure he was following.

Claude smiled at him.

Cawood could not help but feel that somehow Devereux was laughing at him. "Your new clothes don't really suit you well, but it was the best that our friends could do on such short notice. I have just talked to one of our people here. He will send sealed instructions to our representatives in New York. They will 'adjust' the manifest of the ship you two supposedly arrived on from Le Havre two days ago. The records will show you as have having made the journey." He halted waiting for some sign of mastery of this information from Devereux.

Devereux was now openly admiring the brunette. Without taking his eyes from her, he changed the subject. "What will happen to Frank Bowie?"

The day's long mad dash across Maryland had kept Cawood's mind from dwelling on the night's events. He had not expected to conduct the agent team to Baltimore. The thought of having to deal with his friend's body, of the necessity to transport Franklin Bowie's remains back across the river weighed him down. On top of that there was Private Trimble. He would have to bring over another man to help row. This would take time. He was glad that the weather could be relied on to remain cold for a few days. He would take both men home to their kin. They were both from the Northern Neck area near the camp, as he was. Cawood would take them home to their families.

He noticed the intensity with which Devereux was concentrating on the brunette's table. Anger rose in him. *Was it for this that we gave up John Trimble and Frank? The station is full of Union soldiers and this man sits here panting for this piece of fluff?* "Captain, don't you think you should concentrate on the job at hand?" he asked as calmly as he could manage.

Devereux switched his attention to the other officer. "Don't call me that," he whispered. He looked again at the woman, then back to Cawood. "Stop thinking with your emotions and look at those folks. Look at the man. He is not her husband, but he surely wishes he was. There is some interesting story there. There you have a fairly senior naval officer suffering some romantic disappointment. He undoubtedly needs a friend to confide in. Don't you think so? One must start somewhere to 'cast a wide net'."

Responding to Devereux's suggestion, Cawood observed the other table as discreetly as he could, given the proximity. Devereux was correct. The exaggerated deference which the navy man was showing to the brunette would be likely in a married couple only if they were on their honeymoon. Cawood easily recognized unsatisfied desire when he encountered it. "Be careful." He counseled. "He'll carve your gizzard into little bits if he catches you being gallant to her."

Devereux laughed, throwing his head back in appreciation. "Excellent advice! I'll try to prevent such violent thoughts from entering his nautical mind." He looked right at the Signal officer. The blue eyes were cold above the smile. "Don't worry, Cawood, I do believe I've got the details. Why don't you give me the tickets and leave. You did a fine job today. I can't thank you enough. I'm terribly sorry about Frank and the other man."

Looking at Devereux, Cawood perceived the sincerity of this statement. *Astonishing man*, he thought. *I'm happy that I don't have to deal with him every day.* He shook the offered hand and disappeared into the darkened, hostile city.

The train was late, and his damned leg hurt again. It was all that running in the brush, falling and twisting. It would hurt him for days. Devereux kept his seat alone for some time. Using the mirrors, he systematically inspected all the occupants of the buffet, glancing at each in turn, trying not to draw attention. He was surrounded by his enemies. He was surprised to discover the deep feelings which the presence of so many blue uniforms aroused in him.

He had always wanted to be a soldier. He had been raised on stories of the Napoleonic wars and armies. His maternal grandfather had been a colonel of Horse Grenadiers of the Imperial Guard. His godfather was Colonel Claudius Crozet; French engineer officer, emigre, the first Professor of Engineering at West Point, a founder of Virginia Military Institute and a family friend. He had wanted this uniform of deep blue more than anything he could imagine.

His father had not agreed.

Claude had tried to persuade on the basis of the value of a West Point engineering education. Nothing would move Charles Devereux. He insisted that Claude should join him in the bank. It would "steady him." Patrick could attend a military school. Thus would family tradition be respected.

Devereux listened to their voices, sorting them by ethnic origin and region of birth. There were the inevitable foreign born. A surprising number of the officers sounded Irish or Central European. Of the native American voices, he found that the New Englanders irritated him more than the rest. *It's probably the association with Hope,* he thought. *One of these bandbox dandies may be a relative of my sweet bride, one of those priggish little pricks she admires so.* As he watched, another aged female traveler threaded her way through the smoky room to the table presided over by the Yankee naval officer. The buffet had filled to capacity. The old woman stopped by the table to greet her traveling contemporaries. The navy Commander rose awkwardly in respect to her sex.

My God, he is a big one!

The Commander peered about, vainly searching for chairs.

Claude picked up a chair from his table, crossed the short space and offered it at arms' length. "Need this?" he asked.

The naval officer said nothing while absorbing the presence of this new personality, distracted by his own preoccupations.

An embarrassingly long pause developed. The tableau presented by the room full of enemy troops, the table of women, the Northern sailor, and the Confederate spy began to delight Devereux. He wondered how long they would stand there. It seemed forever although it could not have been more than a few seconds.

The brunette broke the spell. "Take the chair, Richard! Miss Harriet wishes to sit."

Richard's arm obediently extended itself. An intimidating paw grasped the curved back of the chair. "Thank you, most kind," he managed, placing the gift in a position convenient for the use of Miss Harriet.

Devereux bowed slightly to the ladies, holding the eyes of the young woman an instant longer than might have been required by the occasion. He moved away to resume his seat.

"A moment, sir! Would you not care to join us?"

He knew who had spoken. There was no one else at that table who could possibly have such a voice. It was a little husky, contralto in pitch and likely to be obeyed by wandering, unattached men. Turning back, he found her pointing to the empty space across the table. He glanced at the naval officer.

The big man's friendly acquiescence was belied by the rigidity of his posture.

Devereux retrieved another chair from his previous table.

She was even more appealing close up. Her hair was a lovely light brown. Her eyes were a deeper brown. Her figure was disguised by the amplitude of the fashion of the day, but she might have been described as statuesque. A wedding ring decorated the left hand.

Claude stood, expecting some further words before he presumed to sit.

"How do you do, sir. I am Richard Braithwaite," the Commander said. "This is my sister-in-law, Mrs. Elizabeth Braithwaite, and these ladies are the Misses Pauline and Harriet Braithwaite, our cousins and Mrs. Helen Goldsmith, a friend." Braithwaite stood as he spoke, to shake Devereux's hand.

"Claude Devereux, Alexandria, Virginia. I am most pleased to make your acquaintance. I have been waiting for this fool train for an hour, bereft of all chance of friendly discourse. It is a kindness to allow me to sit with you." Devereux sat, being careful to look around the table at each in turn.

Commander Braithwaite leaned toward him. "Are you here in Baltimore for the day on business, Mister Devereux?"

"Unfortunately not. I arrived from New York earlier today. A telegram had told me that I should visit a business acquaintance on the way home." He hoped that he would grow more comfortable with this lie. He tried to imagine himself in the train from New York, reached back for the steamship from France, thinking of the details of the voyage.

One of the Braithwaite sisters politely asked if he had been absent from home for more than a few days.

"I have been gone for quite a long time," Devereux replied. "Our family is in merchant banking. We arrange financial affairs for shipping lines and trading firms." Devereux offered that by way of clarification hoping it did not sound condescending. "I have worked in the French branch of the firm for several years."

Commander Braithwaite was now much more attentive. "Your company is called?"

"Devereux and Wheatley. We aren't very large, but international trade is active lately, especially considering the war" He trailed off expecting a renewal of the naval officer's questioning.

Elizabeth Braithwaite blocked that chance. "Wasn't it lonely without your family? Are you married?"

Devereux fumed inside himself. *Damn it, woman! Don't pay attention to me! I don't want his animosity. I want to talk to him.* He smiled pleasantly at her. "Yes, I am married. Regrettably, my wife was forced by a family situation to remain in Alexandria. I was not lonely. I have many French relatives."

"And you are 'en route' now?" Elizabeth asked.

She had a way of looking at you which demanded your attention. Considering the impact of her presence, Devereux was no longer in any doubt of the depth of feeling that her brother-in-law had for her.

"Yes, my father asked me to come home. He and my brother need help in the bank. I am looking forward to a grand family reunion."

"Of course," she murmured, demurely looking at the table and tilting her pretty head in a way that made her look delectable.

This is not going to work, he thought. *She is sitting there, calculating the state of relations between me and my wife. Braithwaite knows what she is thinking and in his state of mind, he will now work up a scheme to do me some injury.*

"What ship did you cross on?" Commander Braithwaite demanded.

"The Marechal Bessieres. We landed three days ago. I have a servant with me." Devereux felt deep gratitude for the thoroughness of Jenkins planning. He now knew it had been ongoing from the time he had gone to France.

Mrs. Harriet Goldsmith had been silent, observing this little drama. Above the rising noise in the crowded room, she raised her small voice. "Is your family included among those Virginians who are loyal to our country?"

It had to come. It might as well start now. "We have always been Whigs," he replied. "The fanaticism of ardent secessionists is something we oppose. My father was a delegate to the Virginia secession convention where he voted against separation on every ballot, including the last one. We own no slaves. Why should we favor the Rebels? We are deeply loyal to our country." *Please! Please!* He begged in his mind. *Accept that! It would not be polite to press me. Let it go that I didn't really answer the question. You don't need to know that my father's closest friend and ally at the convention was Jubal Early and that he is now a major general commanding a division under Lee.*

Mrs. Goldsmith was happy with his answer. Justified in her opinions, she turned to the others. "I have always maintained that there are many Virginians of quality who are not traitors. At last I have met one!"

If you meet any more, you should remember to count your fingers after each handshake, he thought.

Elizabeth Braithwaite spoke. "Mister Devereux, why don't you sit with us on the ride to Washington. We ladies would like to hear from you of the 'goings on' in the City of Light, wouldn't we?" She surveyed the others and saw no overt disagreement. "Actually, Mister Devereux, we are practically neighbors and should become acquainted."

"How is that, Mrs. Braithwaite?"

"My husband, Richard's brother, is presently on the staff of the United States Military Railroad. The headquarters is in Alexandria. We live on Duke Street. I do believe I have met your wife, and your mother. She is French?"

"Yes." He thought his guts might turn to water at any moment. He worked on the mask, feeling the edges of it for flabbiness, willing it into its familiar meaningless affability.

Elizabeth continued to shine her light upon him. "I remember your wife's name, Hope. She's from Boston. Such a beauty." She registered mock reproach at the prolonged abandonment of such a spouse.

Claude's experience of women was sufficient to make him believe that the possession of a wife as beautiful as Hope would serve to make him more desirable to most women. This one did not seem an exception to that rule. He could feel the hollow misery of the man sitting to his right. *If she continues, I am going to start feeling sorry for the Yankee swine,* he thought.

One of the Misses Braithwaite entered the contest. "Elizabeth, did you meet them in your charity work?"

Mrs. Braithwaite brightly replied to her cousin. "Yes, dear, I think it was at a meeting of the Alexandria lodge of the Sanitary Commission."

He remembered Rocklin's rabbit grin. Cast a wide net and listen for the hunger, he had preached. Claude wasn't sure exactly what the Sanitary Commission might be, but it ought to be something of value. "You must remember that I have been away. What is the 'Sanitary Commission'?"

The ladies were surprised and a little hurt. One of the Braithwaite "girls" offered an explanation. "The United States Sanitary Commission," she said, is the army sponsored national volunteer group which does charitable works in the hospitals and at the front. Elizabeth is one of the directors of this organization in your city."

His viewpoint shifted. The brother-in-law was now revealed as a dangerous nuisance whose presence and hostility might hamper the flowering of a beautiful friendship. *How can I rid myself of the interference of this lecherous lout? Stonewall is right,* he thought. *God does favor us. The husband is an officer in the railroad system which sustains operations against Lee and the wife is well placed in an organization with connections throughout the enemy war establishment.* The trick would be to encourage her without causing some sort of crisis of emotion in the future. "I would be most happy to pass on what little I know of the latest 'modes' on the continent. By a happy coincidence, one of my female cousins is obsessed with the subject and spoke to me often of the latest developments." *Among other things …*

The Washington and Alexandria Railroad was one of the shortest in the world. Eight miles long, it ran from the Baltimore and Ohio Depot on Louisiana Avenue to the Alexandria terminal. It would have been a mere convenience for those resident in the Washington City area except for the interesting accident that it was the sole link in the east between the northern and southern railroad systems, a major transportation bottleneck and a sort of funnel through which goods and passengers poured in both directions.

This made the Alexandria end of the line a natural assembly and supply center for the Federal armies in Virginia. From the Virginia town, railroads fanned out into the heart of The Old Dominion. The Richmond, Fredericksburg and Potomac barge traffic from Acquia Landing, the Manassas Gap Railroad, and the Orange and Alexandria all came together in Devereux's native place. He harbored a good deal of bitter ill will toward a Providence which had so positioned his home as to make its early and continued occupation by United States forces a virtual certainty in the aftermath of secession. Only four Alexandria men had voted for Lincoln in the election of 1860. Everyone wondered who they could have been. Bell, the moderate Unionist candidate, received the largest number of votes, but the referendum held on 23 May, 1861 to ratify Virginia's Ordinance of Secession passed overwhelmingly. Alexandrians had not wanted to leave the Union, but they would not part from Virginia, and could not tolerate the coercion threatened against the lower South.

The next morning Northern forces occupied the town. 24 May 1861. That had been the hateful day in which Alexandria had awakened to find itself occupied by Northern soldiers. As the United States Army had entered, landing at the river piers and marching in on the Washington road, the local militia battalion withdrew from the far side, boarding a train which took them to Manassas and enrolment in the Southern army gathering there. Corse, Herbert, Fowle, Jake, all of them had left that day.

Commander Braithwaite left the group when the train arrived in Washington. His destination was the Navy Yard. He had expected to escort Elizabeth and the other women to his brother's house, but she insisted that Devereux could see them safely home.

Devereux made a special effort to be cordial to the big man, assuring him of the care he would give the ladies and asking for the opportunity to meet again at some suitable time.

Braithwaite departed in a cab, having said little to Claude.

The bench seats were uncomfortable in the old cars. A general patina of coal soot overlay everything in the car, especially the windows. The train approached The Long Bridge across the Potomac. The three older women lapsed into a dazed condition, their bodies starved for sleep by the long day of travel, but Elizabeth was awake, smiling at him in an unnervingly familiar way. She did not say anything. She just looked at him.

After a few minutes, he decided that he couldn't sit stupidly silent any longer. He did not wish to be mistaken for someone who would be overwhelmed either by her or such a situation. "Did I understand that you are from Pittsburgh?"

"Yes," she said. "We are all from Pittsburgh, my husband, his brother Richard, and my family, all of us. Richard is a career naval officer, but my husband is in the army only for the war. He's a railroad man, as are my father and brothers. That's why he is working for General Haupt."

Devereux recalled that Haupt was the chief of the Union Army railroads. A new line of inquiry occurred to him. "You have known the Braithwaite family since your childhood?"

She thought that over for a moment, deciding what it was that he wanted to know. "Our families are long acquainted. I met Frederick, my husband, five years ago, when I came out. I did not know his brother until he returned from the Pacific Ocean with his ship. Actually, we met at the wedding. He was 'best man'."

Devereux thought that through. A bachelor naval officer returns from the sea to find that his brother is in the process of marrying this woman. He is overwhelmed with desire. It sets his teeth on edge just to be in her presence. The naval officer is required by the 'decencies' of the situation to act for his brother. Devereux was certain that Elizabeth had done nothing to make life easier for Commander Richard Braithwaite. She enjoyed this sort of thing. She was enjoying it now, anticipating that Devereux would puzzle out the relationships. *It ought to be possible to make use of this woman's character for the benefit of my mission. I think I might enjoy that* "Baltimore is hardly on a direct rail route from Pittsburgh. Why was I so fortunate as to meet you there?" He could see that she appreciated the phraseology.

"I was visiting my parents at home. My cousins.." She indicated the sleeping ladies, "They wished to return with me to Virginia for an extended visit, bringing their friend. The rebel bandit Mosby has made the direct route through western Maryland dangerous. My brother-in-law happened to be in Pittsburgh at the same time." She glanced at Claude to see if he believed that, "and insisted on escorting us back. And so there we were in Baltimore. Who was that young man sitting with you in the station?"

It had not occurred to Devereux that she had been watching him and Cawood in the buffet. It should have been obvious. *Fool! You are more tired than you thought.* "He's from the bank I visited in Baltimore, a clerk, but a promising clerk. We are nearly home. I begin to recognize buildings even this late at night." Extricating his watch from a vest pocket, he flipped open the lid. "Nearly eleven! When we arrive, my man Bill will find us cabs. There are always some about, even this late."

The train decelerated noisily with much clanking, rumbling and screeching of brakes.

Leading the way to the front of the car, Devereux stepped down onto the platform.

White appeared from another car, farther back in the train.

Devereux handed down the ladies and stood with them while Bill reboarded the parlor car to retrieve the women's baggage.

While they were so engaged, Elizabeth Braithwaite emitted a small cry while waving her lace edged handkerchief at someone over his shoulder.

A lieutenant colonel appeared from the darkness to sweep her into his arms.

Another big one, reflected Claude, the family resemblance is striking.

Elizabeth detached herself from her husband's embrace, turning toward Devereux while her husband greeted the other women.

"Frederick! Let me introduce you to Mister Claude Devereux. We met him on the train. He has just returned from France! Richard left us in his care. He is a banker."

Frederick Braithwaite heartily pumped Claude's hand, thanking him for his help.

A guileless soul, Claude thought, *a suitable victim if first impressions have any validity.*

"Elizabeth! I have brought our carriage. May we drop you anywhere, sir?"

Devereux thanked him, but declined owing to the lateness of the hour and the need to ensure that Bill White arrived at his home.

Braithwaite looked at his watch, then at Devereux. "I am afraid, Mister Devereux that the train has arrived after curfew."

"What do you mean, sir?"

"There is a movement curfew on civilians. They may not be on the street after ten thirty. Our troops must be off the streets at nine," the officer hastened to add.

A kind of dull pain set in around Devereux's heart, a sensation of oppression made more rasping because of the civility of the Northern officer. Devereux's silence weighed upon Braithwaite. "Why don't I give you a pass for yourself and your servant," Braithwaite suggested. "I can do that if I don't abuse the privilege."

"Thank you.." *Thank You, you bastard. So you'll give me a pass to walk the streets in my own town! Well, I'll give you something.. Just Wait!*

Elizabeth Braithwaite paused next to Devereux as she passed on the way to the station. Placing a hand on his arm, she looked up at him to add her thanks to those of her husband, saying that she wished to be remembered to 'his lovely wife.'

"Surely, you will come to call," she murmured.

"Your servant, ma'am," Devereux responded.

The Braithwaite party left the scene.

Devereux and Bill White picked up their carpetbags. "Let's go home, friend." Claude whispered. "I am running out of patience." With his hand on his friend's shoulder for support he limped toward the street, hoping there would be at least one cab. Otherwise it would be a long way home.

6:30 A.M., 18 March
(Chester Station, Virginia)

"H" Company lined the muddy shoulder of the simple road. The sun was just drifting up over the edge of the world. The men had become accustomed to pre-dawn summons. They were careful to note the exact locations of their few possessions before they slept. Hard experience had made them able to find their property by touch alone. This morning was exceptionally chill. Overcoats and the 'mackinaw' jackets widely favored by the soldiers had all gone into the regiment's wagons in preparation for the day's march. Tobacco pipes glowed in the dawn. Men stamped their feet, swung their arms, spat richly, and commented, as soldiers do in such circumstances, on the competence and ancestry of those in authority above them. Their breath hung over the road.

The 17th Regiment stretched back into the mist behind "H" Company. The men of the company had noticed and spoken of the frequency with which they seemed to head the column in route marches. Arthur Herbert had been their first company commander. Now he led the whole regiment. He found them congenial company. Colonel Herbert stood waiting at the front of his column in the center of the road, peering into the ground fog, watching for some sign from the soldier he had sent forward as a 'connecting file'. Herbert needed to know when the infantry regiment ahead of the 17th in the brigade order of march began to move. They had been marching down this road for days. Pickett's Division would continue to advance southeast, moving to the line of the Blackwater River for operations against the Union held town of Suffolk which lay behind this stream.

Screening the river was a small Confederate force under General Roger Pryor. Beyond them, there would be the Blackwater itself. Suffolk, farther to the east, was heavily entrenched by the Federals. East of Suffolk stretched the gloom and muck of the Great Dismal Swamp. A traveler who continued in this direction would eventually reach the city of Norfolk, and the Chesapeake Bay.

Several of the regiment's wagons had left an hour earlier under the direction of an officer from brigade headquarters.

Twenty miles they would go today. Their cooks and tents would await them. Seven hours sleep and two meals would fuel their bodies for another 20 miles tomorrow. Snake and Jim Smith would have something good cooking when they arrived.

Lieutenant Jake Devereux's post was at the trail end of the company column. He finished walking the length of the unit, looking at the men and their loads. Beards were widespread, but not universal. Many were too young to grow satisfactory beards. Bodies were thin and hard. *They make me look like an old man,* he thought.

Every enlisted man in the outfit was in Butternut Brown. The most common "uniform" was a wide brimmed hat rolled up in front, a short jacket, rough pants, brogan shoes and a sleeping roll of blanket and rubber ground sheet. A .577 caliber Enfield rifle completed the ensemble.

Jake watched Captain Bill Fowle chat with the colonel in the road.

A taller and older than average soldier sidled up to Devereux. Every fighting organization worthy of its name has at least one perennial private, normally possessed of a rare sense of humor, who wittingly or not acts out the role of unit jester or minstrel. Private Johnny Quick relished this function, considered it to be his by right, hard earned in rain and sunshine wherever they had served. "And how would you be this fine mornin' Lootenant?" he asked.

"Much as yourself, Johnny, much as yourself. How is it that you are not up with them? Jake asked, indicating the two officers in the road. It was well known that Private Quick and the colonel were fast friends. Their jests and ribald humor enlivened the long hours of days like these.

"Well, Lootenant, it's maddened I am, maddened. You know the colonel has been promisin' me leave for months now, months.."

"No leave yet, Johnny? What's his excuse now?"

"It's the military exigencies of our desperate situation. That's what he claims. Shameful it is, to deny a faithful soldier a little leave."

Jake smothered a grin. Johnny Quick had left his family in the 'old country', had lived the life of an immigrant laborer for years before the war and had nowhere to spend his leave in America except in saloons. All previous experience of granting leave to Private Quick showed that the man would end any furlough in the hands of the provost guard. Jake knew that the regimental commander was determined to protect his friend from himself.

In the distance Jake saw the ammunition train of the 15th Virginia lurch into motion.

Arthur Herbert did not wait for word from his runner. He nodded to the regimental color bearer.

The man stepped into the road beside Herbert. Facing down the column, he held the staff hung with the star crossed red flag horizontally above his head.

From his post, Jake found the tableau created by Colonel Herbert, the color sergeant and the square flag, embroidered with their battle honors, to be oddly touching. He blinked against the emotion welling up.

The 390 men of the 17th Virginia fell in on the muddy road in a column of fours.

Colonel Herbert roared, "Forward, March! Route step, March!"

Pickett's Division marched toward the Blackwater.

5

Homecoming

7:45 A.M., 18 March

The first Virginia Devereux had been Claude's grandfather, Richard Xavier. He came from Charles County, Maryland and crossed the river in the last quarter of the eighteenth century to try his luck in the new town of Alexandria.

The family had emigrated to the new world in the seventeenth century as participants in the large scale settlement of British Catholics on the shores of the Chesapeake Bay. The surname was Norman-Irish. The various branches of the tribe had drifted back and forth across the Irish Sea for a thousand years. An old family joke insisted that the Devereuxs consistently produced only three kinds of men, warriors, poets and hard drinkers. That family tradition insured some measure of surprise when the grandfather left the soil in Maryland to apprentice himself to a moneylender and banker. The young man prospered, leaving his master's enterprise within a few years to begin his own. Possessed of a sharp wit, he early grasped the idea that large scale foreign and coastal trade would be the key to wealth in the new port. Shrewd practice and a reputation for dependability in his undertakings insured the survival of his house.

By 1785 he had grown to a stature which invited the attention of men of wealth seeking investment opportunities for plantation profits. "Devereux and Wheatley, Finance Agents and Bankers," emerged from a long and careful courtship conducted between talent and wealth.

Richard Devereux had arrived in Virginia with very little, and had demonstrated for several years a sturdy ability to deal with the world without the shield of servants and family which surrounded the majority of his colleagues. Nevertheless, as his purse grew heavier, he steadily attained the attributes and possessions of a responsible burgher. A house on South Fairfax Street was bought in 1790. House slaves were purchased or brought over from family holdings in Maryland.

A wife was found to grace the household. Catherine Mayo brought to his bed the acceptance which her family had long ago earned in Virginia society. Richard died in 1836, his wife the following year. She declared at the end that life without him was too unspeakably dull to endure for long.

Richard had followed the family pattern. He fought with everyone who opposed him, he drank too much and he could not have been described as excessively pious.

His only son, Charles Francis, held his father in horrified awe. The boy had spent too much time in the company of priests Richard had thought. For a time

Richard feared he might wish to be a priest. This fear had passed when the young man had met his future wife, Clotilde.

From the moment of his father's death it was evident that Charles Francis Devereux would conduct the business of the family on a different basis from that of his father. A devotion to the diligent labor which caused the steady growth of the bank consumed his waking hours. In his stewardship the family business grew to include offices in New York and in Europe. His only recreations lay in the world of Whig politics, his activities as an active communicant of St. Mary's Church, and in his private world in the bosom of his family.

For his wife, he was not the same man that others saw. For her, he seemed to have reserved his inner self For her, he built the Italianate villa which stood among the elms on Duke Street.

The older, smaller house, three blocks away, was used to house visitors, business guests and family retainers.

Claude Devereux and his wife occupied the two story, galleried 'ell' of the big house on Duke Street. At the time of his marriage in 1857, Claude had allowed himself to be persuaded by his mother to live in the wing of the Duke Street house "until you find something of your own." The marriage had not ripened into contentment. At first, it had not been clear to him why this was so. His wife, Hope, was the most consistently fascinating woman Claude had ever met. His desire to possess her never flagged, but she had not found him truly acceptable as her husband. He could not please her. God knew that he wished to do so. He had not met her expectations. It had remained a mystery to him for several years, but at last he had seen that it was not so much him as it was his people and their ways which disturbed her. He felt that this was not his fault. He loved her, but he would not change himself in the ways that she wanted. Nevertheless, his wife proved to be the daughter his mother had always sought. The issue of separate quarters for the younger Devereuxs disappeared. The arrival of children would have brought it to the fore, but there were none. In the end he had left, going first to Europe, and then into the war.

The morning of his arrival, Claude woke in what seemed at first to be unfamiliar surroundings. Often he awoke unable to remember the immediate past, wondering where he might be. This was such a time. Peering around the shuttered bedroom, he recognized furniture which his wife had collected or brought from Boston. Some of the pieces were strange. *She has continued to buy*, he thought. *Mother encourages her.*

The memory of his homecoming came back to him as he lay in bed. He had delivered White to the Fairfax Street house and then completed his weary journey. Descending from the cab which they had found after a long search, he was greeted by Joseph White, Bill's younger brother.

"What are you doing here Joe?" Devereux asked the puzzled footman. "You should be home. Nobody comes this late at night."

"Mister Claude? My God! It's Mister Claude. Are the others with you?"

"Just Bill. I had to leave Jake with the rest."

This fuss in the street brought Devereux's father out, clad in dressing gown and slippers. Holding a lamp, he inspected his oldest son from the brick steps. Surprise and welcome competed for primacy in his face. Charles Devereux's embrace was followed by that of mother and wife.

The newly risen man knew that his clothes would be in the mahogany wardrobe by the wash stand. This had been his bedroom the last year he had lived in the house with his parents. Retrieving a robe from its storage place, he went out onto the second story gallery. The morning air was delicious in its familiar bouquet. The street noise of carts and passers-by meant home.

In the garden, his mother and wife were head to head in a discussion which must concern the coming growing season. His mother's delicate figure displayed its characteristic animation. He could hear the music of her voice and the Gallic intonation which persisted after so many years.

Hope grows more beautiful, he thought. His blonde wife had always been an ornament. Now, in her late twenties, she had attained a ripe perfection. The memory of their happiest times came back to him. He had been twenty-eight, and mourning the passing of a childhood friend who had become something more than a friend, a girl with whom he had shared everything, who had loved him as the young can love best. New York had been an alien and lonely place. The bank did not really need him. He was there "for seasoning." The manager took charge of all significant matters.

Hope Prescott had been visiting relatives. They met at a dinner party. They were naive and lonely. Neither knew anyone in the city. She was beautiful beyond belief. She was always so beautiful. For him it was inevitable. *It's too late, much too late*, he thought. *It had never been a good idea. She looked to be just right, so pretty, so intelligent, so well educated. I should never have become involved so quickly after Caroline's death. I hardly knew her, had no idea what she thought about anything.* He knew that this was nonsense. Looking at her, he could not believe that he had deliberately left her side. His mother and father loved her so. He loved her so. Now she was truly a Devereux and nothing could be done. Claude was reasonably sure that he would not be pleased with the outcome if his parents were ever required to choose between son and daughter-in-law. In any event, all concerned were Catholic. Defeat would never be admitted in family life.

A board groaned beneath him. The two women saw him, and waved. His mother said she would rouse the cook for a special effort and entered the kitchen door.

Hope stood fifteen feet below him, an apricot woolen shawl protecting her shoulders, looking up at him. Nothing was said. What could be said? He went back into his room. Standing by the door, he remembered more. His father had waited for the two women to go to bed, had waited for an explanation other than the paper thin pastiche of fable which his mother had happily accepted.

Hope had not believed him. She would demand the truth eventually and he would give it. It was her right. If she betrayed him, so be it. He had hurt her more in the past than he had ever intended. He would not intentionally injure her now.

He had told his father the true story. Charles Devereux listened without comment, expressionless. When Claude finished, he asked why it had been necessary to leave his youngest son behind. Claude felt deeply the implied criticism. He had known that tone of voice all his days. "I thought it unavoidable," he responded.

Sitting in front of the black marble fireplace in his dressing gown, the older man looked doubtful. "Why is it that these situations always seem to be best resolved in ways that benefit you, Claude," he asked? The arrow went deep into the heart, tearing open old scar tissue. *I must not let him see. I will not let him see!* His father inspected him, looking for something. At last he shook his head slightly and said. "We will, of course, assist you to the extent of our capacity. It is our duty. Welcome home." Without further remark Charles Devereux had risen, bowed slightly and left the room. Thinking of this conversation, Claude felt the tears start in his eyes. *Why don't I just say to hell with it all and leave for Timbuctoo or some other grand place.. Well, maybe later.* After dressing himself, Devereux walked down the gallery stairs, taking his favorite short cut through the kitchen on his way to breakfast with the two women.

6

Fair Play

3:00 P.M., 18 March
(Richmond, Virginia)

The Richmond, Fredericksburg and Potomac Railroad had become a divided parody of its former self. In prewar days, the track had run from the Potomac River at Acquia Creek Station north of Fredericksburg to Richmond, passing through the forested countryside, leaping the rivers on wooden trestles.

No longer. The line from the Potomac to Fredericksburg was now under United States Army management. The company still operated the rest of the route from the firm's main offices in Richmond.

The Superintendent of this enterprise strode along Main Street, enjoying the mid-afternoon sun. Well dressed and well groomed as always, he greeted acquaintances and passers-by alike with the warmth and conviviality that made him a welcome dinner guest, often sought by the most accomplished hostesses of the capital.

His railroad was an absolutely vital artery of supply and commerce between the city and the front to the north. His counsel was sought by congressman and cabinet officer alike. The President himself often requested his opinion. Altogether, Samuel Ruth was a power to be reckoned with in the Confederate establishment.

In the Southern body politic there were some who were doubtful of the loyalty of Confederate citizens who had been so unfortunate as to be born in territory which after secession constituted the United States of America. Those who felt this way generally made an exception for Marylanders, Kentuckians, Missourians and the like. All others were considered to be more doubtful. This opinion of the potential treachery of nonnative Southerners was not universally held. The government's official opinion was that men could and should choose their own allegiance. Such a policy was indeed a necessity. The Confederate forces and economy could not have functioned without the participation of the many Northern born men within them. Their blood had soaked into too many battlefields for prejudice to be effective against them.

Samuel Ruth had overcome these difficulties. Born in Pennsylvania, he had early in life migrated to the South. A workman does not often rise to become the chief official of an industrial company, but Ruth had made the directorship of the railroad his through hard work and innovation.

His brisk stride carried him to the door of the American Hotel, Richmond's finest. The Negro doorman greeted him effusively, knowing that Mister Ruth was ever careful to remember that those less fortunate needed "a little something." Passing through the lobby, he found the key to the "guest suite" which the railroad rented for business travelers and others with whom it wished to ingratiate itself.

He mounted the stairs two at a time, proud of the strength of his body, determined to avoid the progressive enfeeblement which he thought a sedentary life wrought upon so many of his business acquaintances.

Suite 321 was his destination. The parlor occupied one corner of the big building. The windows provided marvelous cross ventilation in warm weather. Ruth settled himself into one of the maroon, plush-covered chairs. In the fashion of the day the furniture was built close to the floor. He sat with his long legs projecting before him and waited for his agent. The motivations which had caused him to begin to spy for the Union Army were so complex as to nearly defy his own analysis. Among them was a belief that the South would eventually be defeated. There was also outraged nationalism which felt diminished by the attempted departure of a portion of the national territory. Buried deepest of all in his heart was the alien unease which he had felt throughout his long residence among "these people." At bottom, Samuel Ruth had decided to side with his own at the very beginning and had never deviated from that course. At first the work had been nearly impossible. The incompetents, poseur dilettantes, and fools with whom he had been required to deal in the staffs of successive commanders of the Army of the Potomac had been destructive in their lack of common sense and application to the job. Of late, the situation had much improved. In the winter a courier had come through the lines to tell him of the appointment of Joe Hooker to command the Potomac Army and of Hooker's new scheme for the administration of the staff. The same man had brought a name, Sharpe. This would be the officer to whom Ruth would direct his reports and from whom he would accept instructions. Skeptical at first, he had slowly become more confident. Step by step the links that connected Ruth's network in Richmond to the North had tightened. Couriers came and went with dependability. Tasks were, at last, clearly stated and the value of his information was explained to him. Ruth's trust grew immeasurably. He began to think that the risks he and his friends endured were justified.

The parlor door opened and closed. The man who entered locked it behind himself. He took a facing chair, and accepted a drink from the silver pocket flask which the big man offered him. The contrast between the two was striking. Samuel Ruth filled the room with his presence. He would have dominated the space the two men occupied even if there had not been such a difference in their size.

The newcomer was a tiny man. His small hands and feet looked like those of a child and his sandy mustache seemed something that must have been glued to his lip.

"Where did you tell them you were going this time, Henry?" Ruth asked, pushing back the leonine, grey streaked mane which threatened to cover his face much of the time. He did not trust this man's judgement. He suspected him of excessive casualness in security matters. It would not have occurred to Ruth to think that he, himself, was guilty of the same habits. In an odd way, his long association with Southerners had made him overly confident of his ability to fool them. Ruth did not think the Confederates would actually kill him if they discovered his secret but it was hard to be sure.

The State Department clerk who sat before him was irritated by the question. Ruth was always asking things like that. Henry Dodge planned to be a power in Virginia once the rebellion was crushed. The Republicans would need many friends to help them reestablish central government control. He would be one of those who succeeded to the power now wielded by the slaver oligarchs. *No one should talk to me in this way,* he thought. *Ruth will regret his words.* "It's a lovely day, Samuel. I have simply gone out for a walk."

The threadbare neatness of this skinny little man amused Ruth. A person of large appetites himself, he had always harbored a measure of contempt for smallness in other human beings. He sensed a narrowness of soul and purpose in Dodge which made his reliability a worry. "Your note suggested with some urgency that a meeting was required," he said to the little man. He hoped that an unneeded hazard had not been created by conferring in the middle of a working day. The wizened little man's very appearance seated in an overstuffed red velvet and mahogany armchair and surrounded by the best that this fine hotel could assemble was ludicrous.

Dodge smirked with self-important pleasure. He paused for effect and then began to talk. "We have a coded telegram from Wood, from Ashland. It reports his accomplishment of a piece of work given to him by the Secretary, Mister Benjamin."

"Do you have it?"

Dodge frowned and sputtered. "No. It would have been stupid to try to walk out of the office with anything. The message was short. I remember it all." He stopped, and sat waiting for approval.

Ruth knew that the clerk would take his time, relishing the fantasy which made a drama of these occasions. The man believed that he exercised more than a little control over historic events. The melodrama of his relations with Ruth reinforced this belief. The spy-master had learned to accept the need to play his own role in the man's dreams.

Feeling sure that he was in control of the situation, Dodge started to tell his story. "The telegram deals with a message transmitted by Wood to a man referred to as Hannibal," he said. "There is a new dossier in our Secret Service archive under this name, but there is nothing in the record, except a note that this is a War Department matter in which we have some interest. The false name is of a kind which the military often uses. Presumably Benjamin is dealing with this affair himself and has made no notes. If he had, they would have arrived at my office unless the papers are yet on his desk. He is a messy man. God knows where any papers on this affair might be."

Ruth reflected briefly on the news. "If Hannibal was at Ashland recently, then he must have been on his way north. Does the telegram say when and where the man might be going?"

"It was several days ago," Dodge replied. "Wood implies that Hannibal will be carrying out Benjamin's instructions and knows that the State Department's business is of greatest importance, and that Hannibal will contact Sophocles when he reaches his destination."

"Isn't Sophocles that Green fellow who lives around the corner from the White House" Ruth asked?

"Yes, he is one of Benjamin's favorites," Dodge said. "I hope no one decides to pick him up. He's helpful as a reference in many of these matters."

"That's a good point. I'll make an appeal for restraint concerning old Sophocles when I report your finding. Is there any indication of Hannibal's identity or task from the military?"

Dodge shook his head. "No. He must be of significance in a major undertaking or Benjamin would take no note of him. He has no interest in the army's informants. He thinks most of them are of no importance, but there is one other thing. Hannibal is accompanied by a young Negro man."

"A courier?"

Dodge was doubtful. "I don't think so. Wood said that the black guarded the place where he and Hannibal talked. Couriers don't do that. This sounds as if the black is part of a team."

Samuel Ruth did his sums. *An important Rebel spy is on his way to Washington. He will contact Thomas Green. He is in the company of a colored man. This should be enough.* "Thank you, Henry. I will send this to Colonel Sharpe immediately."

He looked at the spy reflectively. *I should put some money in his pocket,* he thought. *I haven't done that for a while..* "How are your expense funds holding up?"

The clerk did not wish to take money from Ruth. The taking made a mockery of his pretensions of equality and collegiality. In the beginning Ruth had pressed it upon him, insisting that he would need the funds to operate. Lately the fiction had steadily declined and the raw exposure of the money as payment was only a step away.

"Since you mention it, I could use some money to take several of my associates to dinner."

4:00 P.M., 21 March

The Devereuxs of Alexandria lived their lives by unwritten, but sacred family custom. In the afternoons, Claude had always made a special effort to be home for the daily routine of tea with the family. It was but a short walk from the bank. With his return, he resumed this practice. As part of the ritual, the men gathered for an hour of light conversation that served as prelude to the serious discussions of the day's events which tended to dominate their meals when outsiders were not present. The family assembled for dinner two or three evenings each week. Patrick Devereux, although not resident in the house, nearly always attended in the company of his wife and two small sons. In the parlor the family arranged itself in a fan from the central feature of the room, a black marble Italian fireplace.

Charles Devereux sat in the center of the room, a small table at his elbow. His chair was sacrosanct by universal, unspoken acknowledgment. On this particular day, Patrick and his wife, Victoria, were present for tea.

Claude paid little attention to them. He was lost in thought of the day's business at the bank. This was brought to an end as his wife bent beside him to refill his teacup and whispered, "Look at your brother! He has been staring at you." He looked at her and nodded his thanks for the warning. Claude and Hope had circled each other warily since his return. At first, he had resolutely sought to avoid her company, determined to prevent a resumption of the cruel cycle of passion and recrimination which had marked their marriage. He knew that this situation would not last very long. The attraction between them was too strong for this to continue. He was sure that she must feel the same things. She always had. Meals eaten together were growing longer. Claude could see that his mother had taken heart from their behavior and expected an early reconciliation.

Patrick sprawled in his armchair, peering through the fingers of the hand which cupped his chin. His crutches leaned against the fireplace. His ruined, stiffened leg was on the intricate pattern of the dark Bokhara rug. "It is as if you had never left," he said. "The bank needed you. We needed you."

Claude shook his head. "Rubbish! I never was much of a banker. My only real talent is in the scheming end of things. You and father are the force that makes the company prosper."

The father lifted his head from his newspaper. "It cannot be denied," he said, "that you exercise a great influence with our clients and the staff. Your presence has a positive effect on our affairs." His expression, one of regret, ruined the words.

Across the room, George White, the butler, was removing the remains of a tray of cakes and found himself returning Clotilde Devereux's glance. "Isn't that as it should be?" he said, trying to divert the stream of talk before it became unpleasant. "Jake's the poet. Claude is the speechefier and you two gentlemen are the real bankers." It was understood that George White had the status of "an elder statesman" in the private world of the Devereux household, and that the privilege of general commentary on family affairs was also his. Butler was really not the right title for his function in the house. Steward would have been more correct and traditional, appropriate to the family's old ways. It was clear to all that White did not wish to see this kind of talk continue.

"Why did you have to take the Oath?" Claude's sister-in-law, Victoria said. Unhappy resentment and confusion were plain in her face. "Your mother and Patrick use their French passports and do very well as neutrals. The military government is afraid to restrict their movements. Your father has steadfastly refused the Oath. How could you, when Jake is gone with our men. Perhaps he is …"

"Never say that, Victoria! Never!" her mother-in-law cried out. Clotilde Devereux was suddenly as angry as any of them had ever seen. Her normally pale skin flushed red with blood and her hands shook with emotion. She leaned forward from her perch on the edge of a straight-backed chair, rocking slowly with her arms folded across her bosom. Hope knelt to hold her hand.

Appalled by his mother's tears, Patrick decided he must rescue his older brother, and remove his wife before she unleashed the full fury of her outraged Confederate patriotism against him. "Let's discuss this at home, dear," he said. Climbing awkwardly to his feet, he asked for her help. "Walk me back to the bank first, would you please? I want to pick up some papers that I forgot." His wife handed him his crutches, and steadied him while he got them under his arms and found his balance. Sweeping the room with a smile, he followed her to the front door. George White stood there waiting as he always did. He held wide the door, careful to provide enough space for the crutches to clear the frame.

The family sat for a few moments, waiting for the fog of emotion to clear. Claude had explained the situation to Patrick soon after his return and had thought his brother would have the sense to explain the true situation to Victoria. He had always admired Patrick's wife and did not want to live with her disapproval. He reckoned that the risk from her inclusion in this secret would be less than that which might arise from her anger at his "disloyalty."

"Marie," Charles said from across the room. Claude's father frequently addressed his wife by her first name in the way he had learned in her parents' home long ago.

She had recovered her composure. Hope had gone back to her seat by the fireplace. "Oui, Cher?" Clotilde replied. Her face was still strained, but her voice was calm.

"I think you should give a dinner party to announce Claude's safe return from Europe." He looked decided on this project.

This truly puzzled Clotilde Devereux. "You do? I would have thought you would not want to attract attention to his presence."

There was a moment of silence. This was ended by Hope who walked to the tall, hooded windows. "Non, Maman," she laughed without turning from the street. "They want the attention. Look at their faces."

They did, indeed, appear conspiratorial.

"Ah! Bon!" the Frenchwoman said, clapping her hands in a little show of participation in this game. Only the glistening in her eyes showed that she still felt the hurt of the thought that her youngest might have been injured. "Whom shall we invite?" Marie Clotilde Devereux always relished the thought of an elegant occasion in her home.

"I had imagined you might wish to invite some of Hope's friends from the Sanitary Commission, and perhaps someone from the French and British embassies," Claude ventured.

"But yes! We can invite Colonel Jourdain, the military attache. Do you know someone at the British embassy?"

Claude said that there was such a person.

"As for the Sanitary Commission, they are my friends as well. They care for the wounded of both sides." His mother would not let his wife bear the opprobrium of association with the enemy alone.

"May I pick the Sanitary Commission guests?" Hope asked.

Standing at the window with the light framing her golden beauty, she was an easy reminder of all the reasons the marriage had been desirable. Unfortunately the curve of her neck and the pulse in it just above the lace jeopardized the feelings of nostalgia Devereux felt for their married life. When angered, she often began to seem swanlike. The neck arched and arched while the vein in her throat throbbed so severely that Devereux feared for her. He could see that she was going to torment him over the guests. *She might as well get on with it.* "Of course. Who would you like?" he said.

"A half dozen ladies and gentlemen. I suppose you wish Elizabeth Braithwaite and her husband to attend."

There were not very many people who would have been capable of interpreting Hope Devereux's expression at that moment. He and his mother were among them. The jealousy and suspicion in his wife's face were emotions Claude had not expected. *I had thought all that was gone,* he thought. *Perhaps these things never really die. Surely she does not want me back?* "Yes," he said. "They should be invited, as well as the ladies who are visiting them from Pennsylvania. I met them in the train. I would also like to meet Colonel Herman Haupt. I believe he is Braithwaite's director. I would also want to invite the military governor of the city, General Slough. He's a decent enough man from all I have heard."

Clotilde Devereux turned to her husband inquiringly.

"He is a better man than those who came before him." Charles said to his wife. "Claude will act as host. I will be unexpectedly ill. I think we should invite a number of old Alexandrians to round out the party. There are many citizens who have been forced by circumstance to take the Oath. I will speak to them and seek their agreement."

"We are talking of a dinner party of, perhaps thirty?" Claude's mother hesitated at the thought. Her husband had not allowed social activity on that scale since the occupation of the city.

"Just so," Charles replied, "We should look at the cellar. We may have to lay in some wine for this affair." His mother's happy chatter from below the floor was Hope's signal.

"You won't succeed, whatever it is that you plan," she said. "Your story is absurd. The only protection you have is provided by these and all the other good hearted folk in this place. There are many hypocrites in this city and I believe you must be the worst! You abhor slavery! You thought secession foolish. You and your whole family worked against these things. Nevertheless, in your laziness and self-indulgence you drift along dragging everyone down with you." The vein in her neck was beating and beating. "I can't understand your father. Such a right minded, righteous man. How can he persist in this stubbornness?"

He never knew how to respond to this kind of attack. In particular the references to his character always puzzled him. He knew they must lay at the heart of the matter but he could not see how this was relevant. His inability to do so never failed to infuriate her. "And my brothers? And Bill White?" he asked. "Is it all me?"

She was twisting and contorting a small, lace trimmed handkerchief before her. Holding it to her face, she began to sob, gently at first but increasingly with a force which frightened him. Crossing the room, he took her in his arms. She stood shaking stiffly against him with her forehead on his chest. "I wish I could hate you," she whispered. "I wish I could inform against you. Let me go." For a moment she stood quietly, breathing deeply, her small nose buried in his shirt front. Then she walked away from him. He heard her footsteps on the front staircase. She was running. Her departure from the salon left him surrounded by the aura of her embrace. He had nearly forgotten how well they had suited each other as lovers. He lifted an arm to press the sleeve against his face. He took a deep breath through his nose. The smell of her was intoxicating. Her skin was always the best of perfumes. An artificial scent would have been absurd. *I will have to tell her that..*

7

Smoot

11:30, Monday, 23 March
(Fairfax Court House, Virginia)

Lieutenant Forbes Bradshaw of the 1st District of Columbia Cavalry Regiment was a very young man who liked his present assignment and who, unlike Claude Devereux, did not want to return to duty with troops. He had never enjoyed the company of soldiers in the way that some officers did. They clearly relished being in the field with their men and were unhappy when deprived of the experience by force of circumstance. Not so for Bradshaw, he was quite happy to be away from soldiers who never seemed to hold him in awe as he wished to be held, who never seemed as respectful as was his due. At times he had almost been forced to believe that they might be laughing at him. But that was past now. As Provost Marshal of the town of Fairfax he enjoyed more real power than most colonels commanding regiments. In his present position he was responsible for army discipline in and around his post and for the conduct of legal and police functions with regard to the citizenry of Fairfax County and the guerilla infested hinterlands of Fauquier County to the west. The front line was a long way to the south, and Bradshaw would have been comfortably installed in this outpost if it had not been for the damnable Rebel partisans who made every trip outside the environs of Fairfax Village into an expedition. This particular county enjoyed a certain prominence because of its location immediately across the Potomac River from Washington, D.C. The sleepy little town of Fairfax was only twenty miles from the White House. Bradshaw was 23 years old. He liked parties and pretty girls and champagne. There was nothing in his background that remotely qualified him for his job. His youth alone would have kept him from obtaining such a position in normal circumstances, but there were "considerations." The most important of these were the hopes and aspirations of Colonel Lafayette Baker, Chief of the National Detective Bureau. This organization was the creation of Secretary of War Edwin Stanton who had needed a force to hunting down the host of Southern spies who Stanton imagined correctly to be everywhere in the city of Washington. Colonel Baker was Stanton's man, charged with the task of supplying the information Stanton desired. Baker, therefore, also wanted to have the details of events in the outer ring of Washington's defenses. For this purpose he had volunteered to provide an officer for duty as provost marshal in Fairfax. The war was creating new men, creating them from virtually nothing. Bradshaw, a junior cavalry officer, had been at the right place when a new man was sought. Colonel Baker needed faithful subordinates and the young man's name had appeared on a list of possibilities. It was as simple as that. He got the job.

On this particular morning, Bradshaw had awakened afflicted by a hangover the like of which he had not experienced for several weeks. It brought to mind the aftermath of the grand parties which Brigadier General Stoughton had often arranged in the months and days before his abduction by that devil Mosby. Bradshaw had been at work for two hours and was seated at his desk in the basement of the old courthouse building feeling sorry for himself when the most important event of the day passed, slipping through his fingers without his notice.

A sentry stood by his office door admitting civilians seeking passes and permissions of a variety of types. Another soldier guarded the corridor outside and a third acted as clerk, depositing and removing papers. The three men organized the work and most days he really did not have to pay much attention to what was going on in front of him. He would have been surprised to learn how much civilian money went into the pockets of these three men, placed there by those who wanted "a little something extra."

Bradshaw's headache had reached the diffused discomfort phase when something special began to happen. Unaware of this, he nevertheless began to be more alert to his surroundings. He was seated at his desk with his back to the brick wall. The desk was flanked by the United States flag on one side and a window which faced into the dirt street on the other. Horses restlessly shifted from foot to foot at a rail in front of the building. A mixed group of soldiers and idlers, black and white, laughed and talked in the square.

After rubbing his eyes one more time, Bradshaw looked at the waiting queue of supplicants. They had been neatly shepherded by the guard into a line on a long bench which ran down the side of the office. As each man's case was dealt with, the queue moved along the bench toward official attention. Lt. Bradshaw found that to be a satisfying arrangement. *It keeps the day's business from looming over me.* He smiled at the joke. There were four men on the bench now, four more hayseeds. They all wanted something, something in writing which would allow them to trade, move, sell, buy, something! The next man in line was elderly. The man after him was stocky, brown haired, weather-beaten, like so many of these farmers. His hands were big and hard looking. He did not look particularly bright. He and Bradshaw were about the same size although the farmer must have been in his early thirties. The old man stood up to present his case.

After listening halfheartedly for a few seconds, Bradshaw knew what the farmer hoped for. He wanted permission to cross the lines to visit his children near Gordonsville. Exasperation bubbled to the surface of his mind where it mingled freely with the misery of his sick hangover. "No! No! I have told you people time after time that I have no authority to allow you to traffic with the Rebels for your own convenience. I can't do it! How do I know you truly have children in Gordonsville?"

"Please Cap'n Bradshaw!" the tall, skinny man begged. "You know me. I'm in here all the time with my hardware bidness. I never done nothin' bad. I'm as good a Union man as any in this county. I suffered awful from the 'Secesh'. They hate me somethin' turrible! I got to see my daughter. She's havin' a baby." His voice trailed to a wavering end. There were tears in his eyes.

A thought penetrated the grey fog around Bradshaw. "What about your son-in-law? Where is he?" he asked.

The old man began to look evasive. Agitation and anxiety gripped his scrawny old body.

The Union Army lieutenant watched him closely. His service in this office had made him something of a student of human nature. He felt confident of his ability to catch these country people in their lies.

The stocky, sunburned farmer seated behind the supplicant rose to enter the discussion. "You can't believe old Roberts here! He'd tell you anything to go see that girl of his. Everybody for twenty miles around Haymarket knows the husband, Jim Thomas, is with the Rebs." He suddenly looked contrite, looked as though he thought he had gone too far. "Don't blame Roberts," he said. "Family is family, but no one should have anything to do with the traitors!"

Bradshaw beamed at his informant. "Thank you, sir! I would not have given such a permission in any case, but this intelligence makes me doubly resolute!" Rounding on the old man, he waved him from the room. "Come back, Roberts when you have some valid need for our help!"

Bradshaw lit a cigar. Through a cloud of smoke he expectantly observed the young farmer, now positioned before him. "What can I do for you? Mister ...?"

"Smoot. Isaac Smoot, sir."

Sergeant Smoot left the courthouse folding his copy of the Oath of Allegiance into a suitable size for storage in a large wallet. He collected his horse from the rail and he rode out of the village center to a barn a mile down the Little River Turnpike, the road to Washington.

Sergeant Major Pierce Roberts awaited him behind the barn. The old man had just finished digging two sets of weapons out of the haystack. He returned Smoot's carbine, revolver and sheath knife. "You can carry those openly now, Isaac," he said with a smile. "All us Union men got to arm ourselves against scum like you were half an hour ago."

Smoot took a minute to formulate a response. "Does he always act like that?"

Roberts hooted. "You can't take that seriously! He's just a boy. A pretty, drunken, impressed with himself boy. He says dumb things but he's real easy to get by. The last one was a nasty, tough, lumberman from Maine. He got to be so difficult we had to kill him. That was when they got this one. I don't want to kill this boy, understand?"

Smoot visibly relaxed.

Roberts looked at him critically while petting his horse's nose. "Isaac, you've been too wound up lately," he said. "You're gonna make some bad mistake if you don't accept things a little more."

Smoot deferred to few men. Pierce Roberts was one of the few. "As you say, Pierce. You can tell Lieutenant Morgan and John Mosby that I'm in. I'll just amble on down the road now and find this Devereux."

"Luck, Isaac!" The older man kicked his mount into motion, heading southwest around Fairfax Court House, aiming at the depths of what was already becoming known as Mosby's Confederacy.

◆   ◆   ◆

Hope Prescott Devereux had reached a depth of confusion and frustration which demanded resolution. In the privacy of her bedroom she contemplated her predicament. In the secret places of her heart she knew that the time had come to reexamine the circumstances of her life. *My husband!* The man would drive her into a convent yet. His presence made it impossible for her not to think things through in ways which she wanted to avoid. It was all so confusing. It had always been so confusing, even at the very beginning in New York. He had been so charming, so captivating, so courteous, so witty when he courted her there. He remained so after their arrival in Virginia, and yet from the beginning she felt apart from him. Yes, the problem had started with their arrival in Virginia. There were subtle, and sometimes not so subtle differences in their attitudes toward the things which she believed to be the bedrock upon which every substantial life was built. After a while she had begun to think that the only place they were well suited to each other was in their bedroom. She felt her neck flush at the thought.

One of the most critical of these disagreements concerned his attitude toward work. He was an excellent banker, a businessman with an eye for opportunity and the imagination to see it before others. The customers of Devereux and

Wheatley swore by his instincts and skill at crafting agreements. The employees doted on him, and yet he really cared nothing for the bank. At first she had not believed it, had thought it a pose, perhaps designed to impress her. In the end belief had been inevitable. There was no regularity at all in his habits. She was accustomed to men who went to work at the same time every day, returned late and felt guilty if they were ill. His father was like that.

Claude was nothing of the sort. Neither were his brothers for that matter. Her husband was in the habit of rewarding himself for success in business ventures by absenting himself from the bank. Sometimes this would be for days. At times he would arrive home in mid-afternoon, closet himself with a book of poetry or a novel and while away the hours before dinner reading with a bottle of sherry at his elbow. Bill White was his most usual audience. Claude usually wanted to read aloud to someone. At first he had wanted to read to her, but she had told him that she was much too busy with household chores to waste the day in such idleness. Bill was always there to fetch ice for the sherry. In the first few months he typically seemed to think that she would share his belief that an afternoon of a week day was a perfect time to make love. Hope explained patiently to him that this was not so and that his proper place was in his office. He never replied. *He never replies to any of my complaints about him, damn him!* She thought of his scarred body. *I haven't seen him naked for so long now, not since last Winter.. How many more scars are there?* Tears came to her eyes. She wiped them away with the back of her hand. She thought of the hunting trips. The Devereux brothers owned a farm in the Shenandoah Valley near the village of Strasburg. They liked nothing better than to abandon the rest of the family for days at a time, boarding the train amid much undignified laughter and drinking. Unbelievably, some of the town's most prominent men frequently joined them in these flights from reality. The Corse brothers, the Herberts, the Fowles, and of course Duncan Wheatley, the father's partner, were all frequent guests at 'the farm.' Charles Devereux held his eldest son responsible for much of the dissolution of Wheatley's life.

Claude had once persuaded her to join him and his younger brother, Jake, for a weekend at this place. They had brought a cook with them and had been welcomed at Strasburg Junction by the aged 'ne'er do well' reprobate who acted as caretaker for their retreat. The ancient, rambling farm house tucked in at the foot of the Massanutten range was comfortable enough. The mountain views were delightful, the weather bracing. What she had not liked about her visit were the rough people who lived in the area and the easy way in which her sophisticated husband slipped into the rhythm of their uncouth lives. Their talk of dogs, horses, guns and crops seemed to absorb him fully. Within a few hours, the banker had disappeared. Someone else had taken his place, someone deeply wedded to the soil, someone to whom these people deferred as though he were their chieftain, someone summoned up from deep in the blood. It was baffling and more than a little frightening. *And he lies,* she thought! *He lies nonchalantly, with a smile, and laughs about it afterward. He embroiders his stories constantly. He seems to think it an art form.* She frowned. *He doesn't lie about anything very serious,* she thought, *but whoever knew a man in my family who lied like that?* Worst of all was his unwillingness to explain his actions to her. Questioning of the fitness of his actions was met with silence, a withdrawal into his inner quiet.

He had the strange habit of dragging chance acquaintances into the house in Alexandria. He was apt to show up just before dinner with someone he had met during the day. She had explained to him that this was not a considerate way to treat his mother, moreover, who were these people? "Just people," he would laugh. "Just someone I met today. Would you have me leave them in the street, my dear?" he would say.

His parents welcomed all guests wonderfully. Their circle of acquaintance was remarkably broad. Hope could still remember the dinner party at which Professor Jackson from VMI had dined with former President Tyler. That oddly misshapen man who was Commonwealth's Attorney somewhere down state was there also. *Early, that is his name. Jubal Early,* she thought. *He's sweet on me,* smiled Hope. *Old bachelors are often the most sentimental under all that gruff pretense. I wonder why that man never married. It must be some tragic story.* Hope remembered the fine ham Early had sent the ladies of the house in thanks for their hospitality after his last visit.

The rush of thought had exhausted her. Sunset over the hills west of the city looked beautiful through her window. The awareness of a change in her own feelings about her husband's faults crept over her. *I no longer care very much about these things,* she thought. *He has been gone too long. Nearly all these men are more or less like him. They admire him. He is what they think they are.. Actually, it is what they are.. It isn't bad what they are.. They enjoy life more than anyone in my family. They don't think life is about work. They think it is for the living itself. Why, I think that too. Why did I think I did not. Really, it is his father who is odd here. You can see that the other men in town think that. They accept what he is, but he is not like them. Claude is accepted as a leader, that's why the country people like him so. Clotilde is right about politics. Family is more important.. After all,* she thought. *My Federalist grandfather and his brothers were up to their hips in the secession movement in New*

England in 1815! They actually were at the Hartford convention. The Virginians were the loyalists then! After all..

5:30 P.M., 25 March
(Army of the Potomac Headquarters, Falmouth, Va.)

The courier came in through the picket line early in the morning. It was always an unpredictable process. A certain luck was required, luck which made available pickets who challenged before firing, junior officers who listened to reason, who really listened to prisoners. A lot of luck was needed.

His luck held again.

He walked through the copse of trees to the farm buildings that contained the bureau's offices. His escort kept peering at him surreptitiously, out of the sides of their faces. They knew he was a spy, either one of theirs or one belonging to the enemy. They had said so on the long ride up from the headquarters of the front line regiment through which he had come in. The regiment had been right on the Rappahannock in the Wilderness forest west of Fredericksburg.

The courier was in Confederate uniform. He found that this disguise made the line crossing worse but helped so much in traveling around in the enemy's country that the net effect was worthwhile. He was dressed as a Lieutenant of Topographical Engineers. The papers he had made him a cartographer, engaged in drawing maps for the Confederate War Department. He actually could sketch maps. He thought this was a fine disguise. It had not been questioned yet.

He, and his two cavalry escorts, marched up onto the porch. He would have simply walked in on the way to the chief's room, but the two soldiers stopped him. "If you will wait here, sir," one said. I will find someone."

One of the more interesting things about this disguise was the frequency with which Union Army enlisted men treated him as though he truly were a Confederate officer.

The cavalry corporal emerged. "You can go in, sir," he said and saluted.

The courier instinctively returned the salute. The two soldiers moved off down the path. It was getting dark. *Spring should hurry,* the courier brooded.

Colonel George Sharpe rose as the courier entered the room. "Sergeant Cline! You're back early. I did not expect you until the day after tomorrow."

They shook hands.

Cline sat. He began to feel the tension ebb from his body. He began to imagine the pleasure of a hot bath and ten hours sleep. He began to think about women he knew.

On first contact, Colonel Sharpe always seemed an unapproachable man. Those who knew him well spoke of his intellect, his humor, his inventiveness. A domed forehead loomed above the mustache. This facial adornment had become "de rigueur" in this army. Only the very individualistic chose to flaunt their independence by remaining clean shaven. George Sharpe was not a man to waste his energies in conflicts over such trivia. There was about him something that told new acquaintances that excessive familiarity would not be appreciated. His easy manner did not fully conceal his disdain for the petty nastiness of army politics. He was a lawyer from upstate New York. He had raised a regiment of infantry for the war and commanded it with honor. Joe Hooker had insisted he take this job, that he straighten out the mess that had been the army's intelligence analysis. Sharpe did it well as he did everything well.

Cline noted the presence of another man, a very young man. This man sat in the corner, his chair tipped back against the wall. He had black hair and wore a dark blue suit and string tie. There was something about him that told you he was not a soldier and would not want to be a soldier. Maybe it was the directness of his stare.

Sharpe noticed the courier's point of attention. "This is John Babcock. You have not previously met?" Sharpe was well known for the exquisite consideration of his dealings with superiors and subordinates alike. There was no need for him to explain to Cline, but it was his way to do so. "He is my second in this enterprise."

Cline wondered why the colonel would choose to have a civilian assistant but would never ask. That would be pushing the limits of Sharpe's courtesy just a little too far. "I was going to stay in the Richmond area longer," he said, "but Mister Ruth called me in, using those signals we set up. You know, the ones with the marks on buildings? He was mighty certain that you should have this dispatch. He kept saying something about 'time being on our side if we moved quickly'. Does that mean anything special to you?"

Babcock spoke up. "Did Ruth send this report to General Butler at Fortress Monroe as well?"

Cline shook his head. "The Van Lew woman is still doing that, but I believe Ruth now has it firmly in mind that he works for you, Colonel."

George Sharpe fished a third glass from a drawer, pouring the courier an over-sized drink from the half empty bottle of rye which occupied the center of the field desk before him. "Tell us about this urgent matter, would you please? I'm sure you would like something to eat." Sharpe called his orderly and sent the man to the headquarters mess for food. With his bootheels on the end of the desk, he expectantly regarded Sergeant Cline.

"It has to do with a man known as Hannibal," Cline began. Ten minutes later the false Confederate had finished his story and gone. The two intelligence officers sat quietly for five minutes absorbing the details, each seeking the meaning of his story. Babcock spoke first. "They'll kill him for sure if they catch him in that uniform. Where does Cline come from?"

Sharpe shrugged. "Indiana. He is another of these Midwesterners who wander back and forth across the lines for us. Their accents generally will pass. As for the uniform, it was his idea, John. They would probably kill him anyway. That's what we all do with spies as I recall."

Babcock spoke again. "I can't stress too much how important I think it is to get Butler out of this business. His meddling caused no end of grief to this army over the last year."

Sharpe did not intend to become involved in a struggle with Ben Butler, the Northern commander at Fortress Monroe on the Atlantic coast, east of Richmond, for control of agent networks. "Look, John, let it go," he said. "I think the situation is manageable. Butler is a fool and fools become evident with the passage of time. At the moment I am more interested in the presence in Washington of yet another spy. Like you, I have small confidence in Baker's ability to catch such people. Nevertheless, I think you should take the train and go to him in the next couple of days to pass this on. Tell him that we will be alert here to any signs that this "Hannibal" and his black friend are nosing about. Joe Hooker and I are doing our best to improve secrecy in this army. We expect Baker to do the same thing in the capital."

12:00, Friday, 27 March

"Sir, there is a man I have never seen before who is waiting in the outer room. He says he must see you."

The clerk's name was Fields. Now in his sixties, absentminded and a little feeble, he had been an employee of the firm for many years. Claude Devereux had known him as "Uncle" before the man's last name had come to seem relevant. He talked at times of Claude's grandfather with a reverence and nostalgia which verged on idolatry. Like many of the bank's staff, he tended to come to Claude with personal problems.

"Is his name Smoot?"

Fields was surprised. He had not imagined that Devereux would be expecting such a visitor. "It is, Mr. Devereux. He says he is from the country, from the Piedmont."

"He's an old hunting friend. My brothers and I used to shoot birds on his father's farm. He wrote to say he might want a job. Send him in."

Fields disappeared, returning a moment later with Isaac Smoot.

They shook hands. Smoot's grip was firm and dry. Devereux waved at a chair and they sat across from each other.

Devereux immediately liked what he saw. Smoot smiled across the table at him, clear eyed and obviously interested in his new surroundings. The man had an air of self reliance about him which spoke of his character. The brown eyes matched the color of the beard. His rough clothes completed a picture of rural simplicity.

"Welcome, Smoot." Devereux said. "The door is closed. What are your instructions?

"I'm on your team, Captain, 'til we get this job done."

"You took the Oath?"

"The paper is in my pocket. And you?"

Claude nodded, aware that much might depend on his answer.

Smoot looked at him for a moment, absorbing the idea that the minor betrayal he had been led to expect had not happened. He laughed aloud. "What do we do if we lose the war?" he said.

"We seize Canada and continue the fight from there," Devereux replied.

They smiled together for a second.

"I was joking, Cap'n," Smoot laughed. "I don't plan to lose nothing."

"How long since you arrived?"

"Two days. I've been lookin' around, remembering where things are. I went to Washington City to make sure my papers would work. I wanted to be certain about it before I came here, just in case."

Devereux nodded appreciatively. *This will work. This man thinks for himself.* "Do you think the swearing officer will report your presence?"

Smoot's reaction was to reflect aloud upon the person of the young officer who had interviewed him at Fairfax. "If it was just the puppy who was in charge,

I'd be sure that they wouldn't have a record, but the sergeants in that office were busy writing things down. They didn't do that to throw the papers away."

"Then we should be expecting that someone in this town will eventually have a record that you could be recognized by." Devereux smoked his favorite briar pipe. He blew a few rings at the brass wall lamp set in a sconce next to the fireplace. "Where are you staying?"

Smoot named a boarding house near the waterfront.

"That's no good. I want you somewhere secure and not always in the public eye. The officer in charge of this mission in Richmond suggested that I should give you employment. What would you say to a job as a driver and messenger for the bank? That way you have a good reason to move around and to be often in my company and that of Bill White."

"Sounds workable to me, Cap'n. Is White the nigger?"

The word hung in the air, surrounded by smoke. Devereux bristled. "Bill White is my right-hand man. He is the other member of this team. Are you going to have a problem with this?" He waited for an answer. An unsatisfactory response would send Smoot back south. Devereux tried to read the other's expression. He could see some skepticism. There was also a little resentment, probably at his vehemence, but the main ingredient in the sum total of hints and clues presented by Smoot's face was amusement. *Damn the man! He is laughing at me! At least he is not without humor. We are going to need that!*

"Most of the real rotten people I've been involved with were white, Cap'n," Smoot finally said. "What do you want me to call this fellah?"

Thank God! I really need this man. "Bill would do. You can call me what you like. My family owns a house here in town where we put up visitors, help and friends. Bill and his family live there. I want you there also. His wife and mother are excellent cooks. Any problem?"

"What's the street?"

"I'll walk you there. I was on my way home to lunch. I live nearby."

The tree lined streets rumbled with the sound of iron tires carrying horse and mule drawn vehicles over cobblestones. Walking south on Royal Street, they caught occasional glimpses of the Potomac to their left at the bottom of the sloping shore.

Alexandria had been founded in the mid-eighteenth century. Its domestic and public architecture was predominately Georgian, Federal and Greek Revival. Brick buildings were evident wherever one looked. Wharves terminated the eastern ends of one set of streets. The river and the quays were thronged with transport belonging to the supply system of the Union forces. The low, forested hills of Maryland across the river made a pretty backdrop to the ships at anchor or under way.

The streets were crowded with soldiers. Dark blue was everywhere. Devereux and Smoot were repeatedly forced to step down into the gutter to pass groups of Federal soldiers loitering in front of saloons and other institutions of soldierly recreation. Devereux made an effort to keep Smoot in sight as they passed these men, hoping to detect any overt hostility which might later become a difficulty. There was none.

Devereux did not realise that Isaac Smoot also watched him with concern. Within a few steps of their departure from the bank, the ranger had decided that there was something seriously wrong with Devereux's legs. He watched him from the corner of his eye, and knew that those legs could not be pushed too hard. At one curb, Smoot actually put out a hand to steady the banker, but never quite touched him and managed to conceal the motion behind Devereux's back.

"What do you think of our guests, Isaac?" Claude asked.

"Soldiers are soldiers, Mister Devereux. If they would go home, I would have no further dealings with them."

"I want you to go over to Washington City for me once you get settled in."

"To do what?"

"A Mister Thomas Green lives in the central part of the city. We are going to visit him shortly. He may be suspected of a certain sympathy toward us. Such a suspicion would be well founded. I think it would be beneficial if you would watch his residence to see if someone else is doing the same thing. The gentlemen in Richmond who sent us on this errand are a bit too easy with their arrangements. Your scalp and mine are at risk. I do believe we should check for ourselves."

"To do that right should take several days. I'll need to see if the same faces show up on different days."

"Take all the time you want. We won't approach him until you are satisfied about him."

The two strollers arrived at the big Federal house on Fairfax Street.

Smoot stared at the building. "This is where you put up the help?"

"I can see that you like it. Yes. It used to be the family residence. Come on in and we'll see what's available."

2:00 P.M.
(Southampton County, Virginia)

No one in the regiment was clear on the question of "H" Company's nickname. It had begun to circulate among the men about the time of the Seven Days Battles on the Peninsula. The word spread gradually through Kemper's Brigade, of which they were then a part, then all of a sudden everyone in the division seemed to know simultaneously that "H" Company, 17th Virginia Regiment was just the official designation of an outfit that properly should be alluded to as the "Gypsies."

Why they should be called that was a puzzle to all those then in the company. They were no more nondescript in appearance than the other companies of the regiment. They had no particular claim to special abilities in music or fortune telling. "G" and "I" Companies, the two units of the 17th that had been raised from amongst the Irish immigrant population of Alexandria would have resented such a thought.

The truth was that Major Robert Simpson, third in command of the regiment, had awarded them this title following prolonged observation of their foraging genius during the withdrawal from Williamsburg to the Chickahominy. It was not an original formulation, but Simpson had been heard to observe in wonder that "chickens would have to roost high" to escape their attentions. This was not unfair. It was true that on long marches they eventually began to resemble itinerant peddlers given to the habit of carrying agricultural products about their persons.

Pickett's Division had arrived in the area of Ivor Station, northwest of the Blackwater River the previous evening. The river was no more than four miles distant. The approach marches had been deliberate and moderately paced. Consequently, nearly everyone had reached the concentration area in good order. The men exhibited there the same show of pleased surprise with which they greeted every reappearance of their baggage.

To the south of the railroad, Hood's Division was materializing in a similar fashion. Hood's men had been in North Carolina for several weeks trying to add to the difficulties of the Union forces which garrisoned a number of coastal towns.

Lieutenant General James H. Longstreet, commander of the First Army Corps of Lee's army, was assembling two of his most powerful organizations, Hood's and Pickett's Division, for a strike at Suffolk. Everyone in the force knew this was a sideshow from the main business of defeating the Army of the Potomac in the region of the Rappahannock River, but the prospect of abusing an isolated, and presumably unprepared Union force had a special charm for all concerned. In any event, the aggressive action against Suffolk would enable Southern forces in the Tidewater to expand their program for the purchase and requisition of food-stuffs and fodder. Since everyone in the army wished to eat, this was a popular plan.

Early afternoon of this sunny day found Captain Bill Fowle, Lieutenant Jake Devereux and Sergeant Frederick Kennedy assembled at regimental headquarters. The tents were pitched in the yard of a wooden school alongside the dusty high-way. The three "Gypsy" leaders had been summoned to the schoolhouse by the aforementioned Major Simpson.

Robert Simpson had spent a number of years as a school teacher. His public discourse consistently had the flavor and mannerisms of his profession.

The three men listened attentively to him.

He blinked at them in the bright sunlight and began, "Nice day, don't you think?" He looked around the group in the cheery way that he managed in the most unlikely of circumstances. "Looks like there'll be a moon tonight ..." A slight frown crossed the face.

Sergeant Kennedy watched the major closely.

Simpson rested one hand on a colored sketch map of the district across the river. The map lay on a battered table which must have been carried out of the school.

Fred Kennedy had been in the army long enough to recognize the behavior of a senior officer searching for words to tell you something that you probably would rather not hear. He considered Simpson to be a good officer, better than the average really. *What is this about?* Kennedy wondered. *Why us?*

The afternoon was warm. Simpson removed his grey uniform jacket and rolled up the sleeves of the wrinkled white shirt underneath. He took a red hand-kerchief from a pocket in his trousers, wiped his mouth and cleared his throat.

Fowle took pity on the major. "It's a scout, isn't it?" he asked.

Simpson scratched the side of his face, above the whiskers. "Yes, Bill. The corps commander wants a reconnaissance done of the other bank of the Blackwa-ter. We evidently are going to cross in a few days and move up to Suffolk. I think he must be looking to see if there are any thinly held spots in the line on the river."

"Anybody else doing this?" Fowle inquired.

Kennedy had the same question in the forefront of his mind.

"Our brigade tonight for this division, somebody in Hood's Division tomorrow night."

"Just 'H'?" Fowle asked.

"Yes, just you all. Longstreet wants the venture to mimic the actions of the 'Corps of Observation' that has been here up 'till now. They say they have made periodic raids across the river in company strength, so we are to try and look like yet another. This means you are to take your company across, wander around a bit to see what's there and then bring them all back."

"I rarely seek to leave any of them there, Major." The bite in the words was softened by the smile.

"Yes, yes. That's why you are going." Simpson seemed not to have taken offense at the company commander's remark. "In fact, you are ordered to bring back everyone you take over, living or otherwise. It is particularly wanted that the enemy should not learn as yet that they face newly arrived troops, especially our illustrious selves." Simpson's face took on a Puckish cast. He resumed, "I tried to convince the staff at division that the Yankees would never be able to identify any of your men by their dress and that they were unlikely to have letters in their pockets, but they wouldn't accept my reasoning."

Kennedy was certain that Captain Fowle would not let this slide by.

He was correct. "Your more than usually rude remarks surprise us, Major," Fowle drawled, "but I must say they would have more force coming from someone other than a native of Front Royal."

Simpson had originally been commander of "B" Company. This unit had been raised in his hometown in the Shenandoah Valley. As the only company in the 17th not from the Alexandria district they had long endured more than their share of chaff.

The two officers grinned at each other across the table, enjoying a renewal of the contest.

"In any event," Simpson recommenced, "We will bring 'C' Company up to the river to secure the near bank. He pointed at the map. You are to cross here. There is a ford. This is the lowest one in the river, actually. You should secure the far shore and then send out one or more parties to explore."

"Anything else?" Captain Fowle asked sweetly.

Simpson was relishing this now. "Yes! Yes! Bring us back some prisoners."

"Tonight?" Fowle prompted.

"Whenever you'd like, as long as it is before tomorrow."

I'd be sore at the jokes, Kennedy thought, *if I didn't know Simpson is ready to do it himself.*

"All right, let's say 10:00 P.M. to cross the Blackwater."

"Fine," the major agreed. "I am going to wait up for you with 'C' Company."

"We need to talk to them," Jake Devereux commented.

"They'll be along in a few minutes," said Simpson. "How about a drink while we are waiting?"

Agreement was easily reached and the four men crossed to the school house where the regimental staff had set up a simple mess.

8

An Evening's Entertainment

Sundown
(On The Blackwater)

The moon was going to be half full. Fred Kennedy watched it rise in the late afternoon. It mounted the blue sky like a pale, masked face, half turned across an invisible shoulder. Kennedy looked at the moon and tried to judge what the effect of its light might be on the night's business. On balance, he decided that it would be satisfactory. There would be enough light to see people up close, but not enough to see them at a distance. The shadows supplied by the forest depths would add to the effect.

As the evening deepened, "H" company brought its fifty-four men forward to a meadow a mile from the river. Captain Fowle spent an hour talking to them, drawing diagrams and maps in the dirt, asking questions, probing for the misunderstanding which he seemed always to expect. Finally he was satisfied with their answers and paused.

Kennedy watched him, thinking how lucky the company had been in its leaders. *First we had Herbert, then Claude, now Bill. They were all good, but Fowle is the best. We must not lose him,* Kennedy thought. *He is so careful, so thorough. Claude was a great hero to us all, but Fowle is better for us. There is something frightening about Claude on a battlefield. The ferocity that comes out in him is worrisome. He might do something really foolish. It's funny,* Kennedy reflected. *None of that shows in his brother, Jake.*

Captain Fowle turned to look at the setting sun. "It's six o'clock. They're yours, Fred. See that they get two hours rest. We'll move at 9:15." He collected Jake Devereux with a glance and disappeared into the darkening woods.

Kennedy knew the two officers would be on the river line, listening and scheming until they came back to bring the troops up for the crossing. The company had been together for so long now that preparations for most operations were routine.

In the gathering darkness, he had the more junior sergeants inspect their men, going over the load each would carry, checking to see that the required amount of ammunition was actually on their persons, sniffing to discover what really was in canteens. He watched as each man was made to jump up and down a few times to see what would rattle.

Snake Davis had come with them to feed the men before the patrol. He had a small fire going under a big beech tree. The smoke went up through the leaves, losing its white color as it went.

The soldiers helped themselves to charred sticks from the fire, plunging them into a canvas bucket and using the soot to take the shine off their faces and necks.

Snake was busy with the meal, but took time from this to offer his opinion of the authenticity of their makeup. The resulting exchange followed its usual course and the voices kept rising in raucous hilarity.

Kennedy approached the group. "Any louder and the captain'll be back here to kick my ass!" he laughed. "Snake! You know better than to talk to these boys when there's work to do. They like nothing better than to jaw."

Davis waved his hands. "Here's some food, Sergeant Kennedy," he murmured. "You gonna feel better you eat somethin." The black cook placed a bowl in Kennedy's hands. He had known Sergeant Fred Kennedy all the man's life, had fed him often as a boy when he had come hungry to the back door of Snake's master's house. Kennedy's life was proof that the Northern idea that only the rich had risen in revolt was wrong. The sandy haired, slender man sniffed at the food, and looked at Davis inquiringly.

"Deer meat," the cook responded. "Jim shot it yestiddy noon."

Kennedy had learned long ago to trust Davis, and not just about cooking. "Snake," he said. "There's gonna be an ambulance and a surgeon show up here pretty quick. You tell that doctor and drivers they are to stay 'till we get back no matter what, understand?"

"You gonna leave one of the so'jers?"

"Yes. I'm going put Clark here to guard our bedrolls, but you make sure he stays too."

"All right, Mistah Kennedy, Jim and me, we gonna make them all stay."

6:45 P.M.
(Alexandria)

As dusk fell on Duke street, the cobble stoned space between the curbs filled to overflow with carriages, drivers and tethered mounts. A pervasive aroma of horse overhung the block. Black grooms stood at the head of matched teams. Horses peered around at each other, stimulated by the company of so many other animals. The luckier among them observed the scene over the top of nose bags while munching at their oats. Scattered among the vehicles were military carriages and even that most ubiquitous of U.S. Army conveyances, a light ambulance pressed into service for the evening to transport the guests. The soldiers who had driven these vehicles stood apart, smoking and chatting amongst themselves. Gas street lights illuminated the night and a background murmur of conversation underlay the more specific sounds emanating from the massive Devereux residence occupying the center of the block.

The day had proven to be one of nature's treats, an early Spring opportunity to experience what May would be like. It was deliciously warm. The press of guests within the house could have made the rooms uncomfortable, and to avoid this Claude's mother had opened wide the ground floor shutters and windows.

The soldier-drivers standing in the street looked in the open windows and found themselves virtually members of the dinner party. The golden light of candelabra and chandelier radiated from the large windows. The women guests present for the evening would have been gratified at the interest and admiration which their persons elicited from the gallery of spectators.

Claude's mother had decided to arrange seating for the dinner by placing round tables throughout the dining and music rooms. George White had taken charge of the actual conduct of the party after receiving guidance from his mistress. The relationship between Clotilde Devereux and the butler in major household functions tended to resemble that between director and stage manager in the theater.

Claude, his mother and Hope stood together, condemned to their post in the foyer, to welcome guests. They had been there for forty minutes and were each looking forward secretly to a consensus that all those who were coming had arrived. Claude waited for one of the women to say something, but they did not and he finally decided that it was probably his place to make the first statement on this subject. "Can we possibly leave the door to Uncle George, and go mix?" he asked hopefully.

"No," his mother replied. "Another ten minutes.."

His wife smiled.

Patrick and Victoria had assumed responsibility for the guests already on hand. Pat had put his head out of the parlor twice in the last few minutes and was visibly hoping for relief. Amongst those present was General Slough, the military governor of Alexandria and Colonel Herman Haupt, the commander of The United States Military Railroad System. Claude could imagine how much his brother and sister-in-law must enjoy their company.

George White emerged from the pantry doors at the other end of the foyer. Having found Claude, he came to whisper a message and returned the way he had come. Devereux grinned at the two women. "You'll have to deal with any late arrivals. One of the extra waiters we hired is ill. Uncle George wants me to look at him." With this, he happily left them to wait alone.

After the required interval, the ladies had just decided to join their guests when two more carriages halted in the street. A Union Army officer dismounted from the first, and handed down several women while a very similar man in naval uniform performed the same duties for the second vehicle.

Lieutenant Colonel Frederick Braithwaite followed his wife Elisabeth up the stairs. His brother shepherded the remaining four women who included the three visitors from Pennsylvania. Commander Richard Braithwaite's tall form loomed over these older ladies much as it had during the railroad trip from Baltimore. His gold lace trimmed fore and aft hat, and navy blue boat cloak made an imposing sight in the street and caused much saluting and respectful greeting from the soldiers on the scene. The fourth woman stood at his elbow. She was exceptionally tall and was dressed in shades almost as dark as the naval officer. A white woolen shawl enfolded her.

Elizabeth Braithwaite arrived at the place of reception just within the double front doors. The candle light within glinted on the beveled edges of the glass panes which filled the upper halves of the open doors. Frederick Braithwaite's wife made a pretty picture in a velvet, low cut dress. Her husband's uniform was a suitable backdrop for her. The three women made a striking sight for the men in the street. Hope's blond good looks and Clotilde Devereux's Gallic sense of style completed the scene handsomely.

Elizabeth held out her hand to Clotilde. "It is so kind of you. We were so fortunate to meet your wonderful son in Baltimore." Turning her attention to Hope, "You must be so happy to have him back, and after such a long absence ..." The mischief in the comment caused Hope's ears to burn. She looked down into the street at the tall woman in the white shawl. They smiled at each other. *Well, there is at least one woman here I can trust,* she thought.

"We are all happy to have him back, dear," said Claude's mother. "Colonel Braithwaite," she said to the husband over Elizabeth's shoulder. "I do not believe we have met previously, although we are lucky enough to have the pleasure of the company of Elizabeth in so many of our activities."

"It is my privilege, ma'am," he said. "Elizabeth has spoken of you both on many occasions."

"I do hope you will enjoy our little soiree," she said. "There are other officers with us tonight. Perhaps you know them?" Her own family background in the French Army made her believe that soldiers would always want to be with their own kind. She led her guests away toward the temporary coat closet that had been made of the breakfast room.

Commander Braithwaite was the last into the house and followed the group into the front parlor where he found his brother already deep in conversation with Colonel Haupt and the general officer governor of the city. Frederick beckoned to his naval brother as he entered the room and drew him into the conversation.

The two Devereux women followed their last guests. By the time they entered the parlor, the chatter of thirty people had begun to approximate the roar of surf on an open beach. Hope and Clotilde looked at each other and smiled in the knowledge that thus far the party was a success. Hope studied the scene and frowned. The guests and hosts instinctively had arranged themselves by taste and political attitudes. The old Alexandrians stood in small circles discussing the issues of family and business which had always been their preoccupation. The Union military figures and Sanitary Commission members made up other groups. The foreign diplomats and their wives, as well as the younger Devereuxs, were trying to divide their attentions among them. *This will not do,* Hope thought. *I am not having the damned war reproduced right here.*

At this moment, Claude reentered the parlor through the butler's pantry at the back. He and George White had diagnosed the illness of the waiter as food poisoning and sent him home. He stood inside the door surveying the crowd.

His wife approached, whispering that they should begin with their oldest friends, and that he should try to get people to mix.

Taking a long stemmed glass from a passing tray, he followed Hope to the center of the room where half a dozen older people were laughing and talking. He worked his way around the circle calling on a long and varied acquaintance with these old family associates to make conversation. He spoke with the Wheatleys, the Burkes, the Millers and others whose names he had to strain his recollection to remember.

Hope prompted him, led the discussion when needed and stood ready to deflect the current of conversation when necessary. Excusing themselves, they moved toward the front of the house, aiming at a word with General Slough and Colonel Haupt who were rather boorishly conducting business while leaning against the black marble fireplace.

A shapely hand encircled Claude's upper arm, halting their progress around a group principally made up of women. It was Elizabeth Braithwaite. She drew him steadily toward herself and into the circle. The process made Hope follow. Elizabeth's grip on his arm forced Claude to look down at her. She was every bit as sumptuous as he remembered. The low cut dress provided a vision of milky breast which made it an effort not to stare. The navy brother, stood to the right of Elizabeth. Her stance, half-turned toward Claude, virtually required the navy man to look at Devereux over her shoulder. *My God*, thought Claude. *The view from there must be awesome.* He resolutely looked at the men. "Good to see you again Mrs. Braithwaite," he said, glancing down at her for a second. "Colonel Braithwaite, thank you again for the help the night I returned.. Commander Braithwaite, how fortunate that you could join us. Did you take the train?"

Richard responded smoothly that he had brought a driver and carriage from the Navy Yard since the opportunity to meet so many prominent citizens made this without doubt an official function.

My! My! On duty are you? Claude thought. *What an ass! That will impress her, and all the other ladies as well!*

Devereux instinctively sought to identify the other people in the circle. As he did so, he slowly became aware of the tall woman in dark clothing standing across from him. His peripheral vision had always been good and while he talked to the Braithwaites he inspected her. He could not place her among the visitors he had met in Baltimore. She had said nothing thus far and he decided that politeness dictated a greeting. He took a look at her. *Plain. Homely? No. Not homely. That would be too much. Plain.* At first he thought her very tall, but as he looked at her she seemed smaller, no taller than he, large boned perhaps with graying brown hair and dark, severe clothes. The dress looked almost black in the candlelight but that could not be true, surely! She looked at him once and then away. He found this shyness amusing and a little touching after five months in Paris. *This must be one of Hope's friends from the Sanitary Commission.* He shifted his attention back to the navy man who worried him for some reason he could not have named.

Elizabeth still had him by the arm.

Does she plan to keep me?

The sailor was making small talk with Hope and his brother while Elizabeth prattled on at Claude, somehow including the tall woman whom they all evidently knew.

Devereux was not deceived by the general show of conviviality. *Damn it, woman!* He thought. *Let go of me! Make trouble between the two men you already have!* He was dead sure that nothing in the room existed for Commander Richard Braithwaite except the vision of his beloved's hand on someone else's arm. Devereux cast about for some way to escape the grip of this trouble making female. He caught Hope's eye.

She looked concerned. Her eyes kept returning to Elisabeth's hand on his arm. "Darling, you haven't met Miss Biddle!" she said.

Bless You Hope! he rejoiced. *You are going to save me in spite of my many faults!*

Hope glanced back and forth between her husband and the tall woman.

Claude moved forward, breaking Elizabeth's grip. *Ah! Sweet relief!*

His wife continued to talk, describing Miss Biddle's devotion to the cause of soldier welfare and the care of convalescents.

His hand moved steadily across the open space.

Miss Biddle's hand rose to meet his.

Why am I doing this? he asked himself. It was a strange thing to do. Women did not shake hands with men in his world.

Her hand fit into his.

In thinking of that moment, he later tried to describe to himself the experience. He could not. Something passed between them in the instant of contact. It was a kind of mutual knowledge. There was a horrible feeling of openness, a conviction of vulnerability, an unreasoned awareness that they would somehow be related. He sought and found this plain, middle-aged woman's eyes. It was as if he looked into a mirror.

She looked frightened.

He knew she also felt it. It was as though a telegraph wire ran down the length of his arm, crossed through their palms and disappeared somewhere in her bosom. What ran between them in that instant was electric.

He realized that he still gripped her hand. He wondered how long it had been. "I'm sorry, Miss Biddle," he said. He willed his hand to open, watched it release her. He looked at her. She did not look away. The fright was gone, replaced with something else, something stronger. "How rude of me," he said with a little bow, "wool gathering like that! I didn't hear all of your name."

Hope stared at him. "Amy. It's Amy," his wife replied.

◆   ◆   ◆

Captain Fowle stood in the middle of the clearing and looked at his men. The moon shone into the opening in the trees brightly enough for him to see them. They lay in the grass in a double column with twenty feet between the two files. A line of pickets was somewhere out in the forest, outposts against the remote chance of a surprise.

Fred Kennedy waited in the middle of the formation, squatting in the long grass, chatting amiably with the man nearest to him. There was something very comforting about Kennedy on occasions such as this.

Jake Devereux was at the tail end of the company, talking with the cooks and the medical people who had finally arrived.

Fowle found his watch in a vest pocket, opened the case and held it up to the moonlight. *Time to go*, he thought. With a gesture that mimicked the action, he brought the men to their feet.

Squad leaders faded into the trees, returning with their outposts.

Kennedy swept his head from side to side as he accounted for the returning pickets. He held up a thumb for the company commander.

Fowle walked to the head of the column, clapped his hands once to get everyone's attention and waved the three man point forward into the logging road that lead up to the river. This tiny advanced guard would navigate and protect them from an unexpected meeting.

The double column followed him into the forest, compressing to fit the dimensions of the road as it went. The company seemed to be disappearing into a tunnel.

Fowle glanced back. The clearing was a bright patch of light, on the other side of which he could see the two wagons and the embers of Snake Davis' fire. *They're moving too fast*, he thought in panic. He moved up the column and grasped the lead point man by the back of his jacket to slow him. The soldier nodded without turning his head and eased the pace. With a good deal of satisfaction Fowle watched the men adjust the interval between them to allow for the near darkness. They closed up until he could hear their breathing, smell the wood smoke on their clothing, and sense the soft breaking of twigs on the edge of the track. He would not have allowed talking and except for an occasional cough the column went forward in silence.

The forest was much darker than the clearing had been. It took a few minutes for night vision to reach its full potential but gradually tree shapes began to emerge from the gloom and the bare, sandy ruts of the road took on a faint luminescence.

Fowle halted the column several times to make sure he had everyone. Each time he did this, Jake came up the center of the road and touched him on the arm to report that all was well.

Time passed imperceptibly. Fowle was glad it was not cold. The night was too cool for sweating to have commenced as yet and he felt really good as he often did going into action. Twice the point flinched from night sounds produced by something with feet. One of these was surely a deer. The other seemed to Fowle to be about the size of a rabbit or raccoon.

The walk in the woods seemed endless, a kind of metaphor of the seemingly perpetual stasis of their life in the army. The men in "H" Company had become what they did. Life outside the regiment seemed a distant possibility. They now had a hard time remembering their civilian lives as anything but a faded dream of childhood. The approach march went on and on. The track forked a number of times. At these intersections, the point halted and Fowle showed them the way.

After awhile he began to think of Emily, the girl he had left behind. Home was impossibly far away. He sometimes received letters from her, allowed across the lines by the "kindness" of the Union government, but these had become fewer and an erosion of belief in her constancy had begun to eat at his hope for the future.

He walked into the back of the point, unexpectedly finding himself between two of the men. Corporal Daniels, on the left, held his commander back with his right hand.

Damn! I have to do better than that.

Daniels stood quietly, listening to something inaudible in front of them.

He stood with them, hearkening to the silence.

The leaves rubbed against each other somewhere to the left front.

A sibilant murmur rasped ahead.

"Eight," whispered Fowle.

The leaf sounds ended. There was a pause. "Seven," arrived as a counter.

Fifteen it was, the challenge and countersign for the night.

Daniels stepped forward without hesitation.

Fowle stopped for a moment to give the "C" Company outpost the exact number of men in his force to simplify the process of counting them in, a necessary precaution against an imaginative enemy attempt at infiltration. He halted the company behind a clump of trees which he had noticed earlier. It was almost exactly one hundred yards from the river.

Major Simpson waited for them in the shadow of a huge tree.

The "C" Company commander, Bill Lynch, stood beside him. Fowle could not see the field officer clearly but the tall, stoop shouldered figure with the vast beard was unmistakable.

Simpson held out his hand. "It's right quiet over there," he said. "We've been listening for an hour and have heard nothing but the water and the wind in the trees."

The Dinner Party
(Alexandria)

Hope had planned the seating arrangements for the dinner and Clotilde had selected the guests with help from her eldest son. Hope's only real contributions to the list had been an elderly Presbyterian clergyman from the U. S. Christian Commission and Amy Biddle. She had seated Amy next to Commander Braithwaite at Claude's table in the vague hope that this might in some way improve the spinster's marital prospects. Claude ruined that by insisting, at the last moment, on substituting Colonel Braithwaite for his brother. Claude had said that he wished to speak to the army officer. He seemed to believe, as he always did, that his expressed desire in such a matter would automatically suffice. This habit of mind had always maddened her. It still did.

Hope placed the younger of the two British Army officers, Major Robert Neville at her right hand. She had never seen him before. Indeed, she could not imagine how Claude had conceived the idea of inviting him, but admitted that Neville was a fortunate choice. He was tall, slim, blond, but greying at the sides. The dark green and black of his regiment's mess uniform made a most satisfactory element in the scene. Hope treasured the thought that Neville's presence at her side might cause stirrings of jealousy in her husband. She was becoming increasingly analytic on the subject of her feelings toward him. She now knew that she wanted him. Whatever else there was between them would take a second place to her basic feelings.

Neville had not shown the slightest interest in her thus far. He seemed much more concerned with Harrison Wheatley, who was also seated at her table. The Wheatleys had always been fairly "silent" partners in the bank. This man's father had been a major source of capital for the foundation of the enterprise.

Wheatley did not need to work and had spent his life as amateur banker, lawyer, soldier and historian. He had served in the Mexican War and made a point of telling one and all that only his advanced age prevented his participation in this one. He was having a good time questioning the Englishman about his campaign service. Hope noticed that he appeared surprised and puzzled by the answers he received. Wheatley had a tendency to play with the ends of his thinning, brown hair when distracted. He was doing that now.

Claude's table was the center of a swelling noise of conversation. The French military attache'e wife, Helene Jourdain, was deep in conversation with Mrs. Jane Slough, the wife of the governor of Alexandria. Hope watched this exchange during the soup course. Claude was translating for Madame Jourdain. She saw, with a certain amusement, that it was impossible for him to eat. The two women would not stop talking.

George White hovered near Claude's chair, wishing to remove the soup plates.

Hope watched in amazement as Amy Biddle offered to help with the translation. Claude accepted with gratitude and after listening to her speak for a few minutes, offered some compliment which turned Amy's ears a darker pink.

I never imagined, thought Hope, *that my darling husband would find yet another admirer in this colorless creature.* She contrasted in her mind the image of herself that she recalled from the looking glass in her bedroom with the large, pale, ascetically dressed woman before her. *I thought I liked this woman,* she thought.

She took another look at the British major beside her and saw to her satisfaction that his eyes kept drifting back to her and away from Wheatley.

Hope beckoned George White to her side and in a whisper told him to take Claude's plate away from him. "We can't wait all night while he dawdles, George. Keep things moving along."

George bowed his grey head. "Yes, ma'am." He walked straight to Claude's place, spoke softly to him and removed the plate.

Devereux smiled across the room at his wife.

She could hear that Colonel Braithwaite had taken advantage of Claude's escape from translational duty to attempt to engage him in business talk of some sort. She listened intently, trying to hear what Braithwaite said over the chatter of the two tables. Braithwaite persisted in telling him something about a speculation in railroad construction that he had in mind for the post war benefit of a "select" group of investors. She knew how little Claude thought of people who sought to discuss the bank's affairs in social occasions. She was surprised to hear him suggest that he would welcome further discussion of the idea.

◆　　◆　　◆

Kennedy and his two scouts came out of the forest fifteen yards apart. He had put himself in the middle. As he left the last trees, he passed one of the two bronze field pieces that had been wheeled into position by hand a few minutes before.

The gun crew stood up straight as the infantry advanced through them. The artillerymen took off their hats in a silent farewell, a recognition of the terrible losses that were the riflemen's portion.

The moon seemed terribly bright. The distance to the water's edge grew longer with each step. He came abreast of "C" Company's rifle pits.

The scattered positions were dug along the top of the river bank, two or three feet above the water.

A pale face turned up to look at him as he passed.

The embankment was steep, but not high. He stepped warily into the water, feeling with his first move to know the nature of the bottom. It was soft, too soft. He thought of black, swirling muck and leeches. The water tugged at him, climbing with leaden cold along his calves. The river was loud, running over deadfalls with a noise that rivaled Niagara Falls to his straining ears.

His men moved forward, the water rising against their thighs. Neither soldier wore a hat. Like Kennedy, they held their rifled muskets at port arms. The long bayonets shimmered in the moonlight.

The three men churned onward in the numbing wetness.

Cold water reached his crotch, grasping his genitals in an ever shrinking fist.

He glanced back at the left bank of the river. Nothing could be seen of the Southern troops hidden there. *We must have looked like ghosts coming out of the dark.*

The moon hung low over the grove ahead. It cast a faint shadow behind them. The big trees kept the moonlight from reaching the water in front of the river bank toward which the vanguard of the "Gypsies" advanced.

His chest felt tight. He made a conscious decision to breathe. *My God, I've been waiting for a bullet.*

Private O'Keefe, on the left, reached the shadows.

Private Colonna, on the right, halted, his crossing complete.

Kennedy waded onward doggedly.

The lovely bank came up to meet him. He rested his elbows on it, his rifle pointed into the thicket.

The three scouts stood in the water for a few moments, listening for a reaction to their appearance.

There was nothing.

He waved the two men forward, into the shadowy silence.

They slithered over the lip of the embankment.

He waited for their return, controlling the impatience and anxiety pulling at his insides. He knew what they were doing, fifty yards in, fifty yards left or right, back to the river, then back to him. If they hit something, he would probably get one shot at it before the whole confused mass was in the water with him. *I hope to God that "C" Company and the guns don't get hasty.*

O'Keefe crept back through the brush. "Looks fine to me," he whispered.

A wet noise to one side made the leader turn his head.

Colonna's stocky bulk was at his elbow. "The road is right in front of us. I think I hear a picket somewhere over there." He pointed to the right with his chin.

Fred considered this for a moment. "Go get the company," he told O'Keefe. "Tell the captain what Colonna just said. Tell him I think he should place someone to cover that direction before anything else. We'll be waiting at the road."

O'Keefe slipped into the water, headed for the friendly shore.

The other two men threaded their way carefully through the brushy forest. The moonlight penetrated the treetop canopy enough to outline trunks and deadfalls.

He picked his way among the obstacles, inspecting the forest floor for anything that might snap.

The woodland gloom began to be lightened by a radiant glow in front of them. Abruptly, they were at the edge of the wood.

He found a tree big enough to stand behind, and looked. The road was dirt. It ran in from the right in a straight line that paralleled the woodline and bordered it. It turned steeply to the right just past their observation point and disappeared over a slight rise in the ground. Across the road, to the front, a stretch of open land extended. Several large, irregularly shaped objects occupied the middle distance in this scene. He stared at them, unable to identify them until a familiar sound crossed the intervening space.

"Cows," Colonna whispered.

Kennedy grinned in the dark. *We could use more farm people in this company.*

Colonna grabbed his arm, turning his attention to the right.

Two men in visored military caps were walking down the road. They passed within ten feet of the concealed Confederates. One of them smoked a short pipe. The scent lingered in the air. *All Burleigh, must not be a real Yankee.* The sound of the hobnailed boots rasped on the gravel in the road. The dark uniforms were somehow slightly different from those he ordinarily saw on Union soldiers.

Colonna looked at him inquiringly.

He shook his head. *This must be a change of picket reliefs. Noise will ruin the whole thing, and what will the rest think when these don't show up.* He watched them go. They were almost out of sight, over the hump in the road to the left when he understood what it was about them that was odd. They each had on exactly the same items of clothing and these were all worn in the same way. Even the kepis rode on the two heads at the same angle. *That should tell me something. Where have I seen this before?*

The company came through the underbrush behind him. It sounded like a gentle wind in dry leaves.

Fowle appeared at his side.

He reported.

Fowle listened silently, as he always did.

Kennedy's mind nagged him, trying to remember, reaching back. It was almost there.

Fowle finally nodded. He turned to Jake Devereux, "As planned," he whispered.

The captain found the little group of ten men in his scouting party and moved off through the forest to the left, following the road around the curve and over the rise.

Devereux led the fifteen soldiers allotted to his part of the plan to the right. Keeping just inside the forest, he moved toward the bridge across the Blackwater. That interesting object was found at the spot where this farm road connected at a right angle with the turnpike. There would certainly be a sizable group of the enemy somewhere near the bridge.

Kennedy posted his pickets in a semicircular pattern with their backs to the river. The ones farthest out were in the brush almost on the road. Farther back he set up the main defense position, also semicircular. He had the bulk of the company. He placed the men in pairs, showing them where to shoot.

He had just finished this task and was thinking about how cold his wet legs were when it came to him. He remembered seeing dead Yankee soldiers lying in absolutely straight rows, killed in the ranks. He remembered Gaines Mill, Sharpsburg. On these fields he had seen Federal units who fought as though they were on parade, soldiers dressed with the same fussy neatness and uniformity he had seen tonight.

Regulars! U.S. Army Regulars. Professionals! What were they doing here?

He calculated the chance of finding either of the two officers, and decided against the attempt.

◆   ◆   ◆

Hope Devereux had been a believing, practicing Catholic from childhood.

Her family had brought their religion with them from England. They were proud of the fervor and loyalty which had accompanied their adherence to "the old faith" through the long centuries following the English Reformation.

It was difficult for Hope to admit to herself that she disliked Father Willem Kruger, S.J., the pastor of Saint Mary's in Alexandria. She had seated the parish priest with Claude because she wanted to keep them both in a location in which they could be observed by her, and because the Dutch Jesuit and Claude were friends.

Hope considered Father Kruger to be yet another of the strange, inexplicable people who inhabited the city of Alexandria. The priest had been educated 30 years before at Rome, had served briefly in his native Holland and was then transferred by the Society of Jesus to America. In the United States the man somehow had become an ardent partisan of the cause of Southern rights. She found the priest's attitude so strange that she had once asked him to explain the mental process by which a Catholic clergyman could have become a secessionist.

He had stared at her evenly with the chilly air of aloof and distant intellect for which he had become well known. "Mrs. Devereux," he had said. "First, I think the United States government is totally unjustified in employing force to coerce the states' allegiance to the Union. I think it is wrong and unconstitutional. Second, I do not believe that the great mass of Negroes, those who are employed throughout the South in agricultural work have reached a condition of education and indeed civilization in which it would be humane or responsible to make them suddenly dependent solely on themselves. Third, I have lived in this place for many years. These people have become my people. I will stand with them, confident in the essential decency of this community." She had to admit that he lived by these words. Kruger had steadfastly refused all pressure from the Union Army occupation authorities to take the Oath of Allegiance to the United States. In this decision he was joined by his Protestant colleagues. For his lack of cooperation he had been banned by the United States government from the exercise of his priestly functions in the marriage and interment of his parishioners. His response had been to send his people to Georgetown College in the District of

Colombia to be married. On occasion, he had been known to row betrothed couples to the center of the Potomac River in the night to administer the Sacrament of Matrimony. He felt justified in this since the Potomac River was Maryland territory and did not come under the authority of the governor at Alexandria.

Kruger's acceptance of an invitation to this dinner party in the company of so many of "the enemy" would have puzzled Hope if she had not known of the priest's insistence on ministering to the spiritual needs of all. He had been known to say that it was especially important to care for the Yankees. They needed it more than most people.

To her horror, she heard him ask Mrs. Slough if she enjoyed the house she resided in. The lady so addressed, paused momentarily in her conversation with Helene Jourdain.

"It is quite lovely. The rooms are a little small." She went on chatting with the Frenchwoman.

Hope held her breath. The priest had returned to contemplation of his dinner. He seemed prepared to let the subject drop.

From the corner of her eye, Hope saw Frederick Braithwaite put down his fork, sit up straight and look at the priest. "What does that mean, Reverend?"

Conversation halted.

"What does what mean?" Amy Biddle asked.

Mrs. Slough seemed to have been thinking about the priest's original question. "Do you know the owners, Father?"

"Yes, Mrs. Slough, I have known the Fowle family for some years."

"Are they Catholics?" Braithwaite asked.

A wry smile creased the Jesuit's face. "No, my flock is made up of a few prosperous families like the Devereuxs and many, many Irish and Italian laborers. The Fowles are Episcopalian, but nevertheless friends."

Hope had listened long enough and decided to place herself where she could intervene if necessary. She caught Claude's attention and signaled him to exchange seats with her.

Mrs. Slough wore a look of real concern. "I do not wish to think that anyone has been seriously inconvenienced to provide me with a house. I understood that the elder Mister Fowle had removed to Richmond voluntarily, and the younger ..."

"Is with the Confederate Army," completed Father Kruger.

As Hope approached the table, the gentlemen rose.

"Such a serious lot you are!" she said shaking her blond head artfully and taking a seat at the head of the table. "Where is George? We are having trifle this evening." She looked directly at the detestable priest. "We know how much you enjoy it, Father!"

"Will they not have their home returned after the war?" asked Amy, a look of deep trouble on her face.

Kruger considered the spinster's solemnity. *I should laugh,* he thought, *but that would be unkind.* "Miss Biddle, you must know that the Federal government is requiring in this city that property taxes be paid in person by the owner."

Amy shook her head slowly. "It's stupid of me, but I have been obsessed with the Commission's work. You are saying that the houses of absent rebels are being seized and sold for taxes."

"Yes."

"Many?" she asked.

"More every week," Hope contributed. *Why in heaven's name did I say that?* "Mrs. Slough," she said. "I am sure you don't know such things occur! This is something you might look into." *For God's sake, shut up!* she told herself, but plunged on anyway. "It is unfortunate for the cause of reunion and emancipation that the citizens of this place should be deprived of their ancestral homes through this kind of proceeding." She felt hot anger well up, the product of long months of frustration and humiliation. She had always felt obliged to defend the Federal government's actions, no matter how much she had thought them wrong, now, suddenly, it was all too much. For some reason she looked at Claude who was listening with interest. He nodded. She looked back at her table. She could see that Helene Jourdain was leaning toward Amy Biddle to hear the translation. "Etonnant! Epouvantable!" The Frenchwoman exclaimed and rattled on at some length in a vivid exposition which really did not need thorough translation.

"What did she say?" Mrs. Slough demanded.

An embarrassed quiet filled the room. The Devereuxs had assembled for this evening nearly every person in their close acquaintance who possessed a significant knowledge of the French language. They had wished to avoid situations in which Madame Jourdain would be deprived of conversation.

As a result, Hope knew, with a hollow certainty, that most people present understood exactly what Helene Jourdain had said. In her mind she ran through the list of guests and family estimating the odds. *Kruger. It would be Kruger.*

The priest spoke. "Mrs. Jourdain said that it is astonishing and shocking, ma'am, that your government should do this. She said that the Europeans, in all their many wars have never done this to their enemies." Willem Kruger grinned across the table at General Slough's lady. "I'm European in origin, Mrs. Slough, and I believe that what has been said is something of an exaggeration. Here's George White with his wife's excellent trifle."

"Father, my husband will see to it that our house will be returned to the Fowles." Mrs. Slough was evidently wounded that the Jesuit would think so poorly of herself and the general.

"I'm sure you will ma'am. My outburst was not intended for you personally."

Hope began to congratulate herself on the relatively intact survival of the dinner party. *I'll be damned if I'll ever have that wretched priest at anything again*, she resolved.

◆   ◆   ◆

Devereux and his fifteen riflemen slipped from shadow to shadow. Their task was the simpler of those given to the two officers.

Fowle, by contrast, was headed for a specific goal on the left, a signal and observation tower which dominated the neighborhood and which was visible from within Southern lines.

Jake's job was to block the road to the bridge to protect Fowle's party and the foothold which Sergeant Kennedy held on the near bank of the Blackwater. The young officer strode through the darkened wood just behind the leading man.

Private John Quick was often out in front in expeditions of this kind. He relished the work. His usual jollity left him in such circumstance. It was superseded by characteristics so fell that the authenticity of his comic persona could be questioned.

Devereux caught glimpses of Quick's massive back moving steadily through the dappled night before him.

Just behind Jake there walked another rifleman engaged in counting to himself. 152, 153, 154 ...

Devereux could hear the man muttering softly in the darkness. He tried to concentrate on watching Quick for movements which might betray the presence of the short, stubby branches which could put out an eye. The risk of such an accident at night haunted him.

285, 286, 287 ...

Quick must have been listening as well. He began to slow.

298, 299, 300. "We're here, Lieutenant," his counting man reported.

Devereux disposed his small force to create an ambush. He placed eight men in a row facing the farm road. Three more were positioned in a line at a right angle to the end of the line of eight. Together these two groups formed a kind of letter 'l' with its bend on the road at the point closest to the unseen Blackwater turnpike bridge. The other four he spread across the back side of his 'L'. He then sat down just inside the bend of the 'L' to wait. He could hear the men settling in.

Johnny Quick was in the 'cross bar' of the 'L' to his right. The big man circled in the leaves, like a deer lining his nest.

The night relapsed into an uneasy quiet.

◆   ◆   ◆

They knew the tower must be just ahead.

Fowle had been confident that it would be reached before they had gone this far. He judged that it must be in the pasture to the right of the road.

Where is the damned thing?

The road was only a few feet to their right.

He went to look across at the cows again. He stood on the edge of the thicket, trying to collect his thinking. He could feel panic rising somewhere inside. Thoughts of the other two parts of the company intruded on his concentration. The men were watching him.

He went over the geometry of his march through the darkness, recalculating the approximations of distance and directions which had led him to this spot.

The moon emerged from behind a cloud.

The shadow of the forest fell on the meadow.

To his left front was the outline of a large, skeletal structure lying on the grass, among the quiet, staring animals.

Fowle pointed to the shadow.

Corporal Daniels led the party toward the tower's base.

◆   ◆   ◆

At first Jake thought the sounds behind him came from one of his men in the line covering the back of the ambush. His initial reaction was annoyance. He forced himself to have the patience necessary to remain motionless until the fool quit moving. Irritation was building in him toward action when he heard a stick break back there at a distance which had to be outside his position. He turned his head and found himself watching a Union Army soldier cross the last twenty yards between the river and the road. There was no time to say anything.

The figure in blue-black kept coming. It walked between two men and stopped six feet from him. The soldier spread his feet, fumbled with his fly and began to urinate.

No one moved.

Jake believed his heart was beating so loudly that surely the man must hear.

The soldier's head swiveled back and forth, looking around while he finished his business.

Jake knew that people hardly ever see anything unexpected that does not move against a background. There was hope. *Come on, folks. Nobody move!* he said to himself. *We haven't heard from the captain yet.*

The enemy soldier spat, buttoned himself and stepped out on the dirt of the road, turning to the right and passing in front of Johnny Quick.

That means there are a couple more behind us, Jake thought. *This must have been a corporal or sergeant, checking.*

◆　　　◆　　　◆

Charles Devereux descended from his second floor bedroom as soon as he was reasonably certain that the dinner guests had gone. He had spent the evening in dressing gown and slippers, smoking a clay pipe that he particularly favored, and working his way methodically through a stack of American and European newspapers. Just to be on the safe side, he came down the central stairs wearing an expression of long suffering and stoic resignation to pain. It would never have occurred to him that he might have descended by the back stairway into the kitchen.

He found his family, and Father Kruger gathered in the parlor talking about the musical entertainment which had followed dinner. The general opinion was that the high point of the program had been the light operatic airs rendered by Hope with Clotilde in accompaniment on the pianoforte. The coloratura elaboration of Hope's voice was accentuated by long training, and tended to dominate. Even the most unmusical of guests went away pleased with the picture she made standing by the piano while her mother-in-law played.

"I presume there was some good reason for this whole affair," Kruger asked. "You are asking a lot of your friends. We are all going to be severely criticized for this."

Hope spoke. "On the other hand, you all will now be more popular with the Union population. I suppose that was the point, wasn't it?"

Claude thought she looked splendid. He could hardly remember an occasion when she had been so pretty. Her beautiful skin showed to perfection above the bodice of the blue gown. He smiled at her and she smiled back.

The ladies departed, his mother to the kitchen to supervise the restoration of order to her china, linen and silver, Victoria to her home in the company of her husband, and Hope to the solitude of her bed.

Kruger peered at Claude over the rim of his glass. The black cassock and clerical collar accentuated the ruddiness of his complexion. Straight white hair and round, plain spectacles finished his face. "I am pleased to see that you two are going to stop acting like fools," he said, and dismissed with a wave of the hand the possibility that Claude would deny the evidence of everyone's eyes. "As for the rest, don't tell me." he asked. "It's better if I do not know. If you need help, ask for it, but tell me no more than you can avoid."

"Very well Father, I know where your heart is. Did you like Franklin Bowie?"

"Of course."

"He's gone. We lost him crossing the river."

The priest crossed himself, knelt and asked them to join him in prayer.

◆   ◆   ◆

The platform of the tower was only about thirty feet above the forest floor. It was enclosed by what looked like a rough plank wall. This barrier to inadvertent falls could not have been more than waist high.

"Good evening, gentlemen," Fowle enunciated in a clear voice. He paused, expecting a reaction to this announcement of his presence.

Feet scrabbled on the boards above. A face peered over the edge for an instant. Whispering broke out.

"Who are you?" an unknown voice enquired.

"Never you mind about that," Fowle said. We are here and you are up there, and you'd best come down, now!"

The voices mumbled some more.

"Help! Help!" the same voice cried out. "The Johnnies are here! Tower number 4! Tower number 4!"

Captain Fowle grimaced in the dark. "Daniels," he said. "Put a round through the floor."

"Anyplace in particular, sir?"

Bill shook his head. "Just stop that nonsense up there! We are now in a hurry."
Corporal Daniels' Enfield roared in the night.

A scream emanated from the top of the tower, followed by lamentation and cries of fear and anger.

"Sounds like you got lucky, Daniels," remarked Fowle.

A grunt, accompanied by the rattle of a ram rod was the only sign that the corporal had heard.

"We're coming, don't shoot anymore," the voice declared from on high.

A small square of greater luminescence opened in the floor of the platform. Feet came through the trap door onto the rungs below. The feet resolved themselves into pairs. One, two, three, followed by someone in difficulty managing the ladder.

The first three scrambled down to be met by waiting, searching, hands.

The last man fell the final ten feet, striking the ground with an ugly sound. He lay there in a sodden, moaning lump.

Fowle reached the bottom of the ladder. He had the three uninjured prisoners brought out of the shadows into the moonlight.

Cries of alarm now resounded from signal towers along the river front. The urgent voices receded in distance and shrunk in volume even as the numerical designation of each tower rose or fell to left and right.

The bag held a second lieutenant and two enlisted men. "How's the other one," Fowle asked?

One of his men came out from under the tower to answer. He saw it was Private George Latham.

"He's a 'goner' Captain," Latham murmured. The slug hit him square in the chest. He's blowin' bloody foam out of his lungs." Latham's speech had thickened in the excitement of the moment into the Scots burr of his youth.

Fowle felt that things were closing in on him. *We have to move away from this spot. They will come straight to this tower.* Rounding on the captives he looked closely at the officer. *Small man, young, ratty mustache.* He almost missed the badge in the bad light. It was on the front of the dark frock coat. He grabbed the officer by the loose material in the breast of the coat and dragged him around the corner of the tower into full moonlight. It was crossed signal flags with a torch between. *How nicely symbolic.* "You'll do, Lieutenant, you and one of your helpers. Is either of them wearing chevrons?" he asked his men.

"No," answered Daniels.

"Lieutenant, pick one of your men to leave with him," Fowle said pointing to the writhing outline at the foot of the ladder.

The Northern officer spoke. "Williams! You stay …"

Fowle heard boots on the road, looked up to see a handful of dark figures closing on the tower from the left.

Oh Christ! A picket reserve.

He clutched the Yankee lieutenant harder, shoving him against one leg of the tower while pulling his revolver from the leather holster with the other hand. "At my command!" he yelled. "Fire!"

Rifles cracked in unison.

Men caught moving in moonlight by the volley pitched noisily onto the road. Two kept coming, moving steadily forward.

Fowle cocked the big Colt, pointed at the center of the black figure approaching and tried to ignore the bayonet on the end of the rifle as he squeezed. The pistol banged and jumped.

His assailant bent at the knees, going down like a paper doll folding. The prisoner wrenched away, pulling free of his grip.

"You can't run that fast, Yank.."

The Federal officer turned to look at the muzzle and stopped.

Fowle heard the noise of reloading everywhere in the dark. "Daniels! How are we doing?" he asked.

The tall, skinny corporal appeared beside him. "We killed three, counting yours. Four or five more pulled back into the woods over there," he pointed at the trees farther along the road. "We also shot a cow. Latham's hit in the hand. Let's go now before they come back." There was real urgency in the man's voice.

The party moved away from the road, going back through the woods, dragging their human booty behind them.

◆   ◆   ◆

The Enfield's report rolled over Jake Devereux's hidden position, trumpeting the start of a new stage of the evening's business.

Plaintive cries from 'Tower number four' reached Devereux just before the firing of the rifle. The tidings of trouble now passed from tower to tower along the river. Tower number three seemed to be just to his right.

Jake sensed everyone's renewed alertness. He had a tendency to play with his beard at moments like this. He was doing it now, running his fingers through it from roots to ends in a compulsive, uncontrollable motion. He listened for more sounds from behind his post. *If they are well trained, they ought to stay at their picket position no matter what.* He practiced in his mind the plan for the movement to safety from this spot. *It ought to be possible, if no one..* Thought ended as a stirring in the earth beneath him touched his knees. He knelt behind a large tree that seemed to be a sycamore from the piebald discolorations of its bark. The ground began to stir evilly. He put out his hand to feel the tree. The loose bark trembled in his grasp. The pattern of the vibration was unmistakable. "Cavalry!" he yelled. He looked around the tree and saw them. The pounding mass of horses and riders coalesced under the moon, coming on in a glowing halo of dust and light. He leapt to his feet, drew his sidearm, watching the column of horse approach at a gallop. *This may not be a charge, but it will do. It will surely do.* "A volley!" he yelled. At my command!" Forty yards. Thirty yards. Twenty yards. "Fire!"

The fifteen rifled muskets shook the night almost as one.

The first wave of onrushing death shattered in a devastation of stricken animals and soldiers. The horses screamed pitifully, unable to comprehend the source of their agony.

"Fire at will!" Devereux commanded.

The musketry of his little force ceased for a moment after the first volley. Then it started again, at first scattered, but gathering force as the "Gypsy" riflemen found targets among the unwounded as well as those gathering on the edges of the field of their vision.

The thrashing and moaning in the road subsided somewhat. Jake became aware of the buzzing of leaden bees around his ears. Bullets were crossing his position from the picket post down by the Blackwater. Plunging fire also seemed to be coming from the probable location of 'Tower number Three'.

"Call your shots, men! Call your shots!" he told them. "Enough fire to keep them back, but not so much as to run out of ammunition! Call your shots!"

The cavalry returned. Some of them dismounted. These approached through the woods.

Jake shifted rifles to reinforce the three men in the cross bar' of the 'L'. The pattern looked more like a 'V' now.

Firing built steadily along the line. The "H" company riflemen produced a mass of fire sufficient to inhibit the small number of dismounted cavalry troopers in front of them.

Devereux watched the two riflemen closest to him. They were no longer using their ram rods. One had his tucked under an arm. The other had planted it in the earth near his boot. They were loading by pouring the powder charge in a car-tridge down the barrel, dropping the bullet in on top and banging the butt on the ground.

Jake knew the defects inherent in this method, but was not in a mood to argue. He roamed the rear of his miniature line of battle pistol and sword in hand watching for the enemy's next move.

The fusillade from the dismounted cavalrymen built in intensity. The insect sound of carbine bullets swept the night.

Two of his men went down, one of them dead, a man named Beecham. The other might live. The crying of one particular horse finally forced him to come to the edge of the trees to shoot the poor beast in the head. The blow of a bullet's strike clubbed him in the back as he turned from the road. His first thought was that it was only right. The image of the dying black horse hung before him. He staggered and leaned on his sword.

Private Donnelly pulled him behind a tree. "Get in here, ye bloody fool!" yelled Johnny Quick. "Do ye think we want to figure our own way out o'this?"

Donnelly felt his back. "You're all right Jake," he said. "It just cut you across the shoulders."

Devereux heard hooves. "Here they come again," he shouted. "By volley, At my command!"

The cavalry charged twice more using the fire of their dismounted comrades as cover. He lost another man dead, sabered in the head at the crest of the second attack.

Two pistol shots echoed to the rear, followed by three more.

The signal.

He decided that he would not try to drag the two bodies off.

They're too damned close!

He pulled the men around into two lines and started the process of withdraw-ing by alternating bounds. "Keep up the fire! Don't stop shooting!"

They fell steadily back through the woods.

The horsemen did not press them closely, following instead at a reasonably respectful distance while keeping up a vigorous fire. Bullets buzzed through the leaves breaking branches and flattening themselves in the sapwood of trees.

They had gone back at least half way to the bridgehead. He was becoming hopeful when Private Donnelly moved to his side.

"There's a battalion of infantry in the road, sir," the redheaded Irishman said.

He walked to the left and looked from behind a tree.

The enemy troops were in a column of fours a hundred yards behind the cavalry skirmishers.

What the hell are they waiting for? he thought. As he watched, the column split, dividing itself in a fashion that resembled the opening of a flower. The battalion was in the process of moving into line of battle. "Second squad, fall back!" he ordered.

◆   ◆   ◆

Fowle waited for them at the perimeter's outer edge. He and Kennedy occupied adjacent tree trunks.

Devereux reported as his men came through the line into the perimeter.

Kennedy's pickets opened fire as soon as they were unmasked by the withdrawal.

"Take your people and mine back," Fowle shouted over the rolling crash of rifle fire. "Tell Simpson we'll be right behind you."

Over his shoulder Jake could see a wall of muzzle flash building up. Bullets filled the air with leaf clipped rushing. He saluted and headed for the river.

◆   ◆   ◆

Five minute later, Major Simpson watched and listened in helpless frustration as half of "H" Company fought its lonely battle for existence on the far side of the Blackwater. He had two choices in this crisis. He could cross the river to reinforce Fowle or wait to cover the retirement with fire. He chose the latter. *This is a patrol, damn it!* he thought. *They are not there to fight it out with the Yanks. Where the hell are you, Bill?* By Simpson's calculation there had been three infantry assaults on the perimeter across the stream. A trickle of wounded and a couple of stragglers had come back. He reckoned Fowle must still have something like twenty men over there. There was a great deal of rifle fire in the attacks that had taken place. *Young Devereux must be right. It would be about a battalion.* Captain William Lynch of "C" Company and Jake Devereux stood with him, fretting over the incipient disaster. Simpson heard motion to his left.

The 12 pounder Napoleon field gun behind him spun on its wheels as the crew pivoted the piece to engage a target.

Lynch pointed.

A company of Union infantry was in the water to the left of the Confederate position, some headed for "C" Company, some pushing toward the rear of Fowle's bridgehead.

That's why the fire has lightened. They are planning on over running him with a bayonet charge. They don't want to shoot their own men.

The Napoleon jumped in recoil. The bellow of the gun was followed by the shattering noise of the impact of scores of canister balls in the water and vegetation.

"C" Company's riflemen joined the fight. Smoke added to the bedlam of the scene.

Simpson could see the gun crew hard at work loading.

Four Union infantrymen emerged from the smoke, coming out of the water behind an officer armed with a rifle and bayonet. They grappled with two "C" Company men, knocked them down and headed for the cannon.

They were half way there when the crew finished loading and swiveled the piece.

The five looked down the barrel.

"Don't be a fool!" Lynch yelled.

The blue officer dropped his rifle and slowly raised his hands.

Lynch beckoned them forward.

The fight on the left flank continued. The far bank of the river was strangely silent.

Simpson strode to the infantry line on the river bank. "Captain Fowle!" he shouted. "Come now! They are trying to flank you and will be back with the bayonet soon!"

The "Gypsies" came tumbling out of the wood with blue infantry just behind them.

Simpson had his pistol out shooting at dark forms on the river bank.

"C" Company riflemen were out of their holes everywhere to get the height necessary to shoot over their fleeing comrades.

The two artillery pieces spoke again and again against the attempted envelopment on the left.

Fowle waded up out of the water, hatless, pistol in hand. He drew himself up before Simpson. "I am sorry to report, sir," he began, "that I have not brought them all back."

◆   ◆   ◆

Claude walked the length of the house, down the central hallway. He stopped for a moment to rub the pain in his knee and listened to know if anyone else was still about.

The priest had gone.

Charles Devereux had just left the parlor, climbing the front staircase on the way to his bedroom.

Claude passed through the door into the service wing.

The library door stood open to his right.

The kitchen was abandoned. It had the newly scrubbed look that followed thorough cleaning. He went out the side door onto the brick walk under the second floor gallery. He unbuttoned his waistcoat while going up the stairs. At the top, he paused. A line of light seeped under Hope's bedroom door. The curtains glowed. He knew the door was not locked. *She never locks the door. Someone will kill her eventually. Someone will come in the night. Maybe me.*

She sat reading in her bed, the big walnut bed with finials on the posts that looked like wooden nutmegs.

The night air entered the open door behind him.

Hope shivered and started in the sudden chill. Holding him with her steady, serious, almost solemn face she closed the leather covered volume, putting it on the marble topped night table beside the bed. She turned down the flame of the gas table lamp.

Devereux shed clothes across the room, slipping into her bed with a sigh. "It's been much too long."

"I have finally learned something of value about myself," she whispered into the angle of his neck.

"Yes?"

"Life without you isn't much."

He shook with laughter as he rolled deeper into her embrace.

9

The Hounds

12:15 P.M., Monday, 30 March

It was fairly unusual for a naval officer to call on Lafayette Baker. The Washington Navy Yard was not thought to be a haven for Rebel sympathizers and Gideon Welles, the Secretary of the Navy, would not have tolerated snooping by an Army Bureau in his kingdom on the Anacostia River. Navy men who hoped for promotion stayed away from Army offices. Because of this, Commander Richard Braithwaite's appearance at the Pennsylvania Avenue offices of the National Detective Bureau created a minor stir inconsistent with the somnolence, which normally prevailed among the guards, doormen and clerks of the ground floor.

Troopers of the 1st District of Columbia Cavalry guarded the front entrance of the two story building. Nothing had ever occurred to interrupt the reveries of the guard mounted by their regiment on this post. The soldiers were reasonably content with this situation and most of them whiled away the time in bullying male passers-by and flirting with the girls.

Baker, the regiment's colonel, mainly occupied himself with his duties as counterintelligence chief for the U.S. War Department in the capital region. He was seldom seen by the troops. They understood that the colonel's main function was that of head of the Detective Bureau and that their main function was that of armed force to be applied as needed in support of the Bureau's operations. The men were reasonably sensitive to the ridicule sometimes heaped on them by combat veterans. "Cobblestone Soldiers!" was the gentlest of the abuse to which they were subjected.

The two cavalrymen on duty watched with interest as the tall figure approached along the sidewalk. One of the yellow legged soldiers leaned against the building. The other, the Corporal of the Guard, stood with arms folded in the middle of the brick sidewalk. The stream of pedestrians divided and flowed around him.

Braithwaite wandered about the sidewalk from side to side. There was some uncertainty in his gait.

The corporal in charge remarked to the sentinel that this man didn't seem to know where he wanted to go.

A dozen feet from the entrance, the man drew himself to his full, impressive height and walked straight to the door, and the guard. They exchanged a few words, in the course of which the corporal found himself attempting to stand as straight as he could manage. After holding the door, he conducted Braithwaite to the cubbyhole in which a lieutenant acting as Officer of the Day amused himself through the long boredom of a duty day.

Half an hour later Major Johnston Mitchell sat in a corner of Baker's big office observing the colloquy between Braithwaite and his chief. It was not going well, and Mitchell expected an explosion on the part of Baker at any moment. The security chief was not a man to suffer fools gladly. He had had a difficult morning on Capitol Hill with two senators from the Committee on the Conduct of the War. Secretary Stanton had sent him to soothe them with assurances of the stringent security measures in effect in Washington and the near impossibility of successful Confederate intrusions in this Union "Holy of Holies." Baker had insisted that Mitchell accompany him. The two Republican legislators had not believed them. Senator Ben Wade had ridiculed Baker's certainty on the subject.

Now, Colonel Baker gripped the table before him with both hands as he spoke with an even civility which masked the frustrated turmoil beneath. "Let me sum up what you have told us, Commander. You met this man Devereux, in Baltimore. You traveled to Washington with him, and dined in his father's house. This is the basis for your statement that you think that his actions and his general attitude toward life are consistent with those of a Rebel spy?"

Mitchell believed that Baker's athletic intensity and dynamism often frightened people into speechlessness. The austerity of the furnishings in this cavernous room added to the effect. Mitchell wished that Baker would stop interviewing visitors personally. He was sure that the staff did a better, less emotional job of it. He was correct in thinking that many people left such discussions resolved never willingly to speak to Baker again. Mitchell was an unlikely person in this setting. Balding, somewhat paunchy and more than a little astigmatic, he made a strange figure in the uniform of a major of cavalry. There was little in his experience as a newspaper publisher in Kentucky to prepare him for his present role as one of the leaders of a secret police organization. Like everyone else in the Bureau, he was learning by doing. The country had never before possessed such an organ of government. He knew he should interrupt Baker before the explosion went off and so Mitchell spoke. "Please tell us again, Commander, where you first saw Mister Devereux." He hoped to gently remove the questioning from Baker's hands before an embarrassing scene took place.

Braithwaite described the drama in the station buffet again.

Mitchell found Richard Braithwaite fascinating.

The naval officer sat rigidly upright in the chair.

Mitchell thought that the double breasted blue coat and bullion epaulets looked like something from a theatrical production. The room was not warm, but a thin sheen of perspiration showed on Braithwaite's temples. *This man is not telling us everything he knows or feels about Devereux,* Mitchell thought. *There is no reason that he should be so deeply disturbed about these events if they were exactly as he recounted them.*

Baker settled back in his armchair.

He has decided to let me do the talking, Mitchell thought with relief.

Braithwaite finally ran down to a muttered complaint about the lateness of the hour and business yet to be done at the Navy Yard. He began to look as though he realized how foolish he appeared.

"You say he was traveling alone?" Mitchell asked.

"Yes! Yes! There was only a colored valet with him."

"Did you see the valet?"

Braithwaite reflected for a moment. "Only once, on the 'quai' in Baltimore, when we boarded the train, and that from a distance in not very good light. Why?"

"How did Devereux conduct himself with regard to his Negro companion?"

Braithwaite seemed puzzled. "I'm not exactly clear on what you mean." He halted, confused by Mitchell's Southern accent.

"Was the relationship that of master and servant or did they in some sense appear to you to be colleagues or even friends?"

Braithwaite glanced back and forth between them, evidently uncertain of his audience. "I don't know. I assume that he treated the black the way they all do, like a stupid but useful beast."

God damn it! How dare you assume anything about me! Mitchell thought. After a small moment of silence, he asked for a repetition of the name of the French steamship on which Devereux had crossed the Atlantic.

Braithwaite produced a note on a small piece of paper and spelled the name.

"Why did you make that note, Commander?" Baker demanded.

The naval officer was flustered. "He just did not seem sincere to me. I did not appreciate the way he acted around the women." Braithwaite's head jerked back a fraction of an inch.

The two army officers contemplated him.

It matters not, thought Mitchell. *A jealous heart often is the key that opens the door to our understanding of situations like this one.*

Baker roused himself. "You did say that Brigadier General Slough and Colonel Haupt were guests in the Devereux household on the evening when you were also a guest?"

Braithwaite nodded. He appeared uncomfortable with the payment he was in the process of providing to the Devereux for their hospitality.

Baker continued. "And at this dinner party among our secessionist and disloyal friends in Alexandria, do you remember seeing the same Negro?"

Braithwaite shook his head. "I don't think so, but to be honest I don't really look at them very much."

◆   ◆   ◆

The Regular Army colonel of infantry inspected the four prisoners before him. *Typical hard case types*, he thought. *Two Micks, an Italian and God knows what the other one might be.* "What's your name? That's right, you!" he asked the unidentifiable one.

"Moses Samuels, Colonel."

"And what do you do in real life? You know, when you are not pretending to be a soldier."

The colonel watched with approving interest as the man looked to one of the two Irish looking prisoners for permission to speak.

"Well, can he talk to me, sergeant?" the colonel inquired.

"Yes, sir. He can."

"I am a watchmaker," Samuels declared.

"And you?" the colonel was staring at the sergeant. "What's your name and regiment and has the surgeon examined that shoulder? Your head doesn't look so good either."

"Sergeant Frederick Kennedy. None of us will tell you more. I have no civilian occupation. You seized it for taxes."

The colonel liked what he saw.

"You fellows put up a smart little fight last night. You cost me men I've been training for years. This regiment's been in Texas and New Mexico fighting Apaches, Yaquis and Mexican bandits so long we thought we would never get a shot at you. Now we're here, the big show." He laughed aloud. "You know you are going to lose the war in the end, don't you?"

They said nothing.

The colonel shrugged. "Well, you'll do what you think you must. I can see that from looking at you. Anyone want to join my outfit? I don't see any sense in first rate material like you boys rotting in prison while there is a job of soldiering to be done. I'll take you on, no questions asked. No one will ever know."

John Quick stood. "And what would the colonel's leave policy be?"

◆   ◆   ◆

"Merely a jealous man?" Baker always expected a reasonably quick, not too complicated answer.

"Yes." Mitchell answered. "Nevertheless, there are intriguing aspects to this matter. For example, who really is this man Devereux?"

Baker had learned to listen to his odd looking subordinate. He seemed attentive, but Mitchell knew his attention would soon wander to the political imperatives that surrounded his precarious position in a city filled with ambitious, striving men. Looking at him, Mitchell knew the man would hear him out this time. "Do you remember the information we had from Richmond, through Sharpe last week?" he asked.

Baker seemed blank for a second. Concentration brought the information back to him. "Ah, yes, one of Sharpe's people came to talk to you, something about Green and an agent coming to contact him. You know I don't pay much attention to anything Colonel George Sharpe says. One day I will find a way to bring that collection of cast off infantrymen under proper control from this office."

"Hannibal," Major Mitchell reminded.

Lafayette Baker was, in fact, a highly intelligent man. The press of his Byzantine intrigues and crushing work load sometimes made him forgetful, but this never prevented the eventual recall of significant facts.

"Hannibal had a black man with him," Baker said in a matter of fact voice.

Mitchell's hands made a tent in front of his pudgy face. They almost concealed the bobbing of his head. "It may be," he said. "It just might be. Could we be that lucky?"

"Take charge of this yourself," Baker instructed. "Do we know anything of the family?"

"I brought the file with me when you sent down a note. They are notorious secessionists. So far as we can learn they have done nothing overt as yet. Their bank is doing a large business in Europe, but it does not appear to be connected with the enemy. They have strange, but significant, ties to the French embassy. Several members of the family are French citizens."

"We do not recognize dual nationality!" Baker snapped.

"That may be, but at a time when the issue of French recognition of the Richmond government hangs in the balance, it would be wise to exercise caution in this matter. I don't think you want Secretary Seward to receive a communication from the French ambassador in this affair?"

Baker shook his head.

"There are more varieties of spies in this world than the simple Rebel type we are accustomed to," Mitchell remarked thoughtfully. "I believe we should be very cautious in investigating this. It would not do to find spies where we do not wish to find them."

Baker agreed with that. "Why were Slough and Haupt at this dinner?" he asked.

Mitchell held his hands apart in a characteristically expressive fashion. "It was a major social event. I'm sure they flattered themselves that at last they were making inroads into old Alexandria society. They don't understand that under these circumstances the only people who will associate with them in that town are either newly arrived from the North or such that their company should not be sought. Still, some of these people seem to have been of substance.."

The colonel stared at him, enraged by the words. "At times I wonder ..."

Mitchell flushed. He had become impatient of late with the empty menace with which Baker loaded his dealings with subordinates. "If you can find anyone who understands the Rebels better than I," he said, "or whom you trust more let me know. I have a newspaper waiting for me."

Baker sobered at the thought of the reality of the difference in their relative social and economic positions in civilian life. The war would end someday. Mitchell had significant position in the Kentucky leadership of the Democratic Party. "What will you do?" he asked.

"The usual things."

"Keep me informed. Press the enquiry. I must leave you now. Secretary Stanton has asked me to accompany him to dinner."

2:35 P.M., Wednesday, 1 April

Isaac Smoot was not an introspective man. His upbringing and busy life had not contained the leisure needed to develop a pronounced sense of self. He tended to accept the cards that fate and his superiors dealt him without examining in detail the judgments that lay behind the deal. Smoot placed a great reliance on his own judgement of his leaders. What he had seen thus far of Claude Devereux was acceptable. He would act on that impression until proven wrong. Seeking to carry out Claude's orders, he went to find Lawyer Thomas Green.

He arrived at the parkland across 17th Street from Thomas Greene's house at about 10 in the morning. The park contained the expected benches. He had dressed himself in old work clothes which Bill White discovered in various corners of the house on Fairfax Street. Smoot's experience of police work made him think that lawmen took little notice of loitering laborers so long as the loiterers did not seem to be intent on some unlawful act.

He sat facing the river and the City Canal which ran alongside Constitution Avenue. The Greene house was to his right. The White House gardens were behind him. It was a glorious day, filled with the song of birds and with just enough nip in the occasional small gusts of wind to make life interesting.

During the train ride across the river from Virginia, Smoot had seen small boats filled with anglers scattered across the Potomac. *Bass*, he thought. *I'll bet the river's full of them, like Goose Creek at home.* He was on the hourly train from Alexandria to the Baltimore and Ohio terminal near the Capitol. At the Long Bridge across the Potomac the Provost Guard boarded the train checking 'papers'.

Smoot's rural Virginia voice caused a more than usually careful examination of the pass he brought from the Provost Marshal's office in Alexandria. Looking at the pimply faced youth who fingered the pass and the hated Oath of Allegiance, he found himself trying to memorize the face. *That's no good,* he thought. *There are too many of them for that.*

From the depot, the Pennsylvania Avenue horse cars brought him to the White House. At the corner of 17th and 'F' a large building loomed over the intersection. Army staff poured in and out of the edifice in a continual stream. Pausing on the corner to gaze at the sight in wonderment, he summoned up his best representation of the voice and manner of a rural buffoon to ask a soldier what was 'going on'. The man told him that this building was the U.S. War Department.

He did not welcome the news. Security was certain to be better in a neighborhood which contained both the White House and Army Headquarters. He had brought with him a collection of the last week's newspapers. If pressed, he planned to describe in soulful detail his search for work in the capital.

Four hours was a long time to remain in one spot for a job like this. He took a break around noon time for lunch in a bar on 14th Street. His buttocks were aching from sitting so long on the bench in the park.

About one, Smoot decided he should move. He thought that a patch of woods down to the west on the other side of the City Canal was a likely location.

The watch on Greene's house had not been hard to identify. A man stood at the corner of the two main streets in front of the house. At fairly regular intervals he walked up the block on 17th to the next connecting street and stared at something or someone out of sight in that direction. The watcher was dressed in the clothing favored by small tradesmen, clerks and the like. There would undoubtedly be at least one more watcher on the far side of the building. There was something troubling about the simplicity of the arrangements. After some thought, he focused on the problem. The system of watchers was in itself altogether too obvious.

He decided to move. His backside had endured enough for one day. He reckoned that a stroll down the City Canal and a brief sojourn in the bushes on the other side would give him a chance to see who or what so fascinated the one visible watcher. Perhaps he and Devereux could then figure out what to do next.

He gathered himself up, rising from the bench. From his coat pocket he extracted an eight-inch twist of hand rolled Burleigh Bright. With the Barlow clasp knife that always accompanied him, he cut himself a plug. Having settled the chaw, he resolved to leave.

As he started to move, he saw the front door of the Greene house open. The white Federal house had an imposing overhanging portico. For a second, he could not see whomever it might be that was emerging. By the time this person reached the street he had a clear view of the man. He was middle aged, white haired, well dressed. Followed by a Negro servant, the man strode purposefully north on 17th Street. *If this isn't Lawyer Greene, I'm Abe Lincoln.* By this time, he was on his feet fussing with the pile of newspapers to give himself a greater chance to watch Greene go.

The watcher on the corner was elaborately unconscious of Greene as he passed.

Something started to move back in the park, behind the bench on which Smoot had been sitting. He sat back down and pulled off a boot to fish for a stone. Footfalls approached through the dead leaves. *He should pick up his feet.*

The woman walked out of the wooded park past Smoot's bench. She was intent on Greene's back and never glanced at the nondescript, hunched figure.

A Girl! That's why I didn't notice. Fool!

She passed the fixed surveillance post on the street, following Greene up 17th, nodding to the watcher as she went.

Smoot put his boot back on, gathered up his bits of rubbish, turned and walked slowly back through the park, looking for the others.

◆   ◆   ◆

"How many more were there?"

"Two. There was a Negro across the park on the far side, and a white man positioned about half way between the black's spot under a tree and the place I think the girl must have been. I saw the white man, damn it! I looked right at him a couple of times. I think I may have said something to him when I went to lunch."

Devereux could see that Smoot was ashamed to have missed the most important part of the surveillance for so long. "What do you suppose their system is?" he asked. He thought he knew the answer to his own question, but he knew that Smoot needed to talk about it.

"There are at least two men watching the building itself. These are right on top of it. The one I could see was within 15 feet of the front door! Our Yankee friends obviously don't give a damn if Greene knows about it or not."

"I would think that the idea is to discourage visitors from entering Counselor Greene's abode," Claude commented. "That would mean that the government is worried about Greene's political activity. Perhaps he has congressional acquaintances."

"If that's the case," Smoot replied, "then they may have another set of watchers back farther away, maybe in a building. If they have that, then the house will still be watched even if the ones in the street leave."

Devereux glanced at the window. It was dark. Night had filled the sky while they had talked. *I told Hope I would only be a few moments.*

He and Smoot were closeted in the tiny study cum dressing room which adjoined his bedroom on the second floor of the 'ell.' His wash stand and shaving gear shared the space with a few old pieces of furniture which his mother and his wife no longer wanted to see in the more public rooms of the house.

Just now, Devereux's mind was wandering, not to questions of style in the decorative arts, but rather to his blonde wife. Three doors away, she waited. This evening they had slipped out of the main house for a few minutes alone in her room before dinner.

Smoot had been waiting in the side garden when they came out the kitchen door.

"How did you come to know so much about these things, Isaac?"

Smoot screwed up his face and then replied. "We use the same tricks in the 43rd when scouting for attacks on buildings. I should have recognized that there would be building watchers in one group and people followers in another group further away. I reckon that the openness of the house watch threw me."

"How did Colonel Mosby learn to do this?"

"At Ashland."

Ah, the Indian policemen again.

"What now Cap'n? You're not still planning to go into that house, are you? I take you for a smarter man than that."

Devereux shook his head. "I think we need to know what the police think they are looking for at Mister Thomas Greene's residence. It makes me unhappy that I should have been sent to contact a man so clearly suspected of something."

Smoot was pleased. "I should introduce myself to one of them."

Devereux nodded. "I'll go with you.."

Smoot thought of the legs. "No, sir. This is for me to do. You know that.."

Devereux knew he was right. He also knew that Smoot had guessed the truth. "Very well. Take Bill with you," he said. "He's an excellent conversationalist."

The ranger smiled. "I know you are busy, Cap'n. I'll find the gate."

From the gallery, he watched the man's stocky form pass through the garden gate, disappearing into the night.

10

A Son of Erin

12 A.M., Friday, 3 April

Swampoodle was not an area of the capital to be frequented late at night by the uninitiated, but then, Terence Hennessey would not have been so described. The maze of narrow streets, bordellos and cheap dives just beside the capitol was the home of many of his favorite recreations. This evening had been one of many which he had happily passed there. He had arrived around nine o'clock, sauntering through the swinging doors of Kelly's Saloon and Oyster Parlor with two friends from work. They had walked a mile along Pennsylvania Avenue from the National Detective Bureau. Hennessey enjoyed his work. His neat mind was well suited to the world of archives, dossiers and reports. In Ireland, he had studied a year for the priesthood until awareness of woman drove him to America for escape from the tyranny of aunts who thought no sacrifice on his part too great a price to pay for the appearance of a 'vocation' in the family.

Isaac Smoot and Bill White had stalked this group of police "watchers" all the way from Thomas Greene's house. They had trailed along in the shadows behind them believing that this was a shift just relieved from duty. White had followed the three men closely. He had not previously been near the Greene mansion and he and Smoot thought he would not be recognized. Smoot had followed a quarter mile back, alert to the possibility that they could have been spotted in the crowded neighborhood around the White House.

In the midst of their stroll down Pennsylvania Avenue, the three detectives unexpectedly left the street to spend half an hour in Lafayette Baker's Headquarters. Four men eventually came out, tramping off down the broad sidewalk toward the Capitol. The little group filled the street with laughter. Their coarse joking caused several women to cross the street to avoid them.

Bill had watched them come out onto the street and then moved along the avenue in front of them as Smoot had instructed him. Smoot watched them go and smiled. *That nigger is smarter than most white men,* he thought. Farther down the street, while inspecting the four, he commenced to worry. *Damn! These all look alike! I'm sure the one with the checked coat was in the first group. Which is the new one?*

The policemen turned left off Pennsylvania into the tumbledown buildings and shanties of the Irish slum. They drifted in and out of several pothouses. Their laughter and unsteadiness grew with their progress. Kelly's fine establishment was undoubtedly a favorite of theirs. Its appearance was hailed with yet another chorus swelling into the dusk.

**"I hear orders from the captain.
Get you ready quick and soon,
for the pikes must be together
at the rising of the moon.."**

They are afraid of nothing, Smoot told himself. *I know this manner of thinking. Policemen! Can I go back to that after the war? It is time that these policemen learn to fear.*

He left White in an alley two hundred feet from the doors of the bar. Alone, he entered the bar room, and stepped to one side, just inside the door, looking around, hoping for a corner seat. There were none. In the dim light, he walked the length of the bar. It was hard to see and hear in the noisy, smoke filled gloom. Almost before he noticed them, he was behind the four friends. They stood together leaning unsteadily against the oak for rail for support.

He stood behind them absorbing their presence. They smelled badly of unwashed humanity. Over this were layers of tobacco and alcohol. Two bottles of rye stood on the bar half full. *At the rate they are drinking, it should be coming out through their hides,* he thought. He reached between two of them to wave a hand at the barman. "A glass of beer." he asked.

The man in the checked coat swiveled to stare at this unwanted intrusion into his territory.

Smoot grinned at him. "Sorry, friend!" he chirped. "I reckon I'll be out of your way shortly." He took the offered glass of lager and extracted fifteen cents which he handed over in payment.

The checked coat still glared.

Smoot decided to find out how really mean they might be. Reaching for a second time through the space between the same two men, he picked up a pickled pig's foot from the tray of 'free lunch'.

The Checked Coat gripped his arm as it tried to emerge from the tightly packed array of men along the bar. "Put that back, ye hayseed! Find your own plate of lunch! We don't want you standin' here stinkin' up the place with your smell o' cow shit!"

The other three turned to consider him. He did his best to look inoffensive and unable to protect himself. "I'll just take this and go away. I didn't mean to bother you all. Sorry neighbors." Bowing slightly in submission, Smoot turned away.

Checked Coat yanked him back by the arm. "Drop it! We didn't say you could steal our trotters, did we boys? Maybe we should take you in. You sound like a rebel traitor to me! Doesn't he boys?"

Smoot whined for mercy, pleading that he was a hungry but loyal country man from Maryland.

Checked Coat shook him and shook him until he dropped the foot.

A second kicked it through the sawdust on the floor into a corner. "Get out, ye scum!" the Checked Coat roared. "We want none of your kind here!"

Sergeant Isaac Smoot slunk from the room, cringing from the abuse. He had made his choice, or rather Checked Coat had made it for him.

◆   ◆   ◆

Street lighting in Swampoodle amounted to very little.

Checked Coat materialized and disappeared irregularly, coming dimly into view as he passed half-shuttered windows and the occasional gas street lamp. He was weaving badly, stumbling against buildings, cursing as he waded through the deeper puddles.

Smoot followed him closer than he would have liked. The poor visibility made him fear he might miss a turn in the inebriated and somewhat unpredictable path the man followed.

The badly lit streets were still infested with the outpourings of establishments of the night. Whores, black and white, jostled potential customers in the larger intersections, hoping for a little late night trade to round out the evening's take.

Bill White was somewhere in front of their intended victim. The light was becoming worse and worse. *White should make his move soon,* Smoot thought, *or they would walk right out the other side of this manure pile!* He tripped in a pothole full of liquids and semi-solids, sinking up to the knee. He pulled his leg out, conscious of the noise that inevitably must have accompanied his near fall. He was suddenly aware that the walking sounds in front had ceased. He waited in a half crouch, straining to hear.

"I thought you had learned a lesson and that was to stay out of my way," hissed a voice from a point a foot or so above the level of his head.

Christ! He thought. The man had walked up on him while he waded in the shit! He watched as The Checked Coat drew back a foot.

Smoot shifted his weight to avoid the kick if he could and to try to grab the boot as it went by.

The Checked Coat carefully put down his foot, straightening his back as he did so.

Over the man's shoulder, Smoot beheld Bill White's features. "Stand real quiet, Mister!" Bill declared. "This blade's longer than you are thick."

"Drag your Yankee ass down this alley!" Smoot ordered in a whisper, grabbing an elbow. "My friend is impatient and might want to examine your innards!" They found a cross alley fifty yards deeper in the squalor of back streets. Smoot wanted to be sure that the Checked Coat would not recognize them. He thought the Irishman could only faintly distinguish their features in the gloom. *Perfect.* "Now, Paddy!" he said in a soft voice. "What would be your name?" He was darkly amused at his own attempt at Irish intonation.

Checked Coat stood sullenly dumb.

Smoot hit him as hard as he could, just over the right kidney.

The man commenced to sag at the knees.

Smoot seized him by the elbows to keep him from the ground. "Speak. Paddy! My fists are harder than your guts!"

"Hennessey. Terence Hennessey."

He glanced at White over the Irishman's head and grinned his satisfaction. "Right, good! You'll do! Now tell us why you all are so curious about Squire Greene!" In the thought that Hennesey had accepted his position, Smoot loosened his grip just a little.

The prisoner took the opportunity to knee him violently in the groin. At the same moment, he struck White in the nose with the back of his head. With a mighty effort, the Irishman wrenched himself free of the grip of his two stunned captors.

Smoot was nearly blinded by the pain in his testicles, but staggering to his feet, he gave chase down the dark alley. He could hear Hennessey crashing from side to side in the darkness. He was gaining ground when something large and very fast elbowed him to one side, disappearing ahead of him in the direction of the noise made by Hennessey in flight. A sound signifying the collision of two bodies reached him. There was a cry filled with pain, a cry filled with a despair of the body. By the time he reached them, White had the big Irishman down on the ground. "I'm afraid I killed him, sergeant," the Negro said. "The only way I could stop him was to stick him."

He nodded. His own pain was still so great that he had to keep his teeth clenched to prevent them from chattering. "Turn him over!".

Hennessey was alive. One hand was flat against his side. Blood that looked black ran out between the fingers in the nearly total darkness of the alley. "A doctor!" he whimpered. "Please get me help! I never hurt you. I don't want to die!"

An unidentifiable, apparently female form loomed out of the darkness, stumbling against Smoot, staring down at the Irishman's prostrate body.

"On your way," the ranger counseled.

She scurried away into the black depths of the alley.

He lit a match, and ripped Hennessey's shirt just enough to look at the wound. The long blade had gone in over the liver in a clean incision that might have left the internal organs intact.

He looked inquisitively at White who shook his head. "I imagine his intestines are cut up some," Bill said.

The wounded man looked back and forth between them, finally staring at White.

Smoot could see the humor of the moment. "You didn't expect him did you, Paddy? If you want a doctor, you best answer my questions. What do you folks want with Lawyer Greene? Why are you watching his house?"

Hennessey clutched his side, whimpering softly with the pain. "Please! Please! I'm bleedin' more and more. I don't work on the street. I'm a clerk in the main office."

"Shit!" cried Smoot. He raged at himself for not having the right man. He made an abrupt decision to leave the man in the alley, to expire or crawl away as best he might.

"That's too bad, Clerk Hennessey," White declared. "You're no longer of interest to us." He stood up to leave as thought he had read Smoot's mind.

"No! No! I keep the journal of the Greene case! What do you want?"

White knelt close to the injured man. "What exactly are you seeking to learn in watching Greene's house?"

"Greene's a secret rebel! It's well known! He was one of Rose Greenhow and Breckenridge's friends in Washington. Now he spies for the Rebel Secretary of State, the Jew, Benjamin."

"That's all?" Smoot demanded. "Nothing recent?"

He was gasping for breath now. His chest was heaving with each effort to breathe and speak. "Hannibal. There is Hannibal. An agent in Benjamin's offices told us of a Rebel spy coming to Greene, with a Negro." He stared in horror at White. "You are Hannibal!" he rasped at Smoot.

"That's right!" snarled Smoot. "You can tell that son of a bitch, Baker, that we are going to kill off all you bastards who are harassing Greene. He'll be the last!" *That should keep them going in circles for a while!* He thought.

"Anything else?" White continued as he stared down at the dying man.

"No! Please help me! I am only in the United States five years. I don't care if you are a diff'rent country where you come from! I don't care about any of that. I am only trying to live. A doctor, please!"

Smoot took one arm and Bill the other. They dragged Hennessey through the muck to the edge of the slum closest to Pennsylvania Avenue. There they left him moaning and sobbing successively for them to return and for someone to help.

Three blocks away, Smoot stopped a member of the city police patrol to report the cries of a distressed man coming from the fringes of Swampoodle. The watch hurried off in that direction.

The two men then changed course heading for the railroad station. They could still catch the last train to Alexandria, the one that carried soldiers back to their units from visits to Washington.

7:20 A.M., 4 April

Hennessey lay quiet and still on the medical examiner's table.

The coroner stood next to the body, his shirt sleeves rolled above the elbows. Blood covered his hands and forearms. The blood on his hands was fresh and wet. On his arms it had begun to dry to a color more like brown than red. One hand held a scalpel. The other gripped one side of the large incision he had casually made in the dead man's back.

Major Mitchell stood by the head of the corpse. He watched the pathologist at work.

The physician had tried to avoid soiling his own clothing, but tiny drops of scarlet dotted the dark blue of his trousers.

Mitchell had brought another officer with him from the Detective Bureau offices. Captain Wilson Ford had seemed to think he ought to observe the autopsy, but now, evidently, did not wish to see.

I hope to God he doesn't go down sick, Mitchell thought. *These god awful doctors all think that only they can endure such sights.*

The body had a sickly, pale color. The smell that emanated from the gaping wound made one think of a butcher shop.

The acting medical examiner for the District of Columbia was an army Medical Corps colonel who appeared so ancient that he might have first worn uniform in the second war against the British.

The white haired, pot-bellied old man laid out various internal organs and interesting pieces of tissue on a white enameled cart at his elbow. "He bled to death," the colonel muttered.

"Why? Why do you think that?" asked Mitchell.

"The knife cut the descending aorta. It is the largest blood vessel in the body." The elderly man shrugged expressively.

"Could anything have saved him?" asked Captain Ford.

Mitchell liked the young officer. Ford was Regular Army. He had lost an arm the previous year. The Detective Bureau would never have had his services if the disabling wound had not made a non-combat assignment a necessity. One of the things Mitchell admired about him was the deep sense of responsibility for his men which he always displayed. His question was typical.

The doctor shook his head. "No, Captain, nothing! The aorta was about half cut through." The colonel picked up what looked like gray-pink rubber hose from the cart. He bent the artery to show the slit. "He must have lived around ten minutes. The small intestine was also punctured," the colonel said. "Peritonitis would have killed him in a couple of days. He was essentially dead as soon as the blade went in. Whoever stabbed him used a very sharp knife and a great deal of force."

Major Mitchell suggested that they walk back to the office. The half mile in the open air would do them good, he said.

Early morning Spring sunshine drenched the city. They were followed at a discreet distance by an army carriage which had carried them to their unexpected appointment with the aged colonel and his ghoulish vocation.

"Tell me again," the older man requested. "Tell me the whole story, beginning last night."

In the best tradition of Regular Army deference to superiors, Captain Ford walked to the left of Mitchell. The pinned up sleeve on the right side of Ford's body made Mitchell wonder what particular set of horrors the scene in the autopsy room had recalled for him.

Ford fished in an interior pocket of his blue uniform blouse and extracted a paper covered in the scrawl he had been attempting to improve since the occasion when he and his normal writing hand parted company.

"I was Officer of the Day last night for the Bureau," he began. "As you know, this required me to spend the night in headquarters with the orderly sergeant." He raised the paper to check something. "At about one in the morning, a patrolman from the city police arrived stating that their Pennsylvania Avenue patrol had possession of the body of a man who had claimed to be one of our people. I woke one of the enlisted men on stand-by duty as courier and, in his company, went to the scene with the policeman who had brought the message. It was undeniably Hennessey. He worked in the archive, for me actually. He handled a number of active case files." Ford peered at Major Mitchell to determine if his superior really followed this. "He had been dead for half an hour or so according to the police on the scene. I questioned them. They didn't know much. I saw Hennessey last night leaving The Bureau with three others from a detective team, all Irish. I had them brought in this morning before you arrived. They had all been drinking 'till about midnight in a bar near the spot at which the police found Hennessey. He went his own way when the evening broke up." Ford glanced at his notes. "That was just after midnight.

They stopped on a street corner to let traffic pass in a cloud of horse dust. The lowing of cattle attracted Mitchell's attention to the stockaded pens of army beef animals which surrounded the uncompleted stump of the Washington monument. "What a filthy town this is," he said. "I have the impression at times that we are locked in a struggle for the soul of the city, and that our real opponents are not the Rebels. How much money do you think has been made in selling the army those animals?"

Ford did not seem interested in the thought.

Mitchell sighed. "What did Hennessey say before he died?"

"According to the police, he deliriously repeated the names "Greene" and "Hannibal" many times."

Mitchell stood on the corner, wrapped in apparent contemplation of the massed beef cattle. "How did the police find Hennessey?" he finally asked. "Does the detective team in question have to do with Thomas Greene's residence?"

Ford replied that these detectives were so employed at present. He also remembered that the police had recounted an encounter with two men on the street nearby.

"Was one of them a Negro?" Mitchell whispered.

Ford shook his head. "It was very dark. We could ask them again."

Mitchell smiled. "Do that! "While you are doing this, you ought to check with the railroad staff of the Washington and Alexandria to see if anyone remembers two men, one black, boarding a train after midnight for Alexandria."

"What does all this mean, sir?"

"It means that for once we are hunted as well as hunting."

They arrived at Pennsylvania Avenue within a block of their own building. Mitchell looked longingly at Willard's Hotel across the street. "Captain, I'll stand you to breakfast," said he, "if you will help me draw up some telegrams to New York afterwards."

10:20 A.M., Saturday, 4 April

One of Devereux's vices was his love of old, comfortable clothes.

His mother professed to find in this idiosyncrasy a pronounced resemblance to the behavior of her maternal uncle, Philippe. This gentleman, a 'General de Brigade' of the cavalry of the Emperor's army, developed in retirement the desire to labor in his own fields. This eccentricity initially aroused deep suspicion amongst his peasant tenants. Persistence overcame this. He devoted himself to working seriously at the management of his large farm for the last twenty years of his life. It was a symptom of deeper things. The old man had never accepted the Bourbon restoration and died with Bonaparte's name on his lips.

While Mitchell and Ford breakfasted in Willard's dining room, Devereux sat in the kitchen of the Duke Street villa with his two men. The wreckage and remnants of another of the fine meals regularly produced on short notice by Betsy White littered the massive oak table between the three of them. She had gone.

"Did he know my name?"

Smoot shook his big, square head. "No, sir. He never mentioned you. Not that you could take much comfort from that."

Devereux waited for him to continue. An air of exasperated expectation began to show on his face.

"Mister Claude," Bill recommenced on Smoot's behalf. "It wasn't the kind of situation in which the man had a chance to say all he knew."

Devereux looked at the table for a few seconds and then up at them. "All right," he said. "We will have to go forward thinking that they do have my name, but hoping that it is not so. One can imagine circumstances in which their spy in Richmond could know my secret name and connection to Greene but not have the ability to obtain the additional identification. We will have to hope for the best."

Smoot spoke. "We could just leave."

"Yes," Claude agreed. "That possibility is open. On the other hand, we don't know exactly how much information they have. If they knew everything, I would expect to have been arrested by now. No! We will stick with this for a bit. Isaac, I want you to begin to perform the same service for me and my father's house that you accomplished for Thomas Greene. We might have the opportunity to talk to another of Baker's tribe. Bill, do you remember the address of the terminus of the 'secret line' we were to use in Washington?"

"Yes, the boarding house uptown."

"Good," Devereux said. "Your retention of these things is always better than mine. I'll write a dispatch to Major Jenkins in Richmond telling what we know. Perhaps our communications will work faster than theirs. One can hope."

"Do you want me to go with him?" Smoot asked.

"No. They may be on the look out for the two of you together. Bill, you go alone, and fit yourself into the crowd, understand?"

His pale brown friend grinned. "Don't worry, I'll find a suitably large and invisible bunch of niggers to drift by with."

Smoot gazed in amusement at White. He turned to Devereux. "What will you do now, Capt'n?" he asked.

"I will try to keep moving fast enough to stay ahead of Lafayette Baker."

11
Amy

7:30 A.M., Monday, 6 April

The stockaded barriers in the streets disturbed Claude mightily. Since his return, he had done his best to avoid them, indeed to avoid seeing them. Today that was impossible as he had a meeting to attend beyond the palisade. The tall fences blocked all the streets leaving town. Long, pointed log posts stood planted deep in the brick sidewalks immediately beside the walls of the old houses. The work parties had dug up the eighteenth century brick to find softer going underneath for the points of the posts. The bricks lay heaped around the bases of the posts. Smaller posts extended the walls down into the streets. Gates were planted in the midst of small heaps of uprooted cobbles.

Sentry boxes stood on the inside of the gates. Impossibly young men in blue uniform checked the documents of those who came and went. The difference in the density of traffic inside and outside the barriers made the status of secession minded citizens of the city quite clear. Without a pass from the provost marshal one could not leave the city of Alexandria. These were not easily given to dubious folk.

On this bright Monday morning, Bill White drove Devereux out Duke Street toward the west end of Alexandria.

Outside the barricaded area of the city, one complex of structures was prominent among the surrounding residential buildings. These were the headquarters, maintenance shops, and classification yard of the United States Military Railroad. These buildings occupied the same ground on which the northern terminus of the Orange and Alexandria Railroad had stood before the war. As they drove toward the rail yard, Devereux saw that this collection of sheds and workshops had grown much larger since last he had visited it. *That would have been last winter.* He looked over the fence at the track itself as they drove to the gate, and imagined the line extending beyond the horizon to the southwest. *Burke Station, Fairfax Station, Manassas Junction where it split away from the Manassas Gap Railroad, Bristoe Station, Brandy Station ... Somewhere, far to the south, on the line of the Rappahannock River the presence of blue clad infantry would grow less and less. Finally, there would only be cavalry vedettes, the ubiquitous mounted scouts who lurked at road junctions and in the depths of forests. Finally there would be a burned railroad trestle or destroyed track. Perhaps the rails themselves would be wrapped around telegraph poles, grotesque toys for soldiers amusing themselves with fire. Finally, there would be the mirror image of the military presence on the northern side of the river. Men in butternut brown and grey are haunting the thickets. Fewer, more ragged and not as well fed as the men to the north of the break in the rail line, they would be waiting for Hooker to move.*

Devereux and Bill White sat together on the buggy seat as they were accustomed. White halted the pair of chestnut geldings at the gate of the military railroad compound. The black man began to laugh.

"What is it, Bill?" Devereux asked.

"The fence, Claude, look at the God damned fence!"

He focused on the sight before him. The Federal Army had enclosed the entire rail yard within a massive stockade. It was constructed of logs even larger than those sealing the streets of the city. It marched in wooden solemnity around the site. Trains sat steaming on the sidings inside the wooden barrier. The big roundhouse of the old Orange and Alexandria Railroad dominated the spectacle. "It looks like something you would see in the west," Devereux whispered.

White chuckled some more. "Well, we must be the Indians."

"I had no idea John Mosby was this active," Devereux mused. "Why are they so afraid? This has to be the result of their overactive imagination."

◆   ◆   ◆

It is no wonder that Elizabeth looks elsewhere for amusement, he thought. *This man is unutterably dull.* He had smiled and agreed his way through almost an hour with Frederick Braithwaite, who reintroduced him to Colonel Haupt and then dragged him around the yard to see the facilities, chattering the while. *I should enjoy this,* he thought. *He is suffering in trying to sell me his schemes, and I do like to see them suffer. He is also absurdly eager to please me. I wish he would relax a bit. All this arm waving and expostulation is attracting attention. I don't need to have Haupt start to take a direct interest in me.* In spite of his true sentiments, he nevertheless shamelessly encouraged the man, suggesting that Braithwaite's scheme for a postwar railroad project sounded to him to be a marvelous opportunity for venture capital, implying that Devereux and Wheatley sought such forward looking ideas on behalf of their clients in Europe. He needed Braithwaite. The man could provide transport and sponsorship for trips into the immediate rear of the Army of the Potomac, perhaps even into that army's headquarters itself.

They reached the gravity hump which was the heart of the classification yard. "And here, you see, the cars are pushed to the top by that little switching engine. They then roll down hill into the various branches of track, thus making up the proper trains." Braithwaite was running out of breath.

You silly ass! Devereux thought. *Do you think I never saw a rail yard before? My father is one of the owners of this property which you have seized!* "This is a bracingly cool day, don't you think?" he asked. "Look at the sky. Those high feathery clouds always appear just before the weather improves, don't you think?" He waited for an answer to this nonsense, maliciously enjoying the moment.

Braithwaite's face clouded over. He clutched the large pipe he had been smoking in one hand, attempting to seem appreciative for the wisdom Devereux had shared with him. It was difficult, but he managed.

The Confederate spy saw no purpose in waiting for an answer to this test question. The reaction had been enough. "How do you make up the trains and reverse the engines at the other end?" he asked. "The Rebels hold the yard at Culpeper."

Braithwaite leaped at the chance to continue the conversation, seemingly unaware that he had been mocked. "This is something you must see for yourself!" The tall blue clad man was beside himself with enthusiasm.

People throughout this portion of the yard began to watch.

"Our people have devised ways to avoid this predicament. Could you find the time to visit the front on one of our trains, I would be happy to accompany you."

What a good idea! Devereux knew, at this moment the exhilaration of success. "That's an excellent suggestion!" he said, smiling broadly. "In this way I can view the methods you have applied to these new issues of railroad engineering and at the same time make enquiries on behalf of the Sanitary Commission. Do you think there is a chance I could visit army headquarters? Miss Biddle and I have been discussing ways to improve further the availability of rest camps for soldiers in places closer to the action." *I have to remember to talk to her about this today!*

White watched his commanding officer approach across the open space between the gate and the half dozen sidings. *He's limping again,* he thought.

A train backed slowly into the nearest of the track.

The walking man stopped for a moment to lean against a wall. He looked at the approaching train, and changed direction to be clear when the creeping freight cars reached his point of intersection with the track.

From the buggy seat, White watched the train shriek raggedly to a stop.

The door of the last car slid back. Blue troops jumped down. Their rifles were fixed with bayonets. They took position at the closed doors of the next car. An officer of infantry arrived from a passenger car further up the train. He handed the sergeant in charge a large key.

Bill suddenly knew why there were ambulances in a line to his right. *Yankee wounded,* he thought. The ambulances started to roll. They moved to a car near the engine. The doors opened and men were handed down. Litters emerged in a continuous procession of the mutilated.

The burly sergeant now in possession of the key stepped up on a box to reach an imposing padlock on the wagon door. The sliding door rolled back to reveal the prisoners within. The sergeant waved an arm at a group of armed men in blue, directing them to gather in the center of the open space behind him.

The Confederate prisoners of war in the car blinked in the unaccustomed brightness of the sun. The able bodied climbed down, pausing to help others who could not descend alone. There were many wounded. At the U.S. officer's command, two soldiers grounded arms to help the injured. Bill counted them. Altogether, there were twenty two in the party of prisoners of war. The senior officer prisoner was a first lieutenant. He looked very tired. Somehow he had lost his hat in the long process of capture and transit. His face was sunburned and he would never have been described as tall.

The car load of prisoners milled around in the area between the guards until the Southern officer spoke some unintelligible words to a grey haired sergeant who stood at his elbow.

"Hampton's Brigade! Fall in!" he bellowed.

Cavalry, decided White. *South Carolina probably.* He looked closer. He noticed four men with red chevrons in the ranks. *That would be the battery of the Stuart Horse Artillery Battalion that was with this outfit when some bad thing happened to them.* White noticed a middling tall private in the front rank examining him critically. The man's tall cavalry boots were cracked and falling apart. The yellow braid of the stripe on one leg hung loose. He inspected White hostilely. *Let's see,* White thought. *He's thinking I wish I could kick this nigger's ass for watching me go through this.* He looked away for a second, then back at the soldier. He then took another of the risks, at losing odds that largely made up his life. He nodded to the South Carolina cavalryman.

The horse soldier stared back for a minute, then a big grin lit his homely face. After looking around in a conspiratorial way, he nodded back.

Devereux reached the buggy. It tilted as he levered himself into the other half of the seat. Sitting beside Bill, he was mute for a second. "My God, they look bad. Did we ever look that bad in the regiment?"

"There is no comparison," White said. "There could never be a comparison. We're us, and they're them."

The Union and Confederate officers had finished speaking. The gates of the compound swung open.

The informally selected detail of twenty two, presently representing the cavalry division of the Army of Northern Virginia, marched out of the stockade into Duke Street. Formed into a column of fours, they paraded toward the heart of the occupied city.

A double file of guards surrounded them.

Devereux leaned from the carriage to question a Union soldier with chevrons. "Where are they going?"

"Holding camp on the other side of town," the corporal responded. Twirling his mustache with one hand, he leaned on the buggy with the other. "These are festive occasions in this town," he commented from under the wrinkled brim of his kepi. "Half the women in town will chase them down the streets with picnic baskets. The other half couldn't care less."

"Why is that," Devereux asked?

"No money," the soldier laughed.

Rolling out the gate, Claude and Bill glanced to the right, seeking the retreating little column.

The blue guards were making no real effort to keep people away from the prisoners.

It was a strangely mixed procession.

Driving west on Duke Street from the railroad compound, neither man spoke for several blocks.

"You haven't had much to say about Esther and your daughter since we've been back." Devereux finally ventured. "Everything all right at home?"

Bill seemed taken aback by the question. "Why would you ask?"

Devereux waited for an answer.

White frowned. "My wife and I, we had some bad times when you and I first returned, but I think they are behind us."

"What's the matter, Bill? She objects to your choice of friends?"

White laughed. "That's true! She has a lot to say about it. She points out to me that my brother George, is in the other army. She doesn't see why I should side with the slavers."

"What did you tell her? It seems a logical question to me."

"I asked her if anyone in your family had ever mistreated her, if the people who owned her before me kicked her around any."

"Who was that? I forget."

"That was the Nugents." In response to Devereux's quizzical expression, White elaborated. "Henry Nugent, lumber business mostly."

"I presume the answer was no," Devereux said. "I can't imagine old Nugent or his wife tormenting anyone."

"That's right. She admitted that was true. Actually it's me she wants to fasten on as slave owner. She really wants me to free her."

Devereux thought it over. "Good idea."

"I've been looking for the right time to ask for your help with the papers," White replied. "It's something I have to get done before we leave again."

Devereux shifted restlessly on the seat. "She's right of course. There were always people who abused their servants. There was the matter of your grand-mother.."

White stared fixedly ahead. "We do not judge that to have been abuse."

Devereux brooded on that for a few blocks. "No, I don't either." he finally said.

The number of houses and commercial buildings along the dirt expanse of the street grew fewer and fewer. Shuter's Hill began to loom above them, a low, broad elevation now covered with army camps, a hospital and, on the far slope, an actual fort. The hill dominated Alexandria. It sat jammed in between the roads that extended Duke and King Streets into the countryside. The lower part of the hill was surrounded by a series of decorative wooden, painted arches. As they approached, Devereux could see on them such golden thoughts as might be fit-ting to the celebration of the Christmas season. The references to Yuletide cheer and the Prince of Peace were incongruous. "Must be left over from last year," he commented. "People can be awfully stupid! Imagine leaving something like that up in the middle of this awful war!"

"The glory, jest and riddle of the world," quoted White.

"Where did you get that?" Devereux asked.

"That was in one of the books your momma and Father Kruger were always givin' us to read."

"Sounds like Pope," Claude remarked.

"Could be. I don't remember their names much."

The hill was just before them now.

"Drive on up to that clump of buildings half way up. That's the Sanitary Commission convalescent camp. I must call on a lady."

Soldier's Rest was the camp's name. Earlier in the war, it had acquired a terri-ble reputation as a place in which freshly wounded men suffered and despaired through winters filled with agonies of cold and hunger. The arrival of the Sanitary Commission had been a new dawn. The society women and hard eyed clergymen who made up the Commission tolerated no nonsense from a neglectful government. The army medical corps was happy to have their help.

The buildings were connected by walkways made of wooden 'duck boards'. The one story frame structures could be identified by type without ever entering them. Wards, lounges, messes, offices and outbuildings were present and in heavy use from the amount of traffic to be seen.

As Devereux and White drove in the gate a cluster of patients were deeply involved near the stables in a serious game of horseshoes. White pulled up in front of a ramshackle heap that looked like the main offices. "Go mingle!" Claude told him as he slowly climbed down. "See if you can pick up anything on these people. Units, morale, you know what we want."

White clucked his tongue to the team, and the buggy moved away.

Devereux stepped up onto the plank veranda of what was marked as the main office building. He stood for a moment reading the posted material on the bulletin board thinking about plausible things to say to this woman. He had only met her once. 'Cold feet' might have been a phrase to express his feelings at that point. He heard footsteps behind. She was just stepping up on the boards beside him when he turned to face her. They stood eye to eye a foot and a half apart. Devereux had not been prepared to have her be this close. *I am five foot eleven. She is not much shorter, not much.* His peripheral vision absorbed her clothing. *Ridiculous! She needs to wear things that make her seem more feminine. She dresses as though she were a nun. Black is absurd on her in this weather. Perhaps a white collar with some lace would liven up her appearance.* Devereux remembered women by the way they smelled. *This one smells wonderful. Soap, some type of sachet, a life largely out of doors, and something underneath it which can only be she, herself. Hope smells good too, but different.*

She looked him straight in the eye.

He felt, rather than saw, a definite tightness in her posture and expression.

"What is there on our notice board that would draw your attention, Mister Devereux?" she asked.

He reminded himself to speak without hesitation even as he inspected her. *There's a real body under those funereal rags. The breasts are full and reasonably high. I wonder what her legs and hips are like.*

He used his most winning smile. "Just passing the time. I expected your return." Continuing his survey, he saw that her pale skin was beginning to lose its elasticity. Small lines were starting to score the surfaces of her face around the eyes. *She is at least as old as I am.*

"I enjoyed the dinner party in your father's home," she commented. "I hope he has recovered."

Claude had been wandering off mentally, constructing a map of the directions the conversation should take. Her remark brought him sharply back. He was not sure, for a moment, that the remark had teeth. Her expression changed that.

"Some things are impossible, and should not even be attempted," he said. "My father would never, willingly, offend his friends."

The look that softened her face showed that she was grateful for the frankness of his reply. "How can I be of help, Mister Devereux?"

"I'm concerned with the situation of all these brave men," he lied. *I hope they all rot in hell for eternity.* "Your description of the work done by the Commission, and the further elaboration of this by my wife is inspiring. I want to help you as much as I can. Our business gives us certain opportunities for philanthropy."

She stood in front of him, thinking about that. The color in her cheeks faded to an even more snowy hue.

She doesn't for a minute fully accept this foolishness, he thought. *Now we will see …*

Amy glanced at the horseshoe game.

He followed her lead and looked at the game.

Bill was pitching shoes.

"Isn't that your man? I believe he waited on table at supper."

Very good!

She seemed to make up her mind about something, and turned to open the front door of the wooden building. "Please, come in," she said. "We would be glad to have your help. Hope is already such a benefactor."

He was beginning to know this woman well enough to sense the gentle mockery of the last words. He followed her down the corridor. It ran between two sets of half-open doors. Her hair appeared still greyer in the changing illumination. *Why has she never married?* he wondered. *I do not have a taste for plain women. If I want her, others must have as well.* Her office was very much as he had imagined. Ascetic was not the word to describe it. Restrained and unassuming would have been closer to the mark.

Seated across the desk from her, he remembered the scene in the office of the provost marshal at Wilmington. *You would appreciate him, my dear, He is a butchered bird with red wings and a broken leg, he is just your style, someone to save.* A line of verse floated up out of the reservoir generated by a childhood filled with classics teachers. *'And yonder all before us lie deserts of vast eternity.' That crazy 'artilleur', he would savor that line. What would you do for that death besotted cripple, dear lady? Would you help him? Could you help him? More importantly, what will you do for me?*

She told him in detail of the good works of her comrades and associates.

You good and Christian folk are merely one more enemy, he thought. *You restore the fighting enemy to health. We go to a great deal of trouble to mangle and maim them. You then sweetly send them back for a second chance at us. We don't want to kill them twice, damn it!* "We are, of course, grateful for your presence here, Miss Biddle," he said, "but how is it that you find yourself among us in this circumstance?"

He watched her wrestle with the desire to talk about herself to him. He guessed that against this there struggled a natural reserve and an understandable wish not to appear foolish. The reticence lost. "The beginning of the Rebellion coincided with a change in my life which made it possible to dedicate myself to the work."

Someone died! He reasoned correctly. "But, have you no family? No parents or others who are deprived of your daily company?"

She was looking at the desk top in the same way that she had concentrated on her plate at dinner. Looking up shyly, she answered, "My mother died long ago. I have cared for my father, who was ill, for many years. He died in August 1860. My brothers and one sister are busy with their own lives."

He was beginning to hate this, was starting to dislike himself. "Is there no one else to care for you?" *Damn! Why did I ask? I know the answer.*

Amy colored prettily.

He watched the aching hole in her life momentarily gain control over her conscious functions.

"I mean cousins, friends, someone outside the circle of your work?"

She was mute, confused by the directness of his personal interest.

I had better keep this moving or she may come to her senses and throw me out. "Is the family in Massachusetts?" he asked, dreading the answer.

"New Hampshire," she said. "I have few relatives outside New England. You are lucky to have yours about you here."

Devereux laughed, causing her to look at him again. "Anyone who has my mother and wife for friends can never be truly alone, even if they wish it. But, you must have kin in the government or army?"

"No, only my youngest nephew. He is here, in the Office of the Adjutant General, a lieutenant."

"Good! You must bring him to the house. The ladies will be glad to meet him. Now explain to me the manner in which the finances of this excellent enterprise are arranged. I suspect that it is in that field that I can be of most use."

Her pleasant, but rather severe face, lit at the thought of assistance in an aspect of nursing that she did not relish.

She really is rather pretty in an odd way. The face is too long, but the intelligence and goodness of her comes through.

The woman pulled two large ledgers from a drawer, placing them open on the surface before her.

He picked up his chair, moving to her side, sitting so close that he could hear her breathing.

"An arresting system of accounts," he joked.

"Mine own, I'm afraid," she laughed through her embarrassment and shyness. To speak to him she turned her head.

He saw the nearly invisible sheen of perspiration on her upper lip.

He reached across the desk to point at a column of figures. "And what are these debits?" His hand brushed hers at the extremity of his gesture.

She did not pull away, but he saw and felt the slight tremor that shook her arm.

Devereux had always liked women. He preferred their company to that of men. He felt both protective and affectionate toward women. None of this explained to him the overwhelming desire which now gripped him to seize her, clasp her to his bosom, and make her his own. *Around the bend,* he thought. *You really aren't the right man for this.*

"We have to pay for water supplies," she explained. Those are the charges for the last month." She resolutely did not look at him.

"That's too much," he commented. "I know someone who will.."

White sat in the buggy, gazing down across the broad expanse of Shuter's Hill at the town, the river, the green heights of Maryland beyond.

Devereux climbed in. *She is sitting in her office still,* he thought. He had left her there and had no doubt that she had not moved an inch.

The beautifully matched horses clattered down the hill toward the road, happy to wait no longer. They sensed a return to their stalls and nosebags.

White leaned back, pulling the reins, holding them against their desire to drive straight into the traffic of the intersecting street below.

"So what has Esther done to occupy herself while you were gone. There's not enough to do in those two houses to keep all those women busy." Devereux asked the question absentmindedly, seeking something to say while absorbing his experience on the hill.

"She's been saving money, for a business after the war. She's a good seamstress, you know."

Devereux was absorbed in the memory of Amy Biddle's neck. He did not really have anything in mind as he continued, "Who is she sewing for?"

White cleared his throat, spat in the dust behind the chestnut horses. He was silent a minute, "She's making lots of money doing fancy uniforms for Yankee officers. I inspected some of them. They're right nice outfits."

Devereux had a vision of Bill's mahogany colored wife sitting in the Fairfax Street house with a dark blue garment in her lap. *Bill is right. She makes excellent clothes. We are going to lose this damned war. I can feel it in my bones. I have to keep enough of the family clear of this to give us some chance of survival. Bill, Jake and I will be enough to give up, or maybe just me.* "Good! Fine!" he exclaimed. "You should tell her to keep on with that. Their money is as good as anyone else's, maybe better." He laughed aloud.

White reached for the whip and lashed the air above the team's back.

The buggy rolled on into the city.

◆   ◆   ◆

Charles Devereux enjoyed the verdant intimacy of his garden. He treasured the moments which he passed there. A seven-foot brick wall enclosed it. The sound of the streets was largely excluded from this space by the heavy wall and the English ivy which enshrouded it. The small garden could only be entered from the house or through the pretty wooden gate which opened onto an alley at the back.

He had recently begun to spend the late afternoon hours alone there. He read the newspapers while seated in the white, wrought iron furniture around the fish pond. If Clotilde Devereux were with him, he read them aloud. Sometimes he sat with the day's news in his hands gazing at the colored Chinese carp. In those moments he seemed very old.

This particular afternoon, Hope stood in the kitchen, watching him from the window. She was concerned for her father-in-law. The strain of attempting to operate his business under war conditions was telling on him. He existed in the midst of neighbors who, like himself were supporters of Southern independence, but who were less worried about the ultimate moral stature of their cause in the eyes of the world. Charles had long been known for his views on race relations. He had pronounced them in the legislature and from every other public rostrum available. His peers considered them to be the admirable eccentricity expected of a Virginia gentleman. Most of his friends did not agree with him on this topic. They would not have commented on his ideas, but secretly thought them strangely naive for such a worldly man. Most Alexandrians, in fact, most Southerners, thought the mass of Negroes to be a primitive African people, dangerous because of their numbers, who should be kept carefully under control and forced to do useful work while a lengthy process of adaptation to Western civilization transformed them.

Charles tried hard to strike some workable balance between the needs of his business, his affection and loyalty for his friends, and his total rejection of the legitimacy of coercive armed intervention by the North in Southern life. Over-hanging this was the unending awareness of the positions of his sons and his neighbors' sons and the desperateness of their circumstances. The rending inner struggle within the man had begun to show in his actions.

Looking at him through the window, Hope reached a new stage in her ongoing analysis of her father-in-law. She began to resent him. *Why doesn't he like and appreciate my husband?* She thought. *Has not Claude always been a dutiful son? What right has this man to reject my husband? He has done his father's bidding in all important things. He never wished to be a banker. He has done it in a vain attempt to please Charles.* She was astonished at her own change of heart. She had always held her father-in-law in awe, seeing him to be more like her own folk in New England. She had wished Claude were more like him. *Charles is a respectable person of means and responsibility, like my father*, she thought. *Charles is like my solid New England born and bred father.*

Hope and her 'chere maman' spent a good deal of time in the kitchen experimenting with the family diet and gossiping with Betsy White. A scullery maid did the pots, pans and dishes. Charles Devereux would not have allowed any of these three women to perform the back breaking work that unassisted cooking demanded. Today, Hope had in mind to recreate one of her bygone triumphs in the field of pastry cookery. Claude had a pronounced weakness for fancy desserts.

The more chocolate and flaky pastry these concoctions included, the better he liked them. She stood at the marble topped counter used for rolling out dough.

Betsy occupied herself a few feet away with a large cauldron of simmering savories which was to be the base for a soup.

Hope heard someone come down the central hall of the house. This person took the last door on the right into the library. Through the window she saw her husband walk out of the library, onto the brick paved garden walk. He closed the French door to the house behind him. *He looks nice in that suit*, she thought *He hates frock coats, but they make him seem taller. Blue becomes him.* The irony of the thought struck her. She held up a handkerchief to her face to cover her laughter.

Betsy stopped fussing with the soup pot long enough to be sure Hope wasn't choking.

Claude greeted his father, crossed to the back alley gate, opened it and admitted the new man whom he had hired as messenger and coachman since his return. She had never really looked at him before. The stocky body and round, brown beard seemed of the sort to belong to any of the many Virginia country men who made up the circle of hunters and horsemen with whom the Devereux brothers spent their free time. As she watched, the man followed Claude across the garden. Hope stepped back from the window, unwilling to be seen just yet.

Claude stopped at his father's side.

The banker rose and extended his hand.

Hope heard the coachman introduced as Sergeant Isaac Smoot.

Charles waved them to seats.

"They are here," Hope heard Smoot begin. He was addressing Claude. "You have two at opposite ends of the block and a team of followers at the livery stable on Prince Street. They sent a messenger there this morning when you left and trailed you all the way to that hill outside town and back."

"Were you not observed coming in here?" Charles asked.

"They haven't noticed this back gate as yet, sir," replied Smoot.

The older Devereux smiled his wintry satisfaction at the thought, then turned to his son. "Don't make too much of it, Claude. Our sympathies are not a secret. I would think we have been watched for a long time."

"That may be," his son agreed. "In any event, I think we will continue."

"You are making progress with the Sanitary Commission?" his father asked.

"Yes, the Biddle woman and a couple of the ministers are determined to incorporate me into their assembly of helpful merchants and citizens."

That damned woman! We will see how much time and energy he has left for her to trifle with.

"What about that fellow from the railroad, the engineer?"

"Braithwaite. I visited him today. He's going to transport me into the den of the lion itself."

"Falmouth?" his father asked. "Army of the Potomac, Headquarters?" The old man's eyebrows were arched in amused wonderment.

"The very place," Claude said. "I'm not sure what will happen when I am there, but it now seems I will go."

"Is Braithwaite's railroad building idea worth anything?" his father asked.

"Yes. I think so. If they will let us invest in their country, we might be able to do something with it after the war."

The three men were silent, unwilling to mention the possibility that investment would be a simple matter if the United States were reunited in a postwar world.

"Are there any of your people who might inform against us, Mister Devereux?" Smoot asked Claude's father.

The two women in the kitchen abruptly turned to face each other.

Betsy's pale gold face was expressionless.

What a handsome woman, Hope thought. *What a shame that she has spent her life in another woman's kitchen! My God! She heard it all.*

From the garden Charles' voice floated in the open window.

"No one in my household would ever betray our cause or our men! You need not worry yourself on that account, Sergeant."

It's true! Hope thought. *That tortured old man has it exactly right. They have become more important to me than the politics of this wretched war. I can see it in myself now. I will side with them, against all comers. I should have seen this coming and left. I could still leave. No, I can't. How has this happened? I must have gone mad from living with these genteel lunatics. Little by little they have won me over. I can never go home. That isn't true. I am home. The Dutch priest is not such a fool as I thought.* She reached out and held Betsy's hand for a second. "No, Aunty, I won't abandon your son and my husband," she whispered.

"Let's not listen anymore," Betsy murmured. She put the pot on to simmer at the back of the big coal range. They left to find Clotilde.

The music room was one of Madame Devereux's favorite haunts at this time of day. She was sitting on the piano bench, mending shirts when they joined her.

12

Resolve

Wednesday, 1 April

The afternoon bundle of official mail brought an answer to the question which the Washington headquarters of the Detective Bureau had sent to its representative at New York. Having read the reply, Captain Ford hurried to the third floor room in which Johnston Mitchell spent his days.

The telegram from New York was three pages long, a typical example of the waste so commonly found in the wartime government. When he first had come to Washington, Mitchell's newspaper background had insured that he would be offended by the profligate expenditure of clerical effort and public funds that he found in the government's business, but the longer he remained in Federal service the less it bothered him. He did not like to see this tendency in himself. Looking at the sheets in his hand, he finally found words. "Well, Ford! It seems to be true. Devereux arrived from France on the 'Marshal..'" Mitchell frowned at the name.

"Bessieres," Captain Ford finished. "Marechal Bessieres, one of Napoleon's marshals. He was one of Napoleon's best, actually. And before you ask, yes, that is something I learned at West Point."

Mitchell looked at the young man. It had not occurred to him before, but now he could see that life as a junior Regular Army officer in the present huge volunteer service must not be altogether pleasant. There was a constant temptation for all the "citizen soldiers" to unleash their frustrations and hostility on the handful of professional soldiers who made convenient targets. Ford did not look well. The uniform seemed loose in places which recently had been filled out. For the first time, Mitchell noticed grey strands in the edges of the black beard. "You mustn't let Colonel Baker bother you when he is waspish," Mitchell said. "He means little by it and does not seem to realize how much his comments wound." Mitchell was guessing.

Ford made a small, exasperated gesture with his hand. "No, no. I'm just making small talk. Pay no attention. Colonel Baker is a mystery to me, but that is of no significance."

Mitchell was positive that this was not true. Ford's duties had lately thrown him together often with Colonel Lafayette Baker. "Come now!" he said. "You know that the only thing he really cares about is the importance of the job he imagines awaits him in the first Stanton administration. He is no one without the favor of the Republican bosses. You have the Army, the real Army. He's merely jealous." Mitchell watched a dogged expression come over his young friend.

"No, you are of another world," Ford said. "You don't know my world. The Army was not more than 16,000 officers and men before the war. It will be something like that again. There will be no future in it for one armed junior officers of artillery."

Mitchell saw this must be true. It had not occurred to him, but the iron logic of the situation was evident. "But, what will you do?" he asked.

Ford said nothing, shrugged awkwardly and picked up the telegram. "Do we drop our inquiry?"

"No! Absolutely not!" Mitchell exclaimed. "The more I read the watchers' reports, the more I am unconvinced of Mister Claude Devereux's innocence. His appearance in the midst of war as a loyal man, returned to the bosom of his family, surrounded by his secessionist friends. It is all a bit much."

Ford listened. He was positive that Major Mitchell was justified in his belief. He knew there was something he was forgetting and cast about in his memory for it. He remembered. "I checked with the railroad to see if there were any striking late night passengers the evening that Hennessey was murdered." he said. "There were. A conductor remembered a youngish white man in the company of a taller, light skinned Negro."

Mitchell leaned forward. "Names?"

"He had no idea."

"Passes?"

"They had them. The conductor remembered a soldier at the Virginia end of the Long Bridge walking through the car checking papers. There was no fuss, so he thought no more of it. They did not get off there, so they had to be going to Alexandria. We found the soldier." Ford pulled a paper out of the little pocket formed by the cuff of his pinned up right sleeve.

Mitchell watched him unfold it carefully, working with one hand on the table.

"Private Hiram Ridgely, Company 'F', 1st New York Heavy Artillery. He remembered the two men because it was odd to have them sitting together, and because he was afraid of the white man."

"Why would that be?" Mitchell had his hands folded over his belly, the thumbs caressing each other in a habit that signified contemplation.

"He did not like the way the man looked at him. It was not Devereux."

"Why not?"

"I don't believe our friend Devereux would take to wearing a false beard. He would find it absurd."

"And the passes?"

"Ridgely remembered them as being exactly correct and made out in the Provost Marshal's office in Alexandria."

"Not the Military Governor's office?" The thumbs had stopped.

"No. The names on the passes were nothing we have heard of. I think I know who the white man was."

Mitchell was truly pleased.

Captain Ford smoothed the paper under his hand on the table. A small expression of triumph began to occupy the corners of his face. "Devereux has a new coachman. He is saying that the man is an old hunting friend from the country who has 'refugeed' to escape the war. He is white, bearded, spends a lot of time with the Negro, White."

"And?" Mitchell prompted.

"When I saw him mentioned in the reports, I went to see for myself."

Mitchell found Ford smiling at him across the table. "Yes? What did you see?"

"I saw someone whose trade has become war. I saw my own kind."

"What did Private Ridgely see?" Mitchell asked.

"Private Ridgely insists that the light in the train was not very good and that he cannot be certain."

"Still afraid?"

"Yes, but I personally am secure in the conviction that these two men, Smoot and White, murdered one of my clerks." A grim resolution showed in the one-armed soldier's face.

"Let's see what we know," Mitchell said, ticking off points on his fingers, "Devereux and White did arrive from France by ship at about the time of their appearance here. Devereux has a new servant who you think is a soldier. Do we have this man's Oath form?"

"We are still looking for it."

Mitchell went on with his list. "We lost a man killed by two toughs who sound an awful lot like our friend Claude's people. The 'watchers' say that Devereux is spending a lot of time at the French and British Embassies. Devereux has volunteered his services to the Sanitary Commission and in a very short time has come to be thought of as a major supporter of that inviolable organization. We need to look at the people he associates with there. It isn't much, Ford. It isn't much.. We could be wrong. What do you think?"

"He is a spy and a foresworn traitor."

"That makes three of us, Ford, you, me and that jealousy crazed navy commander. We three all believe that to be true. What do you want to do next?" Mitchell was surprised at the warmth in Ford's reply.

"Sir, I say we should keep looking for the documents on Smoot, the coachman assassin, and at the same time I believe we should write to our consul in Paris to determine what he may know of Devereux and his recent life."

Looking at the young man, Mitchell saw how important this case had become for him. *The smart thing to do is to back away,* he thought. *Who knows where this may take us? I do not want to fight with the foreign embassies. They are outside my experience.* "Good," he replied, smiling. "Excellent. Keep up the watch on all of them."

13

A Turning Point

Saturday, 4 April
(Falmouth, Virginia)

An uninformed observer might have thought it unlikely that Claude Devereux, Confederate spy, the scion of a family known for its disloyal leanings, and newly returned from a supposedly extended residence in Europe should find himself in a poker party with the senior staff of the main field army of the United States. In fact, it had not been difficult to arrive at this social triumph. Union men wanted desperately to believe that the Confederacy did not really exist as a viable national entity, that it was a temporary aberration virtually forced upon the great mass of white people in the South by a criminal, treasonous conspiracy of the privileged planter class. Their ability to credit this fantasy was reinforced by their tendency to think that "The South" did not truly exist as a separate cultural area, that what was claimed to be a different way of life and identity was really only backwardness and a stubborn resistance to the practical, ordered rigor of the ideas which had been brought to America by the Puritan founders of New England. After all, the contest had been settled in England long ago when parliament's forces had defeated those of the tyrant king. The thought that perhaps the contest had now been renewed in America would not have been acceptable. In any event, the leaders and thinkers of the North needed to find Southerners of some stature who would side with them and give credence to the hope that soon the "rebellion" would collapse of its own weight as "sensible" people returned to their true allegiance. For this reason, a man like Devereux could burrow and bore his way into their inner circles like a tree boring insect working its way into the sapwood. There he fed on their desire to believe that there would be an end to the ferocious resistance which their armies had met everywhere. The chance to have the help of people like the Devereuxs of Alexandria, and especially that of Claude, the eldest, was something for which the government had prayed. It would only be rejected if someone could prove him false. This made the process of arrival at Joe Hooker's headquarters quite simple for Claude Devereux.

A steam dispatch packet carried them from the army landing in Alexandria. Standing at the rail of the boat, Devereux had amused himself by watching a man in a ridiculous suit scramble to get on the boat before it left. Once on board the fellow had done all he could to avoid a direct encounter with their party.

Much of the trip on the river to Acquia Landing had been occupied with breakfast with the ship's officers, a long and windy episode. At the terminus of the railroad at Acquia, a special three car U.S. Military Railroad train had awaited them on the siding adjoining the quai. There were two freight wagons and an ambulance car. The latter was just for the three of them.

Braithwaite had been the key to this opportunity to visit the main Union army's field headquarters. He wanted Devereux money for his railroad schemes and to that end the need to display his importance and acquaintance with the mighty had sufficed. It had only been necessary to endure his company and his unending yearning for reassurance of the possibility of postwar riches. Patrick had been a great help. His frank admiration of the accomplishments of the Union Army's railroad engineers went down well with their host.

Claude had always thought his brother formidable in his ability to deal with practical problems and masses of detail. The monumental supply camps which they passed through with Braithwaite depressed Claude terribly. The implications of such organization and resources were clear when contrasted in the mind's eye with the memory of his own army.

Patrick was not affected in the same way. His VMI engineering education made him view the Union Army with something approaching professional detachment. The prodigious staff accomplishments which produced these installations elicited from him a running analysis of the intricacies of the system.

Braithwaite listened in deepening stillness as they rattled along in the ambulance car. "It is clear that your knowledge of such matters is a matter of training," he finally said. "It is sad that we do not have your services in this crisis."

Patrick blinked at that and bowed slightly. "Yes, it is sad, sad indeed that I am unable to serve my country." Braithwaite smiled at him in the belief that he understood.

"And at the head of all this there is, General Hooker?" Claude asked, changing the subject.

"Hooker and his staff, aides de camp, quartermasters, ordnance officers, etc.," Braithwaite answered still looking at Patrick who seemed absorbed in the passing countryside.

"And you deal with these officials frequently in running all this?" Claude asked, seeking to turn his attention away.

"Well, I, in a way, at least in transport matters, yes."

"What is this man Hooker like?" Patrick asked.

◆　　　◆　　　◆

Around the green-covered table the poker players waited for the dealer to call the game. The holder of the cards glanced at them all. He was an elderly major of infantry who looked as though he had been born with a deck of cards in his hands. "Table Stakes, Dealer's Choice. Draw," he announced while shuffling. The cards flashed in his hands as they settled in place before each player. Most of the men in the game wore army blue, but not all. Patrick Devereux sat with them engrossed in his hand. He had his stomach pressed against the table, his elbows planted firmly on the baize cover. It was an unnatural posture, but it was made necessary by his stiff left leg which fit among the other players' extremities only if he sat in this position. A handsome, blonde haired general across from him had bumped it three or four times already, apologizing each time in an off hand way and pulling in his feet.

The dealer spoke again. "Jacks or better to open."

There was a second general officer in the game. This one was younger and junior in grade but seemed to be quite comfortable in the older man's company. As Patrick watched, the young general pried up the edge of his hand from the table's surface. "Ten dollars," he said.

A distinguished looking colonel who gave the impression of participating from a sense of duty dropped out.

Frederick Braithwaite stayed in the game as did the blonde senior officer and Patrick himself.

The dealer went round the circle allowing an attempted improvement of hands.

The young general who had bet wanted no cards.

"Dan, you are the world's greatest fraud," the blonde officer laughed. He reached for the bottle on the table to pour a drink.

A soldier appeared from the shadows to take the bottle from him.

The general made a sweeping, inclusive gesture.

The orderly poured around the table.

The dealer surveyed the faces after his distribution of cards to those who wanted them. He looked at Brigadier General Dan Butterfield expectantly. His first bet stood.

"Fifteen dollars," said Butterfield.

"My God! You're dangerous tonight!" the blonde general officer cried out. "Have mercy! The rest of us don't have your money!" He folded, taking Braithwaite with him. This left Patrick and Butterfield in the game.

"See you, raise you ten," Patrick announced gazing stonily across the green cloth at Butterfield.

Blonde haired and red of face, "Fighting Joe Hooker," Commanding General of the Army of the Potomac, waited for his chief of staff to make up his mind.

"Come on, Dan, take the plunge," he needled his friend and aide. Dan Butterfield was hugely rich. The money came from the "American Express" bank group. It was almost a joke in army headquarters since he made so little show of his wealth, but everyone at the table knew how deep his pockets were. The rich man stared at Patrick, visibly calculating the net outcome of a process in which he drove the betting higher and higher.

Claude Devereux knew his brother's habits at cards. He knew his brother. He knew there was an even chance that Patrick held nothing at all, that he was merely hoping for an opportunity to make a fool of the Yankee officer.

"Call," Butterfield intoned.

Claude searched his brother's expression. There was little there that would cause offense.

Patrick shook his head as though ridding himself of something, and flipped his hand onto the felt. Three sixes.

Butterfield placed his cards on the table, two pair, king high.

Hooker laughed and laughed. "You're lucky tonight Dan. If you hadn't quit, he'd have skinned you for sure!"

The loser seemed to have mixed feelings about his near escape.

Claude sat nearby at a small, round, marble topped table before the fireplace, watching the gathering for some useful opportunity. The colonel who had folded, pushed his chair away from the card table and came to join him.

Braithwaite riffled the cards. "Five card stud," he said.

"I guess I don't really understand why you are visiting us Mister Devereux.." Claude looked to see who had spoken. The officer who had left the game to join him spoke from a chair two feet away. It took a moment to bring himself back from his scrutiny of the card game. "I'm sorry, Colonel I don't remember your name," he said. "I know we were introduced before dinner."

"George Sharpe."

Claude examined the man across the little table; thinning hair, medium build, drooping mustaches, a colonel of infantry. There did not appear to be anything interesting about him but his rank. *Annoying! I need to hear what is said in the game.* "I've gotten involved with charitable work with the Sanitary Commission since my return from abroad," Claude said. "My brother preceded me in this work, as has my whole family in fact. Colonel Braithwaite kindly offered to show us the Army. None of us have much practical knowledge of the subject. He feels that we will be more persuasive in Washington if we have some idea of what we speak." Claude smiled benignly, looking directly at Sharpe. "His wife and mine are thick as thieves in Commission work. I really am just a helper in this. As part of my education, Colonel, what do you do here?"

Sharpe blew smoke rings across the room. They looked to be aimed at the back of Braithwaite's head. "I'm the Deputy Provost Marshal of the Army."

"That is the chief policeman, is it not?" The remark was meant to wound, to send the man away.

Sharpe made a small face. "Actually, no" he said. "General Patrick is the Provost Marshal. I work for him, in a way."

"In what way?"

At the table, Hooker and Patrick were hooting and beating on the green cloth with their open hands in amusement at something Butterfield had said. Braithwaite was nonplused.

The orderly passed around the circle with the bottle.

"I run an office that keeps records of important events in the departmental area of this Army," Sharpe said over the noise.

"A sort of historian?"

Sharpe seemed satisfied with the phrase.

"Of disciplinary incidents, crimes by soldiers?" Devereux pressed.

Sharpe did not appear happy with that. "Not exactly."

Devereux knew how to make it difficult for someone not to answer a question. It was a technique he had perfected early in life. His employment of this trick was among the various traits which caused some people to dread his attentions. Having decided now that he wanted a response, he turned a fixed look on the other man and waited.

"Have you had much experience in the capitalization of railroads?" Sharpe finally asked. "Tricky things. My law firm damned near went bankrupt when a senior partner talked us all into putting up a lot of money on a scheme for a line into Ontario that never quite came to be."

Devereux's annoyance struggled with alarm. "Railroads? We never have had anything to do with them," he said. "Why would you ask that?"

Sharpe pointed at Braithwaite's back with the end of a foot crossed over a knee. "He doesn't do things for nothing."

Devereux glanced at Braithwaite, afraid he might have overheard. The railroad officer gave every sign of being completely engrossed in the play.

Hooker and Patrick were once again surrendering money to Butterfield with good grace. Joe Hooker seemed to enjoy teasing his friend about his riches. "Now, Dan," he said while looking sideways at Patrick. "You know Mister Lincoln will be here tomorrow to visit because he just loves us both. His letters have filled me with confidence for my future but you told me you would look out for me in my old age, and I have decided I'd like a job in one of your banks, maybe in London!"

"We'll give you a job, Joe," Patrick remarked. "Which do you prefer, New York or Paris?"

"You see, Dan!" the general exclaimed. "When Father Abraham finally discovers an excuse, I'll not starve. I have found some true friends." Turning his ruddy, handsome face to Patrick, he announced, "New York."

"Done!" Patrick pronounced, "Subject of course to our father's confirmation." He swung around to peer at Claude.

"A mere formality, General," the elder brother agreed. "You are just the sort of man of the world we need in that branch. God knows, I never could handle the place! Welcome to the firm."

"It's all settled," chuckled Patrick.

Hooker wasn't looking at him anymore. "Yes, it's all settled," he said to Claude. "I have a long memory Mister Devereux," he said in a voice that did not sound at all affected by the whiskey he had drunk that evening. "Let's call it a night. We have to deal with the commander-in-chief tomorrow. I would not want to worsen his impression of me!" He rose.

There was a noisy scraping of wooden chair legs on the unfinished floor. Hooker stopped at the door, turned and looked at Claude. "I will expect you both for dinner tomorrow night in the headquarters mess." With that he walked into the night. His laughter mixed with that of Dan Butterfield, coming in the open door with the sounds of stamping horses.

A minute later Claude found himself outside watching the backs of Hooker's mounted entourage disappear down the road to the staff billeting area. Standing next to him outside the frame farm house was Colonel George Sharpe. Devereux took advantage of the moment to ask what Hooker had meant by his last words.

Sharpe rubbed his lower face before answering. "Joe Hooker is a much smarter man than many think," he said. "He meant it both ways. He did take offense, but he might come looking for a job if things don't go right."

Patrick and Braithwaite came out of the house to stand with them.

The incongruous element in the scene connected in Claude's head. "Why didn't you go with them?" he asked Sharpe.

Braithwaite answered. "He's home. This is his bureau's office. He lives upstairs."

"I was host tonight," Sharpe added. "I hope you enjoyed dinner. Good evening, gentlemen."

Claude kept his reflections on this evening's business to himself during the return trip to the army railhead behind Falmouth. He was plunged into depression by the memory of his inability to move his discussion with Sharpe in the desired path. Braithwaite and Patrick sat in the front of the military carriage, talking to the driver and telling of poker hands seen in games gone by.

The wind stirred old leaves in the little ditch beside the dirt track. Stars glittered through shifting openings in the closely grown forest all around. The return seemed longer than their earlier trip to the card party. At last, the carriage rolled out into an open place filled with rails and railcars and those who served them. Small fires burned throughout the siding yard, lit by soldiers trying to stay warm on a cold night.

Claude climbed down from the carriage alongside their car, impatient and wrapped in his discontent. Still absorbed with his seemingly insoluble difficulties, he slipped in the "right of way's" ballast, twisting his bad leg. "Damn it!" he snarled, and hopped back to the side of the vehicle where he grabbed a rear wheel just as the carriage began to roll forward. The iron tire was wrenched from his clenched fist. He spun on his wounded knee and sat heavily in the mud. Fire ran through his lower body.

Braithwaite and the soldier-driver appeared and dragged him to his feet.

"I am sorry. I think I may have broken something," Claude said.

The two soldiers helped him aboard the ambulance car.

A surgeon came from the hospital train. A perfunctory examination showed nothing worse than an awkward and painful sprain. Fortunately, Braithwaite was outside when the doctor remarked that he would have amputated the leg considering the amount of damage to the kneecap.

"Thank you, Doctor," Claude replied through gritted teeth as the man manipulated the terrible agony that was his right knee. "I was able to persuade one of your colleagues that this was not necessary.." He could hear Patrick outside talking to Braithwaite to keep him out of the car. There would be no satisfactory explanation if the Union officer saw the scars.

"Where did this happen?" the blue coated doctor asked, still holding the leg in his hands, examining it in the lamplight. "Sharpsburg," Devereux answered, still lost in the pain. *Sweet Jesus! They don't call it that!* "Antietam!" he quickly added. "It was just inside the town of Sharpsburg, as the Johnnies were withdrawing."

The doctor never looked up. "That explains it," he said. "This is still unhealed. You should use a cane. I am not surprised that you were released from the army. You were an officer?"

"Yes, yes. I am, I was a captain. Thank you doctor." The bespectacled physician helped him to a chair and departed. Claude listened as his brother intervened skillfully to keep the doctor from describing the true state of his leg to Braithwaite. He heard footsteps crunching away in the gravel and then the sounds of Braithwaite helping Patrick up the iron steps into the car. By the time they reached him he was sitting in a medical orderly's iron chair with a fixed smile.

"Feeling better?" the Yankee officer asked. The look of concern was surprisingly convincing.

"Oh, I'll be fine, stupid thing to do, wool-gathering like that. I deserve it," Claude said. "Pat, sit down, you have more to worry about with that gimpy leg.."

Braithwaite left to settle himself into the separate compartment provided for the medical officer who would normally staff the car.

The Devereuxs sat across the aisle from each other amidst the rows of triply stacked litters. A kerosene lamp burned brightly in a gimbled wall mount throwing yellow light on the walls of the car wherever the shadows of the litters did not interfere.

Patrick began to chuckle aloud.

Claude shook his head. "I don't find anything very amusing in this. I can't see that we did anything this evening except to irritate General Hooker and miss some wonderful opportunity the exact nature of which escapes me."

"No. No." His brother waved a hand, putting a forefinger to his lips, pointing with the top of his head at the wooden partition behind which Braithwaite could be heard moving about. They moved to the opposite end of the car, limping along and holding each other up.

"What then?" whispered Claude.

"Don't be ironic with Hooker again, Claude," Patrick whispered as he shook his head in the dim light. "He picked it up immediately. He seems a very melancholy man to me. We should not make life more wretched for him."

Melancholia is a good description of this, Claude thought. *Joe Hooker and I should be fast friends.*

"Hooker and Butterfield sincerely want us to stay long enough to have dinner in the officer's mess tomorrow night," Patrick whispered.

"Why?"

"They're bored, waiting for the action to begin, whatever it is. They also are looking for allies. Those two men have a deep sense of their isolation from the real centers of power."

"Us? Surely, not us.."

"Why not? Claude, you have created the illusion of our connection to their war effort."

"Who is Sharpe?"

"He is the one you seek here. You told me that you are looking for a clue as to how they can now reason so clearly about Lee's Army.. They, Hooker really, have created something they call the 'Information Bureau.' This man Sharpe is in charge of that and is systematically gathering information of all kind. A group of special clerks are putting all this together and making judgments on the basis of an archive they are creating and the probabilities which are suggested by it."

"How do you know this?"

"You left the room for half an hour about 10:30."

Claude had gone in search of the outhouse and had taken the opportunity to wander about, looking at the clump of buildings. "And they told you that?"

"Hooker told me. Butterfield and Sharpe were not happy with him."

"Why would Hooker tell you?"

"He's looking for someone like us to act for him in Washington, to keep track of plots against him. Our business and diplomatic attachments are appealing." Patrick hesitated slightly, "And I do believe he is sorry for me."

Claude reached for his brother's hand, and pressed for an instant.

"You haven't heard the best, I am to go by Sharpe's offices tomorrow for an extended discussion of 'how it is that we can help them.'"

"And I will spend the day engrossed in the state of grace of every 'soup kitchen' within a day's ride." Claude grimaced in the semi-darkness. "At least I won't have Braithwaite at my heels. He summons up thoughts of revenge."

Patrick glanced at his brother and then away. "You'll never find a better woman than Hope," he said. "Be careful."

"You wrong me," Claude said in the dark, his face only a silhouette. "My reveries on the subject of infidelity run in more dangerous channels than that."

2:45 P. M., Sunday, 5 April

"Stop!" Devereux cried out. "Please stop for a moment. I want to look at the town."

The grave, bearded man beside Claude signed his agreement to the driver and the carriage came slowly to a halt.

"Do you know Fredericksburg well, Mister Devereux?" the other man asked.

Claude clambered awkwardly down from the vehicle. His aching leg making the process tedious.

The Sanitary Commission civilian driver came around to help.

The minister sat upright in the carriage. He looked slightly puzzled.

Devereux had an old prejudice against Congregationalists. They reminded him of the things he had found wanting in himself all his life. He particularly detested their certitude. This one was beginning to annoy him enough to wish for physical space to breathe in. Fredericksburg had come into view as they turned a bend in the road which followed the crest of the high ground on the northern side of the Rappahannock. With the driver hovering at his side, he hobbled along like an old man to a place which allowed him to lean on a big locust tree while gazing his fill at the town. It was an effort to think that the river just below them was the front line. Behind it lay the town. Behind that he could see the mile of gently rising plain across which his blue clad hosts had made their suicidal assault in December. The ridge with a sunken road at its base filled the horizon.

"It looks awful, don't it, sir?"

He had not really examined the driver up till now. The man's rhetorical question made that obligatory.

"Where are you from?" he asked.

"Upstate New York, Troy. It's a different place from this, not wild somehow."

The driver's shaggy hair, rough clothing and rubber boots seemed very appropriate.

Fredericksburg was a deserted ruin. The sweet harmony of the place in Devereux's memory was destroyed by the desolation of its empty streets and roofless shells of buildings. Stray dogs haunted alleys. As he watched, he saw two brown figures with rifles cross a distant open space between buildings. *Pickets. From what Harry Jenkins told me, they are probably Early's men.*

"Mister Devereux! Don't you think we should be getting on? We have many more miles to go today!" The preacher was impatient.

The driver shifted from one booted foot to the other. Devereux knew he would speak soon, afraid of displeasing the reverend Doctor Moulton, afraid for his job.

Devereux wanted to say something ugly to Doctor Moulton. He also knew he could not afford to indulge himself in that way. He looked down at his own mud coated boots. He saw spots of brown on the skirt of his black frock coat. From the corner of his eye he saw a puff of white smoke across the river. The snakelike hiss of the passing bullet frightened the horses. The crack of the rifle's report arrived.

The driver ran to seize the bridles.

The minister stood in the carriage, wild eyed with fright, speechless for once.

Claude limped away from the tree. *Must be 700 yards,* he reflected? *Probably one of those telescope mounted English guns we had on board "Let Her Rip."* He watched the buildings for activity.

Another puff of smoke announced the impending arrival of a bullet. It 'whacked' into the locust he had just left. *God Damn It Jubal! Are you letting them shoot obvious civilians now? Steady. If they wanted to hit you, you would be down by now.*

He pulled his large white linen handkerchief from a pant pocket, tying it quickly to the end of his stick. He stopped, faced Fredericksburg, and waved his white flag in a big arc over his head. For just a second he saw the glint of a piece of glass looking at him from a foundation, then it was gone. A moment later a grey figure wearing a kepi stepped from a doorway in the building which held the sharpshooter's lair in the basement. The tiny shape waved a white cloth back at him and disappeared.

He made his painful way to the carriage. The driver came round from the horses' heads to help him in.

The minister was still standing, his eyes moving back and forth between the ruined town and the man before him.

"They won't shoot again," Devereux told him. "It was their idea of a joke."

8:30 P.M.

Taken as a group, there were many things about the inhabitants of the North that Claude Devereux found offensive. Among these, their assumption of their own moral superiority was for him the worst. To Devereux the unending recitation of the evils of slavery to which Southerners had been subjected for decades was but one of many provocations which New England had inflicted on his countrymen.

Like many of his people he found the Puritan ethic with its embedded identification of work with virtue to be repugnant and demeaning to the dignity of man as one of the creatures that nature's God had made to populate the earth and be happy in it. He believed that man was intended to live in harmony with nature and that to attempt to make of man a being possessed of godlike qualities not in keeping with his place in God's plan was an abomination. If Southerners would rather read poetry than scripture, if they would rather sing and dance and hunt and make love than paint their houses and grub for more money, then this was their right, indeed their duty to the true nature of man, to their nature. He had no thought of ever accepting the opinion of the Yankees that somehow God Almighty had given them sway over the earth, in particular, his earth, his land. He reasoned that the blacks were men like him, but that they had emerged from a background so different that there must be many years of adaptation to white civilization before the masses of them were ready to be free citizens. The ever growing Northern obsession with the institution of slavery he thought the grossest hypocrisy, a pretext for domination of the South. Surely, the more intelligent Yankees knew that if the slaves were suddenly freed, a cataclysmic social and economic crisis would follow, a crisis that might so embitter relations as to forever keep the Negro from his true place in American society. For these reasons, he had seen the creation of the Republican party in the years before the end of the old Union as a trumpet call announcing the marshaling of the superior forces of the North against his region. The election of 1856, he had seen as a turning point, even with the clown abolitionist Fremont as candidate of the new party. The emergence of Lincoln in the late '50s as a spokesman for the more radical elements in the Northern states he saw as a death threat against all he held dear. Devereux was deeply empathic. He could listen to a man's words, watch his behavior with others and judge what was in his heart. He judged Abraham Lincoln to be in the thrall of a great idea, the idea of Nation, the belief that for some reason God had made America for his own purpose and that the United States was somehow greater than the sum of its parts. Devereux feared and hated this idea. He saw that it would make the South the servant of alien interests and ways and that it would condemn his people, his Virginia to an eternity of subjugation to whatever foolishness might seize the minds of the growing nationalist forces. Lincoln served for him as symbol of all that must be resisted and overcome.

Devereux was prepared to dislike Lincoln, and therefore it is surprising that, in the end, he found that he liked Abraham Lincoln as a man. The process that led to this remarkable outcome began that night. On this particular evening he had the experience of watching the President of the United States and General Joseph

Hooker circle each other warily for hours. The commander of the Army of the Potomac was patently ill at ease in the presence of his political chief. Joe Hooker had suggested the night before that all was not well between him and Lincoln. The expressions on their faces at dinner confirmed that.

Lincoln had arrived at the dinner in Hooker's headquarters mess just after the Devereuxs. His appearance, descending from an open carriage caused a stir. Officers ran about moving chairs unnecessarily while enlisted orderlies watched them in amused exasperation. In Lincoln's party were several men whose identities were immediately known to the Devereuxs. Edwin Stanton, the Secretary of War, was one. In close association with Stanton there was a military officer who seemed to have the ear of both Stanton and the President.

Claude asked Braithwaite who this might be.

"Colonel Lafayette Baker. You want to stay away from him."

"Why is that?"

"He's the head of Stanton's secret service in Washington. He is the principal spy catcher."

"You don't think me a spy, do you?" Claude asked with a raffish air. Braithwaite waved a hand. "Don't be silly, but I nevertheless think it would be a good idea for any Virginian of quality to avoid involvement in his affairs in the present state of things. A good way to do that is to avoid him." A small gesture of the head made it clear who was meant.

Claude nodded and stood beside Patrick studying his opponent.

The man was large, muscular, and bullet headed. His face wore the marks of a life filled with the need to control self expression, to subordinate emotion to ambition, to hang on every word of those who might be of help.

This fellow can wipe out my family with a gesture, he thought. Hatred welled up in Devereux, unreasoning, murderous hatred. As he watched Baker, George Sharpe appeared in the room.

Sharpe worked his way through the crowd to shake Baker's hand.

The guarded facial expressions and tense atmosphere between the two made it clear to Claude that Sharpe shared at least some of his animus for Baker.

As Claude watched, Sharpe's eyes focused on the Devereuxs across the smoky room. Claude tried to seem reasonably unconcerned as he saw words pass between the two officers.

Baker looked up, searching the room.

Sharpe's head was turned away from Claude, but he knew that a description of himself and Patrick must be the subject of those whispers.

Baker found them, and looked carefully from one to the other.

"Patrick! Claude! Come here I want to introduce you!" Hooker beckoned across the room.

From the corner of his eye, he saw Baker start to move toward them, leaving Sharpe standing alone.

"Mustn't keep the general waiting," the older Devereux said, pulling Braithwaite forward. He and Patrick limped across the room together. A cane borrowed from the ambulance car helped him on his way. Patrick's crutches cleared a comfortable path as usual.

"Want to have you meet someone," Hooker said as they arrived at his side.

The subject of this remark, a heavy, elderly looking officer turned to look at them.

"Henry Halleck," he said, holding out his hand to Claude. "I understand you are from Alexandria and are a firm supporter of the Sanitary Commission."

The General in Chief of the Union Army! "I am that," Claude replied," but I am also one of your reading public."

"Really!" Halleck responded. "How unusual to meet someone who has read anything these days. What are you referring to?"

"'Elements of Military Arts and Sciences,' and your translation of Jomini's *'Vie Politique et Militaire de Napoleon'.*"

"My God!" the general exclaimed. "I had thought that only my mother and the printer had read those! Do I understand from General Hooker that you are newly returned from Paris?"

He said yes, sensing Baker's approach even as he spoke. *Don't be too eager,* He told himself. *That may have been too much, too much, too quick. Don't frighten them off.* "May I introduce my brother, Patrick?"

Baker appeared at Claude's left, listening to the talk, standing so that he could interpose himself between Devereux and Halleck if the occasion should require it or the opportunity present itself.

"Do I also understand that you two gentlemen are half French and fluent in that most lovely of tongues?" Halleck continued.

"Mais, bien sur, mon General," laughed Patrick.

"Aha! Joe, I have just found my dinner companions of the evening. You can deal with the president and Stanton tonight. Care to join us, Colonel Baker?" Halleck swept toward the dining room a hand on the sleeve of each of the Devereux brothers. "Tell me, what do you really think of this man, Hugo? he asked.

"Somewhat overrated and tedious," Claude ventured. "'Les Miserables' does, in fact, make me miserable."

Patrick glanced at him reproachfully across the back of Halleck's grey haired neck.

The General in Chief nodded gravely, "I am glad to hear you say that. I find it has much the same effect on me."

The three swept across the room toward their table. It was next to that at which Abraham Lincoln was already seated watching with his deep-set eyes as the room filled.

Baker followed in their wake.

Claude did his level best throughout dinner to balance attention given to Halleck and Baker with an overpowering desire to listen to the conversation at Lincoln's table.

Patrick was a great help. His engineering knowledge fit squarely with many of Halleck's major interests. Unfortunately, the general's literary fancies left Claude's younger brother fishing for witticisms and stalling in hope of Claude's intercession. The conversation rambled on in French. Baker understood not a word of it. This created a problem in which prudence and a certain sense of fair play seemed to demand periodic digressions into English. The ministrations of soldier-waiters added to the noise and confusion causing people to speak louder than they otherwise might have done. The glittering polyglot chatter of their table soon absorbed the attention of most of the room, including that of those at Lincoln's table, who seemed happy to have an excuse for their inability to talk to each other.

In a lull at his table Claude heard someone say, "Henry, you have at last found someone pleasing to talk to. I am so glad. Washington is at best a dull place. I often wish for some diverting company there myself." It took Claude a second to realize that this statement had been inserted into a small hiatus in the conversation by the President of the United States. Halleck's back was to Lincoln. A nasty hush settled over the room as the various possible interpretations of the remark soaked in. Devereux peered through the lamplight and smoke at the tall man's table. Joe Hooker looked thoughtful. Lincoln waited for some response from his principal military advisor. The color of Halleck's face deepened noticeably. *What a cruel, pointless thing to say!* Claude thought. "Mister President," he said at last. "General Halleck has been so kind as to give us his views on a number of subjects in which I have been unaware of recent developments because of prolonged absence overseas. I fear we have monopolized his conversation." Claude caught a fleeting look of gratitude as it crossed Halleck's face.

Hooker cleared his throat. "I have not had the chance to introduce these young men, Mister President. They are supporters of the Union and friends of the Sanitary Commission."

Claude now found Lincoln's undivided attention centered on them. Nothing was said for a moment while the tall man's looked at the two brothers. "From your voice, sir, I would say you are from one of the border states," Lincoln said.

"Actually, Mister President, I am from Alexandria," Claude replied.

"A lovely place, we are happy to have been able to keep some of you Virginians with us. Mister Devereux, is it?" Lincoln asked. "There is at least one of your fellow Alexandrians who I wish had thought longer before he made his fatal decision two years ago."

Claude gazed blankly at him.

"The President is referring to Robert Lee," Halleck suggested.

"Oh! Well, he would do whatever he thought best. It is his nature," Claude replied evenly. *Your grandfather was one of us, damn you! What is it in Illinois that makes the blood run cold? Is it all the lovely Yankees who went there to mix with our people?*

"You know him?" Edwin Stanton rasped.

"Family friends," Patrick said. "Our grandfather took a special interest in the family after the death of General Lee's father in the West Indies."

"I have never had the pleasure," President Lincoln said. "I suppose he is only a few miles from here, somewhere on the other side of the river. If he were with us tonight, how would I find him at table?" A sad, wistful smile appeared on the dark features.

"You would like his company, Mister President," Claude replied. "He is a gentle, courteous man who could not speak French to save his soul."

Heads swiveled all through the room as staff toadies sought cues from which to organize their reactions to this effrontery.

Halleck, Hooker and Stanton seemed to harbor a tentative and surreptitious pleasure in the scene.

Abraham Lincoln showed not the slightest displeasure with Claude. He bowed slightly. "Mister Devereux, from all I hear the man is a virtual saint, and single handed is the biggest obstacle to peace which exists in this country. I keep telling Generals Halleck and Hooker and everyone else who will listen that it is Lee and his army which are the major riches held by Jefferson Davis and that they should be the objects of our attacks not Richmond. What do you think?"

Claude felt within himself for reserves of composure. *Don't tell him he's right. For God's sake don't tell him.* "General Lee will defend Richmond to the death, always," he finally said.

"Why?"

"Because it is the center of his world."

"And not yours?"

Claude did not like this. He sought some artifice with which to turn Lincoln from interest in his motivations. "I am only a banker, Mister President. My world must necessarily be more diffuse in its concerns."

Lincoln was silent a moment, bowing his head again slightly in a perceptible gesture of regret. "Has he no weaknesses, no faults, other than an inclination toward treason?" he finally said.

"He is excessively polite," Claude replied. *Surely, that must be safe.*

"Could you explain that a little?" the President asked. "I see that his Old Army colleagues agree with you."

"He has a hard time being perfunctory or peremptory in dealing with others, any others," Patrick said. *I don't believe he can make use of this. But can I be sure?* "I saw him often when he lived at Arlington, Mister President," Patrick continued. "I was acquainted with some of his children."

Yes. You damned near married one of his daughters, Claude thought.

"And?"

"He always made suggestions to his wife's servants with regard to gardening or.."

"You mean slaves, don't you?" interjected a tall, bearded civilian several tables away.

"Yes. That is exactly what I mean," Patrick said, facing the civilian. "We do not call them slaves unless we intend to sell them." He turned back to Lincoln, ignoring the angry muttering at the civilian's table. "Lee needs willing, disciplined helpers, because of his, character. From what I have heard of his army, they are not always at hand. This is a weakness."

"So it is!" said Lincoln. "So it is. He is not alone in having this problem."

Hooker and Halleck looked at each other.

"You must come see me at the White House, both of you," Lincoln said. "I would like to hear more about him. I can see from your choice of table companions that you are already well connected with the War Department. Perhaps we should find some way to make your help official." These words hung pregnant with meaning in the air.

Claude stole a glance at Lafayette Baker and then at Sharpe.

Baker seemed stunned. A fixed smile gripped his features between the enormous sideburns.

Sharpe squinted noncommittally across the room.

"We are at your service, sir," said Claude.

14

Women's Work

Noon, 7 April

Major Johnston Mitchell and his friend Captain Ford listened in astonished disapproval to Lafayette Baker's account of the presence of the Devereux brothers at Hooker's dinner party and worse yet of their dazzling and sudden entry into the inner circle of the War Department. Having heard the whole story twice, they tried to find some way to react.

"We must go to the president with our suspicions!" Ford declared, sure that Lincoln could be relied on to stop Devereux's progress toward his goal, whatever it might be.

Baker laughed nastily, rose from his chair behind the massive desk and paced in front of the open window. He stopped and looked out at the traffic on Pennsylvania Avenue. "Captain Ford," he said. "The President has asked them to the White House to discuss that damned traitor Lee. He wants their view of the man, 'as his neighbors'. We must be careful, very careful," Baker said to no one in particular. He was still looking out the window. "Colonel Sharpe would like nothing better than for me to make a mis.." He remembered that he was not alone and turned to face them. "What will you do?" he asked.

Ford knew that he had the answer for that, and spoke. "We are increasing the number of watchers on all of them and most especially are trying to understand what it is that he is doing with the foreign diplomatic missions here in Washington."

Baker nodded his agreement. "Good. Good! We must find something, soon! Keep me informed, Good Day!"

The hounds were not alone in seeking ways to exploit Devereux's luck. The day he returned from Falmouth, Claude suggested to Hope that he would like to see Major Robert Neville again.

I remember him, the blonde man in the gorgeous uniform, she thought. "Why," she asked.

He looked at her in the particular way which she knew meant he was thinking of dragging her upstairs.

Without changing his expression, he said, "I need to use him, most ruthlessly I am afraid," he said, and with that he reached for her hand.

Thus it was that when Major and Mrs. Robert Neville of the Military Attache's office of Her Britannic Majesty's Embassy accepted an invitation to lunch at Willard's Hotel with Claude and Hope Devereux they were accompanied at a more or less discreet distance by a group of Baker's detectives. These came together in the lobby with the team which had followed the Devereuxs from Alexandria. There followed an awkward and clumsy moment in which the followed pretended not to notice the followers. This passed and the luncheon foursome settled easily into Willard's massive chairs, menu in hand.

Hope Devereux and Simone Neville looked at home in the sumptuous atmosphere of the big hotel's dining room. They seemed at ease with each other although the two ladies had met only three times including the dinner party on Duke Street. Nevertheless, there appeared to be a natural sympathy between them. Hope was the younger by a few years, but a shared taste and many of the same interests cause their conversation to be animated on subjects of mutual concern. Both women were blonde and handsome and a stranger might have thought them kin.

The Willard was a grand hotel. Placed at the corner of 14th Street and Pennsylvania Avenue, it was a gathering place for the capital's prominent, a clubhouse for the powerful. Significant visitors knew that they could not afford to stay elsewhere. The hotel was an unofficial extension of the government's premises. It had been the site of last minute attempts to negotiate a compromise between the freshly seceded Confederate states and President Lincoln. The eclectic opulence of its decor complemented well the silk and lace of the two women.

Major Neville chose this day to come to lunch in uniform. The forest green and black of the 60th Rifles' "walking out" uniform made a somber but dignified picture against the color and activity in the room. Black bone toggles which served for buttons on his jacket scraped against the table's edge occasionally. The sound made Devereux envious of the man and his freedom to be what he was and not what someone else wanted him to seem to be.

While thinking this, Devereux finished telling of his recent encounter with President Lincoln. The two women listened to this with attention, but as he watched, Devereux saw that their concentration began to return to each other. He had been asked by Neville to interrupt their discussion of a recent charity bazaar at the British embassy to tell his story, but the moment had passed. Simone Neville wanted to know if his wife might want to take part in future activities of this nature. The answer was evident in Hope Devereux's expression.

A Negro waiter arrived with coffee.

"I thought it a wonderful story, old man!" Neville said with a smile. "I can't think why these two lovely creatures are not equally fascinated. How often does one meet a head of state in this country?"

The two women paused just long enough to give Neville a blank, slightly annoyed look.

Devereux had taken some pains to cultivate Neville. He had let it be known that the banking necessities of the British Embassy community would receive favorable attention at "Devereux and Wheatley." The attention had been welcomed by the Nevilles and the English couple were on their way to becoming habitues of his parents' house, a situation that Neville clearly relished. *I hope to God that the Indian Policemen had the right name,* Devereux thought. *I would hate to be wasting my time! He thought about her reactions to his planning for this luncheon.* Hope had warmly approved of this luncheon. "Don't you think they are splendid people?" she had asked. "Simone knows everyone in the government and the diplomatic corps." "What about him?" "I don't know what to think about Robert," she had said. "There is something odd, veiled, in him. Do you agree?"

The watcher in the corner sat a little too far from their table for easy eavesdropping. The man was obvious behind a newspaper that seemed to have only two pages with anything of note in them. Devereux considered speaking louder to give him something to report about. He decided against it. That would be too much.

Neville was looking at him strangely.

I've done it again! "I'm terribly sorry," he said, "lost in my recollections of that evening, I'm afraid. What did you say?"

Neville shook his head.

The two women announced their desire to absent themselves to the 'powder room'.

The husbands stood as they departed.

From the corner of his eye Devereux saw the watcher shift a little in his seat to observe the ladies' departure.

"You probably think I have forgotten that you asked me for the names of men I think would make good hunting companions," Devereux said.

Neville stirred in his seat and shook his head again. "I would never presume to think you had forgotten something, Claude. Never.."

Devereux reached into the pocket of his frock coat. A long, narrow, envelope emerged. He slid it across the table, pushing it with the heel of his hand. "There you are. Unfortunately, most of these people live in places difficult to reach at present. Some are debatably behind rebel lines. In other cases it is hard to say. You might want to exercise a certain caution, and hope for better times ahead."

The black waiter returned, coffee pot in hand. He stood staring down at the envelope on the table between them.

Another one?

"Thanks so much," said Neville, picking the thing up by one end, fanning himself with it absentmindedly. "Do you suppose he got all that, Devereux," he asked while waving the envelope at the watcher nearby? "Or would you like me to take it out and read it aloud? Read something aloud at any rate?"

The two women were returning. They rose.

Devereux looked at the Britisher. A close examination was needed to see beyond the well mannered friendly face, to see the outrage inside, to see the calculation. Neville smiled. "Just remember, Claude," he said. "Nothing is free, nothing at all." With that the intelligence officer placed the envelope carefully in an inner pocket and turned to the ladies.

11 April

Corse's Brigade crossed the Blackwater on the road to Suffolk with a minimum of commotion. The 30th Virginia drew the assignment to lead the dawn advance. The 17th's scouting expedition the night of the Devereuxs' dinner party had led Montgomery Corse to believe that the brigade might have to fight for the far bank. Because of this, the nine rifle companies of the 30th gathered in little clumps of silent men in the early morning darkness. Someone on high had arranged for boats. When these arrived, they were an odd collection of flat bottomed river craft. Clusters of boats slid into the inky and menacing water. As the 30th rowed across the river, men pulled in their heads in imitation of a turtle's reaction to threat. They would not have admitted it, but many prayed silently in dread of the volley which they knew might come from the far bank. Three hundred fifty odd soldiers paddled and rowed as hard and as rapidly as they could manage with the strange assortment of implements which they had found for themselves. Higher headquarters had thought of boats, but not of oars.

Not a shot was fired. Boats grounded in the mist. The wave of troops splashed through the shallows, sliding in the mud, coming up over the bank on both sides of the bridge nearly together. The bluecoats were not to be found. Warm campfires and heaps of refuse showed they had been there, but they were gone.

The bridge itself was too massive a structure to have been much damaged by infantrymen intent on leaving. There were a few burnt timbers, but it was not serious. Dawn found the brigade's Pioneer Company busy removing the railroad ties and intertwined *chevaux de frise* with which the former occupants of the spot had blocked the span. To the north of the bridge, a party of engineer troops arrived to drag pontoons from a long train of wagons. Two bridges would be better than one.

All four regiments of the brigade were across by seven.

The day promised heat.

The 17th crossed last. Corse let them detach a small party to search the site of the night action. There was nothing. The disintegrating bodies of animals marked the scene with their smell of death. Captain Fowle's bleak face silenced the soldiers as he led them back to the Suffolk Turnpike. The regiment's trains waited by the bridge as they reached the road. The "H" company commander shook his head in answer to the mute question in the faces of his drivers.

Snake Davis cursed once, vilely.

Fowle lengthened his stride. It would take a lot of walking to catch up with the rest of the brigade's column of march.

8:35 P.M., 14 April
(Duke Street, Alexandria)

Charles Devereux applied an inflexible standard of hospitality to all who entered his door. Guests who abused his generosity, who proved to be offensive or boring might not get a second chance to appear in a better light, or then again they might depending on his judgement of them, or Clotilde's insistence. As paterfamilias, Charles felt a certain obligation to listen patiently to the opinions of his guests no matter how tedious. Nevertheless, at dinner this evening, he found it difficult to keep his mind from straying.

Lieutenant Warren Knowlton Biddle was the reason.

Charles had spent most of an active political life in pursuit of moderate political positions which sought to accommodate both his populist Jacksonian Democrat friends and the ever more nationalist views of his Whig political associates. He was accustomed to the need to accept the differing opinions of others. He was not accustomed to being attacked with such violence by those who broke bread with him in his own house.

Amy Biddle's facial expression had changed over the last hour as she listened to the talk at table. Her features had assumed a more and more fixed look as the meal progressed. She loved her brother's boy, had loved him all his life, had held him in her arms as an infant. He had arrived in the family when she was yet a girl. His presence had always compensated her, to some extent, for her own lack of children. His behavior this evening was a revelation. He had always been a rather withdrawn, perhaps even shy young man. As a youth he had never shown any interest in politics. He was hardly more than a boy now. He looked so strange in Army Blue. She had not imagined that he would be so forceful in his opinions. It was strange. By the time dessert had been cleared from the table, she was hoping for an end so that she could go home and sort through her reaction to what she had begun to think of as his rudeness.

"I am a little unclear as to what additional steps you think we should have taken to prevent the 'current disaster'," Charles said, taking advantage of a momentary pause in the spirited debate between his sons and young Biddle that had gone on throughout dinner. George White stood at Charles' elbow, a silver tray in his white gloved hands.

Charles reached for the creamer from the tray. Both he and the butler had their eyes on the lieutenant.

"Yes, you do know we personally opposed secession, don't you?" Patrick asked.

White reached Claude's side with his tray.

Claude glanced up at him and reached. "Perhaps you think we should have taken more direct action, but we have the disadvantage of a fondness for legal process in this family," he said in explanation of their apparently insufficient activism in 1861.

Warren Biddle look around at them all. "I accept the fact that my critique of the failure of men of substance to take action against the 'slavers' does not apply here. If I have offended. I ask your pardon and that of the ladies."

Charles shook his head slightly, "It is not a serious matter, but I do not believe that you should eliminate the possibility of further change in your opinion. Situations are often more difficult and tangled than an outsider might imagine. In defense of my neighbors and friends I would point out that their constitutional beliefs are, in fact, the older, and in many ways the more original conception of the nature of the Union and the relations between the states and the central government."

"Older, but not better," the young man said. "The time has come when a superior definition of the power of the national sovereignty over the states must be acknowledged."

"Why?" It was Amy Biddle who had spoken.

Her nephew flushed deeply, sensing the displeasure which must lie beneath her question. "The national purpose demands united action. Too long has virtue been frustrated by the selfish obstructionism of petty local factions, and party demagogues."

"You have in mind the Democrats?" Patrick asked.

"Not all. There are many who are loyal."

George White came to Lieutenant Biddle's chair with the tray.

He waited patiently for the young officer to finish speaking. "Milk or sugar, sir?" he asked.

"And who can doubt the immorality of the Rebels when there are evidences everywhere in the South of the sins of the flesh?"

George had bent slightly the better to hear Biddle's wish for improvement of his coffee. His face was not more than a foot from the lieutenant's. There was not a great deal of difference in their complexions.

Hope had been quietly translating the discussion for Madame Helene Jourdain.

"Mon Dieu!" hissed the Frenchwoman.

Claude turned to look at his wife across the snowy field of the tablecloth.

She had grasped Helene Jourdain's wrist. She was looking from George to Claude's father, and at each of the sons.

As he watched, her knuckles began to turn white. *I thought she knew,* he thought. *Surely, I must have told her. Surely, one of us told her. Surely, she would have seen..*

Bill White took a step away from the fireplace behind Warren Biddle's chair.

Clotilde stopped him with a look.

Charles slowly flattened his hands on the linen.

"I'm sorry, sir. I didn't hear which you wanted," George said into Biddle's ear.

"Neither, thank you," the young man replied without looking at him.

An hour later the men were alone with Claude.

"I am surprised that the government is not eager to get a likely fellow like you up to the fighting," he remarked.

"Well, they are not," Biddle said. "My family's associates here all want me to stay in army headquarters."

"You are in the Adjutant General's office?" Claude asked.

Biddle wasn't good at billiards, but he was making an attempt to hold his own in a 'head to head' game with Claude while Colonel Jourdain stood by leaning on a cue, to take on the winner. The third floor billiard room was a snug and masculine place. The hipped roof arched in over the table. Gas lighting gave off a pleasing, hissing illumination. A 'Sennah' patterned oriental rug was centered beneath the table. The three players made a striking group around the green-covered table. Claude and Colonel Jourdain wore evening dress. Biddle was in uniform.

Pretending to be a soldier.. I'd like to stuff the insolent little bastard out one of these windows. What say, Bill? Which leg do you want?

Bill White stood by the side board to refill glasses from the decanters at his elbow.

"Not anymore," Biddle replied to the question about his job. "I moved to General Halleck's personal staff last month." He made his shot.

Claude could see before the cue ball struck that the angles chosen would be useless. He held his tongue.

"I believe that you know this man, Halleck, do you not, Claude," asked the Frenchman.

Squinting down the length of his stick at a combination of balls, Devereux replied, "Yes, met him last week at Falmouth." He turned his head to smile at Biddle. "We share an interest in Victor Hugo."

"What do you find to occupy yourself with in such a large organization," asked Jourdain. "I have always found that junior officers have little of interest to do in general headquarters, other than to carry messages about."

"Lately I have been taking charge of the arrangements for the general-in-chief's correspondence," Biddle said. "But in fact I am mostly occupied with the appointments of army visitors from the field who come to Washington."

"Such as?" Claude demanded, making a banking shot which dropped a ball in a side pocket.

Biddle walked over to Bill and handed him his glass. "Captain Ulric Dahlgren."

"The admiral's son?"

"Yes."

"Why is he of interest?"

"He is the most clear thinking man on political matters of great importance of anyone I know. He is destined for high position, if not in the war, then in the new republic to come."

"Does he share the ideas that you championed at dinner?" Jourdain asked.

"Yes! We have had many discussions. I think he will someday be president."

I saw this paragon of Puritan zeal last week. He must be at least 25 years old.

"These new principles for governing your country are not well understood in Paris," Jourdain said. "I should hear more of this, perhaps we.."

"May I invite you to our mess for lunch next week?"

"But, of course!" responded the military attache of the French Empire. "Lunch is what I do for a living these days. General Halleck will not object?"

"Of course not!" Claude interrupted. "You and he can have a splendid talk about 'Les Miserables'."

♦   ♦   ♦

Devereux enjoyed watching his wife brush her hair. Seated at the delicate "coiffeuse" with its inlaid ebony edges and arched, mirror she worked the brush through her golden locks. The silver brush shone in the light of the table lamp on the stand beside her. The shadows cast by her moving arms danced on the walls. Blue flocked wall paper had been chosen to show her coloring to perfection. In the private world of her bedroom she seemed truly a queen. He lay sprawled on her bed, head on the massed pillows, slippered feet pointed at her back. His jacket and waistcoat were on the boudoir chair where he had dropped them.

She looked at him in the glass. "Darling, don't encourage Amy," she said. "She is a very lonely woman. I feel sympathy for her, but not enough to put up with having to witness her wistful yearnings for you."

He deposited the small glass of apple brandy from which he had been sipping on her night table. "What did you think of the nephew?"

She turned to face him. "He has little sense, and less manners, although he does appear to admire me."

"Yes, he does, damn him! The Biddle taste for the Devereuxs is evidently widespread."

"Amy apologized for his bad behavior," she told him. She was still looking at him in the mirror. "Vicky and I sewed with Mrs. Slough and Elizabeth Braithwaite yesterday. Women are sometimes very talkative. Sometimes they are unhappy and want to tell their friends things to see if the friends understand them the same way they do themselves. Mrs. Slough is afraid that her husband is not thought enough of a radical on slavery. She's afraid that several Republican congressmen are attempting to turn Stanton against General Slough by saying that he is too easy with us here. She wanted to talk about army politics. I think it was to see if we would agree that these things are often exaggerated in importance."

He waited for her story, knowing there must be more.

Her eyebrows narrowed as she returned his look. "You do want to know, don't you?"

He could see that his surprised silence was irritating her. "Of course I do, dear. What is it?"

"Mrs. Slough told us that Stanton and Lincoln are already impatient with General Hooker and seeking a replacement."

"Do they have someone in mind?"

She looked at him again, suspicious that he might be humoring her. "They have several generals in mind as possibilities." She saw now that he really wanted to hear. "There is someone named Grant, from the West? I think I have seen his name in the newspapers."

He sat up on the bed. "Anyone else?"

Now she knew he truly wanted her help. Happiness surged through her that she could be part of something so important to him. "Reynolds. Major General Reynolds, a corps commander in Hooker's army, a man from Pennsylvania. General Slough thinks he is the most probable choice."

"My God! A truly valuable friend, Mrs. Slough, I hope you are planning to continue your association with her."

She nodded, looking at him seriously. "There's more. Elizabeth is vexed that Frederick has been gone so much the last month. General Hooker's army will march south just before the end of the month. Elizabeth said that her husband told her that the military railroad is hauling forward rations for 130,000 men and placing them in 'depots'." She looked at him inquiringly, puzzled by the word.

"Storage places."

She was satisfied with that. "Elizabeth also said that Frederick has had to visit these 'depots', and that this has caused him to spend much time at Falmouth and near Rappahannock Station. She is terribly unhappy with his absences. He was on one of these trips when he went to Falmouth with you."

He rose from the bed to cross the room and held her head in his hands and kissed her.. "You are a treasure," he said. "Patrick has wrung out the details of Hooker's Information Bureau and now this! That fool Biddle told Edouard at billiards that the cavalry began to move yesterday in 'something big'."

"Oh yes!" she cried out. It came now in a rush. "Frederick told Elizabeth that vast amounts of horse feed were needed near Rappahannock Station because the whole cavalry corps would be gone for "a couple of weeks."

He stood quietly for a moment.

"What will you do," she asked?

"I will send a message to our friends. I will send the message and pray that it arrives in time. Thank you, my dear."

"I should have been told about George White, all the Whites," she said sadly. "You all owed me that. I feel like such a fool. Why did none of you tell me? I thought he was.."

"Uncle George? Yes. We did owe you that. I always assumed that you understood. We simply do not talk about it. Did you not find us odd? Surely you guessed?"

She focused on his face. "Yes, I must have. It made everything too hard to understand then, but now I see things differently, and it makes perfect sense. They could not be anywhere else, could they?"

"No. My darling," he whispered to her. "It would not be bearable to think of them somewhere else."

15

Paris

Thursday, 16 April

There were not many patrons in the District of Columbia Main Post Office at eight o'clock of a Thursday morning. The white people present paid Bill White no mind at all and the few colored folk merely glanced at him. Bill dropped the envelope in the slot provided under the words "United States Mail." He tapped the metal surface to make sure the letter wasn't hanging and then left, going out the front door and walking slowly away. He turned right at the first corner, and went down Seventh Street. A block away he paused at the curb for several men on horseback to pass in a cross street and then strode on toward Pennsylvania Avenue.

A heavy set, white haired postal clerk stood behind the marble counter surrounded by an ornate grating. He seemed to be installed in the middle of a picture framed in bronze. The curlicues and tendrils of reddish brown metal surrounded him entirely. He lifted his head to greet two odd men who appeared before him.

There were a tall pale one and a short, darker one. The cheap suits and waistcoats were a sort of uniform for their kind. The tall one held open his coat so that the post office man might see the badge. "Open up," he said, pointing to the slot in the metal grating into which Bill had placed his letter. "We want the mail bag just behind this slot."

The clerk leaned forward to better see the lettering on the shield.

"Get the door open, man. We want that bag."

Slowly, more slowly than the situation might require, the clerk walked to one side of the window and rotated a butterfly latch to admit them. They brushed by him and halted behind the bronze plaque and its opening. The bag was bloated with mail.

"Don't you empty these things at the end of the day?"

"Yes, yes." The clerk appeared only now to have noticed the fullness of the bag. "I was off yest'iddy, must be Herbert Rasmussen was on. Must be. He's a little forgetful these days."

In the time of the great war the cryptanalytic capability of the United States government largely resided in three young men who labored in the central War Department telegraph office on 17th Street Northwest. Two of them were present when the mail bag was brought in. It soon lay deflated in a corner of the room.

Major Mitchell had arrived with the bag. He stood at a window with his back to the work table. The White House was across the street. The view from the third floor window was not reassuring to him. He was disturbed by the look of normality that the street below conveyed. *It looks*, he thought, *as if all were well, as if we were yet one country, one people, as though nothing had changed. I must not think that. We are one people!*

"Nothing, not a damned thing." Captain Ford said. He stood by the table with the two telegraphers. The white and brown detritus of the contents of the ravaged mail bag littered the tabletop and floor.

"Are you certain there was something, something secret that was to be communicated?" one of the telegraphers asked.

"We brought it to you directly from the Post Office because we were sure there would be treasonous communication among the letters," Ford said.

Mitchell spoke from the window. "The man does not have an extensive correspondence. If he mailed something, it was for his master." He held up a hand. "Excuse me, I meant for his employer. There is a Post Office in Alexandria. Why would he have come ten miles to mail a letter?"

"Very well, sir," said the chief telegrapher, "then I suggest that there is another explanation for our inability to find some significant message in all this." He waved an arm at the litter. "That would be?" asked Mitchell.

"Invisible ink."

"Have you seen that before?" Ford asked.

"Just in the last few months," added the second telegrapher. "We found mention of this in a British embassy telegram from Canada. There was a reference to their belief that the Rebels would soon begin to use such a practice. Their embassy here is very active in information gathering." He looked embarrassed to be talking so much.

How very young they are, Mitchell thought.

"But then, you would know that," continued the telegrapher, making an unwarranted assumption. "A week later we received a captured courier pouch from Colonel Sharpe. He wrote that there was something wrong with it. Nothing in the pouch meant anything of note, and there were no ciphers. It was like this actually."

"And it was?" asked Ford.

"Invisible ink, urine, actually, was the liquid used. There are other possibilities, of course, blood, lemon, etc."

"Where did you learn to read 'secret ink', Mister Bates?" asked Mitchell.

"We found a chemist at the Smithsonian Institution who has investigated this subject as a sideline for some time."

"Of course," said Ford. The sarcasm in his voice made the telegraphers visibly uneasy. He had the field soldier's disdain for scholars as a class. He found them to be "idle" and was always surprised and a little chagrined at their occasional usefulness.

Mitchell was thoughtful. "How do you come by British embassy telegrams, Mister Chandler?" He spoke now to the more senior of the telegraphers, Frederick Chandler.

Chandler hesitated a moment.

"Come now, sir!" said Mitchell. "Surely we are colleagues?"

Chandler and Bates considered the matter momentarily and decided that must be so. "The Telegraph Cable Company provides them to us."

"Ah! How helpful. I would suppose they also provide the telegrams of other embassies?"

The man smiled. "Yes, the Post Office helps us with, other correspondence."

"I am happy you have told us this, gentlemen. We did not know they were so helpful. It will be so useful in the future. Did it occur to you that it might be a good idea to share this source of information with the Detective Bureau?"

An awkward silence resulted. *You little sneaks!* Ford thought. "The British message about the invisible ink," he asked. "Where was it coming from?"

"Toronto. It seemed strange to us. How would the British government in Toronto know that the Rebels would use such a method?"

"How indeed?" murmured Mitchell.

1:30 A.M., Sunday, 19 April (Paris, Virginia)

The 2nd New York Cavalry Regiment lived by its wits in an unending game of hide and seek played with the lives of real people as stakes. The hauntingly beautiful fields, hills, villages and stone walls of Fauquier, Loudon and Clark counties were the playing field upon which this contest was waged. It was a game they had little chance of winning. Their opponents were the Southern guerillas who infested all the Virginia counties west of Washington. The guerillas were sprung from this ground and they had the unwavering support of the vast majority of people there. The regiment had learned to live with the unending, unbending hostility of the inhabitants, had come to long for the occasional return to friendlier areas close to Washington. These periods of respite were terribly needed to recharge the well of fortitude.

The Rebel guerrillas were everywhere. Several different bands roamed the area. Elijah White's 35th Virginia Cavalry Battalion sometimes returned to Loudon from its service with Jeb Stuart's division. Harry Gilmor frequently brought his mixed force of Marylanders and Northern Virginians into the Valley of Virginia.

Hanse McNeill's mountaineers raided from what the Federal government claimed was the new state of West Virginia with some regularity against Union Army supply trains. These organizations came and went. They were present in the countryside as circumstances required, but Mosby's men, the 43rd Battalion of Virginia Cavalry, were always there. From eastern Fairfax County to Fisher's Hill in the Valley they were an ever present menace to the U.S. Army and its friends. For a federal horse soldier of the 2nd New York, it was largely beside the point that the actual front line between the armies lay far to the south. For them the war was a matter of midnight raids and sudden, merciless ambush. Into this lovely countryside so stained with death and war Isaac Smoot rode to deliver Claude Devereux's message of warning for General Lee.

◆　　　◆　　　◆

In the quiet of the night, the cavalry captain sat his mount on the long grassy slope above the village. "D" Company, 2nd New York lounged in their saddles behind him. The column gave off its own restless music. Saddle leather creaked, horses snuffled in the darkness, as whispering passed from man to man.

The village was small, two streets in all. They crossed in a 'T' at the far end. There were perhaps twenty-five houses. The inn stood at the crossroad, on the right from the Union officer's point of view. The glow of candle light made it easy to locate the wooden buildings. "D" Company had been there before. This little town lay squarely in the center of the company's normal patrol area.

The officer's horse began to shift nervously between his legs. The big, bay gelding shook his head. He raised first one forefoot and then the other. The horseman removed a gauntlet to touch the animal's shoulder. He buried his fingers in the hair, kneading the muscle beneath, stroking. The animal quietened.

This operation had been well thought out. The approach march had been made in darkness. Ten miles of cross country movement had ensured the probability of an undetected arrival at the target of the night's activity. Small parties of troopers now occupied positions from which they could block flight from the village along the two roads that led away from the far end.

Most Union Army officers were citizen neophytes, new to the trade of soldiering. In this second year of war they were fast becoming professionals. Marco Aurelio Farinelli, Captain, US Volunteers, commanding "D" Company, 2nd New York did not fit this description. This was his sixth year of combat. He was an old man in a young body, a foreign volunteer come to America just for the war, a professional.

His foreignness was thought to explain much about him. His men had come to watch for the inexplicable in his behavior and to recognize and respect in him dark silences that should not be interrupted. As their time together passed and his command of English improved they found that he sometimes could be made to speak to them of other places and other wars, of Garibaldi and Solferino, of the long struggle for Italian unity and constitutional government. He was in many ways a puzzle to them. Some of the men were troubled by his lack of animosity toward the Rebels. He generally shrugged off their expressions of anger toward their enemies. "Good fighters. They take care of horses, better than you. They are good fighters," typified his comments. The slightly built, olive skinned man always gave the same reply when asked why he had crossed the ocean to participate in this struggle, "For the Republic," he would say, and walk away.

Captain Farinelli sat contemplating the village. *There is much more light than there should be at this time of night*, he thought and turned in the saddle to look back at the men. Just behind him his guidon bearer held the wooden staff in his gloved hand. The red and white swallow tailed pennant hung limp along the top of the shaft. The butt end fit tightly in the socket attached to his stirrup.

Private Williams, the bugler, was next to the guidon bearer. He clutched his instrument against a thigh, waiting.

Farinelli looked for a second at the officer beside him, a lieutenant. This man had brought word to regimental headquarters in Leesburg of a suspected spy trailed out of the Washington defenses into this western end of Fauquier County. It was Forbes Bradshaw, a long way from his comfortable post at Fairfax Court House.

The colonel commanding the 2nd New York knew John Mosby well, knew his penchant for late night conferences in distant hamlets. His decision came easily. There would be four raids, simultaneously. Farinelli would lead the attack most likely to strike home.

The Winchester road ran over the Blue Ridge through Ashby's Gap behind and to the left of the raiding party's position. A wagon, unaccountably, improbably, came over the crest of the gap. It rumbled down the dirt road toward the village. The clatter of the wheels on the stony surface grew steadily. Farinelli saw the moment of opportunity. The noise of the wagon would cover that of his attack. He rose in his stirrups, and rotating an arm to the front, ended the signal to advance with his gloved hand pointing at the end of the village's main street. He squeezed the horse. The willing beast surged forward. He felt the barrel of the horse fill. The air began to flow past his face. Behind him hooves thudded on meadow grass.

The wagon was almost abreast of the column. It rattled on down the road.

"D" Company gathered momentum and speed. Farinelli drew his saber, carrying it across his torso.

The horse was at a canter.

The open, near end of the short street materialized. *200 yards!*

Someone to his left rear fired a round. It sounded like a rifle. *The wagon!*

The charge in 'column of fours' pounded toward the beckoning street. *100 yards!*

Firing began in the small, white frame buildings on both sides of the street.

Farinelli extended his saber to the front, rotating the elbow to lock his arm. He looked back, then forward. *50 yards!* "Bugler! Sound the Charge!" he cried.

The hiss of bullets and the report of the guns punctuated the first notes of the call. Houses flashed by to left and right. Doors began to open. The far end of the street grew larger and larger. The horse was flat out in a gallop.

A man in dark clothes carrying a weapon ran from a building. He leapt for a horse's back pulling the animal's head around to flee the thunder of the charge.

The gelding's speed carried the Italian soldier past the fugitive before the other horse could gain its stride. As they passed, the downward pointing tip of the cavalryman's saber entered the back of the man's neck. The momentum and weight of the gelding were transferred through the medium of Farinelli's body and locked arm. A foot of the sword ran through the man's neck before the changing angle created by the horse's passage ripped the blade out the side of the throat. Ahead of him, he saw activity around the old inn. It looked like the swarming of wasps from a disturbed nest. Soldiers, and men who ought to be soldiers, poured from the various openings of the building. A small, slight man in grey uniform wearing a flat hat dashed out of a side alley. His mount had been hidden behind the inn. He was headed for the Left-hand choice of the two roads out of town.

Close behind him were two more riders. One was a near giant, mounted on a horse which would have been absurdly large for a smaller man. His blue trousers and short, grey jacket were striking. The second was in civilian clothes. As they made for the crossroads three of Farinelli's men closed on them. The group of six met in a swirling melee. Pistols banged. Sabers swung. One of the Federal cavalrymen crashed to the ground. Around the inn, fighting continued. Farinelli cut at a man attempting to free a horse from the bucking, plunging line of animals tied to stone posts in front of the structure. His blade glanced off the head, laying it open to the bone. From the corner of his eye he saw a civilian step into an open door in the house next to the inn.

In his hands there was a shotgun.

Horse pistols roared from the street. The man with the shotgun was knocked backward into the room behind him.

A woman screamed.

Farinelli heard shots outside of town. *Fugitives striking the outposts.*

Quiet descended on the crossroads. The doors and windows of the inn stood open. Curtains blew in and out.

A woman wailed beside the body of the much shot civilian.

The captain dismounted. Part of the company spread out to secure the town. The rest began to search the surrounding houses. "We lost one man, sir," the company First Sergeant reported. "The townspeople have nothing to say of course," he continued. "There're three enemy dead, the man in the door there, the one you killed, and one other."

"Where?"

"Behind the inn, Schmitt shot him as he was making his run with the other three. Sir.."

"Yes?"

"The men all think the little one, all in grey, was Mosby himself."

Farinelli sighed. "That may be."

"Jurgens says he cut the bearded one with his saber in the fight over there." The sergeant pointed to the middle of the crossroads where John Mosby and his two companions had struggled with the Union cavalrymen.

"Captain! Captain!"

The officer from the District of Columbia cavalry stood over the dead enemy trooper behind the inn.

"Yes, Lieutenant Bradshaw. What you want?" They stood together over the body.

"I know this man," Bradshaw said. "It isn't the one we were looking for, but the last time I saw this man he was with the spy, Smoot."

"His name?"

"I don't remember, but it will come to me. He had this in his hand." Bradshaw held out a crumpled sheet of paper.

Farinelli did not take it. It had the rebel guerilla's blood on it. The mess that had been his face was more than he wished to deal with just now. He turned and walked to the street. His men were all out of the houses now. The doors and windows had returned to their tightly shuttered, silent state.

There were three dead horses in the street. He walked to the bay gelding. The big troop horse stood expectantly in the space in front of the inn. A shallow, freely bleeding cut ran across its shoulder. Farinelli paused for a minute to look at the wound. The massive head turned to nuzzle him.

"Glori'Iddio, mi' amico" he murmured. "Viviamo ancora."

16

At Wits End

8:32 A.M., Sunday, 19 April
(Before Suffolk)

The long march of Longstreet's force finally came to an end as the Confederate force closed on the city of Suffolk. The 17th Virginia Regiment occupied the extreme right of the line of encirclement formed by Hood's and Pickett's divisions. All in all, ten thousand men in grey stood before the Union occupied Virginia city. The Dismal Swamp defined the right flank. A strange, marshy crossroads aptly named The White Swamp bounded the 17th's left. The other units of Corse's Brigade stretched out to the left beyond the crossroads. Somewhere past them was the rest of the division. The idea that all the rest of Longstreet's Corps lay even farther to the west and north, in a vast incurving arc coiled about the city was too remote to deal with.

The Yankee army which they had trapped in Suffolk was not behaving properly. For three consecutive days they lashed out in well run, heavily supported attacks. The Regular Army troops which The Gypsies had met on the Blackwater were prominent in all of them. The first of these morning assaults had been uncommonly unpleasant. The blue attack had come out of the dawn mist without a sound. Major Simpson was commanding the regiment in Herbert's absence. He watched in dismay as the enemy skirmish line rolled across the 17th's pickets like a breaking wave. Half the men in the main position behind the picket line had still been asleep. They lost most of their meager creature comforts in a scramble to get back half a mile to a woodline that could be held against the cheering Federals. The sight of a number of their comrades being marched away under guard from the overrun picket line added to their unhappiness. To make things worse, they soon knew that the advancing Union infantry was not alone. Artillery batteries and squadrons of neatly attired and beautifully mounted cavalry emerged from the broken, wooded country to the front. The weight of the force moving upon them had seemed more than they could hope to resist. In the ranks, the men scrabbled in the soft ground with shovels, mess tins, boards from ammunition boxes. They knew they could give up no more ground. It was stand or run.

Major General George Pickett arrived at the right flank in midmorning. With him were the 57th and 3rd Virginia Regiments. He appeared unexpectedly, almost mysteriously in their midst. He was cheery as always, a dapper dandy of a man with curling ringlets. "Simpson, I am here!" he announced. "You did not think we would allow you to have all this to yourselves, did you? Ah! Here they come again!" The general officer commanding had then taken it upon himself to organize and lead a counterattack which cleared the lost ground. He left the field at sundown promising to return in the morning.

3:00 P.M.
(National Detective Bureau Hqs., Washington)

Mitchell and Ford rose to their feet in a display of respect for the entrance of their commanding officer.

"Who's that sitting out there?" Baker demanded after he reached his desk.

"That is John Babcock," said Mitchell. "He works for Colonel Sharpe."

Baker's eyes shifted from Mitchell to the door. "He's a civilian?"

"Yes, Colonel. He prefers to remain a civilian. He's Sharpe's closest associate"

Baker snorted in disbelief. He shook his heavily whiskered head. "One might expect some such nonsense from Sharpe. What does he want?" He kept looking back at the door as though he might go examine Babcock again.

"They have heard from their most important agent in Richmond," Ford reported. "He told them that he has lost the informant from whom they knew of Hannibal."

"How?"

"The Confederate cabinet office in which he worked conducted an investigation. One day, he simply stopped arriving for meetings with Sharpe's agent. The agent is terrified. He expects to be arrested any day." Ford paused.

"What does Babcock want?" Baker repeated.

Ford stared at Baker. *Don't you care at all about the war?* he thought. *Don't you want to know the truth? Can you think of nothing but yourself?*

Mitchell broke in, afraid from the look on Ford's face that something irreparable was about to happen. "You know what Sharpe wants. He reasons that something we did with the information he gave us caused this. He thinks you have found Hannibal."

Baker's face took on an air of guarded assurance. "But, we have not found Hannibal. We have no idea how the Rebel police may have gotten onto Sharpe's man. It is no problem of ours!"

The morning sunlight seemed too clear for this room.

Ford cleared his throat. "There was the matter of Terence Hennessey."

"What of him! A drunken Irishman! Cut in a barroom fight. It proves nothing."

"He died trying to tell the police something about Hannibal," Ford said.

Baker was temporarily without a reply.

Mitchell reached across two feet of space to take a brown folder secured with red ribbon from under Ford's only arm. As he untied the ribbon of the folder, Mitchell felt the hush in the room deepen. He glanced at Baker.

The secret service chief was not looking at Mitchell. His eyes were still fixed on the door, behind which sat his rival's emissary.

From the edge of his field of vision Mitchell glimpsed Ford. The young officer had gone pale. He was rubbing his stump with his remaining hand. The empty blue sleeve showed how pitifully short was the remnant of the arm.

Mitchell withdrew the two pieces of paper from the folder and put them on the table.

Baker looked down. "What's this?"

"These are two letters which have relevance to our work. One of them is from a woman resident here in Washington. It is addressed to her female cousin in the town of Salisbury, Maryland. The other letter, the wrinkled one, is the message of a doctor in Warrenton, Virginia to his brother in Harrisburg, Pennsylvania.

Baker lifted his eyebrows in impatient expectation.

Mitchell extracted a box of matches from a pocket, struck one, and holding one of the letters passed the match rapidly back and forth just behind it. Block printed letters appeared in brown rows between the lines of handwritten text.

Baker took the paper from him. "Code.."

Mitchell nodded.

"Are they both the same?"

"Yes. The ciphered text is the same, and written in identical ink."

"What of these documents themselves?" Baker asked.

"None of the four people mentioned in the letters exists so far as we can tell. The letter from the woman was actually mailed. The postmaster in Salisbury must be part of this …"

"We can deal with him," Baker muttered.

"The crumpled one was recovered in a cavalry raid in western Fauquier County," Mitchell said. "I don't believe it was ever intended that it should be mailed."

Baker now had both letters in his hands. He inspected each thoroughly. "This is a woman's hand."

Mitchell agreed.

"And the other is written by someone with bigger fingers and less grace," Baker said. "What about the paper?"

"No watermark," Ford said. "They are also made by two different companies in New York."

Baker harrumphed again.

The three officers surrounded the table upon which lay the evidence of treason.

"You have had the cipher solved?" Baker finally asked.

"The telegraph office people went through it quite effortlessly," Mitchell said. "It's in the standard Rebel code system, the one they decipher so easily."

"And?"

Mitchell fished another sheet of paper from the brown folder and handed it across.

"God damn it!" swore Baker after he had read both.

"Is it accurate?" Ford asked anxiously. "We have no way of knowing."

Baker looked thoughtful. "It isn't complete, thank God, but it would be very helpful to Lee. Very helpful." Baker continued to turn the paper over in his hands, looking first at the back and then the front. "This man knows a good deal about our friend Sharpe and his methods."

"Clearly, that is true," Mitchell agreed.

"This means that he may have penetrated the inner circle of Colonel Sharpe's office."

"Perhaps," said Mitchell reluctantly.

Baker looked from one to the other. "I am sure there is more you wish to tell me about these letters."

"The one addressed to Salisbury was mailed by Devereux's Negro," Mitchell said.

"And the other?"

"A team from here and the Fairfax Court House provost-marshal trailed Devereux's coachman, Smoot, into the guerilla country near the Blue Ridge several days ago. We have them all under observation," Mitchell offered as an explanation.

Baker appeared preoccupied and frustrated. "Yes! Yes!" he said.

"They lost him there," Mitchell continued. "The cavalry garrison in Leesburg went into several places to search for him. This was found on the body of a dead Confederate partisan after a fight in one of these operations."

"This was when?"

"Last night."

Baker seemed pleased at their enterprise. "You haven't wasted any time. That's good! It wasn't found on Devereux's coachman?"

"No," said Ford, "but the dead man was a known associate of his. Lieutenant Bradshaw, from Fairfax, who was present, reports that he thinks he saw Smoot during the fight, but he isn't sure."

Ford cleared his throat. "Sir, we did not actually catch White, the Negro, with the letter. Our men saw him mail something. We confiscated the bag. A search showed the letter to Maryland to be among the contents."

Baker thought about that for a minute. "How many pieces of mail in the bag, Captain Ford?"

Ford's pallor was disappearing. His ears took on a rosy tint. He looked confused. He cleared his throat yet again. "Two hundred and fifty-two."

"Was there any other mail that could have been from the black?"

Ford looked as though he might become ill.

"Captain Ford?" insisted Baker.

Mitchell watched his young friend closely.

"There were two letters, or rather notes from men who are nearly illiterate. They were to women, women not their wives."

"Obscene?" Baker asked.

"Yes."

"He mailed this where?"

"Here," Mitchell answered.

Baker threw up his hands. "Well, there you have an explanation for that! He would be recognized in Alexandria. What is it that you gentlemen wish to do?"

Ford seemed beyond speech.

"We want to arrest Devereux," Mitchell said.

"Out of the question! This city is filled with Southerners and enemy spies. Any mail bag you picked would have some treasonous communication in it. A perfectly reasonable explanation for the mailed letter is that this nigger can't keep his pants done up, a notable failing of his race. In the case of Devereux's coachman, you have nothing at all! As I remember the file on him, he is from Fauquier County. How do you know that he was not simply going home to visit family? You did not obtain this," he gestured at the letters, "from him. Bradshaw is a most unreliable officer. We should do something about him. You gentlemen are going to get me into a lot of trouble! This man Devereux is a friend of General Halleck, and, others. You will have to come up with better information than this before I will authorize his arrest! After all, there is such a thing as a tradition of judicial fairness in this country."

They were speechless.

Ford began to speak, then caught a glimpse of Mitchell's stony expression and said nothing.

Baker continued. "Be sure you say nothing of this to this man waiting outside! What's his name?"

"Babcock," Mitchell answered.

"Nothing at all. It is clear to me that Colonel Sharpe has failed to keep enemy infiltration from his staff. I will have to speak to Secretary Stanton of this. Nothing at all, do you hear me? Captain Ford, do you hear me?"

Ford nodded. "What shall we do with him, sir?" he asked.

"Take him to dinner! Take him to the Willard. Use our confidential funds. Take care of it! Good night."

"Shall we continue with the Devereux investigation?" Mitchell demanded.

Baker looked hard at him for a second. "Yes, of course. Use your judgement. Bring me whatever you develop, before you act on it."

Monday, 20 April

"But, damn him!" Captain Ford cried aloud. "How can he think that such a falsehood can stand? Devereux is so palpably guilty that the truth is bound to come out in the end!"

Mitchell held his young friend in a regard at once gloomy and affectionate. "Speak more softly" he said. "Someone may hear you. But why, why do you think that it is bound to come out?"

Ford sighed. He placed his hand on his knee and looked at the small hairs and wrinkles on the back. "Because we are not going to let go!"

"The more interesting question," Mitchell commented "is how much our beloved colonel actually has managed to believe of what he told us yesterday."

"You think he does?"

"Certainly, to some degree. Men never wish to be on the side of evil. They always try to persuade themselves otherwise. He is no different."

"Your wisdom amazes me Mitchell," Ford said with a smile. "But, he's destroying our organization! What do you think Colonel Sharpe will give us from now on?"

Mitchell held up a thumb and forefinger linked in the perfect circle of negation. "Tell me about the news from Paris," he asked. "It's a pity we didn't have this yesterday."

Ford grimaced in agreement. "The consular officer involved, a man named Cole, writes that Devereux is a well-known figure in Parisian society. His inquiry at their bank offices, which are near the 'bourse' produced a veritable biographic brief on the subject of our friend Claude. This was from the manager, who it seems is a relative of some sort on the mother's side. When Cole, the consul, pressed Monsieur Berthier of Devereux and Wheatley for some statement of the last time he had seen his cousin, the man became rather vague. Cole writes that he never, in fact, answered the question. On the subject of the Negro, White, Berthier had nothing at all to say other than that he knew him. And that was that."

Mitchell gestured impatiently. "Go on! Please go on."

The young man continued. "The evasiveness present in that conversation caused Cole to seek others who might know him. He found many."

Mitchell was visibly crushed.

"But those that he discovered fell into two groups." said Ford. "The first was made up of people who evidently knew our man, Claude, but were determined not to speak of him, and a second group who were puzzled as to why the embassy of the United States would be asking after him. The most extreme of these was an elderly uncle who wished to know if this meant that we were all friends again."

"What else did he say?"

"Someone took him away after that."

"And what does Consul Cole think of all this?"

"He believes that Devereux has recently been in France, but that there is something irregular about that fact, something hidden." Ford rubbed his eyes with his hand. "It is unfortunate," he went on. "that we do not have a portrait of Devereux to send to Cole for use in his investigation."

"Do you mean something like a miniature painting?"

"Or a Daguerreotype. It would be quite helpful I'm sure."

Mitchell considered this, then shrugged eloquently. "What will Cole do now?" he asked.

"Continue. He will continue. The ambassador has now taken an interest in the matter. They intend to press the search for Claude across the length and breadth of France."

Mitchell nodded and then said, "I'll tell you what we will do, Ford. We will search for a break in this man's armor. There must be one, and when we find it we will bore right in through that hole!"

17

Lee

Tuesday, 21 April

Army of Northern Virginia headquarters was in an elm and oak grove which surrounded a crossroads in the forest of the Wilderness west of Fredericksburg. The white tents stood back away from the road in the hope of avoiding the worst of the dust and mud. Horses stood in patient lines under the trees waiting for they knew not what.

A quarter mile from the crossroads, Major John Mosby led his little group through the shimmering sunlight on the forest track. They had come almost to the end of their long and desperate journey. He and his companions had slept little in the past days. In the cool of an April morning, they walked their weary mounts slowly in single file on the red dirt road. The trip had been hard. The manner of its beginning had set the pattern. After the fight in Paris, the riders had not dared to halt to count their surviving comrades until they had broken through Farinelli's outposts and reached a friend's farm some miles down the dirt road to the south. Isaac Smoot's wound was not properly dressed until they reached the town of Culpeper. He had not really noticed the blow at the moment of its impact in the melee in front of the inn. The cavalry saber's edge had seemed blunt. The impact had nearly unhorsed him, but there had been no feeling of hurt, none at all. In the excitement of the escape he had felt nothing but an ache above his ear. It was only later, standing in the farm yard, in the dark, that he felt the warm wet soaking through his shirt. A match's light revealed a deep gash running from his left ear to the angle of his jaw.

"It's beginning to clot," a familiar voice told him. "The flow will stop soon. Don't laugh too much, Isaac, it will only bleed more." The thin faced little man with the wolf eyes stood behind the soldier with the match. The friendly grin habitually seen on this face seemed to war with the chill of the eyes. John Mosby turned away to remount his horse.

They rode on, down to the Rappahannock River through the rolling, broken ground of the Piedmont. Kelly's Ford or any of the other major shallows were certain to be outposted. They would not cross there. Mosby's partisans avoided such places unless they had some reason to test the resolve and strength of Northern cavalry. They swam their horses across the river in a sheltered spot known only to men who had once been boys in the neighborhood.

Smoot's wound then began to bleed again, torn open by the violent motion of his horse as the beast tried to scramble up the far bank. He began to roll in the saddle, weakened by the trauma of his wound and loss of blood. The giant Lieutenant Tom Morgan held Smoot's arm across the gap between their horses. "John!" he yelled at Mosby. "You have to stop. I have to bind up his face again." The party had emerged from the river and raced south a quarter mile before he had felt it was safe to call out.

Mosby reined in and walked his horse back to see for himself.

Light was beginning to brighten the eastern sky.

"You feeling poorly, Isaac? he asked. "Your face surely needs some repair. I've been planning to get you sewed up as soon as we can reach a surgeon. Are you going to be all right that long?"

Smoot considered Major John Mosby in the gathering morning twilight. *You bastard.. You'd leave me in a minute if you could,* he thought.

Tom Morgan was busy making another bandage out of a spare shirt.

"I'm all right, sir," Smoot replied. "Did you see Pierce fall?"

Mosby looked away at the wood line to their left. "There are only so many men like Pierce Butler, Isaac. He was on the ground as we broke out into the street in front of the inn. That was quite a thing the way they charged right down that street in the middle of the night.. They are learning." He looked back at Smoot. "We will miss him, won't we?"

Morgan had finished.

They moved on.

An army doctor in Culpeper cursed and waved a fist at them when he saw Smoot's face. "He could have bled to death, you damned fool!" he told Mosby. "He might yet die of inflammation. Why didn't you leave him to be taken prisoner? They don't kill prisoners." They waited impassively for him to calm down and sew up the damage. Then they rode on, ignoring his protests and futile threats of court-martial charges against Mosby.

They found Stuart's cavalry present in ever greater numbers as they rode east along the Fredericksburg turnpike. General Stuart himself they came upon as he sat his horse alongside the road, watching one of the South Carolina cavalry regiments from Wade Hampton's brigade flush Union sharpshooters from a wood near Bailey's Tavern. It made a striking tableau. Stuart lolled in the saddle aboard his favorite charger, "Virginia," his stocky body looking so comfortable in the saddle that he and the horse gave the impression of unity of purpose. His features were hard to see behind the famous mustaches and red beard, but his high boots and feathered hat made him instantly recognizable. The cavalry division staff surrounded their chief, chatting among themselves and watching the action while Brigadier General Hampton walked his mount back and forth nearby, listening to the scattered shots from the hardwood forest. Dismounted butternut troopers could occasionally be glimpsed among the trees across the turnpike.

Mosby and Stuart conferred.

Smoot inspected Stuart minutely while they talked. He watched as the general's attention wandered back and forth among the sounds of fighting, Mosby's story and Hampton's pacing. *When he gets to be my age, he'll be fat,* Smoot thought.

As if he had heard the thought, Stuart glanced up and caught Smoot's eyes. He nodded, evidently in acknowledgment of Mosby's account.

A soldier with a banjo slung across his back sidled his mount up to Smoot. "How're you today?" he asked.

Smoot thought this a strangely inapplicable pleasantry considering his present appearance.

"My name is Sweeney," the man continued.

"What's going on over there?" Tom Morgan asked, meaning the fight across the road.

"The Yank cavalry has been pushing hard with its scouts all along the upper fords for the last few days," Sweeney said. "They come across last night again. It's on'y a couple a miles to the river from here, don't you know?"

Morgan and Smoot looked at each other after a moment. *Just wait a few days, banjo-man. You'll have all the Yanks you want,* Smoot thought.

Mosby waved at them to come forward. They rode past Stuart's little command party.

The cavalry leader followed Smoot with his gaze, seemed about to say something.

A riderless horse came out of the wood and ran through the clearing.

Stuart pulled his mount around to speak to Hampton.

The road ran on like a tunnel through the woods.

Robert Edward Lee was shorter than Smoot had imagined. His torso was long, but the legs were not. His beautiful grey head and the fine look in his eyes were so familiar from newspaper engravings that you thought you knew him, but you didn't. Smoot had never seen him before, had not expected to see him even now, and for this reason was surprised when a soldier from the headquarters guard battalion, Coppens' Zouaves, had come to fetch him from the field hospital where yet another doctor had been fussing over his face. The Louisiana soldier led him through the camp with its tents and wood smoke and restless animals. Smoot's face had a big bandage around it and it made him feel conspicuous and a little foolish. In the midst of a group of blazing campfires he caught his guide by the sleeve to ask how much farther they were going. The grey and red figure stopped and looked at him. "Jus' a liddle more far," the man replied and walked on. Eventually they came to a large wall tent inside which several lanterns and voices were heard. After a few minutes the Zouave came out and held a tent flap open for Smoot to go in.

The tent seemed very full of people, but there were really only four. Lee himself, Smoot, Mosby and Major Charles Venable. A map table occupied the center of the space, under the lantern. A metal cot stood one side of the shelter. Smoot had heard that Lee would not stay in anyone's house because he feared that the Union Army would burn the house if they learned of it.

Mosby introduced him to the other two men. Lee shook Smoot's hand. Shyness came over him looking into the old man's face. Lee asked what had been done for his wound, and how it had happened. "You rode this far like that?" he asked after listening.

No one said anything.

"You have my apology and your country's gratitude, sergeant, for your suffering." He looked at Mosby. "I want to talk to you after we are through with this ... Sergeant, please tell us all you can remember." Smoot knew with a great certainty that Major John Mosby's indifference to his pain and injured humanity would be the subject of that talk. In the army that lay gathered in the wood around them, the soldiers believed that Lee was in a real sense their father. For him, they would fight, kill and die. Isaac Smoot now understood that feeling. With Lee watching him, he told Devereux's story, explained that the mass of Union cavalry would cross the Rappahannock and Rapidan rivers very soon, and that they would cross just opposite the sector in which Stuart now found them to be pushing for footholds on the southern side of the rivers. After the cavalry moved, the main force would cross in the Wilderness itself, aiming to cut the main road to Richmond behind Lee's army.

General Lee paid close attention, asked a few questions directly of Smoot and then started making his queries to Mosby who had heard all of this several times. He wanted to know how Claude had learned these things. Mosby explained the role that women's gossip was playing as well as the help provided by the foreign diplomats. Smoot was offended at first that Lee did not ask him, but then saw that he was simply trying to save him needless suffering from the pain in his face, from the wound that had started to bleed again from the movement of his jaw..

As Mosby spoke Lee watched Smoot for signs of disagreement. There were none. John Mosby's abilities did much to compensate for his failings.

At last Lee swung his silvery gaze full on Smoot and said, "I can't begin to tell you how important this is to us, Sergeant. Men like you and Captain Devereux will be the margin of eventual victory for us. Thank you so much for all of us. Thank you for your service to our people." He turned to Mosby. "Major, this man is not going back to Alexandria, I trust."

"No, we will be keeping him with us for a while. His wound needs to heal, and I think the Yankees must be too aware of him. I will send another to take his place, probably Lieutenant Morgan."

"Good."

"You don't believe it?" Major Venable asked.

Lee looked at the tent wall, judging whether or not Mosby's group had moved far enough away. He turned back to Charles Venable. "Major, it is not important whether I believe it or not. In fact, I do believe it."

"Then I do not understand, sir." Venable was visibly disturbed.

Lee sat in his camp chair, his chin down, looking at the map. "Because we cannot afford to act on it," he said. "We will have only one chance to do what we must against Hooker's army. They are so much stronger that although we must risk all, we cannot afford to do so until I am sure that my opponents are committed to a particular course of action. They must actually move before we can believe. This is the only way to reduce the danger to an acceptable level. It is regrettable that this is the case. If we were just a little stronger, then I could take more risk, perhaps.."

"So you will wait?" Venable's impeccably uniformed figure loomed over him in reproach.

Lee nodded from his seat. "I must see which way Hooker goes, to our left in the west where Stuart is meeting them now, or downstream, below Fredericksburg." He shook his head, "No, I must wait. It will not be long."

Venable squeezed one hand in the other. His knuckles cracked.

"What is it?" Lee asked without looking up.

"Perhaps, sir, in view of the very considerable danger to the parties, to the Devereuxs, to people like this man Smoot.."

Lee sat back in the canvas chair, looking at him. "You want me to stop it?"

"Sir, if we cannot derive some benefit from this effort on the part of Devereux, his family, and others.."

With a sigh, the old man, old before his time, put down the dividers he had been holding over the map. "Unfortunately, I cannot do that either. This is technically a War Department scheme. I know that I could influence them to some extent to stop it, but the Secretary of War himself is involved and the scope of the operation extends beyond the boundaries of my Department. That being so, I am not confident that such an intervention on my part would be proper."

Venable stood wrapped in reproachful silence across the table.

"And then," Lee went on, "there is the undeniable truth that Devereux has done so well. He was always such a bright young fellow.. I wonder how his brother, Patrick, is getting on. He was a great friend of my daughter.. This, thing, that Claude is building in Washington is of value. Would it be right to interfere?"

Venable said nothing.

Lee began to look exasperated. "Major," he continued, "I have made a bargain. This undertaking is part of that agreement. It should be no secret to you that it has been necessary to accommodate a variety of different conceptions as to what our government should try to do this summer. I now think we will have a relatively free hand. This was necessary to that end. Thank heaven it is also useful."

Venable's face cleared. "How can we make this work by Devereux serve that end, sir?"

"Good, that's the way!" Lee said. "Let us think of that. Once we have dealt with Hooker, Devereux might have some chance to benefit us."

18

A Change of Heart

8:00 P.M., Tuesday, 22 April

As potentially useful loyalist citizens, the Devereuxs of Alexandria now found themselves much in demand among those adherents of the Lincoln administration who were actually responsible for martialling support for the government. Functionaries found them less attractive, but since the power did not really lie in their grasp, what did it matter? A kind of courtship began in which the various factions of the government sought to attach the Devereuxs to themselves. In the course of that process, Claude and Patrick found themselves invited one rainy night to a "smoker" at the White House. The party was intended to serve as a forum for political discussion in support of the administration. Two dozen of Washington's congressional, military and business elite filled the big room. The gentlemen sat about in overstuffed armchairs dimly visible in a gaslit atmosphere which reeked of cigar smoke and whiskey. War Democrats and Republicans peopled the room in roughly equal numbers.

Pat Devereux enjoyed watching his brother carry on in situations of this sort. Claude stood across the room beside the tall windows leaning on the shawl draped piano. A congressman from Wisconsin was at his side hanging on his golden nonsense. From his seat by the door, Patrick could clearly discern the words. "Railroad construction incentives, new markets, pent up venture capital, return to normal conditions of trade, emergence of new constituencies." Claude's standard chatter floated across the room. It was designed to seize the attention of those wise enough to have some thought of the need to prepare for the future and for post war life.

I once found it amusing that he could make commerce sound like romance. I thought it was droll, but I can see now that I was jealous as well," Patrick thought.

"I was much taken by listening to your earlier discussion of Napoleon and his Grand Armee, Mister Devereux," someone said from behind Patrick's chair. Abraham Lincoln's deep, Midwestern voice could not be mistaken by those who had once heard it.

Patrick reached for his crutches.

The President's hand fell on his shoulder. "Just sit there. I'll pull up a chair." Lincoln dragged a chair to Patrick's side, finding it in the grouping in front of the fireplace. A footman followed him with hands extended, seeking an opportunity to take it from him. Settling himself, the tall, slightly bent man spoke. "Did I understand that you share the generally held view that we are in the midst of a war in which Napoleon would have been quite comfortable, in which he would not feel out of place?"

"Yes, that is correct, sir." Patrick grinned wryly. "I have a good deal of time available in which to consider these matters and I am sure that the professional education and experience of the leaders, especially those who served under General Scott in Mexico, was such as to make it unavoidable that they should have a mental lens made up of Napoleonic tactics, weaponry and general method through which they see the possibilities. They are comfortable with that understanding of war. There is actually some justification for it."

"Why is that?" Lincoln asked. "I knew just about nothing of military and naval affairs when we began in '61. I keep trying to learn, but there are few who know much of value. I have been more and more aware of the newness of this war. After all, Napoleon did not have railroads or telegraph. Neither did his soldiers have the advantage of rifling in their muskets to give them more range."

"That is so, Mister President," Patrick answered, impressed with the quality of the questions. "But the sorry truth is that most men never learn to shoot well enough to obtain a great advantage from the additional range furnished by rifling in muskets. As for railroads and telegraphy, he would have brought those things into his system of warfare without the need to change anything very much. He marched his forces vast distances across Europe, bringing them together on the field of battle, as Lee tried to do in front of Richmond last year. He failed then, but succeeded later at Groveton. Austerlitz was the best example of Bonaparte's mastery of that form of maneuver. The modern tools you spoke of would merely have speeded up the process. No, I think that the 'style' of the armies has not changed. Nor have their organization, the tactical ideas of leaders, and the belief that an enemy can be brought to final, decisive battle."

"You do not believe that is possible?" Lincoln asked. He leaned forward to hear well above the noise of the many voices.

"I believe it will be necessary to destroy the Confederate armies utterly before you can succeed in bringing the Southern states back into the Union, if that is what is envisaged."

"What do you mean, Mister Devereux?"

Patrick felt caught in a net of his own words. He glanced about the assembly of prominent men. "Congressman Thaddeus Stevens over there," he said, "is rumored to favor redrawing the seceded states' boundaries and to wish to 'redistribute' the white population of those states, filling the void created by that with colonists from the North."

Lincoln put a hand on Patrick's sleeve. "He will not be in a position to make such policy. I will. I want to see the country whole again. You did not finish answering my question."

Patrick cast back through his memory for the question. "Sorry, I lost the thread for a second. I remember now. I think Lee's army is so tough and resilient a military instrument that it is unlikely that a battle of annihilation can be achieved against it."

"And that means?"

"It means that most likely you will have to grind them down until they are nearly gone, until all hope is gone, then the leaders will try to save what is left."

"You mean they will surrender?"

Patrick nodded. *I should not be saying this. I will regret it. Claude would handle this better.* Jake's image flashed up at him for a second. This man's face was so earnest. It was compelling. "They are not extremists. Very few of them are like *that*," he said, waving a hand vaguely in Stevens' direction. "You know who they are. Many of them were your colleagues in the old Whig party, as was our father."

Lincoln appeared pained. "Well, Mister Devereux," he said finally. "Things do move along. There is no longer anything that could realistically be called the Whig party. The future belongs to the heirs of the best of Whig thought, we Republicans."

The best of Whig thought, the best of.. My God! The best of Whig thought! You Republicans began as an alliance of nativist industrialists and transcendental New England preachers. Onto this was grafted the Know Nothing rabble, the abolitionist fanatics, and a menagerie collection of European radicals! The best of Whig thought.. Patrick saw his brother watching him across the room. *Claude! Come help me! I must shut up!*

Henry Halleck and another officer were immersed in conversation with Claude.

"Your brother tells me that your father has decided to join our party. I find that encouraging," the Illinoisan said with a wide smile. "My whole idea of renewal of the Union demands the adherence of men like the Devereuxs in order for it to work." Lincoln looked up at someone behind Patrick. "Hello Edwin, glad you could come. You know young Devereux here, I believe."

Secretary Stanton walked around into Patrick's field of vision. "I'm happy to hear you are joining us, happy indeed."

Patrick held Stanton with his blue eyes. "Yes we are, we have decided. Virginia will have to be rebuilt. Our participation will be needed. We will join your party, all of us." *God forgive us! Please God..*

"Claude, I do not want to talk to that man, anymore."

The oldest Devereux swayed back from the carriage window through which he had been surveying the dripping Washington night on 15th Street to peer at his brother. "What are you talking about? I thought it went exceedingly well. There did not seem to be one among them who rejected the notion of our connection with their egregious party."

"Does that not feel unnatural?" Patrick asked. "We have carefully avoided any connection with these people until now. Why do they so evidently wish to accept us?"

"It is especially because of that. This is the 'prodigal son' phenomenon at work. Most of these people are dying to see the sinners redeemed. They attribute our change of heart to my return. In addition to this, they see what they wish to see. Papa's long standing reputation for moderation on the slavery question now stands us in good stead."

"Do you not think it conceivable that there is an ongoing search for your past, Claude, for your recent history?"

The carriage clattered on the wet cobbles. A voice outside called harshly to the driver. The vehicle creaked to a halt. The sentry at the District of Columbia end of the Long Bridge came to the carriage window, holding a lantern high to see their passes.

"Where've you been this miserable night?" the soldier asked, his face invisible beneath the visor of his blue kepi except for the ends of his long blond mustaches. The hunting horn of the infantry adorned the flat, inclined top.

"We've been at the White House for a visit with Father Abraham. He asked after you," Claude answered.

The silhouetted figure stared in at them for an indeterminate period of time. His breath hung in the damp air. "Very well," he finally said. "Good night to you both." An arm gestured in dismissal to the driver.

Claude rapped on the hatch behind the coachman's seat.

Bill White looked down through the opening. His large form was enveloped in a rubber cloak. The rain pelted in through the hole.

"How are you doing up there, my good man?" Claude asked.

The looming figure shook its head, unable to see the humor of the remark on a night like this. He slid shut the little door.

"Why not? Why don't you want to talk to him?" Claude asked, turning again to his brother.

Patrick Henry Devereux struggled against the frustrations of an unfulfilled career, against his innate sensitivity, against his tears. "Because I find that I want to tell him the truth, to inform him, because he reminds me of Papa. I fear I will tell him too much. That is why. You should deal with him. You were always better with words. There is something about his face, his ridiculous folksy stories.."

"It never did me much good with our father," Claude replied. Well, I am truly sorry Pat, but you are going to know him as well as he wishes. He told me tonight that he and Stanton think you should be a sort of private unofficial counselor available to talk to them about Napoleon, Jomini, and that German fellow. What his name?"

"Clausewitz. I do read, you know," Patrick said. "Berthier sends me books from Paris. Clausewitz isn't published here yet, although he is by far the best thinker of the lot. My interests may not be as wide as yours, but …"

Claude held up a hand.

"And what are you going to do?" asked Patrick.

Claude shrugged in the darkness. "I am going to wait for orders from Richmond."

19

Old Friends

Saturday, 25 April

The little group of men and women sat at two square rough board tables in the center of a sizable space in the middle of the mess hall. A pot bellied black iron stove dominated one side of the building near the entrance to the kitchen by the wooden stands on which serving vessels stood at meal times. A small fire glowed in the stove's belly. It helped in driving the damp from the room.

Rain beat against the windows of the plank sided structure. Rain had fallen for days, softening the ground to a mushy mess of loam, clay and sand. In the first day of rain many said that moisture was sorely needed for new crops in the fields. The second day ended such talk. Now, in the fourth day of rain, grim determination was the general mood. Hope was widespread that the downpour would end soon.

Devereux leaned against a window, one hand gripping the molding above the upper pane. He was bent a little at the waist, peering out and upward, staring at the cloud cover. His black broadcloth suit and white shirt seemed almost excessively elegant in such humble surroundings.

At the two tables, discussion centered entirely on the intricacies of Sanitary Commission business. Fund raising, relations with the local military command, the moral and physical condition of their charges; these were the topics of disputation.

Hope sat with her back to her husband watching Amy Biddle's face.

The older woman occupied the seat at the opposite table which directly faced Claude's wife.

She knows I am looking straight into her face, and she still can't stop gaping at him, Hope thought. *I shouldn't take this seriously, but I don't like it.*

At Amy's table, Patrick finished delivering a report of the availability of commissary supplies from the quartermaster-general's department. An elderly lawyer from New Jersey favored him with a motion to accept the report verbatim. This was seconded by one of Amy Biddle's black gowned colleagues, a schoolmistress from one of the Midwestern states. Patrick tried not to watch his brother's stance at the window. *Damn him!* He thought. *He has gotten me into this business with these prune faced Yankees. He should at least make it seem plausible that he cares about this. The sad stupid and ironic truth of it is that I can't help being caught up in the organizational side of the Commission's work. And then there are the men themselves. When I walk through the wards, I don't care which army they came from.*

He felt, rather than saw Amy draw a small, sharp breath beside him. Glancing at her, he turned in the direction of her gaze and caught a glimpse of Bill White's profile disappearing from the framed view of the yard provided by the window.

Claude returned to his chair, sat for half a minute and then rose to excuse himself.

White waited in the shadow of the entrance to the camp's stable. "There's someone in the prison ward who wants to see you," he said. He stopped because of the look on Claude's face. Devereux could think of only one possibility. He tried not to imagine the extent of his brother's injuries. *How will I tell my father?* he asked himself. "Who?" he finally managed to ask.

"Fred Kennedy. He got hurt and captured down near Suffolk after we saw him last. He thinks Jake was all right," White added in reaction to the worry that clouded Devereux's face. "He was taken in some kind of skirmish and they have sent him and another man here to recover before they go to a prison camp."

"Why here?"

"The Yanks know they are from this town. They want Fred and Moses to take the oath."

"Samuels?"

"None other."

"Do you think either or both could be persuaded to do that?" Claude asked.

Bill grinned into the rain beyond the stable door.

"What are you so happy about?"

"I told them you would be wanting them not to go back on exchange or to a prison, that you would be wanting them to stay here with you."

"And?"

Bill grew more serious. He seemed to ponder the rain. "This must be raising the rivers, don't you think? It has to be hurting Hooker's plans." He looked at his friend for confirmation.

"Without a doubt. What did they say? Bill. I'm going to be missed in a minute. If my wife doesn't wonder where I am, the Biddle woman certainly will."

Bill White shook his head at the other man. "Claude, you are in for some rough times with these two ladies. Things would be simple if you were just usin' Miss Biddle, but that would be too easy for you. Sergeant Kennedy will stay if you want. You are still his company commander, in spite of everything. Samuels says he won't stay. He will bet on getting back to the regiment."

"Why? Why?" Devereux cried out.

White peered anxiously around outside, afraid of the noise.

Claude held the front of White's raincoat. "I want you to tell them both that I will, we will put together financing from banks here and in Washington to put them both back in business, in a small, discreet way. They can stay here, and serve the cause at the same time."

"They won't listen to that, Claude. They know what that is, it's just a way to get what you want. Kennedy will stay for you. Samuels won't. He's a Jew. He won't have it be said after the war that he took the easy way out. I understand that."

Devereux rubbed his face with one hand. He watched the mess hall for signs of impatience with his absence. "Tell them I'll be around to see them tomorrow. Tell Samuels we'll find some way for him to 'escape'. Tell him, never mind I'll tell him myself."

White watched him splash through the muddy yard on his way back to the meeting. "You are a worrisome man, Mister Claude Devereux," he muttered, "a worrisome man."

20

Several Awkward Moments

Friday, 26 April

"I spent two months in a camp just like this one," Ford told her.

Amy Biddle looked formidable seated behind the roll-top desk. She had swiveled the chair so that she faced him. The severity of her way of dressing made her seem someone newly risen from a memory of grammar schools and spinster teachers, but the kindliness of her expression softened the impression for Ford. For him, she brought to the front of his mind memories of nurses in lamp lit wards and the rustle of starched petticoats heard when you were only partly awake.

"Where was that?" she asked with a rather pretty smile.

"In New Jersey, I was shipped out of Fortress Monroe after the amputation began to heal. The convalescent camp was in Patterson, New Jersey. As I said, I was there two months."

"And then you went home on convalescent leave?"

He laughed a little. "Yes, yes I went home. I went up to West Point and stayed in the bachelor's quarters there for another month, and then I reported down here."

"Why did you go there? Where are you from?" She looked surprised and concerned for him.

He found that astonishingly touching. He discovered that he did not want to say anything that would worry her. "California," he said. "Sacramento. The family is widely scattered. My parents have been dead some years. It was the best thing to do."

"California! It is so far away! And now you are a, detective?" She was clearly mystified by trying to imagine this bearded, one armed soldier as a policeman.

He found that pleasing. He did not want anyone to think of him as a policeman. He squinted at her as he sometimes did when suppressing a smile, and said, "well, not exactly. I am assigned to the National Detective Bureau, but I oversee detectives. I do not ordinarily interview citizens myself." He waited for the obvious question.

She just sat smiling at him.

This is not going to be easy. "In this case," he began lamely, "we thought an officer should come to speak to you because of the prominence of the gentleman who is the subject of our inquiry."

She did not rise to the bait.

"Claude Devereux," he said.

She turned her head just enough so as to no longer hold his eyes with hers. One could easily think that she was looking at the patients who had just walked laughingly past her window. Ford could see a small vein pulse in the side of her throat. He wished that this woman would feel this way about him.

"Is Mister Devereux in trouble?" she asked without much change in her face. She was still looking in the general direction of the window.

"Not at all, nothing like that, we are making some inquiry in preparation for his acceptance of a post with the government." Now she was looking him straight in the eye again. *My dear, the only post in the government I would wish to give him is the one we will tie him to at the end of this.*

"What a good idea!" she said. "Claude and his brother, Patrick, are so eager to help. It has occurred to several of the staff here and at army headquarters that they must be given a wider opportunity for their efforts. The Reverend Joshua Moulton wrote me from our lodge at Falmouth to recount several incidents he observed in a recent visit there by Claude." She seemed to notice that she had begun to use Devereux's Christian name. A slight flush spread across her face. "These incidents made Doctor Moulton a firm supporter of the Devereux brothers," she continued. "They have begun to make such a difference in our finances here." She seemed embarrassed at having said so much."

"We understand that all the Devereuxs are in one way or another involved with the Commission?" he asked.

"Yes, that is so, except for Charles. He really is much too occupied with the bank for that."

"Anyone else?"

She was perplexed by that. "Well, there are Bill White and his father. They do odd jobs and run errands, and there are the diplomats."

"They come here, the English Major ..."

"And the French colonel and their wives," she finished for him. "Yes, they come more and more often." She paused for a moment and then looked right at him. "Aren't you going to ask if he has spoken to me of information that he wants?" she said without change in her tone of voice.

"What do you mean?" he whispered.

Her eyes were no longer friendly. "Elizabeth Braithwaite came to see me yesterday. She told me that a detective had visited her at her husband's office. The man told the Braithwaites that someone named Baker is suspicious of Claude, that he thinks Claude is somehow a spy. He wanted their help watching Claude."

A leaden cold surrounded his heart. He somehow managed not to be afraid for himself. *It must have been Turner, he would do that. Poor Mitchell.* "There is always some poor soul who does not understand his task," he said. He watched her face, looked at the eyes. *She doesn't buy it. She doesn't know what to think, but she doesn't buy it.*

She blinked her eyes and opened a drawer to retrieve a watch. "Elizabeth is having tea with Hope and Victoria Devereux in an hour," she said. "I do not think you deserve to be embarrassed by what will happen after she tells them this.."

He rose abruptly to his feet. "Thank You. You will excuse me madam? I now remember a pressing engagement I had forgotten."

He was gone, leaving her door wide.

Through the window she watched a patient hold his horse so that he could mount.

◆   ◆   ◆

Almost exactly six hours later Mitchell and Ford found themselves waiting in Colonel Lafayette Baker's anteroom.

Ford went over the events of the day in his mind. *I don't see what we could have done differently.*

From Baker's room could be heard the subdued tones of conversation.

They had waited for almost an hour. A summons had brought them from the ground floor at six thirty. They had been waiting all this time. Ford recognized the sound of feet approaching from inside the double doors which led into Baker's office.

A man peered out through the opened left-hand door.

Mitchell knew him to be a minor official in the Secretary of War's inner office.

He beckoned.

They rose to follow.

In the room were four men, Baker, the War Department official and the two Devereux brothers. Looking at the scene, Mitchell knew instantly that they were in deep trouble. Baker would never have consented to such a gathering if he had any control over what was happening.

"Major Mitchell, Captain Ford, I believe you know these gentlemen," Baker said quietly from his seat behind the desk. Ford waited for an invitation to sit. There was none.

"You probably do not know Mister Davenport, "Baker said. "He is Secretary Stanton's assistant for diplomatic affairs. He works closely with the State Department, don't you know, and brought this matter to my attention this afternoon. It seems these two gentlemen have been told indirectly by one of our detectives of an active inquiry into their loyalty. Mister Davenport finds this difficult to believe, that we doubt them, I mean."

Mitchell had been looking at Claude during this speech. He wondered what it was that the man saw at the indeterminate point in space upon which his eyes were focused. It was certainly not Mitchell. "May we sit, sir?" asked Mitchell.

"Of course, my God!, slipped my mind." Baker indicated chairs across the space in front of his desk from the brothers and Davenport. "I have explained the chain of events and information that has caused us to seek additional facts concerning Mister Claude Devereux. Mister Davenport agrees that this was only prudent on our part given the, confidential information we had of new Confederate spies in the capital. I mentioned that we had recently lost a man under suspicious circumstances. I showed them the two cyphered letters and described the ways in which we had come by them."

Ford thought Claude Devereux was very nearly the saddest man he had yet seen. The composure in the fellow's face was so complete as to resemble the face of a statue. He recognized what lay behind the rigid mask. He saw a man who believed himself defeated, who grieved for a friend he had sacrificed uselessly. *Baker has not told this man that Smoot lives. Good! Let him suffer like the rest of us.*

Beside Claude Devereux, his crippled brother stared at Mitchell with undisguised hostility.

"It proves nothing," Davenport said. "A tissue of circumstance and chance. None of it in any way connects these two gentlemen with spies, Confederate plots or anything else of the sort. Secretary Stanton feels certain that you have made some mistake in this matter, don't you agree, Colonel Baker?"

Baker swallowed convulsively while reaching for the water jug always present on his desk. Having taken the time to pour himself a drink, he fixed Mitchell with a hopeful, but neutral scrutiny. "I have not had the opportunity as yet to mention the communication you have received from France."

Ford was gratified to observe the undivided attention which Mitchell's words now received from the two Virginians.

"We took the trouble to ask our legation in Paris to make inquiry concerning your activities and reputation in that city, Mister Devereux," Mitchell said.

"And? You learned what, Major Johnston?" Claude demanded in a tone at once courteous and firm,

"Mitchell," Baker interjected. "His name, is Mitchell."

"You are known, sir, and thought well of by your relatives and French friends."

The brothers seemed riveted to their seats in their concentration on his next words.

"No one can remember seeing you recently, but then memory is an undependable thing."

Davenport broke in. "Are you telling us, Major, that nothing untoward was discovered concerning this gentleman in Paris?"

The tension in the crippled brother was such that Ford could not help but wonder what would happen in the next few minutes.

Baker's bewhiskered features swung from Mitchell to Davenport to Claude and back in restless search for escape. His trim, athletic form was neatly framed by the heavy drapes of the window behind his desk.

"No, there was nothing you could really put your finger on in Paris."

The unspoken remnant of this statement hung nearly visible in the air amongst them.

Claude laughed softly but deep in his chest. "You won't keep us waiting long for the rest, will you, Mitchell?"

Ford found himself talking. "The consul from the embassy sent some of his men around to check on a variety of details. According to the records of the *Societe Maritime de l'Ocean Atlantique* in Cherbourg neither you nor your Negro servant took passage on the *Bessieres* at the time you claim."

Baker stopped fiddling with the small objects atop his desk and leaned forward slightly. "What do you say to that, Mister Devereux?" he asked.

Davenport began to have an air of puzzlement about him. He turned to observe the response.

Claude chuckled again. "Well, Colonel, I can see that your people are too thorough to be taken lightly. The decision that I should return to America was sudden and the timing was not of my choosing. The ship was booked full. A Monsieur and Madame Henri Cormier were rather rudely informed at the last moment that I would require their accommodations. Evidently those who affected this change saw fit to leave the manifest as it was." He smiled again. "I am not surprised; if you knew them you would not be either."

"Them?" Baker asked.

Davenport replied for Claude. "The Quai d'Orsay, the French Foreign Ministry, they are addicted to secrecy in the most trivial of matters. Secretary Stanton thought it best not to inform you of this, Colonel Baker, but Mister Devereux very properly advised the Secretary of his relationship with the government of Louis Napoleon as soon as they became acquainted."

Claude shook his head. "It would have been much better if this had not been necessary. It would be better if you did not hear this. I was asked by the French to return and take up my old life in order to assist the Emperor's government in their assessment of the general situation with regard to the stability of our national life and the likely prospects of our government." *Will they accept this? It is our last chance. Hare told me to be ready, to have stories within stories, within..*

Baker smote the desk top with the flat of a hand. "A spy! A damned frog spy at that!" He began to rise.

"Much too harsh a term, a better description would be a patriot seeking to do what he can.." Davenport commented.

"What? What did you say?" cried Baker.

"Mister Devereux freely, and at his own initiative told us of this 'arrangement' of his with the French government," Davenport continued. "We have discussed him with Colonel Jourdain several times. He speaks so glowingly of you, Claude, that we can only believe he is seeking to support your efforts here in Washington."

Baker lapsed into silence.

He is calculating the odds, Mitchell thought. *And we are going to lose in that arithmetic.. The probability that leads to his survival will win.* Mitchell spoke, his eyes on Claude. "So it has been decided to employ this man to communicate to the French government that which they should learn."

"Precisely, Major, precisely," Davenport said. At this delicate moment in our efforts to prevent improvement of the Rebel diplomatic position, such a channel is invaluable, absolutely invaluable." Davenport was immensely satisfied at the prospect. He pulled out his watch. "We will have to be off, unless you have some other points, gentlemen."

"Who made this decision?" demanded Ford.

"The highest authority, Captain, the very highest. Goodnight, Colonel Baker."

21

A Hollow Victory

Saturday, 27 April
(The French Embassy, Washington)

"Colonel Jourdain will see you now," the young man announced.

Devereux went in and closed the paneled chestnut door to the colonel's office behind his back. "Edouard, so good of you to receive me without announcement," he said "I would not interrupt your morning, but something was said yesterday by one of our mutual acquaintances that troubles me."

Colonel Jourdain's polished good looks and impeccably tailored civilian suit made him appear part of the furnishings in the somber, masculine beauty of his office. He shook Claude by the hand, looking down at him with friendly welcome in his features. The ramrod straight posture of the man always made him seem stiff to Claude, but Patrick and Clotilde professed to find in Jourdain the image of many of their European relatives.

"Who is it that voiced this perturbing thought, Claude? Coffee?" Jourdain rang a small bell to summon a member of his staff. The same young man who had shown Claude in appeared for the purpose of receiving the request.

"William Davenport," Devereux replied after he left.

Jourdain considered him for several long moments. "Yes, he has taken the opportunity to speak to me of you on many occasions. I have done my best to do well by you in these little talks, as has our ambassador. Ah! The coffee. Put it on the credenza, Felix. Thank you." Jourdain busied himself with his duty as host for a moment. "Claude," he began after a moment, "Father Kruger is my confessor. A most admirable man, don't you agree?"

Devereux put down his cup and saucer. "Of course, he is my confessor as well. I take it that my dear mother is responsible for his pastoral relationship with you?"

Jourdain smiled and nodded. "But, of course. Your wonderful mother introduced Willem Kruger to Helene and myself upon our posting to Washington last year. At some point during the autumn, he mentioned to me that both you and your younger brother Joachim were absent in the Confederate forces."

Devereux grinned at the other man. "And so when I 'miraculously' appeared from Paris, you wrote home?"

"Just so, my friend, just so. It does not seem that the United States authorities had a great deal of success in establishing your true identity and pattern of recent activity in our country." He shrugged. "But, then, they had, disadvantages. Your relatives are loyal to you and we dealt with any others who might have been, indiscreet. I gather that you must have been smuggled into the South some-where?"

"Yes."

"You have many friends among us, Claude. Indeed you are one of us.. The judgement was made here and at home that you would probably succeed in establishing yourself among your enemies. We are instructed to assist you, within reason. I presume that you are able to have them believe that we are, how shall I say it? 'associates'?"

Devereux smote himself upon the thigh. "That's good! By God, that's won-derful! I told them I was helping you because it was logical, and they jumped right on it. They want me to report to you the very things Richmond requires me to study! Well, at least some of the things." He grew thoughtful. "Is that what you want, information?"

"It was logical," Jourdain said smiling. "Impeccably so. You are to be congrat-ulated. Our actions have been an unintended consequence of your logic." He seemed immensely pleased with the idea. "My friend we do not want you to tell us anything."

"No? What is it then?"

Jourdain went to a safe in the corner of the room. He returned with a sheet of paper.

Devereux took it from him and read.

> **The cavalry under Stoneman will advance two weeks before the infantry. Starting from the upper Rappahannock fords they will march to Gor-donsville and thence along the Virginia Central to Ashland. In this posi-tion they will sever Lee's supply line.**
>
> **Two army corps will demonstrate at Fredericksburg to fix Lee in position.**
>
> **Three army corps accompanied by Hooker will march west to the inter-mediate fords, cross the two rivers, and circle into Lee's immediate rear.**
>
> **Two more army corps will be held in reserve.**
>
> **Hooker knows Lee's strength. It is 60,000.**

"And the date?" Claude demanded.

"General Stoneman tried to cross the upper Rappahannock fords with his troops on the thirteenth of April," Jourdain answered. "The rains, and Stuart's men have held them back."

"The twenty seventh. Hooker's infantry marched today," Devereux murmured almost to himself.

Jourdain examined the man's face and posture.

Devereux momentarily seemed crushed by the weight of his burdens.

"You knew these things, did you not Claude? This is not the first time you have learned this? I was sure you must know and so felt no urgency in giving you this. I have been waiting for an opportunity for a talk like this."

He regained control enough to respond. "We discovered most of this a month ago. How did you obtain this information Edouard? No, forget that I said that. I know you will not tell me. I must ask again what is it that you want from me?"

"Are your communications good?" the French officer asked. "Can we expect that you can dependably cause this and, other information we might give you, to arrive safely in Richmond?"

Understanding showed on the Virginian's face. "You wish that I should act as a post office for you, for transmission of the product of your efforts here."

"Exactly! As you know, the Emperor's desire is to enter the war on the side of the South at the first chance. Until such an opportunity occurs we must do what we can. In answer to the question which you withdrew, I would say, that we have several very sincere and worthwhile friends in the Lincoln government, the army and Congress. Until now we have had no good procedure with which to forward our wealth of knowledge to Benjamin."

"To Judah?"

"None other. The possibility of such cooperation was discussed in Paris with Senator Slidell some months ago. He insisted that Benjamin would be the Confederate official involved."

Devereux rose, the paper in his hand. "It's too late to do anything with this, Edouard, but I accept your offer. I am in fact in Washington on business for Judah Benjamin. I will act as postman. My communications are excellent. Please remember me to Helene, don't forget our dinner engagement next week."

◆   ◆   ◆

Mitchell retreated from Baker's door in utter silence.

The adjutant looked up from his papers in the outer office, grasped the significance of Mitchell's expression and attempted to appear sympathetic as the other passed.

The fat little major went down the wide wooden stairs with an easy step. The farther he went from Baker's door the more light hearted, almost gay, that he felt. On reaching the ground floor he turned into the corridor running the width of the building, and knocked on a painted door almost at the end of the hallway.

A familiar voice spoke from within. "Come in."

Mitchell found his junior colleague seated in the swivel chair at his roll top desk.

The habitual neatness always evident in Ford was not apparent at this moment. The one armed man sat with his boots on the window sill. The open casement window let in a pleasant breeze, and his blue uniform jacket was unbuttoned. The curtains billowed around his legs. Mitchell's wife, a sweet tempered Kentucky lady, had insisted on her privilege as an older woman to mother Ford, a man whom she could only think of as maimed. As a result, his little office owned one of the only windows in the building with lace curtains. A bottle of rye whiskey stood uncorked on the sill beside Ford's highly polished boots.

"Come in, Major! Do come in!" he said. "I presume that you will be leaving as well?" Ford put down the tea cup from which he had been drinking and searched through the desk for another.

Mitchell dragged another chair up to the window and accepted instead a badly chipped glass from the young man.

Ford poured a solid shot into the bottom. "Watch your mouth on the edge, it's a mess," he said. "Was he polite?" Ford asked gravely. "He was terribly polite with me."

Mitchell sighed. "I accepted command of the New York City office. He would have liked to fire me, but it wasn't possible. I went around to see someone last night after our, discussion, with him, someone Democratic. What about you?"

Ford sipped. "He has remembered that I am an artilleryman. He very sweetly asked if I would not be happier with troops of my own arm, if I would not relish a return to the field."

"And you replied?"

"My God, Mitchell! I have dreamt of nothing else! The damned surgeons rejected all my pleas! He has arranged a place for me on Hunt's staff, the artillery reserve of the Army of the Potomac. I have been punished with a silken whip."

"Actually, I arranged it, Ford. He had in mind to recommend my discharge from the army for inefficiency and your reassignment to recruiting duty."

Captain Ford scrutinized him, and poured another round. "Who the hell do you know?" he demanded.

"People from New York," Mitchell said. His florid, rather fleshy cheeks quivered in outrage at the thought of the appeals he had been forced to make to his party allies. "In New York, Ford, the Democracy still lives and must be reckoned with. Lincoln and his friends cannot succeed without the help of the New York Democratic leaders.. And so I am off to deal with the enemies of the Union in the Empire State, and you.."

"I will go back to what I know best; ordnance supply, horse maintenance and gunnery." Ford swiveled to look at Mitchell. "Major, I must admit.."

"Yes?"

"I had begun to enjoy the work."

"Do not let it trouble you. It is not a work worthy of you," Mitchell replied. "Are you available for dinner today? Mary will miss you, I will miss you."

"Johnston, we were not wrong," Ford insisted. "He is a terrible menace, damn him!"

"Go back to your guns and horses, Wilson. Leave it to me. I will not relent. Devereux must suffer for his treason. We Democrats will have his blood if the Republicans will not. The men who saved us from destruction have added this matter to a long list of grievances against Lafayette Baker, and his masters. Will you join us this evening?"

"Of course, but first I am going to take the train to Alexandria. I have found someone whose beauty is not measured by the years of her age, someone whose loyalty to these benighted traitors is offered in innocence. I want to make sure she knows that I admire her before I go."

22

Absolution

3:46 P.M., 28 April

Water dripped from the verdigris stained metal roofs of Alexandria. Dark, low hanging clouds ran wildly across the sky. They came from the west, crossed the town and the river, and plunged on toward the impossibly near horizon line dividing the Maryland landscape from the heavens.

Devereux liked to look at the roofs. He cherished the bricks, mortar and ivy of the old city. The truth was that he felt rooted in this place. He had once heard Robert Edward Lee say that he thought himself strange for the feelings which filled him whenever he returned to Virginia. "Actually," he had said in his soft voice. "I find myself nodding to the very trees."

Devereux climbed the low steps of the church in a state of mind that had something in it of preoccupation but more of despondency. He opened the heavy door and crossed the foyer, pushing through the double doors that opened into the nave of the church. He stood for a time, looking at the altar. His head began to fill with the old church smells; incense, candles, hymnals, the ancient dust itself. In the dim light he could see his grandfather's open casket draped in black crepe. Saint Mary's had been crowded to the doors. His grandmother had borne it well, with the dignity expected of her people. The White family had sat in the Devereux pew for this solemn transition in the life of their collective household. The Devereuxs occupied the inner seats, the Whites the outer places. He remembered that George White had held his own mother's hand tightly throughout. The old woman had lived her whole life amongst the Devereuxs. She had been born among them in Maryland and had come with Richard when he established himself in Virginia. To Claude, she had always seemed one of his grandmothers. *That was long ago. Everything is different now..*

This rainy Tuesday afternoon brought few visitors to the church. An elderly man prayed in a front pew. Devereux heard his rosary beads rattle on the wooden rail. The sanctuary lamp burned red within the communion rail. He moved up a side aisle to the confessional box. The priest's name sign on the center door showed that Willem Kruger had received his message.

He shut the door himself and knelt to wait in the dark. The little wooden panel between confessor and supplicant slid open. "Bless me, father, I have sinned," he began from habit.

"We have all sinned, Claude," Kruger responded. "What is troubling you today? Have you been drinking too much? I can smell it on you."

He shook his head. "No, Willem, it is not so easy as that. I have failed terribly. Men have died again, this time for absolutely nothing."

The Dutch priest leaned toward the screen between them. "Tell me, my friend, tell me.."

"I killed George Daingerfield."

Kruger sighed. "We have talked of this so often.. You repented and were absolved of your guilt. God has forgiven you this sin. I do not wish to hear of it again! You did not come to me for this. Tell me now."

The telling did not take long. He had rehearsed it in his mind as his nature required. Kruger turned away once as the other man found it necessary to wipe his eyes. At last, it was finished. "It is not permitted that you should despair, Claude," Krueger said. "It is not possible. God does not forgive despair. It implies a lack of confidence in his providence which is unacceptable. You have done nothing which I find morally wrong in the context of a just war. The enemy chose to make war upon us. This is a defensive struggle. As your pastor, I cannot give you absolution because nothing of what you have told me requires it. As a fellow citizen I must urge you to continue your work. You must not, cannot, give up. Have you spoken of this with Hope?"

"Yes."

"Good." Kruger was silent a few seconds. "Claude, the Biddle woman has asked me to give her instruction in the Faith. She is a charming person, a very elevated mind. I, I would not see any of you hurt, Claude. Be careful."

Behind the screen, he nodded and thanked the priest. He crossed himself and opened the door to leave.

Bill White sat in the pew immediately outside the door. He looked up at Devereux. There were tears in his eyes.

He heard it all. "Yes, Bill, what is it? he said. "Have they come for us?"

The Negro looked uncomprehending for a second, then he smiled. "No, Captain, you should look up into the choir loft," he said.

Standing in the aisle with the open door in his hand, Claude Devereux raised his head. The long talk in the dark booth had dilated his eyes. The loft was dimly lit. The gloom of the rain contributed to the darkness. For a moment he could not see the man seated above in the shadows, and then Lieutenant Thomas Morgan leaned forward into better light. He was wrapped in a rubber poncho. Water ran down it in little streams. He acknowledged Devereux with a faint smile.

"He came after you left the bank," White said quietly. "He has been trying to get by the watchers for several days. He says they all were withdrawn yesterday. He wants to know why. You've won. You've won again."

"Where did he come from?" Devereux asked, still staring up at the Rebel cavalry officer.

"From Major Mosby. Isaac, Sergeant Smoot, got through. They delivered the mail to General Lee a week ago. He says Major Jenkins is coming to see you soon. I would not bring him to you until he told me."

Behind them in the thin walled box the Dutchman's voice was heard. "The Society of Jesus would survive my arrest, but God's house is neutral ground."

"Thank you for your counsel, Father Kruger," Devereux said to the voice. He beckoned to Bill. Together they walked for the entrance to the church.

Above them a bulky figure started for the stairs.

9:35 A.M., 29 April
(Alexandria)

Mister William Fields had worked for the house of Devereux for forty years. Throughout, he had been a member of the Democratic party. Politics was the sole area in which he parted company with the present generation of Devereuxs. He thought Charles Devereux the finest man of finance in all Virginia. The two banker sons of the house he had known since their birth. Altogether, he held the Devereux clan in high regard. As cashier of the Alexandria branch of Devereux and Wheatley, he felt it a duty to the firm to exercise the benevolent watchfulness incumbent on his many years of service. For this reason he found the recent announcement of the adherence of the family to the Republican cause to be odd in the extreme. Fields had shared the political beliefs of the founder of the bank. He and Richard Devereux had taken second place to no one in their support of Andrew Jackson. They had struggled for the spread of their party's ideals of popular democracy. Charles Devereux's defection to the cause of Whiggism had never sat well with Fields. That had been bad enough. This was baffling.

Among the items of baggage which Fields carried with him from his partisan political background was an abhorrence of nearly all things British. It was, therefore, with some reluctance that he announced to Claude Devereux the arrival in the bank's premises of Major Robert Neville.

"Show him in, Mister Fields. Give me a minute and show him in," he instructed the older man. He glanced about the room, searching for anything left carelessly in the open.

Footsteps echoed in the corridor, the sound of leather on hardwood flooring.

Fields opened the door to reveal the visitor. "Mister Neville," he said.

Neville stalked across the red and blue Turkey carpet, a wide smile on his handsome face. "Devereux, how good to see you! How is our lovely Hope? And your dear mother?"

"Fine, Major, just fine. What can I help you with this sunny day?"

"It is rather lovely today," Neville drawled, "isn't it? One becomes so fatigued of the rain."

He wants something. "Yes, is there some difficulty with your account, your office's account?" Devereux asked. He picked up a bell to ring for a clerk.

The Englishman extended a kid gloved hand, palm up. "Nothing of the kind. We are most pleased with our arrangements. I particularly want to thank you for the assistance you gave our consular officer in New York in the matter of those lost crates of furnishings for my secretary, most helpful!"

"If you do business with enough shipping companies and freight agents, almost anything becomes possible. May we offer you tea? We have some decent China tea." Devereux still had the bell in his hand.

The gloved hand stabbed at the air. "No! Not quite yet, if you don't mind, Claude. I need some help." Neville glanced at the glass paned door.

"There is no one within thirty feet," Devereux commented. "Our employees do not sneak about. What is it?"

The British officer blinked at him, seeming suddenly owl like. "What are they doing, the Americans, the bloody Union Army? You must know. You are here to learn these things. I have tried every officer and congressman we know and have learned next to nothing. My ambassador is disturbed at the lack of precision on our part as to Hooker's actions. It is clear that he has moved, that the cavalry has disappeared, more than that, we know not." He looked very like a man whose position was threatened by a failure of performance in a crisis. The grey leather of his glove stretched tightly across the brass knob on the end of his walking stick.

"My, my, Robert," Devereux said. "I had no thought that such things might be hidden from you. I had imagined that you would have many friends among the 'saviors' of liberty."

Neville clearly was discomfited by the irony of the words. "Not as many as you might presume," he replied. "And, one of our best, was posted away, inconveniently, in March. Philip Hare advises me from Toronto that you should be requested to help us in this."

"Hare?" Devereux spoke the name to the room, as though expecting a footnote to appear upon the air. "Ah, yes! The big one! He remembers me, does he? So he's in Canada. I'll wager that was an exciting voyage!"

Neville was not amused by this whimsy. It showed in his face.

My word, Major. You 'chaps' are reputed to have a better grip on things than this. There must be something interesting brewing in Whitehall. Could it be that you are about to face up to the prospect of our survival? Devereux suddenly tired of the Englishman's unhappiness. "You said to me some time ago that 'nothing is free'. Do you still hold to that belief?" Devereux asked.

Neville began to flush red. He fidgeted with the head of his stick. "Do not mock me, Claude. We will need each other in the future."

Devereux nodded solemnly back at him. "I do believe you are correct. Yes, I do." The banker found a key on the ring in his pocket and opened a drawer in the desk at which he was seated. A large, iron bound box came out of the drawer. Another key produced from the box a folded sheet of ivory colored writing paper on which the French report of Hooker's plan was written. Devereux held it out. "This is what you want," he said.

Neville held it in the light from the glass door to read. After a moment, he looked at the other man. "It is most thorough," he said.

Devereux agreed with a silent gesture.

Neville contemplated the paper for another moment. "It answers all our questions. You would not tell us how? No, I thought not. Very well. We are grateful. How long have they known?"

"My courier tells me that General Lee received the identical report from his hands on the 15th of April." *I hope to God that it was not soaked in Isaac's blood,* he thought. "President Davis will have it by now, of course."

"Of course," Neville said. "Do you believe he is acting on the basis of this? Lee, I mean."

Devereux shrugged expressively. "One can only suppose."

"Yes, of course. What is it that you wish in return?"

Devereux squinted across the room. "I will undertake to keep you informed, Neville, but Her Majesty's Government must undertake to accept for refuge such persons as I shall nominate, if the worst occurs.."

The British agent pursed his lips. "I have no authority," he began. Seeing clouds gather in Devereux's eyes, he hastily continued, "but I will forward your, proposal, to London, and we will see. Is that acceptable?"

"Yes, make it clear that without this commitment, there will be no more help from me. Can we give you that cup of tea now?" he asked.

Neville rolled the paper into a cylinder before sliding it up a sleeve. "Thank you, no. I must get this back to my code clerk. I'll see myself out."

His departure left Claude standing at the glass topped door of his room. He closed it, rotating the handle, watching the mechanism pull back the latch. He began to hum an operatic air. A gratified look came over his features. He whispered softly to himself. "An excellent case of American intervention in Franco-British affairs." He gathered up his hat and gloves.

On the way out the door of the bank he informed William Fields that he would be available at home for the rest of the day.

23

Jubal

12:07 P.M.
(Marye's Heights)

The group of horsemen occupied the shady spot beneath the trees in the beech grove atop the ridge. From his seat on the grey horse Lee could see nearly every house in Fredericksburg. His field glasses extended his view across the river. On the other side, the Federal artillery looked impressive in its battalion positions. The guns had been dug in behind horse shoe shaped mounds of earth. The crews seemed tiny stick figures among the battery horses and limbers. In the town itself infantrymen could be seen excavating trenches in back alleys and gardens.

"And how long have those people been there, General Early?" Lee asked.

A big, stoop shouldered, mean looking man in stained, worn clothes eased his horse out of the crowd and alongside Traveler. He looked sideways at the army commander. Something remarkably akin to reverence showed in a face which did not seem designed for it. "They started to come over in the night. They drove Barksdale's brigade out. I thought it best to pull back to this ridge.." He waited for some sign of approval from Lee. Anxiety could be seen in the restless way he shifted a wad of tobacco from one cheek to the other.

Without lowering the glasses, Lee commented, "You did the right thing, exactly the right thing."

The massive shoulders sagged slightly in relaxation. Jubal Early spat over the shoulder of his mount into the mud in front of the horses. The red brown stream of tobacco juice described a long arc. Early's horse shied slightly from the sudden appearance of wet soil under its nose. It moved to its left, crowding Lee's mount, causing the beautiful beast to back away.

Robert Lee was still looking at the town through the glasses. He absentmindedly reached down to pet the horse.

Early stretched from his seat to try to grasp the grey's reins.

Traveler kept backing away, looking at the strange man with obvious distrust.

A captain in the staff group behind the generals nudged another officer in the ribs in the hope that they would all see Early make a fool of himself.

Lee lowered the field glasses, taking in the scene with an annoyed look that quickly softened in comprehension. "He is not a trusting animal," he said. "It is a defect of his character." The army commander waved a hand at the town and the enemy forces on both banks of the Rappahannock to the front. "I do not believe that this is real. They would be moving forward if it were. Major Marshall!"

A tall, dark, bespectacled man with a Louis Napoleon mustache and beard answered from ten feet away. "Yes, General Lee?"

"Please recount for General Early the information we received this noon from the cavalry."

Early's negative attitude toward cavalrymen was well known. The infantry division commanded by him included some of the toughest soldiers in the Army of Northern Virginia. Amongst them, the Louisiana brigade of infantry had a particularly fearsome reputation. Their pelican flags were dreaded by enemy commanders and Southern civilians alike. Jubal both loved and hated them. He loved them for their fighting hearts but despised the things they did to amuse themselves at the expense of the helpless. For all his gruff manner and careless appearance, he was a rigid disciplinarian who watched his men closely for violations of army regulations. The cavalry arm in general, and Stuart's division in particular, offended him. He had no time for soldiers who had the inherent ability to ride away from situations that they wished to avoid. Perhaps his long career as a prosecuting attorney had influenced his thinking. He tended to deal with most people as though they had something to hide. His opinion of Stuart's horsemen was neatly summed up in his nickname for them, "Buttermilk Rangers."

"General Stuart reports," Marshall began, "that a large force has crossed the rivers in his front and on his left flank. He reports his position as about ten miles west of the Chancellor house on the Orange turnpike. He has taken prisoners from three different infantry corps." Charles Marshall pulled a scrap of paper from a pocket and read. "They were, the Eleventh, Twelfth, and Fifth. He also believes that large numbers of cavalry are moving around him to the west, crossing into his rear, behind the enemy infantry."

Lee held the field glasses in his hands, looking at Early, waiting for comment.

The chewing stopped momentarily. Early spat again. "I suppose Jeb will be right in this," he said. His eyes were fixed on the older man.

Lee searched among the staffs for a face. "Major Venable?"

The possessor of this name raised a gauntleted hand from his place beside Marshall.

Lee glanced at Early. The hulking, unconsciously threatening figure had focused fully on the two staff men. "Tell your tale, Major, tell it," Lee said.

Venable cleared his throat. "We have a, friend, in Washington who was able to send his opinion on Hooker's plan. It is, not inconsistent with what seems to be occurring."

Early's large head swiveled back to Lee. "And so you believe that this spy's report illuminates the situation before us? I had thought that you did not credit such people over much!"

Lee sat the grey horse calmly, examining Early as one examines a scientific exhibit in a glass-covered case. "I have known him for many years, General. I think you have as well. Major Venable, write the name."

Early received the folded order book sheet, opening it slowly. He looked at the name. "His father is my friend," Early began. He stopped himself.

Lee's arm swept the horizon. "What is your opinion, General?" he asked. "Should we accept the man's information as explaining this? After all, he is an infantry officer."

A half circle of smiles surrounded the two commanders.

The chewing recommenced. Early nodded once, decisively. "I would," he said. "They are all good people in that family."

After considering that statement for a moment, Lee started to speak. "Very well. Colonel Chilton, where is General Jackson?"

"He was here with me forty-five minutes ago," Early interrupted. "He has gone down to the picket line to talk to Barksdale."

Lee looked at him sharply. "I have said before that all of you expose yourselves too much! I know that you do this as well, General! I cannot spare you! Do you hear me, General?"

Early appeared to be unable to decide whether or not this might be praise. "Yes, sir," he said. "I do hear you."

"Good," Lee continued. "Colonel Chilton, dispatch a galloper to bring General Jackson to me, here. Send another to General Stuart to instruct him to withdraw his force toward us in such a manner as to cover the movements of the enemy cavalry while delaying the advance of the enemy's infantry mass to the east."

Chilton dismounted and found a stump to sit on while he wrote. Marshall walked his horse back into the cavalry escort to pick the riders.

Lee's eyes met Early's. He began to speak again. "I will ask the President to give us back Pickett's and Hood's divisions, but I fear they will arrive when the crisis is passed. We will push with the force we now have on the left, Anderson's and McClaw's divisions. They must hold back the infantry that confronts General Stuart until we can further develop the situation. Those people over there," he said, pointing at the enemy, "must believe that I have no choice but to fall back, or to be pinned here by their demonstration until the rest arrive in our rear.

They have three infantry corps to our west now. They will try to uncover Bank's Ford, just there." He pointed in a northwesterly direction at a spot several miles away where the Rappahannock traversed the fringes of the forest of the Wilderness. "If they are allowed to do that, they will bring yet more infantry to our side of the river. They will then make a concentric attack to crush our left. They will fail in this. I will not withdraw, and we will not wait for them to act."

Early's heavy brow rose in mute inquiry.

"I will ask General Jackson to go to the left," Lee said, "to reconnoiter and take such action as may be necessary. I will bring his divisions to the left as rapidly as can be managed, all except yours."

Early turned his head from Lee to the sight of the massed enemy forces gathered within sight of the ridge. He saw that engineer troops were now beginning to erect two pontoon bridges. He could just see the heads of the soldiers working atop the pontons on the river.

Lee spoke his name. "General Early, you will hold them here, all of them, while we deal with Hooker in the west. Can you do that?"

The massive, whiskered head came up. The bulldog line of the jaw showed under the beard. "Just my division?"

Lee pondered that. "Barksdale knows the town," he finally said, seeming regretful of the fact. "To remove his men from Fredericksburg would reveal our intention to make a change in dispositions, I think you will have Barksdale's people as well as your own, but no more!"

Early grinned his assent. "Barksdale took a prisoner from the Sixth Corps right down there, this mornin'. That's John Sedgewick! You remember John, do you not?"

Lee thought for a moment. "You are classmates, are you not?"

"Absolutely! Sedgewick always was a careful man. Take your time, sir! Take your time. John and I will be here growling at each other for some days. Take your time."

24

Old Jack

8.00 A.M., 1 May
(West of Fredericksburg)

The Orange turnpike ran west from Fredericksburg into the green depths of the Wilderness. Ten miles west of town it passed a small, white framed chapel. The humble structure was on the south side of the road on top of a gentle rise in the ground, a rise so slight it would hardly be noticed in normal circumstances.

On this day, the sunshine of a May morning painted the landscape in gold and green. Birds sang in the cool, shadowy trees. The forest crowded close to the turnpike on the north. To the south, behind the church, the ground was more open. Another road lay there, leading off to the southwest, into the hidden fastness of the forest.

Zoan Church served the local farming community. It had done so for forty years. For all that time it had been the central reference point in the lives of the many small landholders who lived nearby. It had never been witness to anything like the scene around it now. North and south of the turnpike, and all about the church, long, wandering lines of entrenchments scarred the land. Confederate infantry filled these defenses, if "filled" really described their meager strength on the ground. To their rear, behind the gentle slope of the ridge, wagons and teams sheltered in the shallow terrain "shadow" provided by the ground.

In the fringes of the looming jungle of woodland to the west, an ever shifting array of blue clad soldiery gathered. Their scouts could be seen from time to time as they looked out at the grey enemy.

The Confederate troops dug in across the turnpike had fought these same Yankees the night before several miles to the west around the Chancellor House crossroads. There had been too many to hold back, and the Southern commander, Major General Richard Herron Anderson, had pulled back far enough find the open ground he needed for fields of fire. He found the area to either side of Zoan Church satisfactory.

Richard Anderson was a veteran of the "old army," the regular service of the United States. His steady, reliable manner and solid background of achievement made him an officer of whom Robert E. Lee seemed always to expect much. He seldom disappointed. From a position within the horse shoe shaped earthen shelter of a 12-pounder Napoleon field gun, he watched enemy staff officers move about inside the wood line to his front. The battery whose position he shared, kept up a desultory fire against these targets, and the entrenching blue infantry around the guns. In the interval between the thunderclap reports of his artillery,

Anderson carried on a pleasant, seemingly unconcerned conversation with the men around him. Officers and men alike shared in the warmth of his benevolent attention. It would have required a particularly acute observer to notice the worry that inhabited the corners of his eyes as they sought the limits of the hostile line of battle.

The commotion of approaching riders on the road from Fredericksburg turned heads to the rear. Four men rode toward the gun positions beside the road. At the head of the group, a general officer sat a small and somewhat nondescript horse. This rapidly approaching figure attracted considerable comment from infantrymen in reserve positions behind the rise. Their special interest was aroused by his uniform. The Rebel riflemen pointed open mouthed at the splendid martial dress of the figure which passed before them. The beautiful French grey tunic, and deep blue trousers made a fine picture. A double breasted coat was closed by two rows of gilt buttons grouped in threes. The sleeves were heavy with the gold braid of two enormous Austrian knots. On the collar the wreath and stars of a general officer of the Confederate States Army completed the ensemble.

The little cavalcade halted among Anderson's artillery pieces. The division commander hurried to the side of the newly arrived senior officer. Among the gunners and drivers of the battery a name ran around like a whisper of the wind, "Stonewall, Stonewall has come." By the time Anderson reached his side, the Second Corps commander was deep in inspection of the enemy position. From his elevated viewpoint on the diminutive horse, the bearded man peered across the temporary "no mans' land."

"That's a right pretty suit of clothes you have there, General," Anderson offered.

The field glasses slowly descended, coming to rest in gauntleted hands resting on the saddle bow. Pale blue eyes peered down over sunburnt cheeks. A suspiciously deep shade of pink began to suffuse the one ear that Anderson could see. The sartorial splendor of the man was undisturbed by speech.

A Union battery to the northwest barked nearly in unison. The fall of shot whizzed by, clearing the crest of the low ridge by a few yards. Men and horses reacted with hunched shoulders and tossed heads.

Neither general officer paid this passage of tangible, spherical destruction the slightest attention.

Stonewall Jackson's Calvinist convictions against worldly displays of "vanity" were well known. His usual clothing often seemed to have been made up of "hand me downs" from Jubal Early who was generally thought the next most disreputably dressed officer in the army. Confusion and embarrassment radiated from Jackson's stern features. "General Stuart," he stammered. "He was so kind as to have it made for me, London, I believe, my, my birthday you know.."

The bearded, youthful soldiers gathered round to see legend speak, and were astonished and pleased that legend had human feelings like them.

Richard Anderson considered the man. From the viewpoint of the professional soldier, Jackson could not be other than bizarre. The man's very existence as a senior officer, an Army Corps Commander no less was baffling. He was a professor, of all things! For eleven years he had been Professor of Natural and Experimental Philosophy at the Virginia Military Institute. College professors do not emerge from obscure lives of pedagogy to blaze across the sky as meteors illuminating the firmament of military history. In addition, this professor's eccentricities were such as to make sober men whisper of possible instability. Even now, Anderson could see his own men waiting expectantly for some sign of the special mark upon the man, of God's intent. Anderson himself waited.

"What will you do, General?" the deep voice asked from above. The blue eyes held him, demanded something of him, something unreasonable.

Anderson blinked to clear his mind. The sun was beginning to seem excessively bright. He glanced at the waiting soldiers, at the blue tinged forest, back at Stonewall. "I will defend on this ridge until the army comes up," he said. "It is the best ground to be found."

Jackson stared down at him. "You are extended to the river on the right?" he asked.

Anderson shook his head. "No. McClaws' division is on my right. I only reach about three hundred yards north of the road."

Jackson sat quietly on the little horse for a moment, thinking.

Anderson waited, pondering an indisputable fact. *Thomas J. Jackson is not my corps commander, not mine nor Lafayette McClaws' neither. To hell with him,* Anderson thought.

Jackson's left arm shot out. "Is there a road there, running from south of us into the forest, toward the Chancellor house?" His arm swung, describing a diagonal line leading into the enemy's right rear.

Anderson cast back in his mind for the record of the previous night's wanderings in the jungle of woods. "Yes. Yes, there is such a road," he said.

Jackson's head bobbed in agreement. "Good! Good!" he said. "Major Hotchkiss, my cartographer, was sure such a track lay there.

"Then, we will attack." Jackson said in a clear, unhurried, certain tone.

Artillery fire from the opposing force was building steadily. To stand much longer on this slope, in the open, discussing operations would be foolish. *What shall I tell this man?* Anderson thought. *Will he listen to the simple logic of the numbers? He must know that McClaws and I have but a handful of men against this vast and swelling sea of blue coming to meet us. What will happen to the army, to the country, if we lose them?* He looked up at the strange, intense, exalted face.

The eyes burned down at him.

If we wait here, Anderson thought, *they will come in all their numbers and in the end we will be forced back. How far? To the North Anna? And then where? Richmond?* Anderson placed a hand on the shoulder of the ugly little horse.

The scrawny beast swung his head to look at him.

For an instant he wondered if the soldiers' story about this horse was true, *Does it really sleep curled up like a dog during halts on the march and come when he whistles.*

"You mean to shock them?" he asked the professor.

"Indeed, that is so," Stonewall answered.

God help me, but I am going to do it, Anderson thought. *Please God! We are your loyal sons..* The professional soldier nodded his agreement to the schoolteacher. "What are your orders, sir?" he said.

"McClaws will press straight ahead," Jackson answered. He was pointing with his left hand now. "Your division will attack astride the road on the left there. We will gain their rear. I will accompany you."

"When?"

Jackson looked at his pocket watch. "Eleven o'clock. Send gallopers to McClaws and General Lee. I will reconnoiter this road of ours."

With a twitch of his heels, Jackson was gone, galloping to the left, his small escort struggling to keep up.

Richard Anderson walked to the rear, searching for his chief of staff.

6:45 P.M.
(Washington)

Abraham Lincoln had an ingrained prejudice against dandies. They made him uneasy. In the western region from which he had emerged, men dressed plainly, or roughly, but never obsessively. Lincoln found it surprising that the War Department staff officers who regularly briefed him were such dandies. Their bandbox perfection of dress and physical beauty puzzled him. He asked Henry Halleck why they all looked the same.

Halleck had not at first understood the question.

The president restated it another way, asking if they were all West Pointers.

The general in chief at last grasped the nature of the president's inquiry. He had shown both sympathy and amusement. He told Lincoln that this procession of the well born, well connected and well dressed was really the outcome of a process of "natural selection" as Professor Darwin would describe it. He gave it as his opinion, based on long observation of army politics, that nothing in the nature of a permanent change could be expected in this process. It was just the nature of things that the "rich got richer" in the army as in all other spheres of human effort.

One of these gorgeously uniformed creatures was attempting to brief him now. It was hard to focus on all the details. He looked out the tall windows at the sunlight disappearing from Seventeenth Street. The White House looked golden in the fading day. His legs ached. Sitting in these low chairs made his knees hurt after a while. The briefing officer paused, uncertain of the degree of attention he was receiving from the commander in chief. Lincoln looked at him, indicating that he should continue. The youthful major tightened his grip on the wooden pointer in his right hand. "And thus, Mister President,' he said. "You can readily see that it is most likely that the Rebel attack against General Hooker's main force which occurred west of Fredericksburg this noon must be a diversion intended to cover his withdrawal from the defense positions which he occupies in strength just south of Fredericksburg." The slender, handsome major held the point of his stick on the big, hand drawn map which covered most of the wall behind him.

The president found the maps produced by the Army's topographic engineers to be art objects in their own right. This one was a mass of brown contour lines, blue streams and green forests. The watercolor washes which made up the larger blocks of color gave the room a strangely gay aspect.

The major's stick still showed the area of the Southern attack that seemed to have frightened Hooker so. The point of the stick lay on the eastern edge of the big green wood near a symbol which identified a church. Abraham Lincoln fished in a vest pocket for something, finally retrieving a scrap of paper. He looked at it for a few seconds.

The roomful of officials and officers waited.

"And so, Major," Lincoln began. "It is the opinion of the General in Chief that Lee is going to retreat?"

"Yes, Sir. He has no practicable alternative. He cannot take the risk of destruction of his army that the present situation imposes if he continues to defend behind Fredericksburg. General Hooker's plan has succeeded."

Lincoln looked around the room. Secretary Stanton and General Henry Halleck were conspicuous by their absence from this late afternoon presentation of information to the chief executive.

A general murmur of discontent ran round the room. Resentment at the role assumed by the briefer and his presumption in drawing a conclusion of this importance was evident.

"How far south do you think he will go?" Lincoln asked. "I mean Lee," he said. His heavy eyebrows knit together in concentration.

Confusion and a trace of fear manifested itself in the major's handsome face. He did not like the audience's reaction to his earlier remark. "I, I do believe he will have to go back to the North Anna, Mister President."

Lincoln leaned forward. "And that is where on the map?"

The major's stick traced the alignment of the Telegraph Road south from Fredericksburg to a wide blue line running west to east at right angles to the road. It was the North Anna River.

The distance was impressive.

Lincoln considered the map. "Twenty-five miles?" he asked the major.

The young man swallowed twice and nodded. "Yes, Sir," he said.

Lincoln meditated upon these matters a moment. He then turned to a brigadier general seated at the large table with him. "Philip," he said. "Why has Hooker drawn back if all this is as described? The opportunity lies before him." He raised the hand containing the small, irregularly shaped morsel of paper. "According to this note, which I made at one of these sessions a week ago, Lee has something like, 70,000 at most and our army around 120,000. Lee is divided between Fredericksburg and wherever it is that he is, over there in the west, by the woods." He waved at the map.

The major hastened to show the probable position of the Rebel force on the edges of the Wilderness.

"Why doesn't Hooker attack? Now!" Lincoln demanded of the brigadier general.

The general flushed red to his collar line. He attempted to make a good case for General Hooker's need to "straighten his lines." He explained that the forest itself was a major obstacle and factor in the operation. It surely had caused a "disturbance" in the organization of the army. Hooker would undoubtedly attack in the morning in accordance with his original intention.

Lincoln listened quietly, respectfully. His hands made a tent before his features. "Mister Devereux?" he finally said without turning his head.

"Which of us do you mean, Mister President," Claude asked from his seat four rows back.

"Patrick," Lincoln said. "Will Lee think he must retreat?"

Heads turned toward the two men in civilian clothes seated side by side in the back of the room. It would have taken a keen observer to interpret the almost imperceptible nod which passed from one to the other.

"The logic presented here is impeccable, Mister President," Patrick said, "but he will also reason that he must fight you somewhere and turn back your army or face eventual defeat. Would the North Anna be a better place? I think not. The men would be discouraged by the retreat itself and he would be afraid they might not fight as well as they would farther north.."

Lincoln pulled his chair around to face them, and the rest of the group. His back was to the major. "You are a judge of men I think, Claude. Why has Hooker stopped in this way?"

Claude looked at his brother.

Patrick would not meet his eyes.

"There is something terrible in Robert Lee, Mister President," Claude began, "something, savage. It is normally hidden, but it emerges at times like this. The numbers, the geometry of that map all support both General Hooker's plan and the major's explanation, but I would guess that there was something about that Rebel attack today that did not fit with the logic of anything. Lee attacked as though he is not compelled to do anything! General Hooker is a smart man, he must be trying to figure out what it is that Lee is really going to do."

Lincoln swiveled around to stare at the brigadier general.

The red faced man shook his head. "No. No. General Hooker will attack in the morning. Lee will withdraw," he said.

Lincoln glanced at the major. "You do not seem as certain, young man," he said.

The staff officer did not respond.

The President of the United States left the room without goodbyes.

9:35 P.M.
(The Wilderness)

The heavy firing died away with the passing of the light.

Anderson's column of attack had swept forward through the woodland, swinging from the left like a boxer throwing a round-house punch and then cutting in toward the roads which led directly to the rear of the Federal army. The effect was something like that obtained in using a long pry bar to move a boulder. Anderson's Division was jammed into the sensitive spot where real leverage could be found. As they drove forward, the men could feel their weight begin to disrupt the fabric of the blue army. Resistance began to fall away, and all at once the forest was full of Union troops pulling back toward the Chancellor House crossroads. They did not run, and they continued to fire, but they moved steadily away from contact with Anderson's men.

Lafayette McClaws' soldiers could be heard to the northeast, pressing, demanding the attention of the enemy, holding them in contact so that they could not be used elsewhere on the battlefield.

The Orange Plank Road running southwest from Zoan Church formed a kind of intersection with another dirt road that ran in from the northeast and disappeared into the woods to the southwest. It was a place of no importance whatever except for the accident of location which made it a convenient meeting place that night. Anderson's attack lost momentum as the light failed. In the infantry, men gradually stopped moving for fear of blundering into the enemy. Soon the front line fell silent as riflemen stood and listened, and then, it was dark. The little crossroads seemed almost hushed for a time. The war had moved a quarter mile away to the west. In the darkness, staff officers arrived. Orderlies and cooks tried to make the space around the intersection usable for rest, food and planning.

Robert E. Lee and Stonewall Jackson conferred around a tiny fire under the hardwood trees. Engineer officers were dispatched down the roads, seeking information. Silence closed in around the little fire.

3:10 A.M., 2 May
(The Crossroads)

The two generals sat by the coffee pot waiting for it to boil. Upended cracker boxes made seats. Both men were known for their patience, but it had been a long night.

A Negro cook waited with them, enameled tin mugs in hand.

The regiments of Richard Anderson's division stirred to wakefulness around them in the impenetrable blackness of the forest. Out of the shadows floated the voices of the army.

"So Bones, he chased this old she coon up one side and down the other of the run," a voice announced from nearby. "You could hear him snufflin' and moanin' to hisself, smellin' first one tree'an thann another."

"But, I heerd you say you wanted him to tree the little'uns," responded a second disembodied voice.

"That's right. I surely did, but old Bones he never accepted that anythin' but a giant boar coon or such like that was good enough for a fine Red Bone like him. So he kept on searchin', and searchin'."

"What happened?" asked the second soldier.

"Well, we had this nigger huntin' with us that evenin'. His name was Jackson, like the gen'ral, you know. I don't believe they are any kin."

Hooting, howling raillery shook the underbrush.

"I don't know what you fellahs are laughin' at, they could be," the first man said. "He hunted with us some. He had this black Plott hound, big dog, good for rabbits, coons, squirrel, good nose. Jackson bought him from old man McClung in New Baltimore. It was right dark, so I stood still for a while, afeerd of fallin'. I jus' stood there and listened to Bones attackin' evur tree he could find."

"And?" prodded the other.

"Well, Jim Jackson he spoke my name from about ten feet away. 'Mister Walker,' he said. 'Come over here.' So, I had him keep talkin' until I could find him. It was so dark it was hard as hell to find him and that black dog."

"Come to the point, will you Walker," asked a third person "I have to go find the colonel, but I want to hear the rest."

"You should tell him this story, Cap'n!" said Walker "He knows this Jackson, and both these dogs. Anyway, when I got to Jackson he was standin' by a big water poplar, pointin' up with his shotgun. The Plott hound had one foot on the trunk and was lookin' straight up, straight as a tent pole. Up in the tree was this she coon we'd been after. She was splayed out on a branch lookin' at us as calm as she could be."

"So, what did you do?" asked the second man.

"We stood there, the three of us, enjoyin' the noise that Bones was makin' on the other side of the run. He was near in a frenzy by then. Then I called him. He didn't want to come at fust. When he did, I held him up so he would see the coon. The poor thang! He was so embarrass't he jest walked away with his head down, wouldn't look at the other dog, didn't come back for three days."

"Where was this?" asked the captain.

"Over to the west, in Rappahannock," replied Walker, "near to Sperryville, behind these Yanks here, God damn them!"

By the fire, the cook poured a mug for Lee, then another for Jackson, who looked up at him. Jim Lewis was Jackson's personal cook. He had come from home with him. Lewis could not help grinning in delight at Walker's story. Jackson just shook his head. "As you can see," he said to Lee, "they are in fine spirits after yesterday.

The army commander smiled. "We should all be happy for what was done. What more have you learned since last night?"

Jackson rubbed his chin before answering. "The cavalry is correct," he said. "Hooker's right flank is open to the west of us, and we have learned that there is a route which would take us there." He picked up a stick and began to draw in the damp earth. He first drew double lines to show the imagined position of the enemy. It was a half circle with a road running through it from east to west. The western end of the enemy half circles barely reached the road. He then drew a larger, meandering circle having its starting point at their present location. He accompanied the drawing with a description of the various forest tracks which made up the route. It became clear from his explanation that the larger circle would reach the east-west road just outside the place where Hooker's line of battle ended.

Lee pondered the drawing. "What do you propose to do?" he finally asked.

"Go around there," Jackson said, waving his stick at the outer circle, pointing ultimately at the western end of the Union army line.

"With what force?" Lee asked.

"With my whole corps," Jackson said.

Lee sat back slightly and considered the other man.

Jim Lewis stood with the coffee pot in his hand, staring at the drawing. He had done a fair amount of soldiering and could see several worrisome things about this crude map. The route was ten or twelve miles long. Jackson's corps had more than 25,000 men to Jim's certain knowledge. It would fill the whole route when marching. The route passed fearfully close to the Union lines throughout. Jim began to wonder where he, personally, would be during this march.

"And what will this leave me?" Lee demanded.

Jackson had anticipated the question. "With the Divisions of Anderson and McClaws," he replied. No trace of humor or irony marked the Second Corps commander's face.

Lee contemplated the man for a moment. "Well, go on then," he said.

Jim poured General Lee a second cup of coffee.

"I'll have my men on the road by four," Stonewall pledged, climbing stiffly to his feet.

All that day the serpentine column of men struggled to make its way past the face of its enemy. The Second Corps of the Army of Northern Virginia tramped doggedly through the eery forest with its dank hollows and boggy little streams. To the right of the marching men and rumbling wheels, the Army of the Potomac lay paralyzed by the spell that Rebel daring and desperation had laid upon its commander. The massed blue strength just a few hundred yards away could easily have swept away Jackson's Corps which was spread before them like a banquet by this roll of the iron dice of war. With the death of the Second Corps would inevitably have come the end of Lee's proud army of farmers, planters and working men. They were the best the South had to offer, the finest of their people. If they were destroyed, then the Confederate States would soon be gone as well. In a special sense, they were their country, for there were not enough men in their country to replace them if they were lost.

Several of Hooker's generals discovered what was underway and tried to warn him. He could not hear them. All he could see was the image of danger and strength that Lee and Jackson and their tattered ragamuffins had fixed on him. This was a curious thing. Joe Hooker was a fine general and deserved his nickname, "Fighting Joe." At Sharpsburg his attack on the left had nearly destroyed the same army that now held him in a spell woven of so many threads. In spite of him, Hooker's army surged against the limits he had placed on it. Federal probes into the right flank of Jackson's Corps cost him regiments he could not spare. These had to be left behind to block the Yankees from certain knowledge of the enormity of the folly into which Jackson had launched the Corps. All day, the ugly little horse carried his master up and down the long column, while he encouraged, pleaded, and urged them forward. Men would remember to their deaths his pale eyes and the words, "Press on!" The infantry, forbidden to cheer because the enemy would hear, waved their hats and patted "Little Sorrel" as he passed.

At last the vanguard of the infantry reached the turnpike west of Hooker's position. Stuart's horsemen waited there, and commanding them Jackson found black bearded Fitzhugh Lee holding the all important road junction through which his twenty-five thousand rifles would pass, deploying to face the enemy's exposed flank. Stonewall waited with Fitz while the infantry divisions filed into position north and south of the turnpike. In these positions their many long lines would be perpendicular to the end of Hooker's line of battle, somewhere to the front down the road. An hour and a half passed. Jackson said nothing. He waited patiently, sometimes looking at his pocket watch, occasionally peering at the sun setting in the west behind him. As he waited, he sucked on half a lemon from a bag hung behind the saddle. To the south and east rumbling cannon showed that the men he had left behind along the route of march were still fighting. Finally, it was done. The staff reported that all were ready. Young Major General Robert Rodes waited beside him. Rodes' division was first in the massed column of attack. Behind him were stacked up the old "Stonewall Division" under Raleigh Colston and A.P. Hill's "Light Division." Rodes and Colston were colleagues from the faculty at the V.M.I. He believed deeply in them as friends and hard fighters. Hill's record spoke for itself. Jackson looked at Rodes. He was still holding the lemon. "Well, General Rodes," he said. "You may go forward.."

Robert Rodes stood in his stirrups and pointed with one hand at the wood line to the front. As far as you could see into the woods to either side of the turnpike, the solid lines of riflemen started forward behind their red flags. Rodes touched his horse with his heels. He and his division staff went forward at a walk with the infantry, leaving "Old Jack" sitting there.

The regiments now saw him as they passed and, uncaring of what the enemy knew or thought, they began to cheer him as they passed in the golden light of dusk. It commenced as ordinary "huzzahing," but soon it changed to the wild, shrill call with which their hungry, savage hearts spoke at times like this. Jackson took the battered old cadet cap from his head and held it before him on the little horse's neck.

Three quarters of a mile east on the pike, troops of Major General Oliver Otis Howard's Eleventh Corps of the Army of the Potomac were lounging comfortably around their campfires. They had just eaten their evening meal and most were looking forward to a nice nap. Some faced west in their camps, but most were there to block against whatever it was that made so much noise in the dense woods to the south. Since the river crossing several days before they had seen no Rebels except for a few cavalry to the west. Most of these "Yankees" were German immigrants and the talk around their fires was as much of Bavaria and the Rhineland as it was of Cleveland or Chicago.

Unexpectedly, deer began to run out of the forest to the west. At first it was only a few. Men ran for rifles, hoping to bag venison for their messes. Ten deer broke from the trees together, followed by a black bear. Then they heard it. It was the sound that had frozen their blood on a dozen battlefields. Faint at first, but rapidly growing in volume, they heard the insane, high pitched, cackling sound that they called the "Rebel Yell." Soldiers ran in all directions to find their units and equipment. Ranks formed facing west as the sound grew and grew. A battery of Napoleons waited for the demons behind that sound to emerge from the woods.

The forest moved, seemed to come alive and the first brown ranks swept upon them still driving the game before them. The Union artillery battery fired one volley and then was silent, carried away and destroyed by the avalanche of screaming warriors coming out of the trees. Howard's men ran. Those who did not, died or were captured if they were lucky. Those who ran, ran fast and hard. Some of them ran all the way through the army's position and out the other side. Indeed, they ran right through Hooker's headquarters astride the pike at the Chancellor House and ended four miles from their starting point in Richard Anderson's Confederate lines where they were taken prisoner.

The Second Corps assault poured through the hole where Howard's people had been. The right flank of the Army of the Potomac folded up like an accordion. The massive phalanx of Rebel infantry drove straight forward aimed at the enemy's most vulnerable points. These were the fords and pontoon bridges across the Rappahannock River behind the fighting troops.

As night fell, forward motion slowed as regimental officers straightened out formations scrambled by the rapidity of advance and the dense undergrowth. They aligned the brigades in the dark to continue the attack until the river was reached. Everyone knew that the Yankees were badly off balance and that this might finally be what they had wanted so much and fought so hard for, the destruction of the main Union army and the end of the war..

Afraid that they might lose the way to the river in the darkness, Jackson rode forward of his lines into "no man's land" to personally reconnoiter. He had done this many times before. His faith in divine providence and Christian resignation had often led him to disobey Lee's order that he might not so expose himself. Now, God turned his face from the cause of Southern independence.

North Carolina soldiers mistook Stonewall's staff for enemy cavalry in the dark wood and fired a volley into them. Jackson was struck in the arm. Enemy artillery opened fire, raking the groud onto which the wounded general had fallen.

The same soldiers who had fired the volley then spent half the night trying to get him off the field under fire, but the damage was done. Jackson's arm was amputated by his staff surgeon later that night.

The Second Corps assault was over.

When Robert Lee was told the next day, he said,"General Jackson has lost his left arm, but I have lost my right."

25

A Meeting of Two Minds

Monday, 11 May

The couple picked their way between the bivouacs and camps atop the hill to reach the gate of the earthen work known to the engineers who had designed it as Fort Ellsworth.

Amy Biddle watched as her escort spoke to a sentinel. The blue of her skirt and the white, high necked blouse made a pretty picture. She gathered her shawl about her against the hilltop breeze. After some hesitation the soldier raised the hinged wooden rail which prevented casual access to the fort.

Ford held out his elbow to her. Together, they strolled across the interior of the fortification. Passing soldiers saluted Ford's rank. Unwilling to release her he nodded gravely to each in return. An artillery major emerged from one of the frame buildings within the walls. Seeing them arm in arm, and noting Ford's condition, he waved a hand at Ford in passing, and tipped his cap to Amy. "Good afternoon, ma'am," he smiled.

They climbed the gentle interior slope of the southwest corner of the redoubt. Side by side they stood near one of the big guns and looked out in the direction of the lowering sun still shining in the west over the valley of Hunting Creek. The Orange and Alexandria Railroad ran away down the valley. A road crossed the same space. It was filled with horse drawn traffic.

"It still does not seem right to me," she said, "that you should be required, or allowed to participate in battles. Are there not enough men with two arms left?"

"It is not the point," he said. "I am lucky to be on the artillery staff and, in any event, I do not fight with my arms. An officer's head is supposed to be the most useful thing about him."

"But, you were at Chancellorsville, were you not?"

He shook his head in self-deprecation. "Only at the end." "I arrived at General Hooker's camp during the meeting in which he ordered the Army of the Potomac back across the Rappahannock."

"Did he have a choice?" she questioned. "I read that the army was surrounded by Lee's men."

Ford laughed.

She turned to look at him in surprise.

"I'm sorry, my dear lady," the soldier said. "The main thing that was surrounded by Lee was Hooker's belief in himself."

"I do not understand."

"The staff, or rather a colonel named Sharpe, gave it as his opinion at the crucial meeting that the 'surrounding' force could not have more than 40,000 effectives. Everyone present knew that Hooker at that moment had over 80,000 men within the 'encirclement'. Many of them had never been in action."

"Then, why?" she asked shyly.

"Why did he withdraw us? Why indeed! What better position could one have had! His enemy was spread paper thin all around. His own force was concentrated in the center with his supply line well established. He just gave up. Lee and that devil Jackson wrapped him in a web of illusion as strong as bands of iron. Forgive me, I should not criticize the general officer commanding."

"Why not?" Amy asked, sincerely puzzled about reasoning which would protect dangerous incompetence.

He said nothing, seeming to cast about in his mind for a good reason. "A habit," he eventually answered. "Perhaps not a good one. I hope you will not mind if I continue to call on you as the opportunity presents itself. My duties will bring me to Washington regularly for meetings with the Ordnance Bureau."

Amy tightened her grip on his arm. She could feel the muscle and bone through the blue serge. The thought that he had been deprived of an arm exactly like this one made her feel sick. "You know the answer to that question," she whispered. "I am happy that you are no longer involved with the detectives."

Ford looked at her carefully. "You mean you are pleased that I am no longer an accuser of your Devereux friends," he said. "You needn't worry yourself! They no longer have accusers. One cannot accuse the newly found friends of the Republican establishment. That is finished!"

She colored slightly, bending her head in apparent inspection of the ground. The grey in her hair shone almost silver in the dimming light. "Would you be unhappy with me if I became a Catholic?" she asked.

Ford had been somewhat distracted by admiration of the strength of her profile as seen against the sinking sun. It took a conscious effort to recall her words. "Catholic?" he said. "Why would you want to?" His brows came together momentarily. A tightly controlled whiteness spread across his features. "Ah, yes, I see now."

Amy watched him closely. "I have been taking instruction from Father Kruger," she said. "My family is a mixed group in matters of religion. Some are Congregationalist and others Unitarian.. I now see that one faith is too cold for me and the other too formless. Perhaps I could be happy as a Catholic."

"Do you have in mind that you might stay here, after the war?" he asked.

"I may," Amy responded. "This is a pleasant place. It is easy to imagine oneself among these people, forever."

Ford shook his head, glanced sideways at her and smiled.

"What is it, she asked?"

"It must be the climate, or the water," he said wryly. "Or perhaps it is merely the much reported charm of these Virginians."

She began to detach herself from his hold on her arm.

"No, please," he said gripping her forearm more tightly with his elbow. "I need you, badly. I don't care what church you habituate as long as you will let me take you there.

She held his hand in hers and looked away to the south. The river was crowded with traffic. White steam and black smoke drifted from the ships.

Anger boiled up in him. "They are all liars." he told her. "You must not believe them! They are our enemies. My friends and your patients are their victims! It is the worst thing about them that they are so easily believed in their lies! They hate us! Don't you know that? Many of them will never think themselves our countrymen again, no matter what the outcome of the war! Claude Devereux! He would sell his soul to the devil for 'Southern rights'!"

"But, they are accepted by the government!" she cried. "The president.."

"Yes! Yes! the president!," he said. "Devereux, he was too clever for us, too clever by far! Now we cannot touch him, and he is installed in the center of government, like an ulcer lying along a bone! You care for his family? They are all traitors to the Union, and the Constitution!"

Tears had come to her eyes. "Not his mother!" she plead, "not Clotilde and Hope."

Ford stared, wild eyed. He shook himself from her grip to unbutton his uniform coat. He produced a folded sheet of ivory paper. He had not planned to show her the note, at least he did not think he had intended to do so. Mitchell had written to ask him to do this, but he had thought he would not.

She took it and read. "This is impossible!" she declared.

"Why?"

"Because it is Hope Devereux's hand, but the letter is from someone named Taylor in Washington and is intended for her sister in Maryland."

"Ah yes," he whispered. "We wondered if that might be true, if it was her hand. How interesting, Boston born and bred.. I kept this, in the belief that someone might recognize the writing. It was posted by the Negro, White in Washington."

"But, what is the point? Why would she write to someone who does not exist?"

Ford handed her a box of wooden matches. "You will have to light one of these. There are some things I have not mastered as yet."

After seeing the enciphered text, she began to speak with some agitation. "Do you think this, spying, was of importance in the battle at Chancellorsville," she asked?

They had walked back in silence from the fortified heights. Her office seemed a refuge from the world.

"How could it not have been?" he answered.

"I don't know what to think," she said in a low voice. "I love these people." Tears had come again.

He gave her a handkerchief. "I do not believe that you care for them enough to join them," he said.

She wiped her eyes. "No, if there were no war, I would be happy to have them accept me, but there is a war and I know my duty. We Biddles always know our duty." she said with a wry expression. "What is it that you want from me?"

He was startled by the new chill of her voice. "Dear lady! I want but two things. The first is that you might inform my friend Mitchell in New York of anything serious that you observe. Here is his address. We must not let this treason prevail! The second is that you would accept the love I feel and will always feel for you."

Amy shook her head. "You cannot deprive me of new found family and in the next breath ask for my love. I will not have it. I will write Major Mitchell if I find it necessary. Please go."

"May I return?

She sat quietly, her eyes on the white wall in front of her desk. "You may, but do not do this to me again!" she said. She caught her breath in a half sob, and turned from him.

He stood and bowed slightly, reaching for her hand to kiss it. "I hope you can forgive me." he whispered. *Mitchell,* he thought. *I told you I didn't want to push her. If you cost me this woman..*

15 May
(Richmond)

The cabinet room door opened to permit the departure of the great and the nearly great. Major Charles Marshall rose to greet each man politely. Harry Jenkins emerged at the ragged end of the outpouring of cabinet officers and officials.

"I had no idea you were in there," Marshall began.

"Just making notes for Mister Benjamin, I seem to be doing that for him lately." Jenkins smiled at the thought.

"Not in the army any more?" Marshall said.

Jenkins wore a black suit.

"Not so! I have been asked by the Department of State to come 'en civile' to these meetings when I am helping their Secretary. I now have an office in their rooms as well as at the War Department. Things seem to be going that way in our business."

"So I hear," Marshall said. "Is Seddon losing his grip? The rumor is all over the army that you secret service people will be Benjamin's soon."

Jenkins looked about. He checked to insure that the cabinet room door was firmly secured, and then pulled a chair up next to Marshall. The two men were clearly of an age. The dark and soldierly good looks of Marshall seemed unrelated to Jenkins' ungainly and angular fairness, but their body language bespoke a familiar and close relationship. "Look, Charles," Jenkins said. "We've known each other a long time, since school really. I don't like the way things are developing in my little sphere."

"Don't want to work for Benjamin?" Marshall asked with a small smile.

"Not particularly, I preferred things the way they were." Would General Lee have me on the staff if I need to leave Richmond?"

"Of course!"

Jenkins appeared to be comforted by the words. "I do not understand it, Charles," he muttered. "The man's organization is a shambles. The War Department cannot get a straight answer from them most of the time, and their field operations are rotten with people working for both sides!" Jenkins seemed to brood on this. His head of red hair bobbed in agitation. "Several months ago we caught one of his clerks digging in the most secret of archives. We wormed a confession from the man. He had been passing details on one of our best efforts in Washington to the enemy."

Charles Marshall's eyes narrowed. "This wouldn't be the Devereuxs, would it?" he asked.

Jenkins was startled. "Venable must have told you!" he finally said.

"That is correct," Marshall said. "He tells me all these things. What happened to the clerk?"

"We have him in Castle Thunder on bread and water. He refuses to tell us to whom he reported. I told him last week that he will rot there forever if he does not."

"And, what does he say to that?"

Jenkins laughed. "That he will remember my name."

"This did not damage Benjamin's position?" Marshall asked.

"No! No!" Jenkins laughed again bitterly. The sound of his own voice made him glance at the closed door. "Consider events! Claude Devereux managed to extricate his people from a trap created by the State Department's poor arrangements. He also contrived to reach us with valuable intelligence." Jenkins looked at Marshall for confirmation.

"It was certainly helpful," the other officer agreed.

Jenkins looked disappointed with this. "All of this worked to Benjamin's benefit," he said unhappily. "He made the argument that greater efforts to exert a close control should be made in order to avoid such situations in the future, and that the talents of such valuable officers as myself would be better used if applied to the operations of all the secret services."

"The President accepted that?" Marshall asked.

Jenkins nodded. "He wanted to accept it. This conforms to his own beliefs in these matters."

Marshall meditated on this for a moment. "What the devil are they doing in there!" he growled in frustration.

"Oh! I am sorry, Charles," said Jenkins. "The President is giving General Lee his consent to the summer offensive campaign plan. An obsession with my own troubles has robbed me of my manners. I left to give them the opportunity to question him concerning the size of the force he will leave to cover Richmond."

Marshall frowned. "He can't leave much behind, Harry," he said. "We don't have men to spare to defend this city. Our forward motion will protect it!"

"That will not be well received," Jenkins said. "The loss of 'Old Jack' is deeply felt in there." He tipped his head toward the door. "My God, Charles. We were both Tom Jackson's students. He was mad as a hatter in some ways. Is it true what is said of his death?"

Marshall lowered his chin and his voice. "Let us cross over the river,"

"And rest in the shade of the trees," Jenkins concluded. "So it's true. He really said that at the end. Where on earth did that come from?"

"Beats me. He didn't have a poetic bone in his whole body."

"You should have seen the funeral procession down Broad Street here with Sandy Pendleton supporting the widow and Jim Lewis leading "Little Sorrel." I almost forgot the rotten grades he used to give me because he didn't understand the lesson.."

The latch shaped doorknob revolved. As it opened, it could be seen to be in the hand of Robert E. Lee.

Jenkins and Marshall rose to their feet.

With his back to the occupants of the cabinet room as he emerged, Lee's face was a study in mixed emotion. Satisfaction and frustration seemed to struggle within him as he reviewed the conversation just concluded and swung to face what he thought momentarily to be two officers of his own staff. His eyes met those of Jenkins. The mask slipped into place. The general's features took on the familiar look of marble civility. With a gesture of recognition he swept by, gathering up his staff officer as he went.

"Major Jenkins.." Judah Benjamin's voice summoned from within the cabinet room.

President Davis, Benjamin and Secretary Seddon were grouped around the far end of a well-polished ebony table.

The high backed chairs matched the long table and were curiously carved with tropical animals and African heads. The Confederate national flag was draped as bunting on the mantel piece below an engraving of Washington.

Jenkins took a seat on one of the side chairs which lined the walls. He selected a chair near enough to participate in the discussion as needed, but not so close as to include himself in their number.

"James, he must leave us enough men to be secure in the capital. He must! You will ensure that this is so!" Davis's words fixed Seddon to his duty, without the possibility of evasion.

Seddon blanched at the thought of a confrontation with Lee. "I believe General Lee intends to do what you wish, Mister President," Seddon offered in remonstrance at the suspicion evident in the chief executive's words.

The baleful look which Davis set upon him caused Seddon to quickly add that he would enforce compliance with Davis' wishes in the matter.

"Now, what was that business about Hannibal that he mentioned? I never took General Lee to be much of a scholar of the classical world, and what does Hannibal have to do with the battle at Chancellorsville?" Davis seemed puzzled. He looked at the three men.

Jenkins waited for a cue from Benjamin.

"This would be Devereux," Benjamin said softly.

"Who?" Davis demanded.

Exquisite embarrassment suffused the room.

Jenkins inwardly prayed for invisibility.

"Captain Claude Devereux, Mister President," Seddon said firmly. "He is in place in Washington City for General Lee, and Secretary Benjamin. We all sent him there some time ago."

Davis still looked blank. Hostility began to creep into his face.

Judah Benjamin interrupted the growth of the expanding bubble of strain. "This is the man who is making a particular study for you, Mister President, the officer suggested by Slidell."

"Ah, the banker from Washington, Yes! Now I recall the man. This is important. He has made some progress in his task? Good! But, what has he to do with General Lee?"

The two cabinet officers sat in silence.

Davis looked from one to the other, awaiting a response.

Neither man spoke.

Seddon appeared to be focused on the portrait of General Washington above the fireplace.

Judah Benjamin smiled calmly at his friend, the president.

Irritation began to show in Davis' sallow, haggard face. He gathered his shawl around his shoulders, wrapping himself in its woolen comfort. "Major, Jenkins, isn't it?" he said. "Tell me about this since no one else will."

Jefferson Davis waited for the door to close behind Seddon. They sat alone by the black table, he and Judah Benjamin. Davis traced the grain of the wood with his fingertips. Worry creased his forehead. "Don't overreach yourself, Judah," he said slowly. The army does not like you. A country at war for its life must listen to the army. It is clear that they think you are taking this man Devereux from them."

"They are correct," Benjamin replied. "The appreciation of Northern weaknesses which he is acquiring and reporting to my office is more portentous to our national survival than any details of information which he may pass to General Lee. I would like your permission to halt the War Department's communication with him."

"Why?"

"They risk his position by forcing him to perform too many duties. To learn what they want, he must actively seek the intelligence. He has achieved a notable standing for himself and his brother. They are familiars of both Lincoln and Stanton. We now have unmolested mail communications to them."

"How is that done?" the president asked.

Benjamin's beatific smile embraced the thought of Devereux's resourcefulness. "He uses the mail facilities of the United States Sanitary Commission. His family's position with the Commission causes them to receive mail through this body. He mixes his correspondence into the stream of official letters."

Davis loved the minutia of government business. This description of Devereux's ingenuity held his attention. "And then," he pressed.

"The mail," Benjamin responded, "is addressed to one of our friends in Maryland who passes it to a Signal Corps courier." Benjamin knew that the questions meant he had nothing to fear from this conversation. Davis never wished to hear the details of plans he meant to cancel. "My belief," Benjamin continued, "is that Hannibal, and his brother, should confine themselves to observation of the inner workings of the Lincoln government and ought not to do anything that might call attention to themselves."

"But, do I understand correctly that Captain Devereux, and his brother, are advising our enemies?"

"Yes," Benjamin answered evenly.

"Are they providing sound advice?"

"Yes, Mister President. There is no other way. To do less would be to destroy the basis of their acceptance by the Yankee government.."

Davis rubbed his eyes slowly before speaking again. "Does the army know all this, Judah?" he asked.

"Only Secretary Seddon, and Major Jenkins. He is managing this affair personally for me."

Davis frowned at his friend. "It is not surprising, Judah, that the army does not trust or admire you. The generals would never accept this.. You must use your own judgment in this business. You must decide for us how far it can be allowed to go. You may not, however, forbid the War Department's employment of Hannibal."

"Sir! the risk to.." Benjamin began with a rush.

Davis waved him to silence with a bony, long fingered hand. "Come, Judah. Think!" Davis insisted. "If I allow you this, surely James Seddon or Major.."

"Jenkins," Benjamin reminded.

"They will take the news to General Lee. You can see it in their faces, can't you? Do you wish to discuss the matter with Robert Lee?"

"No."

"Good. That is settled. You should do as you think best, but do not obstruct the army's use of the man. Do you think he will be able to maintain himself in Washington for long?"

Judah Benjamin shrugged expressively. "One cannot know these things. The Papal Nuncio recently asked me how it could be that a Confederate officer should be seen at the White House. His colleague in Washington saw Hannibal at a reception. Somehow they know who he is."

Davis permitted himself a silent laugh. "Do not let that disturb you. The Catholic Church knows much, but will tell the other side nothing! The New England factory grandees and their efforts to transform their Irish workers into something more to their liking have gotten the attention of the Churchmen."

"Slidell writes from France that the Quai D'Orsai goes to some pains to speak well of this man Devereux, and his family."

"That is more worrisome," Davis remarked. "Now I recall that he is a French citizen. Hmm! Judah, you must make it clear to friend Hannibal that we will not forget him, and his. Whatever can be done, should be!"

"I will see to it, Mister President."

26

A Family Reunion

18 May

Claude woke abruptly in the darkened bedroom. He lay quietly for a time in the warmth of the big walnut bed trying to recollect exactly where he was. After some thought he remembered the night before, remembered the theater, and a late supper at the British embassy. He also remembered Hope's dress. *My God, she does look fine in it.* He felt with one hand for her beneath the covers. His fingers reached the far edge of the mattress. All at once he knew why he had awakened. The night air was cool on his face. A slight breeze stirred the curtains by the partially open window. Turning his head he could just see her silhouette against the moon glow. She sat by the window in the flowered chair. "Can't sleep?" he asked, hoping she was not ill.

She swung round to face him. Her profile was outlined in the outer luminescence for an instant.

He wondered why she had been looking out the window. "What did you think of that actor fellow?" he asked.

"You asked the same thing last night," she replied. "Why are you interested in him?"

"I don't know." Devereux murmured. "I thought his performance was admirable, but if we had not met him at the Simpsons' dinner, I suppose I would not have given him another thought. There is something odd about him. He is looking for something."

"He asked me if he might call on us," she said.

"And?"

"I told him yes. Why not?" she answered, a little defensively. "Did you get his name?"

"Not really," he said. Everyone seemed to know him, but not me. I suppose that I was in Europe too long.. It's something like John Boone," he replied. "John, something Boone, a pleasant young man, perhaps a little too serious. I wish I could remember his name."

"I have it somewhere on the play program," Hope told him. "I will find it for you tomorrow." She was quiet for a brief moment. "I don't like Amy Biddle's nephew," she said.

"No? The idiot lieutenant?"

"Claude, He is a hypocrite. He preaches all the time, the fool! And I do not fancy the experience of having this rude boy stare at my bosom in any more drawing rooms!"

He grinned at the darkness. "He has good taste in women, but you knew that."

"He has no taste at all!" she exploded. "And, I am sick to death of the endless drivel he mouths."

Ah! The convert's zeal. "It isn't all drivel, my dear," he said. "It is merely the evidence of his hatred for us and it is richly returned. He watched her ghostly outline with satisfaction while thinking that young Biddle wasn't such a fool at all. Her shadowy figure recalled something dimly remembered from a childhood fancy of summer nights and friendly spirits. He could hear her breathing across the room.

She sighed deeply.

"What is it?" he asked.

"Patrick, it's Patrick," she whispered. "You don't comprehend how much it is injuring him, what you are doing."

"Do you imagine that I enjoy this myself?"

"It is not the same," she said. "He is.."

"Innocent?"

"Perhaps," his wife commented. She laughed musically. "There is something in you, my love, that few would call that." The sound of her voice died away. She sat in silence for a moment before beginning again. "Your brother would have been happy to have them out in front of him," she said. "Fair targets! That is what he would wish. It is not to his taste to lie to them! You, we, will all pay a terrible price."

"Don't be morose," he said. "Surely, you have not been there at the window brooding on this? Come back to bed."

Hope leaned out the window. "Come here, Claude," she told him.

Closing his dressing gown about him, he stood behind her chair, one hand on her shoulder.

The second floor gallery of the ell occupied the space beyond the window. A pale yellow light fell upon the brick walk in the garden below. The shape of the illuminated patches imitated the hooded windows of the ground floor. Someone was in the kitchen below.

"I heard them downstairs," she said. "It woke me."

"How long?" he asked.

She shook her head. "I have no idea. Perhaps an hour.."

"Let's go see," he said. Halfway down the stairs an old board creaked loudly complaining of the night damp.

The subdued murmur of voices in the kitchen ceased.

Devereux opened the pantry door and limping badly, entered the kitchen. The icebox resided across the room beside the sink. He nodded to the people around the table and then searched for a glass in the cupboard beside the door.

Aunt Betsy rose from the table to take it from his hand. "What do you want at this time of night, Claude," she asked.

He tried to look at her, and not at the group around the table. She had on a nice dress, something she would normally not have worn at work. Devereux considered her. Anxiety showed in the almost furtive way she approached him. He smiled at her while trying to absorb the impact of the blue figure at the table. "I'd like some buttermilk Auntie. Too many late nights have taken their toll I think." He held his stomach with one hand as he spoke. Claude had called the elder Whites Aunt and Uncle all his life as any well brought up Southern boy would have done.

She went to the icebox with his glass.

Her departure removed the screen behind which Devereux and the men at the table had avoided looking at each other. All the White men were there. George Senior, Bill and Joe occupied the far side of the table. George Junior sat at the far end, next to his mother's empty chair.

"You look healthy, George," Devereux ventured. "The army must be doing well by you."

Bill White and his soldier brother exchanged glances. Joe studied the grain of the tabletop.

Betsy returned with a moisture beaded jug and a glass of milk.

"Thank you," Devereux told her. He watched George Junior's eyes as they followed the glass. "Want some?" he prompted.

The soldier took a glass of milk from his mother.

Devereux sat down. "What is it?" he asked. He examined the pendulum wall clock. "Why are you all here at four thirty in the morning?"

"My son has deserted from the army." George White stated evenly. "We have come to talk to your father."

A variety of emotions and thoughts raced through Devereux's consciousness. "How long have you been gone?" he asked.

"Just since yesterday," George Junior replied.

"They maybe don't know he's gone yet," Bill commented. "His friends said they would cover for him. They told him he should not go."

Devereux began to see the familiar figure at the end of the table in a new light. The memory of his own soldiers started to fill the room. "What happened George?" he asked.

The mulatto fixed him with a chilly stare. "I don't want to be with them no more. They are no different from you all! They don't like us colored folks! I'm tired of it all! I'm tired of doin' nothin' but guard and fatigue duty. I joined to whip the people who need whippin'. They're never going to let us fight you! I'm sick of officers who say they are our friends, but wash their hands if they touch you. Most of them could not be officers in a white regiment. Some of them are just trash."

"I doubt if they are quite that bad," Devereux observed. "You never did know when to stop talking."

"The worst are the Irish," George Junior exploded in resentment. "The damned, nigger beating Irish! I hate them the most!"

His mother began to weep softly into her hands.

Joe White, her youngest, went to her, to hold her close against the pain.

"Do you want to hate yourself, boy?" George Senior growled. "What do you think you mostly are?"

"Uncle, you don't want to tell father this," Devereux told George White.

The old butler shook his head.

"He has to go back, Claude" Bill interjected. "We've been telling him that all night."

"Yes," Devereux agreed. "You must go back George, now, before they miss you!"

"Who are you to send me back to the United States Colored Troops?" the soldier demanded. Who are you, of all people to do that, you and my dear brother?"

"You chose your path," Devereux answered coolly. "We chose ours. You were raised in this house. You belong here. You are one of us.. We do not desert! My father would accept this no better than yours. You will go back!"

George Junior rose from the table to hold out his arms to his mother.

She left one son for the other.

"I don't want no more of it! I want to be here with my own! Do you want this, too, mama? Do you want me to go back?" George asked.

"I don't want you to be there," she said through her tears, "but you belong there now. You joined them. And they are fighting for the freedom!"

Bill White rubbed his face with one hand. "This way some of us are bound to be on the winning side." he said.

The Union soldier sighed aloud. "All right! How can I get back? The provost guard will pick me up for sure! I was real lucky to get here."

Devereux made an expressive gesture with his hands. "Bill and I will take you back after breakfast," he said. "I have papers that make that a small matter. Let us say nothing of this to anyone else."

A small sound caused them to turn to the pantry door. Hope stood in the tiny room. "So many men to feed, Betsy" she said. "I do hope we have enough on hand!" She walked across the kitchen, gathering the older woman's arm in hers as she went.

Joe White left for the garden wood shed. The big kitchen range needed a lot of fuel.

27

A Visit

Wednesday, 23 May

Devereux had not expected a summons to the offices of the military government of Alexandria. He had imagined that his new status as a loyal Republican would protect him from such inter-ference. A soldier clerk had brought him the folded sheet of paper containing a terse invitation to the provost marshal's headquarters. Devereux would normally have simply gone out the door to walk the short distance from the bank, but on this occasion he decided to assemble his men to support this expedition into the lair of the beast. It was probably the tone of the note that caused him to do this.

Bill White drove the carriage as was their habit since Isaac Smoot had left. Lieutenant Tom Morgan trailed the vehicle on foot across town, ready to provide "muscle" for an escape attempt if this were needed. Sergeant Kennedy came from his new stable to take a position by a window in the bank from which he could see if anything changed in the neighborhood in Devereux's absence.

Five minutes after their arrival at the police headquarters, White sat on the driver's seat behind the chestnut team outside the old commercial building which housed the offices of the military governor.

Devereux walked down the hallway that extended through the center of the structure. He concentrated on the leg, willing himself not to limp, thinking about what he was going to say. He looked at the glass topped doors and the names painted there. "Charles Browning, Major, USV, Provost Marshal" was printed in gold lettering on one. The door opened into a small ante room. A familiar face and form occupied the room. The short, fat, middle-aged man rose from his seat at a dark wooden desk. His frock coat was cut in a style so modern that it made one think of the engravings in "Harper's Weekly." Devereux was always interested to see what sort of silk cravat this man might be wearing on a particular occasion.

"Hello, Claude," the man said, plainly glad to see his visitor, "good to see you.. We haven't seen much of you at the Lyceum since you've been back."

"Good morning, Mister Ellis," Devereux responded. "Is Major Browning in?"

"He has gone out. I imagine he'll be back shortly. You can speak freely."

"What's this about, Jeff?" Devereux asked. "You're not in trouble, are you? I keep worrying that he will discover that the office is short pass blanks."

The other man solemnly shook his head. "It would never occur to him. I was here before he was assigned, and I'll be here when he is gone."

Devereux had brought this man into the world of secret work in January 1862 during his first trip into occupied Alexandria. His father had suggested Ellis as a man whose working skills as an accountant would naturally recommend him for employment with the occupation authorities. Ellis had been very willing. The Union Club of Alexandria was always in search of new membership. In the winter of 1861 they were especially welcoming. Ellis did not complain of his work for the provost marshal. He simply did the work. He did the Union army's work, and did it to the Confederate Government's satisfaction.

Devereux released the shorter man's hand. *The ties are getting a little worn,* he thought. *I'll ask Hope to pick out a half dozen new ones for him in Washington. They will make an acceptable gesture of appreciation on his birthday.*

Ellis did not have the opportunity to explain Devereux's summons. They were still standing together in conversation as the door to the corridor swung wide to admit two men, a Union Army major and a tall, blonde civilian. The newcomers halted momentarily just inside the door.

"Ah! Major Browning, you have not met Mister Claude Devereux I believe," Ellis began.

The officer seemed rooted to his place on the threadbare carpet. He looked at Devereux with an expression both guarded and noncommittal.

Devereux returned the scrutiny. A pleasantly welcoming smile spread across his face. He extended a hand.

The officer looked down at it, then up at the Virginian. He did not move.

Devereux felt his heart beat faster. He searched for the edges of his self control.

The provost marshal began to speak. "I did not send for you to shake hands."

The blond man stepped around him to grasp Devereux's hand. He shook it heartily, smiling broadly the while. "Glad to meet you, Devereux," he said. "I'm Lewis Galbraith. I've been looking forward to this opportunity since I've come to hear so much about you.."

"Thank you, Mayor," Devereux answered. "I had been planning to call at your offices, but the moment never quite seemed right, our family have been supporters of Mayor Price for many years. Now that he is gone, it is a delicate situation."

"A sad business!" the mayor replied. "I do hope you believe that I had nothing to do with it, nothing!" The smile had changed to the sincerest regret for the unpleasantness of wartime life.

Devereux was spared the need for a reply by the intervention of Major Browning. "Come into my office, Devereux. I want to talk to you about an incident which occurred a few days ago involving a colored soldier." Without further elab oration the man opened a door behind Ellis' desk. A larger room containing a desk, several chairs and various piles of paper was revealed.

Before Claude could enter, the voice of Lewis Galbraith was heard. "Major, I would like to sit in on this meeting, if you do not mind."

Browning had reached his desk, was standing behind it in a magisterial pose waiting for Devereux to arrive before him. Doubt marked his features. "This has nothing to do with the tax sale."

"Mister Devereux is one of our most prominent citizens."

"Very well," the military officer said with visible reluctance.

The two men in civilian apparel filled the space before his desk.

"Why, why don't you sit down, gentlemen?" the officer requested with obvious doubt, trapped in the necessity of avoiding insult to the Union mayor of the city. "Do you know the soldier, George White?" he asked Claude.

The mayor frowned slightly turning to Claude. "Those people work for you, I believe."

"For my father, really, they have done so for many years." Turning to the provost marshal, he spoke. "Yes, Major, I know Private George White of the 2nd United States Colored Troops Cavalry Regiment. I took him back to his camp on the morning of the 18th, as is reported in that note in front of you." Devereux referred to a document made up of several sheets of paper pinned together at a corner.

The owner of the desk had retrieved the papers from a heap in the center of the piece of furniture. He raised his head to glare angrily at Claude, stung by the tone of the words. "Were you harboring this deserter?" he demanded.

"Of course not!" Devereux protested. "He left camp without permission for a few hours to see his mother, my father's cook. When we discovered his presence, I took him back, immediately!"

The eyes across the desk narrowed speculatively. "So, his mother harbored him?"

Devereux felt odd, a little light headed. He began to see the man in a different light, began to see him bleeding and broken on the floor He could see himself hammering the man with his silver headed cane. "Yes, she did," he said between his teeth. "Perhaps you should …"

"Come now, Major," the mayor expostulated. "The man took a few hours off to visit his parents. Devereux took him back. There's an end to it! I think you have enough to do without harassing loyal citizens! General Slough is a personal friend of this family, as are others in the government.."

Browning colored at the rebuke, but he was apparently unafraid of the possibility of political repercussions, and plunged on. "You will have to understand Mister Devereux, that although Mister Galbraith and I are both from Vermont, he is an attorney and understands the niceties of such a situation far better than I."

"And what were you in civilian life, Major?" Devereux asked politely.

"We run a quarry in the north, near the Canadian line. Montreal is the nearest big town."

"A charming place," Claude replied smoothly.

Browning was somewhat taken aback by the response. Doubt began to show in his eyes. Nevertheless, he chose to continue. "You will have to tell me how you got through every check point between here and Upper Marlboro, Maryland," the Union officer said abruptly.

"I thought we were finished with that," the mayor expostulated.

Devereux stopped him. "No, that's quite all right, Mister Galbraith, here it is," he said, retrieving a folded, official looking paper from a coat pocket.

The military police official leaned back and held up the document to examine it in the light from the window behind him. A frown gathered on his craggy features. He seldom saw Secretary Stanton's signature on documents of this sort.

Bill White stood outside in the street next to the chestnut pair. He absentmindedly petted the animal closest to him. The horse shook his head appreciatively.

Down the street, Lieutenant Morgan leaned against the doorpost of Snelling's Tobacco and Sundries Emporium. In his dress he had tried for an effect which would be acceptable to casual observers. A checked, soft cap was pulled low over the violet eyes. Workman's overalls and a rough jacket made him the very type of a lounging idler. Passing women glanced at him, looked away, and then back again. He tipped his hat to each in a gesture so much a reflex that he was not aware of it. Since Devereux's entry of the military government building, the partisan cavalry officer had spent a pleasant quarter hour engaged in conversation with two Union Army enlisted men from New York. Morgan's older sister lived in that state with her farmer husband's family. Morgan had visited her home at Sackett's Harbor on Lake Ontario several times before secession separated him from his sister. He missed her. It was still possible to send letters, but it was difficult and dangerous. The news from upstate New York was welcome.

At the far end of the street, Frederick Kennedy waited in Devereux's office. The room occupied a corner of the brick Devereux and Wheatley building. It looked out on the intersection of streets which bounded two sides of the structure. Kennedy sat with his face half averted from the open window. Thus far he had seen no one truly inexplicable in the spaces surrounding the bank. As he watched, a slender, blond, deeply tanned man in a dark coat approached the bank's front door. He asked the Negro doorman something, nodded at the answer, then strolled away in the direction of the provost marshal's office. Kennedy watched him go.

A few minutes later, Morgan took notice of the same man as he walked along the street. The discussion with the two soldiers distracted him somewhat, but he found himself glancing back at the oncoming stranger. The man stood out among the general passers-by. He did not look like someone who really belonged on this busy street. A new image of the same man swept through Morgan's consciousness. The figure in his mind's eye was in Confederate uniform. *I know him,* Morgan thought. The tanned man saw him and began to cross the street. He was midway across when two burly, mustachioed civilians emerged from the tobacco shop to seize Morgan by the arms.

"We've been watchin' you, fellah!" one cried. "What'r you doin' in the middle of a work day loiterin' outside that buildin'?" He indicated the provost marshal's offices with a tilt of the head.

The two New York soldiers tried to shield Morgan from his assailants. "Who the hell would you be?" one yelled. "He was just jawin' with us! His sister lives near my folks!"

The blond man stood silent across the street.

Traffic stopped at the noise.

One detective held Morgan's shoulders against the brick of the tobacco shop wall. The other felt his body beneath the bulky clothing. One hand closed on the Army Colt secreted beneath the waistband of Morgan's trousers. The detective smiled full in Morgan's face from a distance of less than a foot. The man's breath was disgusting and his teeth needed repair. Over the other detective's shoulder, Morgan saw the courier start once more across the street. Holding the other Confederate's attention Morgan shook his head slightly. The man gripping his shoulders began to rotate his head to discover the object of Morgan's attention. The pinioned man brought a knee up hard into the crotch of the policeman with the groping hands. The man's grip slackened as his face suffused with blood, the mouth opening convulsively. Morgan bent one leg enough to retrieve with one hand the six inch, narrow bladed knife that normally resided in his boot. With that hand he drove the blade into the abdomen of the detective holding his shoulders. The restraining pressure disappeared instantly as the gut-hurt man collapsed on the sidewalk. At the same time, the policeman with crushed genitals sank to his knees, hands crossed over the damaged organs. Morgan then extricated the pistol from his waist bad, cocked it and shot him through the left eye. The other detective writhed on the sidewalk in agony, clutching the wound in his belly. The Ranger took careful aim and shot him in the head.

The two unarmed New York soldiers recoiled in astonishment and fear from the scene.

Morgan considered them for a second. He grinned wildly at them. "Run Yanks!" he shouted. "Go home! Home where you belong! Go!" With these words he spun on his heel and disappeared in an alley.

Shouting in the street interrupted Major Browning's scrutiny of Devereux's "Laissez Passez" from the Secretary of War. Browning had just reached the conclusion that he had badly overstepped his authority and the interruption was welcome. A shot outside the window brought the three men to their feet. Jefferson Ellis rushed into the room from his post in the next chamber.

Browning reached the window first. "I saw him!" he cried. "A man in old clothes! He ran down that alley!" Without further words he ran for the door.

Devereux, Galbraith and Ellis watched the spectacle from behind the glass of the office window. A small crowd had instantly gathered about the prostrate bodies of two men. Neither moved. A soldier held back the throng while another stared into an alley behind the group.

Browning roared for the sergeant of the guard in the main corridor of the building.

As he had reached the window, Devereux glimpsed Tom Morgan's disappearing back. *My God! They'll run him down and that will be the end of us all,* he thought.

"What could that have been?" the mayor exclaimed.

Browning pelted across the street and into the alley. Behind him were three cavalrymen carrying Sharp's carbines.

At least a minute had passed since the shooting.

He may escape, Devereux thought. *It is just possible.* "Probably a deserter," he told the mayor.

"No, a deserter does not fight like that," the mayor said slowly. "We now have much experience with the race of deserters in Alexandria. Men with uniforms and guns to order us about, sometimes they do not even have the uniforms.."

Something in the man's voice made Devereux look at him. Lewis Galbraith stared down into the street. There were tears in his eyes.

"They will run him down," Devereux said slowly, experimentally. "That will be the end of it. One less traitor."

"It is not as simple as that," Galbraith said without looking at him. "You know that. There is right on both sides of this, this calamity of a war."

Devereux and Ellis exchanged glances. "Why is it that I did not meet you before the war?" Devereux asked Galbraith.

The mayor laughed aloud at that. "We do not move in the same circles, Mister Devereux. I moved here eight years ago from Burlington, Vermont to work for the railroad, The Orange and Alexandria. I almost joined the militia in '58." He laughed again. "God knows where I'd be now if I had."

Devereux did not answer at once. His attention was on a face that had turned upward to confront him from the crowd. It was Lieutenant Howard Cawood. His tan seemed deeper than ever. It contrasted strongly with the white of his collar. "I look forward to our future association, Mister Mayor," Devereux commented. He held out his hand. "Don't concern yourself too much about having come from Vermont. You are here now."

That Night

Cawood told his story and left. The meeting with Harry Jenkins would be the next day. The Signal Corps had safely brought him to Washington. After Cawood's departure, Claude and Patrick Devereux, Frederick Kennedy and Bill White remained behind in Claude's room at the rear of the bank. The rump meeting was dominated by an empty chair. Claude sat in front of one of the heavily draped windows. To his right hung a portrait of the bank's founder.

Grandfather would be proud of you, my brother, Patrick reflected. *You and he, you are the type to so ably endure these appalling conditions. I will do my best.*

"Is he dead, Captain?" Kennedy asked.

Claude flinched from the question. His face pulled to one side in a tic of nervous expression. "I think it must be so," he said. "Ellis informs me that there was a further encounter in the boatyard near Jones's Point. He killed another one. They think he was hit several times. There was a lot of blood. They have not been able to find a body."

"Maybe he got away. He was, is a mighty tough man," Kennedy insisted.

"I believe he must have crawled off into a hole somewhere," Patrick said. He looked at the others almost apologetically.

Claude nodded slowly. He did not say a word.

"We must continue to search for him," Bill insisted. "We were not friends, but …"

"Yes, we will search," the leader agreed.

Sunday, May 24

"You caught the spy himself, but you do not know to whom he reported?" Devereux looked disbelieving. "Was there no one who appeared to be a probable suspect?"

Jenkins looked across the table at the banker. *My God, but it would be easy to dislike this man*, he thought. "There were," he said, "in fact, there were several. Unfortunately, the evidence was not compelling, and they were all of a position in society which would not allow of frivolous accusations."

"Ah, yes! Of course! How foolish of me!" Devereux responded. "We know how this works, don't we Fred? Patrick?"

Kennedy looked on impassively from a chair against one wall. He acknowledged Devereux's question with a slight smile. Patrick looked away, embarrassed by his brother's bullying of a friend.

"You can't expect that we will be comforted by this news, Harry!" Devereux exclaimed. "How long before that clerk's former master, whoever he is, finds someone new to unmask us! My wife is involved in this now my friend! My family, nearly all of them are in it. Sergeant Kennedy here, and there others in this town. What about the priest, the two ministers! Damn it! You know who they are!"

Jenkins squirmed in resentment. "We are doing everything we can to deal with this danger," he said. "It is for this reason, among others, that I now work directly for Secretary Benjamin. I handle all matters involving you personally!"

Devereux digested this, and looked at Kennedy for a comment.

"We are going to go on with this, aren't we, sir," the sergeant said? "Why bother ourselves with worry in this?"

"That's right, Claude," Patrick exclaimed. "Leave poor Harry alone!" His expression showed how much he was displeased by Claude's show of bad temper.

"All right, Jenkins," Claude said, turning back to his visitor. "Leveler heads prevail. You say our information was useful at Chancellorsville?"

"Extremely so. General Lee would not have moved without it!"

"That makes a lot of this worthwhile. What does Venable say? Does Lee want more of the same kind of thing?"

"Of course! Charles sends his regards and thanks you with the rest of us. Claude, the army is going to invade the North again."

"Why are you telling us this?" Claude asked, alarmed that such information should be freely given.

Jenkins looked exasperated. "Why!" he cried in frustration. "Because we need for your group to play a role in the campaign. That is why!"

"When?" Patrick and Kennedy asked in unison.

"The worst thing about them is the plausibility of their lies …"
The phrase rang through Amy Biddle's head as she watched them walk away.

"A distant relation," Claude had said. Just in from Kentucky, in tobacco brokerage, from Frankfort. I have been showing him the camp."

Lies. All lies! She was now sure that they must be true, the things Wilson Ford had said. The very grace and assurance with which Claude said these things added to her belief in his deceit.

They had used Devereux's office room in the old administration building for a meeting of some kind. The redheaded cousin from Kentucky seemed very little like Claude. The man possessed a gravity and slightly unbending decorousness that reminded her of Patrick. The four men moved steadily away from her across the yard of the convalescent camp, Patrick managed his crutches well, she thought. Once again she noticed that Claude tended to lean on someone's shoulder in walking any sort of distance. *What is the matter with his leg?* she thought.

She went down the hall to her room.

That strange, quiet little man who had taken the Oath of Allegiance in the hospital and who now ran a livery stable had been there. He and Claude seemed inseparable these days. Amy did not like the way this man looked at her. At times, his face held nothing but a careful politeness. At other times, when she managed to catch him off guard, she saw something else in him. Pity for herself was not an attitude she would accept from anyone, least of all someone who had so easily changed his coat.

She was mindful of the letter from Ford which lay in the center drawer of the desk at which she sat. He wrote that for the present he would be absent in Ohio seeking horses for the artillery. He had told her in past conversations that the constant death and maiming of artillery horses was, for him, the greatest pain of all in warfare. He had spoken of the ghastly necessity of shooting wounded horses after every action. Amy had asked him why he did not have someone else do this since it hurt him so. After all, he was an officer. He had shaken his head, saying that it was "just one more score to settle with the rebels."

It may have been the presence of Devereux's "cousin" that decided her course of action. She searched in the desk for the address of the friend in New York whom Wilson had recommended to her. *Here it is! Major Mitchell.*. Devereux had just now mentioned the unexpected necessity of a trip to New York City. Amy had expressed regret that "the Commission" would be deprived of his help for a time. "At least they would still have Hope to call upon," she remarked. He had smiled engagingly while announcing that Hope would accompany him, that, in fact, she was "looking forward to the shopping and the theater.."

Something must have shown in her.

The three men seemed at a loss for words momentarily.

Devereux had finally suggested that perhaps she, too, would benefit from a short absence from her heavy schedule. 'Could she accompany them?' He had accepted her regretful excuse with undue ease.

As they turned to go, she caught the little Kennedy man's expression. The sadness in his eyes was unbearable.

"So you actually offered to take her with us to New York?"

Devereux knew from the tone of his wife's voice that he had done something of which she disapproved. His own feelings about the incident were a complex mixture of guilt and regret that he was unable to find some way in which he could enjoy the company of both women. "Yes, I did. She refused. You don't think it was a good idea, I see."

Hope said nothing. What could she say?

In the privacy of the sitting room off their bedroom, she wore a silk dressing gown over what he remembered to be a very appealing lace night dress.

"Where is he now, this mysterious major?"

"In Maryland, somewhere. The Secret Line will try to take him back across the river tonight."

"Tell me the rest, Claude. I want to hear everything he said to you. I am involved in this as deeply as any of you! I want to understand what we are doing!"

"Are you sure you want to know?"

"Claude!"

"Fred Kennedy has been commissioned in the Signal Corps."

"That doesn't mean much to me," she said.

"Nor to him," her husband replied. "Jenkins showed me Daguerreotypes of several men. He had me write down their names. They are additional couriers they may use to reach us."

"Did he tell you what General Lee will do next?"

"No," he lied.

"What else did he say, Claude?"

"He asked Kennedy to leave the room. That was a little odd in itself, but then perhaps it is not so strange since he claims that the president is directly involved in what we are doing. Someone made this suggestion to me once before, but I paid it little mind. From one so principled as Harry Jenkins the claim carries a great deal more weight. According to him, he was instructed to tell me that they consider all this to be 'absolutely essential'! He said that they, the president and Benjamin, want me to dig myself and Patrick in deeper and deeper, 'like ticks on a dog', until we are in a position to influence events and.."

"And what?"

"And then, we will be able to identify the key weakness of the North."

She inspected him carefully. Doubt began to cloud her face. "No."

"No, what?"

"No, that's not true. It's absurd."

"Why isn't it true?" Devereux asked softly.

A frown obscured her beautiful features. "Don't be clever. We both know you are not telling me the truth. All this can't be happening just so that you can write some damned report! That's ridiculous! You can't tell me what it is you are trying to do?"

"No," he lied. *She has put her finger on it! This must have more importance than a report! It must!* "It would be foolish to do so," he said. "If it becomes imperative, I will tell you. It implies no mistrust of you, my dear."

"I will accept that, Claude. I do trust you. By the way, Mister Booth came by today, and left his card."

"Who?"

"Don't be impossible! The actor! You told me you wanted to talk to him some more."

"I thought his name was Boone." He tried to remember why he should have found this actor to be worthwhile.

"I asked if this was a social call," Hope went on, "or business." She peered at him. "Claude, I tire at times of waiting for an indication of your interest."

"Please. Continue."

"He said that he has successfully placed money in petroleum wells in Pennsylvania. Do you know what that is?"

"A substitute for whale oil, what else did he say?"

"He told me, and maman that he might wish to make some business arrangement with the bank, but in fact, I think he merely wished to speak to you. Something in your conversation with him at the Simpsons' party has made him want to know you. What did you tell him?"

Devereux searched his memory. "I told him of our family interest in the arts. I told him how difficult life had become for most people in this town. I said that the Yankee government had much to answer for. He agreed. When did he say he would call again?"

"He was unhappy to have missed you. He will be absent from Washington for two months. I did not think I should press him."

"No, of course not. Well, it matters not."

28

The State of the Union

Monday, 25 May

Hope found the trip to the North to be something different from her expectations. She had been endowed by her upbringing with a mental image of the northeastern part of the country as a land of industry, thrift and common sense. An underlying assumption in the picture was the notion that a certain uniformity of purpose, custom and belief pervaded the region. Her years in the South had inexorably altered her allegiances, but the image of her homeland remained. Hope found that the journey strongly supported her belief in the economic vitality and wealth of the North. The evidence of money, goods and development was everywhere to be seen. The commonest sort of people appeared to be well fed, well clothed and possessed of funds with which to indulge their ordinary whims. The railroads themselves gave evidence of a national capacity for procurement of capital goods. Cars, tracks and locomotives were all of the best and latest manufacture. Altogether, the trip was a sobering experience for Southern partisans.

The Devereux passage to New York along the steel rails was interrupted at several points by Claude's need to conduct the bank's business. They descended from the train at Baltimore, Philadelphia and Newark. As the long trip progressed, Hope gradually began to see that other interests than the bank's were being served by the calls. In Baltimore, stops in the premises of two steamship lines were followed by a visit to a firm of commission merchants who reacted at first to Devereux's unexpected appearance with a circumspect courtesy which recast itself to genuine warmth after the exchange of private words between her husband and one of the company's partners. After watching Claude in conversation with this man for a few minutes, she was sure that her husband had not come here to discuss business.

Hope Devereux considered herself to be a committed helper in her husband's secret work. In recent weeks she had attempted to support his mission in every way she could. Nevertheless, she sensed in him hesitation to involve her fully in the details of things. She was determined to beat down this reluctance. She had struggled for years to achieve real understanding of her husband's inner life. Having finally, truly, made him her own, she wanted nothing about him to be closed to her. To that end, she eavesdropped shamelessly. From across the room she listened to Claude's small talk of shipping rates and insurance syndicates. She kept her face averted from the men. In her handbag, she carried a new issue of the "Revue des deux Mondes." It made fine camouflage. Her husband's tone of voice changed slightly. The Baltimore merchant bent forward and listened closely as

Claude spoke to him in a near whisper. She heard the names of places; Pennsylvania, Harrisburg, Baltimore. Her husband felt in his coat pocket for something as he spoke. He showed the merchant several small, flat objects, daguerreotypes. More names crossed the room to her; Harrison, Stringfellow, Alexander, names unknown to her, names that must be of importance. The merchant wrote them, repeated them to himself. At last he tore the small piece of paper with the names into tiny fragments. The man listened intently to Claude's low voice. He began to nod. The nodding grew more and more vigorous. The two men stood. The merchant shook Claude's hand. He held it with both of his. His voice rose with emotion. "You may rely on me in this final crisis, sir! You may rely on us all. Constitutional government will be restored with the downfall of the tyrant! You will then see a voluntary reunion of the states!"

"Who is that man, Claude?" she asked when they had left the building and were safely wrapped by the walls of the hired carriage in which Bill White had driven them about the town.

"A friend. Well-meaning friends abound in the land of our enemies," he answered.

"It is not true, is it? The South will not return to the old Union. I cannot imagine you and your brothers and friends accepting that, after all this!"

He looked at her. After a moment his face softened. "I think not, but let them believe it. It harms nothing, and we are quite willing to be their, neighbors."

The Newark stop was particularly long. Devereux visited a variety of commercial establishments. In most of them he passed a few minutes, signed a document or two and departed. Emerging from one of these places, he handed Bill a folded note. Looking at it upside down, she could see that he had written upon the paper the names of two intersecting streets and a time. "Let's be there then. I would not keep this man waiting. Jenkins was particularly insistent that I should take his measure. He is the leader of the most violent anti-draft men."

White drove the unfamiliar vehicle and team well, with the skill he consistently displayed in such matters.

She and Claude discussed the manifest evidences of material wealth and prosperity which abounded in the streets about them. He told her that the contrast to Richmond or Wilmington, North Carolina could not be more striking. "Clearly, the United States is in the midst of a flourishing of industry and commerce the like of which it has never seen," he remarked. "I have been gathering published evidences of this for some time. Our own observation of this wealth confirms my view of their great material strength. In a business climate of this kind, stimulated by immense government expenditure, there can be no chance of finding weakness. They move from strength to strength! Jourdain gave me figures some benefactor of his filched from the Quartermaster General's office. Production rises steadily, everywhere!" He looked more than a little wild eyed. A kind of sad desperation was in his utterance of these thoughts. She looked out the small, square window, seeking words of consolation and encouragement. "Claude! We have passed this corner twice before, have we not?" she asked him.

"Yes, but he was not there yet!" Devereux pointed with one gloved hand at the window closest to the curb.

Following the line of his arm she glanced out to see a thin faced man in a bowler hat and brown suit. She was sure the figure had appeared in the two or three seconds during which her attention had shifted to her husband.

Devereux opened the door of the carriage as it approached the corner.

The thin man stepped up into the vehicle as it made the turn. Shutting the door behind him, the newcomer removed his hat in courtesy to Hope as he settled into the seat across from his host and hostess. "Good day to you Missus!" he grinned, looking at her for a long instant. "And you would be?" he asked.

"No names! You know that. No names," Devereux responded sharply. "This is my lady wife. She is completely in our trust, but no names, neither ours nor yours, Mister Smith."

The other smiled and showed his acquiescence with an inclination of the head. "And what about the nigger?" he asked, cocking his head toward the place where the driver's back would be found on his seat above.

"He knows nothing," Devereux said. "A local livery driver, hired for the day."

The Irishman kept his eyes on Hope throughout this exchange. He seemed to like what he saw. "And why does Richmond send such a proper gent as yourself to speak to the likes of me?" he asked.

"My superiors wish to know of your intention regarding the Draft Law."

"Ah! Yes! They would, would they not, ma'am?" The man addressed himself to Hope, seemingly unable to take his eyes from her face. "So, the powers that be in Jeff Davis' government wish to know the plans of a lot of hapless sons of the 'auld sod stranded here amongst the robber bankers and Yankee politicians. I find that amusin'. I surely do! My comrades and me, we yearn for Mister Davis' approbation, we do, yearn for it! What will we do? What will we do?" His face grew stern. It seemed drawn, almost haggard. A light began to glow from within his skull. "We will not fight for the damned English, Yankee, Republican bastards! That we will not do!" he cried. "Them as wanted to do that have already joined! The rest of us will not be had by that ape, Lincoln, and his scurvy crew! We don't mean to die for their precious nigger pets!"

"What about the German workingmen?" Devereux asked. "Do they feel the same?"

The man stared at them. "The squareheads will do some damned thing, some foolish thing! They will protest the drawin', but then someone will explain the rules and offer to compromise and they will go quietly home! An undependable lot!" 'Smith' gazed about the carriage as he spoke. His attention returned to Hope.

She stared back at him.

He abruptly swung his attention to her husband. "If you're so keen on things military, your honor, why aren't you in the army, yourself?" he demanded. A fine gentleman like you should be in the field inspirin' the peasantry to acts of patriotism! Isn't that right ma'am?" He was happy with himself for making this statement, and grinned at them both.

Devereux squared his shoulders against the attack, but did not respond.

Hope colored at the man's insult. "My husband is an officer of the Confederate Army!" she said with heat. "He has done more than his share of fighting!"

Smith smiled at her. "Very good, missus! Very good! We should always see a wife defend her man!"

"You were a soldier, weren't you, Smith?" Devereux asked.

Surprise appeared in the Irishman's face. Puzzlement replaced it. "That I was, Colonel. That, I was. Seven bloody years in Victoria's bloody army! The Mutiny, you've heard of the Mutiny, Colonel? Of course you have. The siege of Sevastopol? Good! The lads should not be forgot." He laughed aloud, throwing back his head to do so. "Corporal Bloody Paddy Smith I was, of Her Britannic Majesty's Tipperary fools." The laughter disappeared from him. "No more for me! Or my mates! We will fight no more for fine gentlemen who would not spit on us for aught else! That's why we are all Democrats, like you Rebs! We all voted For Breckenridge! Nearly every mother's son of us! You fancy gents went for Bell and elected the monkey, Lincoln! We're not so clever as that, not by half!"

After a moment's silence, Devereux lifted his head to address the other man. "Will the Democracy's political leaders stand by you against the draft?"

"Well, they may, and then again they may not," 'Smith' answered him. "If they are clever and thinkin' of their tomorrows and not of their pasts, they will back us. There is no really good reason why Lincoln cannot be brought down. All you need is for there to be enough of us in the streets! Enough noise, enough fire, enough dead niggers and bankers! That's the ticket."

Hope blinked back the evidence of the violence of her emotions and looked away, looked out the window at the passing traffic.

"The colored people have nothing to do with this!" Devereux snarled. "Take your anger out on those who oppress you!"

'Smith' examined him with new interest. "A Reb nigger lover! Somethin' new. Don't you worry, Colonel we know our enemies. We pick 'em ourselves!"

"I am not a colonel," Devereux said. "Captain will do.."

"Infantry?" asked Smith.

"Yes."

"Been wounded?"

Some mad impulse to justify himself to this man, to make another soldier know him for what he was made Claude pull up his right pants leg.

Smith bent forward to look. "Beggin' your pardon, Cap'n. You've been there," he said at last. His face seemed different now. The hostility was gone from it. "Stop the cab," he said. "I'll walk from here." Standing in the street 'Smith' stood with his hat in his hand to speak. "Good Day to you, Missus! Take good care of this man of yours. His heart is too sweet for this world!"

His thin, slightly bent form retreated from their view down the lonely crowded length of a city sidewalk. The figure disappeared around the corner of a bank.

29

A Prince of Denmark

Tuesday, 26 May, New York

"I really do believe that you will enjoy the play," Devereux told her. "You admire George Latimer's taste in these matters. He thinks John Wilkes Booth's Hamlet is superb!"

She inspected his face in the golden shadow of the gas lit bedroom. The rosy light of a springtime evening was fast disappearing behind the heavily draped windows. Velvet hangings nearly succeeded in deadening the noise of Fifth Avenue. "And you will be closeted somewhere with the seditious elite of this city?"

"Not immediately. I am having dinner with Strong and Olmstead first. The Union League Club can not be neglected in this city of doubtful allegiances. After all, they are our friends. People of such profound fidelity cannot be slighted."

"Which 'our' is this, Claude?"

She had begun to ask such things in the last few days. At first he had allowed himself to be provoked by the implicit criticism, but reflection had shown him the justice of her questioning. He knew she was worried about his mental state. "This is the loyalist Virginian and War Department counselor speaking. The other Devereux will meet with Fernando Wood, and his brother tomorrow, just for balance.

"They are the anti-war Democrats?"

"The very best and richest. It was Secretary Stanton's thought. He wants to see if a loyal 'Southron' like myself can bring them around. You really will enjoy the play."

"You did not know Booth was playing here?"

"Of course not! You were with me downstairs in the lobby when we spied the playbill! Why would I deceive you in such a way? What is John Wilkes Booth to me or mine?"

She rose and searched about the elegant room for some of her possessions, disappearing for a moment into the sitting room, and reappearing with a small embroidered bag from which she began to extract the implements of her toilette. Seated at a dressing table, his wife began to brush her hair, looking at him in the glass as she did so. "You should not be required to deal with such evil riffraff as that Smith person," she said. Her eyes had taken on a surprising glint in the reflected light of the crystal wall sconces.

Later, amidst the dark and bulky forms of men clothed in evening dress and blue, Hope resembled something newly emerged from a Rococo dream of godlike shepherds and the athletic deities that with them populated impossibly lovely forests and meadows. She knew well the flattery which the richness of blue silk gave to her complexion. Men craned their necks from around the hall to better see this lovely and unfamiliar woman. She had never been afflicted with the growing prudishness of her time, and Claude encouraged her natural desire to be seen in the best possible light. As a result, she dressed in accordance with the requirements of European fashion, and not to please the Boston society matrons among whom she had been reared. She seemed this evening to be the radiant centerpiece in a magnificent display of golden hair and mature beauty. The bodice of her velvet gown served as frame to her portrait. The whiteness of the skin of her shoulders ran down into the rounded loveliness of her bosom.

Bill White sat above and somewhat to her right in a position from which he could assure himself of her safety and still view the performance. He watched with amusement the ever increasing number of heads turned in her direction. White considered the play in silence for a time, seeking to enter fully into the spirit of the thing. Elizabethan English was not a major difficulty for him. The Devereux inclination toward literature had provided many opportunities to hear the family in dramatic readings. He found Booth to be annoying. At first it was not possible to locate the source of his discontent. It seemed odd. The actor's diction was perfect. He did not pace extravagantly in the manner of so many thespians of the day. At last, he had it! The intensity of feeling which radiated from Booth was unsuitable. The man addressed the other players with a directness and fervor that ill suited the melancholy Dane. The gestures were too strong. Having decided this point to his satisfaction, he gazed about the theater. He had frequented such places in Europe. In France it had not been necessary for him to sit in the balcony.

"A dream itself is but a shadow!" Booth's declamation of the line caused White to shrivel up inside himself. *My, but I wish there were more dreams in which to hide,* he reflected. *More dreams for us all!*

In frustration with the play he began to inspect the assorted members of the audience. There were the expected officers of the Union Army and Navy. Some appeared to be permanently installed in the New York establishments of the government. Their girth and age provided unmistakable evidence of this. Others were indisputably visitors from the field forces of the Northern republic. *Convalescents and people on leave,* he thought. He finished looking at the boxes across the yawning pit of the theater's hall and commenced a survey of those seated in the orchestra.

Motion across the way in the third box from the stage captured his attention. As his focus shifted, he saw a woman lean back into the interior of the box, back behind the heavy red velvet curtain which outlined the opening of the tiny room. He saw her for an instant and only with the corner of his eye. The angles involved made him believe that the woman had been looking at Hope. For a second he dismissed this as the usual curiosity which women display toward each other's appearances. The woman in the far box was only a dim shadow. Part of one of her shoulders could be seen extending beyond the draperies' fringe. The man seated to her right turned to whisper some few words to the unseen presence. He smiled and swung to the other side to speak to yet another woman seated beside him. With this one, he seemed more relaxed. White could see that their shoulders were touching. The heads inclined together for a second. *That's his wife*, he reasoned. The man in the box was dressed in civilian clothing, a dark evening suit. As he watched, the balding, chubby man began to lift his head, and an absolutely compelling conviction came over White that the fellow was to going to look right at him! White turned away, peering down at Booth and his colleagues on the stage. After a time, he felt rather than saw a shift in the bald man's attention. A glance at the box showed the man to be in deep conversation with the hidden lady. Bill rose quickly, and hastened to the shelter provided by the nearest stairway.

After the play, in the Devereux hotel suite, the three conspirators leaned close to each other about the little hotel parlor table. The gas table lamp cast a deeply shadowed light on them. Hope's face reflected her worry at the news delivered by White. Devereux inched still closer as if to remove barriers to his comprehension through reduction of the intervening space. "Tell me again what he looked like, the man in the box seat?"

White repeated the tale.

"Mitchell. It sounds like Mitchell. One of Stanton's people told me he was in New York. Damn!" He shook his head in frustration at the idea. "It must be coincidence," he finally declared. "It must be. The play is having a good run! Why shouldn't Major Johnston Mitchell go to the theater with his wife? Why should we find anything strange in that? It is normal!" He sighed in relief.

Hope was watching White. She saw that the worst had not been spoken. "He hasn't finished, Claude," his wife said. "Tell us the rest, Bill. It's the other one, isn't it? You were not in the lobby after the last curtain. You were outside waiting for them to come out.."

"Yes. I mixed in with the coachmen and stood with some Negroes among them. They came out, the man and two women. I know it was dark, and the women had on bonnets, with the sides, you know, but I do believe that the one behind the curtain was Amy Biddle!"

No one spoke. The silence grew thicker and denser.

"I suppose it must be true," Devereux murmured at last.

"It is such a shame," Hope answered. Sarcasm colored her voice. "You had them all shoved out of the picture, the detectives, Baker, all of them. Let me see, how could this have happened? It would not have anything to do with your actions, would it? You encouraged her, damn you! And now she has turned on you! Why wouldn't she? How will you feel when they arrest me, or your mother or Victoria?" Rage distorted her beautiful face.

Devereux knew that tears would be next.

"Please," White broke in. "We can't do this."

"Baker does not know of this," Devereux said, his eyes fixed on the table, ignoring her anger for the moment. "Mitchell is isolated here among his Democratic party friends. She has come to him with information, but they will not know what to do with it. We must assume that Mitchell has had us followed around town. Fortunately we have done nothing that is unambiguously criminal or disloyal up till now. He will go to the Democratic leaders here with his suspicions. I am meeting with some of them tomorrow. Among them, there are some who fear that I might speak too ill of them in Washington. They dread persecution as rivals of the administration who are at the same time soft on treason. Others will want to speak to me after the larger meeting. They will want to talk of the possibilities presented by the Conscription Law. It should be possible by manipulating their fears and hopes to make some further serious difficulty for Major Mitchell, but in the end he is too dangerous. He will have to be dealt with ..."

"Your nemesis?" she asked with a mocking smile.

"Or I am his. We shall see."

White shook his head. "Why do these Democrats want to help us?" he asked. "What do they want?"

Hope laughed aloud. Her merriment seemed to echo around the hotel bedroom. "I know the answer to that! My family are all Democrats! They were robbed of the White House in '61 by their own foolishness, Bill! They allowed the party to be split along regional lines, and Lincoln was elected by a minority. Now someone they regard as far worse than Jeff Davis rules the land. They wish to see Lincoln fail. They think they will pick up the pieces afterwards."

"And they don't care if we are independent?"

"No!" She laughed again. "They would let you go your own way if that is the price to be paid for the destruction of Lincoln's band of revolutionaries." Turning to her husband she frowned prettily. "What about the Biddle woman?"

"We have to get out of this city tomorrow." Devereux said. "Mitchell can act against us here. Amy? Now that we know that she betrays us, it will not be a problem. Did she see you," he asked White? "More importantly, does she know you saw her?"

"I don't believe either one of them think they were recognized. I never saw Major Mitchell before in my life, and Amy was hidden by the curtain."

"Good! Then we'll be on the train for Washington early tomorrow afternoon."

"What about Booth?" Hope inquired. She produced a leaflet program from her handbag. "This says that he will be in Cincinnati for two weeks and then will play in Baltimore with this same production. I watched him again tonight. Perhaps I watched him too closely. I did not see Amy."

"Forget Booth. We have other.."

"I think not!" she snapped. "You were right. There is something intriguing in him. You must speak with him again, soon."

He thought about it. "As you wish, my dear," he said.

30

Across the River,
and Into the Trees..

Wednesday, 27 May

The rain poured down in a roaring, rushing torrent. The engine rolled screeching into the steamy, enveloping, smoky shelter of the terminal station. Devereux peered at the dimness of the platform. Dirty windows obscured the image of home that filled the scene.

Hope stirred restlessly in her seat, disturbed by the lurch of the cars across the merging pattern of the railyard tracks.

"Wake, sweetheart," he whispered. "This long day is coming to an end."

She stretched appealingly, managing to look better in her weariness than most women could manage with an hour's preparation.

Devereux gathered up the odd bits and pieces of their belongings.

She stood to arrange her hair. A mirror in his grasp provided the tool for the arrangements needed to achieve perfection.

As she fussed, he wondered what news might greet him on the platform. The train had halted on the Virginia shore to admit the usual group of Union Army enlisted men checking papers and tickets for God knows what imagined defects. Devereux kept his eyes away from them even as he presented his papers to a youthful private with a Midwestern voice. Through the sooty window, he had watched a solitary passenger approach the sentry and conductor to display some small flat object. *A ticket,* he thought.

The conductor waved to the second class car, the next in sequence behind the compartmented wagon in which Claude and Hope had made their journey. Bill was in that car.

The boarding passenger passed his window. The man, as if by random choice, turned his face to the light in crossing the space illuminated by Devereux's compartment.

Joseph White smiled up at his friend.

The two White men were waiting for them on the quay by the time Devereux and Hope stepped down from their car.

Hope gave her hand to Joseph in a spontaneous gesture of happiness at the sight of his familiar and reassuring face.

He held it awkwardly for a second and then released it, glancing about the platform.

Devereux was rooted to the spot on which he had descended. An unpleasantly cold mist hung over the station. He waited for the news. It had to be bad if they had thought Joe should join them on the train.

"Morgan is alive," Bill told him.

"Where?"

"He's in Father Kruger's rectory. Workmen from the boatyard brought him. They hid him for days."

"He bled a lot," said Joseph. "The carpenters hid him with old man Jones and his wife. They couldn't get a doctor for him. He was in awful bad shape, so they took him to Father Kruger."

"Who is caring for him?" Hope demanded.

"Mamma and Madame Devereux," Joseph answered. "They want to move him, Mister Claude. They say they are running out of reasons to be in the rectory.

"Let's not stand here to talk about this," Bill said.

"No, no you are right," Devereux agreed. "Lead us to the street, Joseph. No more talk about it here."

Wednesday, 3 June
(The War Department, Washington)

"But, I tell you we have no one better!" the white haired old man snarled. Resentment showed in the grey eyes. "The President wished to give the command to someone else."

"Yes," Claude Devereux replied. "I believe John Reynolds was made the offer and declined it several days ago for reasons not altogether clear to me." He stopped talking and waited in his chair. His slouch was meant to convey the idea that he felt relaxed in this setting. In fact, his leg hurt so much that he was trying to find a comfortable position in the low chair. An open casement window behind him admitted a pleasant breeze. The day had been warm and the breeze was very welcome. Washington is noted for its hostile summer climate. This year it seemed to be setting in early.

Patrick Devereux rubbed his eyes with one hand. He stopped long enough to speak his mind. "It's clear enough to me," he said. "President Lincoln would not give him enough of a free hand to make it worthwhile."

"How do you know that?" rasped the old man. He was unhappy with the badgering tone of this talk. The fingers of one hand drummed on the desk top, while the other hand felt in a pocket for what must have been a watch. A vein beat slowly in his temple. The angles of his face held hints of a purplish color which could not be healthy. This man had spent a lifetime subduing the complaining and the outraged in a succession of courtrooms. He did not mean to be put into a corner by these two amateurs.

Patrick did not intend to let him off the hook. "Judge Renfroe, I was asked my opinion in this matter by John Loring, Secretary Stanton's appointments clerk.."

"I know who he is," growled the old judge.

"I had to be told enough to make an intelligent comment," said Patrick, trying to be apologetic and reasonably deferential in his manner. It was difficult, but necessary. A man who is both an assistant secretary of war and a former federal judge could be treated in no other way.

"Why would he ask your opinion in such matters?" the judge said in exasperation. "Why do you two young men have so much to say to so many people, and why do we listen?"

Claude laughed, throwing back his head to do so.

Caleb Renfroe glowered.

"I am sorry!" Claude offered in apology. "The desire of the president and his cabinet to have the advice and assistance of so many private citizens is something which, I too, find surprising. Everywhere I go, I meet someone who has recently been closeted with Secretary 'so and so' or Admiral 'what's his name'. This is an astonishingly accessible government.

The old man 'harrumphed' in discontent with the thought. "It may be so!" he said, "but this is a vestige of another era. The government is too large now for such foolishness. We must stop this! A giant, commercially complex country cannot continue to conduct its business in such a way. It is not modern!"

Claude contemplated a peaked tent made of his fingers. "You are, of course, correct, Mister Secretary. It must stop, but at the moment my brother and I find ourselves among the hordes of well-meaning dilettantes of government who are called upon for counsel. I can understand why it is that such august personages might want the advice of Patrick. His grasp of military affairs astounds even myself, and I have been listening to him all our lives. Their desire to learn my views is unaccountable!"

Renfroe pondered that notion. "You will pardon my skepticism as to the sincerity of that last statement," he commented. Then, a few minutes later, having subsided into quiescent resentment of the two intruders, he seemed to make a decision regarding their relative weight in the world. "You are perfectly convinced that General Hooker is unfit and should be removed from command?" he asked. "Perfectly sure?"

Claude possessed the ability to project such assurances in a way that forbade consideration of the possibility that he might be wrong. "There is no doubt of it," he said firmly. "His failure of nerve at Chancellorsville will be repeated 'ad nauseam.' He should be replaced with someone more solid."

"And you have in mind?"

"George Gordon Meade, the fifth corps commander."

"An engineer, like McClellan," Caleb Renfroe commented.

"An engineer, like Robert E. Lee," Patrick rejoined.

Knuckles resounded on the office door.

"Come!" cried the judge.

A junior clerk in a black frock coat appeared to deliver a note. "Now?" the judge asked. Impatience marked his features.

"Yes, sir. He said now.."

"You gentlemen will excuse me for a few moments, I am sure. My master calls," he said with a sardonic smile.

Judge Renfroe's footsteps receded down the naked hallway, echoing the whole way from plaster walls and hardwood floors.

"You are wrong to do this, Claude," Patrick said softly. "You must stop. We know nothing of this man Meade. He could be anything!"

"Or nothing!" snapped his older brother. "I want Hooker removed! The man is a much better general than they think him. We don't need to have him lurking on Lee's flank during the march north."

Patrick raised a finger to his lips.

Claude listened intently. There was nothing to be heard. He crossed to the door, throwing it open to reveal an empty corridor. He winked over his shoulder at his brother.

The seated man bristled visibly. "I don't care if you laugh at me! You have always thought yourself so damned clever! You must stop helping them. I am finished! You are giving them too much! I will no longer participate in this foolishness!"

When they had finished with Caleb Renfroe, the Devereux brothers rode home in their father's open carriage behind the chestnut geldings. The clatter of the wheels on cobblestone could be heard in the family parlor long before their arrival.

Their two women sat together in front of the black fireplace. A warm wind rustled leaves in the elm beside the open window. Victoria Devereux tilted her head in the direction of the street. Her husband could be heard above the rumble of iron shod carriage wheels. His words were inaudible but the tone was clear. Anger and frustration filled his voice.

The vehicle drew near.

Claude could be heard speaking in a manner which she had come to characterize as "Claude talking us out of," or "Claude talking us into.."

The driver pulled the team to a halt at the door. Springs creaked with the motion of the passengers. Victoria heard the small, dull sound of her husband's crutches on the brick sidewalk. The heavy front door swung inward. Claude entered, to stand in the foyer, looking back, holding wide a round topped door.

Through the beveled glass pane, she watched her husband struggle to enter his father's house. The two men looked so alike. Patrick would have been the taller, had been the taller.

Claude shut the door.

The brothers seemed simultaneously to take note of their wives. Whatever had passed between them disappeared, succeeded by the familiar Devereux demeanor.

Claude looked back and forth between the two women, taking in their somber faces. "Where is he?" he demanded, making light of their mood.

Neither woman spoke.

"The cat, I mean! No cat can eat our canaries and live to tell the tale!"

Hope choked against emotion and buried her face in a handkerchief.

Claude went to her side, taking one of her hands in his own.

"It's Morgan isn't it?" asked Patrick in a soft voice.

Victoria crossed the room to him, helping him to a chair. "Yes," she whispered. "He's dying."

"How could that be!" Claude asked. "How can it be? I visited him yesterday! He was weak, but.."

"In the night!" Hope sobbed. "He suffered a reversal in the night. Doctor Harrington says such things occur in injuries so, awful. Something came apart inside. He is hemorrhaging terribly! So terribly!"

"Who is there?"

"Your mother and Betsy … They sent us away."

Claude did not stand more than five feet ten inches in height, and he seldom found the tiny rooms of old Alexandria houses to be oppressively small. Nevertheless, the passage to Kruger's attic room made him feel that the walls were squeezing in upon his shoulders. A painted door of pine planks barred access to the chamber beyond. A murmur reached his ear from beyond the wooden barrier.

He knocked and the door was opened. Clotilde and Willem Kruger knelt at the foot of the bed. A rosary hung from his mother's hand.

Betsy White sat on a stool by Morgan's side.

Charles Harrington stood behind her. On a table nearby were surgical instruments and a mound of bloody bandages.

Doctor Harrington turned to study Devereux's appearance. In answer to his mute question the older man turned away to his patient.

Morgan could be heard speaking behind the shield of Betsy White's back. "My property should go to my sister's boys. We have no other close kin anymore, not anymore.." The murmur ceased as Claude approached. Morgan focused his violet eyes across the dim space. "Hello, Captain, Good of you to come by, your women folk have been taking good care of me.."

Devereux could now see that Morgan's right hand was grasped in Betsy White's upon the coverlet. "Don't talk, Tom," Devereux entreated. "Save your strength."

The long, pale figure made a gesture of dismissal with its free hand. "Not to worry. We both know that. I haven't been right in the head the last few hours. I'm glad you've come when the fog has lifted a little. I want to say to you.." The voice became indistinct. Morgan coughed hard. Bloody foam covered his lips.

Devereux's mother rose to wipe it away with a towel.

"Thank you, ma'am," Morgan whispered. Turning his face to Claude he spoke firmly. "Devereux! If they win, we will be at their mercy forever! Nothing will be our own again, nothing. Don't listen to anybody who wants to give up! Do what you think is right! Promise me you won't let them win! Your word, Sir!" The cavalryman's voice had risen in pitch and volume. A desperate, almost frenzied look had come over him. His fading color was terrible.

"My word, Tom. You have my word. We will do what we must. I swear it.."

Morgan's large head fell back on the pillow. His eyes closed.

Betsy wiped his face with a damp towel.

Devereux turned away.

His mother and the doctor followed him down the narrow stairs to the landing below.

His "aunt's" voice came to him down the tunnel of the stairs. "You were praying, Lieutenant, go on."

"For thine is the kingdom ..."

"He will be gone within the hour," Harrington said.

Claude nodded. "Betsy? What is this about?" he asked his mother.

"He became unable to recognize us several hours ago. He wanted Betsy to hold him. He called her by some other name, someone at home, I think."

"Forever, amen," echoed in the stairwell.

"Perhaps his nurse," the doctor suggested.

Claude kissed his mother and shook the doctor's hand. "Thank you, Charles, do what you can," he told the physician.

Harrington made a dismissive, even irritated gesture.

The two silent figures watched him descend the long staircase.

Morgan's failing voice followed him down to the foyer. "Try me, O God, and seek the ground of my heart …"

Kruger's housekeeper waited for him to wipe his eyes before she opened the door to the street.

As he walked away down the warm, sunny street, his thoughts drew in upon themselves. He withdrew into the hidden, adamantine center of his being. He passed men he knew as he strode along the familiar streets. They greeted him, some raising hats or waving in friendly anticipation of the legendary courtesy of the family. He saw none of them. He walked on and on, unaware of his destination. His leg hurt him terribly but he limped on, indifferent or perhaps welcoming the pain. At one point, he found himself in front of the Daingerfield house on Cameron Street. He looked up at the second floor window. For a moment he thought there was someone..

At the stockaded gate on Prince Street a sentry thought to challenge him, but then recognized the man he had so often passed through the barrier, and was silent.

He walked up the hill, into the grounds of "Soldiers Rest."

She saw him coming through the window, put a hand to her throat, and went back to sit at her desk.

He closed the door behind him, and crossed the room to stand looking down.

"I have wronged you," she began. "I have betrayed you all.."

He pulled her out of the chair and into his arms. "No! If you do not say it, it is not true. We all do what we must! You will help me save the family, I know. You love them." He held her face in his hands. There were tears in his eyes. "God help me, Amy, but I do love you both! Life is too short.." He kissed her.

It was the kiss she had dreamt of, had never thought she would really have. It was all she had imagined. It was like the moment in Clotilde's parlor when she had first touched him. They seemed to flow together, to merge in some way that denied the separateness of their bodies.

He stepped back from her, to look into her eyes.

The light of this long June day had faded into golden shades of twilight.

"We can't do this," she said. "Hope is my friend. What would your mother think?"

He stood with his weight on the better leg. A low groan escaped him. The iron grip of the misery in the bad one was really catching up with him now. She helped him to a chair, and then pulled up his pants' leg to see. "Oh, my God!" was all she could say for a moment. He felt her tears on the awful mess that was his knee. He stroked her head. "Don't trouble yourself, my dear. It looks worse than it is.." he said. Her tear streaked face turned up to him was more than he could bear. He pulled her up and into his arms.

After a time, he said he should be getting home. Amy found him a cane and insisted that he use it. She sent for an army buggy. As the driver helped him in, she stood on the board sidewalk watching. "Mister Devereux twisted his knee," she told the soldier. The man nodded and touched the bill of his cap.

Claude looked down at her from the seat. "Don't forget dinner Friday night," he said.

"Yes.."

The carriage rolled away down the hill carrying him home to the wife he so loved.

31

The Road North

Thursday, 4 June

Seated in his walled garden, Charles Devereux sipped the dark, strong coffee which his wife had spent many years teaching him to prefer. Crickets sang in the night. They lived in the ivy which covered the six-foot brick wall. Flambeaux in iron mounts provided light. A pleasing and refreshing breeze flowed from the river, clearing the oppressiveness of an unseasonably warm day.

His sons whispered together. Their speech was no louder than the wind in the elms.

"Harrisburg?"

"I believe so," said Claude. "The Second Corps will lead the advance, the old 'Army of the Valley'. Baldy Ewell can be expected to push hard and all those Shenandoah men will be eager to get back into their own country. They will slide to the left from their present positions near Culpeper, leaving a small force to deceive Hooker at Fredericksburg.

Patrick nodded in understanding. "They're going to break contact and get behind the barrier of the Blue Ridge for the move north. When will this happen?"

"They have already gone. Longstreet and the First Corps started to pull away from the Fredericksburg area yesterday. I expect that Stuart will be hard pressed to keep the Yankees from understanding what is happening as Lee moves away to the west, but then, he is good at that, and can manage."

"Likely!" Patrick agreed. "So then the army will march north in the Shenandoah Valley, cross the Potomac and go into Pennsylvania in the Cumberland?"

"Exactly! The valley system swings to the east up there. They will follow it around in the direction of.."

"Harrisburg, the Pennsylvania state capital," his brother said, completing the thought. "Kennedy and I will be there waiting for them? Splendid, Claude! This is inspired on your part. What do you have in mind for us to do?" Patrick Devereux's face and body showed an enthusiasm and a welcome for the adventure which had been absent from him for too long.

"I believe you should place yourselves in the city where you can best get detailed knowledge which would help Lee in capturing the place with the least possible destruction and loss of life. You can then fall back to Philadelphia or Baltimore to do the same things there. It may be necessary for you to separate in order to be in more than one city. You will have to judge for yourself."

Patrick looked at his brother. "Fred should be in charge. He's an officer."

"Is that what you want?"

"Yes."

"Very well. I'll tell him. I'm sure it would not have been an issue either way."

"No. Do you have any idea how we may get through the lines to reach Lee from Harrisburg?"

"None whatever. You will have to work that out between you. There are going to be scouts working for Lee out in front of the army. They will arrive on the scene before the cavalry. I have pictures of some of them and their names. You will have to do your best."

"What's our reason for being there?"

His father interrupted. "Money, my boy! We are bankers."

"Frederick Braithwaite," added Claude. "He is eternally pestering me about his damnable railroad schemes. His putative partners are in Harrisburg. That should be enough! You will have to work something out for yourselves in the other places. Jenkins gave me the names of three members of the Pennsylvania legislature who would help you."

Patrick reached across the space between their black, wrought iron chairs to take his brother's hand. "Thank you, Claude. I want to help so much, but I just can't. It's killing me.."

"Say no more. I only wish I could give you what you really want."

"And what of Jake?" their father said, interrupted once again from the other side of the pond. "What of our little Jake, our baby boy?"

"Pickett's Division will be in this invasion," Claude replied.

"Let us not speak of that to your mother!" their father replied. "Let us pray for him, for them all!"

Tuesday, 9 June
(The French Embassy)

Devereux held the cream colored sheet of paper up to the window's light to read. The clatter and smell of downtown Washington streets drifted up from below.

Provost Marshal-General's Office
Army of the Potomac
May 27, 1863

Brig. Gen. S. Williams, Assistant Adjutant-General:

Sir: By direction of the general commanding, I furnish the following memoranda of the position of the enemy and other data obtained within the last few days:

1. The enemy's line in front of us is much more contracted than during the winter. It extends from Bank's Ford, on a line parallel to the river, to near Moss Neck. Anderson's division is on their left. McLaw's is next, and in rear of Fredericksburg. Early is massed about Hamilton's Crossing, and Trimble's is directly to the rear of Early. Rode's (D.H. Hill's old division) is farther to the right, and back from the river, and A.P. Hill is the right of their line, resting nearly on Moss Neck. Each of these six divisions have five brigades.

2. Pickett's division of six brigades, has come up from Suffolk, and is at Taylorsville, near Hanover Junction.

3. Hood's division of four brigades, has also left from the front of Suffolk, and is between Louisa Court-House and Gordonsville.

4. Ten days ago there was in Richmond only the City Battalion, 2,700 strong, commanded by General Elzey.

5. There are three brigades of cavalry 3 miles from Culpeper Court House, toward Kelley's Ford. They can, at present, only turn out 4,700 men for duty, but have many dismounted men, and the horses are being constantly and rapidly recruited by the spring growth of grass. These are Fitz Lee's, William H. Fitzhugh Lee's, and Wade Hampton's brigades.

6. General Jones is still in the valley, near New Market, with about 1,400 cavalry and twelve pieces of light artillery.

7. Mosby is above Warrenton, with 200 men.

8. The Confederate army is under marching orders, and an order from General Lee was very lately read to the troops, announcing a campaign of long marches and hard fighting, in a part of the country where they would have no railroad transportation.

9. All the deserters say that the idea is very prevalent in the ranks that they are about to move forward upon or above our right flank.

GEORGE H. SHARPE,
                    Colonel.

(Indorsement)

Hdqrs. Army of the Potomac, May 27, 1863

Respectfully forwarded for the information of the General in Chief. Colonel Sharpe is in charge of the bureau of information at these headquarters.

JOSEPH HOOKER
Major-General, Commanding.

The ambassador's brows knit slightly in concern. "A certain discretion must be maintained," he began.

"You need not concern yourself, Excellency!" Devereux assured. "All my communications are in code and are carried by hand."

Behind his ambassador's back Colonel Edouard Jourdain looked at Devereux and frowned.

The diplomat departed for another appointment. The two soldiers smiled him out of the room.

"Are you using the cipher device we suggested to your State Department?" Jourdain asked abruptly.

Devereux scrutinized him closely. He had lived with treachery long enough now to suspect it in anyone.

"Don't trust it, Claude," Jourdain whispered. "Take my word in this matter. That little machine will betray you! I don't want my name used in messages encoded with that thing, understand!"

Devereux had not seen the Frenchman in so agitated a state. "And him?" he asked tilting his head in the direction of the departed man.

A truly malicious expression came over Colonel Jourdain. "Him? You must be joking! That pathetic creature can think of nothing but the possibility that Mister Davis might ask that he be the first chief of a French diplomatic mission in your capital." Jourdain laughed nastily, almost silently for a moment. "He is torn between that aspiration and the terror which grips him at the thought that our true relationship to you should come to light!"

Devereux shook his head. "But, he knows that the Union government wishes me to serve as a bridge to you all. I do not understand!"

Jourdain took on the aura of paternal counsel. "He thinks they may be playing you against us."

"But, they are!" Devereux exclaimed. That is their stated intent! I told you that. I am a vehicle for their supposed control of your views of the political and military situation."

"Yes, yes, I know," Jourdain agreed. "But, he fears that there may be a yet deeper level of this affair, one in which they have deceived you as to their intent."

Comprehension swept over him and Devereux leapt to his feet. "You gave him this idea, Edouard! You did, didn't you? And now he clutches the thought to him in his fear!"

Edouard Jourdain made a scornful gesture. "How could I know that the fool would seize upon the mere possibility? I should have followed our normal rule with the diplomats. Tell them nothing!" Jourdain glanced at Devereux. "It is his fault, my friend, that I did not provide you this document earlier. He is making for me a rule that I must not meet with you except in his presence. I have written to Paris, but it will be some time before instructions can arrive to relieve me of this burden!"

A gloomy silence filled the room. This confession of human fallibility somehow made the elegance of the decor less persuasive.

"It does not matter," Devereux said quietly. "Someone told me of the existence of this document four days ago. I have sent word across the lines. I don't know if the news will make any difference. It should not."

Jourdain was visibly shaken by Devereux's attitude. He seemed to gather himself for an assault on this incomprehension.

The American held up a hand to hold back the flood. "No! No! Spare me the explanation! My informant took some pains with the news of the arrival of this appreciation in General Halleck's offices. He learned that Colonel George Sharpe's admirable work is for naught. They didn't believe him."

"Not at all?"

Devereux shook his head slowly, savoring the discomfort experienced by the other man. Jourdain had become much too haughty of late. "Where did you get it, Edouard," Devereux asked? "I do not often question your sources, but in this case, you must have someone in the inner circle of the War Department. I have to know with whom I am dealing. I give you my word I will not touch him."

Jourdain rose and paced. "We will make an exchange," he said from the other side of the room, his back to Devereux. "A mutual violation of confidences ... I want to know who told you of this paper!"

Devereux gave him the name. "It was Robert Neville."

"L'Albion Perfide!" sneered Jourdain. "We are instructed to help them here! You see how they can be trusted! He did not tell me! He told you but not me! Bon! Merde!" The French officer caught the look in Devereux eyes, and began to see the humor in the situation. "But, come now," he said with a laugh. "You would not expect me to inform him before you!"

"Of course not, never.." Devereux replied softly. "I should leave now, but you have not given me your half of the bargain."

"Lieutenant Biddle."

"Amy's nephew."

Jourdain shrugged. "Such personalities are trivial in their availability. An ego of such enormity is, perhaps, the most profound of weaknesses."

"The little bastard! The wretched, conceited, pathetic fool!"

Jourdain was alarmed. "Claude, I could not allow you to damage my source of information. Be careful."

"You need not worry, Edouard. He can scream their secrets on every city street, if he wishes. It is nothing to me, nothing at all."

"Bon, one thing puzzles me, my friend."

"What is that?" Devereux had risen, levering himself to his feet by means of his chair's broad arm. He searched the room for his hat and gloves.

"If Hooker and Halleck do not accept Colonel Sharpe's exquisite analysis, then why has the cavalry of the Army of the Potomac attacked across the rivers toward Culpeper?"

Devereux stood rooted before the fireplace in the act of reaching for his possessions. "When," he asked? "I have not been to the War Department today."

"Mon Dieu! It was this morning, at dawn. The cavalry corps has driven forward in great strength. The telegraph speaks of heavy fighting and many losses." Jourdain smiled. "'The little bastard' has gone to much trouble to inform us today." He was speaking to Devereux's back. From the window he watched Claude scramble through the open door of a carriage.

At the War Department on 17th Street, he climbed the steps two at a time, indifferent to the pain that would come later..

A sentinel stood by the door, his rifle butt grounded by one boot, the muzzle held before him in white gloved hands.

At the top Devereux looked back at the cab in which he had traveled from Jourdain's offices.

The driver sat, whip in hand gazing up at him, puzzled by such a display of energy in the June heat and humidity.

Devereux smiled at him.

The hiss of the lash over their backs started the team in motion.

He stood still for a moment, allowing his breathing to return to its normal rhythm.

Pulverized horse dust eddied in small clouds around the hooves of passing animals. The familiar smell of equine urine hung about the dirt street.

He turned to face the building.

The sergeant of the guard stood just behind him.

Devereux began to search a pocket for the much folded form which gave him the right of admission to the War Department.

The sergeant, a grey haired, middle aged, regular army soldier stepped back and opened one of the doors to let him in. "We don't need that, Mister

Devereux," he said. "As much as you go in and out, we'd be a sorry lot if we couldn't recognize you. Come in out of the sun, sir."

The steps to the third floor seemed endless today. He passed the telegraph office door and wondered if the president would be there. Lincoln seemed to live in the three white walled rooms whenever a crisis arose.

Judge Renfroe and William Davenport waited in the younger man's rooms at the end of the hall. Devereux could hear their voices as he came down the corridor.

Davenport's military assistant ushered him through a small ante room filled to bursting with men in dark suits. They stared hostilely as he swept by under escort by the rather prissy captain who controlled entry to the inner office.

Davenport and Renfroe sat in barrel backed chairs beside a large working table.

The judge had removed his coat in self defense against the heat. It lay on the table amid the orderly heaps of paper.

Davenport waved him to a third chair.

Devereux's anxiety overwhelmed him even in the act of sitting. "I thought that Hooker was going to sit and stare across the river at Fredericksburg until winter. What is this that I hear about Pleasonton and Culpeper?"

Judge Renfroe shook his large, white fringed head in silent disapproval of the casual ease with which Devereux learned the army's secrets..

Davenport opened his mouth once, closed it slowly, and spoke. "I am happy that you are on our side, Claude. I truly am. Wherever did you hear that?"

"People tell me things, William. You know that. It has been described as one of my most useful attributes. You must tell me what is going on! I am eaten by curiosity."

"Hardly a sufficient reason to be told anything," growled the judge.

Davenport thought for a moment. He inspected the fingernails of one hand. "We will not want the French government to be informed of this, Claude."

Renfroe's big head swiveled enough to bring his bloodshot, yellowish eyes to bear. The heat had made him sweat.

Devereux could smell him from across the table. "You know I tell them only those things which Secretary Stanton wishes." He felt the table with his fingertips. The scars of long government service were deep.

Davenport's expression softened. "There have been reports of rebel movements to the westward, tending in the direction of the passes over the Blue Ridge. Hooker can't account for the continuing strength shown by Lee on the Rappahannock around Fredericksburg. He has decided that what we are seeing must be a massing of cavalry for a big raid into western Maryland, the kind of thing Stuart did last winter. He is afraid that Lee is trying to draw him westward to make possible some sort of forward movement by the rebels from their present positions in the east."

Devereux's fingers made a tent before his features. "What if Lee is moving around Hooker's right flank?" he asked. "He has been known to attempt such feats." *Might as well see if they really do know..*

The War Department officials scrutinized him momentarily. Davenport's attention returned to his nails. Judge Renfroe cleared his throat. The timbre of his voice seemed more than usually rich with the phlegm that old men carried with them toward the grave. "Someone suggested that to General Hooker. The idea was sent here. Hooker does not think so. Halleck and Stanton accept Hooker's judgment. We do not. I have finally come to agree with your opinion of Joe Hooker. He must go!" The vituperative fire in the assistant secretary's eyes' made Devereux shrink inwardly, feeling for the irreducible self that could not be threatened by such hostility.

"And the president?" Devereux asked.

Renfroe shrugged.

Davenport answered for them both. "It matters not. We will wait for the result, and point to the obvious necessity, when the time comes."

"What do you want of me?" asked Devereux. "You both are too busy to have felt a need for my company today."

Davenport found such bluntness disconcerting. He rose and tugged at his waistcoat. "Claude, the Army of the Potomac will surely be going north. All three of us believe Hooker is utterly wrong about Lee's intention. It has become Secretary Stanton, and President Lincoln's custom to place an 'observer' with armies in the field to be certain that they have all the details of the picture at the front."

Devereux struggled with the news. He now knew what they wanted. He turned to Caleb Renfroe.

The old man grinned at him in unalloyed enjoyment. "That's right, my fine young gentleman friend! They are making a spy of you! You will have the opportunity to inform against whomever it might be who will have the privilege of facing that traitorous man, Robert Lee!"

"The judge has a deft touch in the explanation of such things," said Davenport. "In the event, you will be appointed a special assistant secretary of war, with the appropriate papers. We would prefer, however that you not reveal your true status, if that can be managed."

"And what shall I be to the uninformed?"

"A Sanitary Commission Inspector."

"Attached to Army headquarters?"

"As you wish."

Devereux grimaced, stood and started for the door. "I will assemble a few men and a wagon," he said. "This is the usual Sanitary Commission inspection party."

"You will need a uniformed officer to escort you at some points."

Devereux was rooted by the door. "Very well."

"Good! Good!" exclaimed Renfroe. "We have a young man who is burning to get to the front, a lieutenant in the Adjutant General's office, name of Biddle."

24 June

The 17th Virginia Regiment hungered for the road. On the 9th of June Pickett's Division had marched away to the west. Now only Corse's Brigade remained behind on the North Anna. Grumbling was heard in the ranks. Men questioned the judgment of those in high places who chose to leave such soldiers as themselves to defend a river line on the road to Richmond while others marched to glory.

This river line, that of the North Anna, had been to the rear of the Rappahannock River front until the Army of Northern Virginia began its progress toward the Shenandoah Valley. That movement had begun cautiously. During the last weeks, A.P. Hill's new army corps, the Third, had gradually thinned its lines before Fredericksburg, slipping away to the west, contriving to make a convincing show of immobility for their enemy. Now there was little left north of the railroad bridges held in strength by Corse's men. A screen of a few hundred of Hill's soldiers strove to create an illusion of strength just south of Fredericksburg. If that broke down, the defense of the North Anna bridges would be all that stood between the capital and the invader.

Today, more than a hundred men waited at the railroad junction. They gathered throughout the morning, arriving in threes and fours, messmates come to see if it would be true. They were nothing much to look at, and the heat and dust made them appear shabbier than they truly were. They didn't really look bad. The brown and grey of their clothing somehow blended into a harmonious, if uneven effect. Their detractors often described them, and all those like them, as being nothing resembling a 'real army.' An English journalist who had visited this army in the previous springtime had thought them to be inconsequential at first, but puzzling. He could not account for their continued existence in a contest against the well regulated forces of the United States. After a time, he came to see them differently. He began to write of their passion for home, and their right, of their unending talk about the proper limits of the powers of democratic govern- ments. Eventually, he wrote a long column on the subject of their rejection of the tyranny that they believed was threatened by the North and the Republican Party. Most significantly, he started to see beyond the rough clothes and worn equipment, to comprehend the depth of feeling carried by these soldiers for each other, and for the man who led them all. In the end, he saw that threadbare men could march in straight lines with clean weapons. He commenced to see into their secret hearts.

A knot of officers stood to one side, mindful even in this citizen army of the need for some small distance between leaders and led. Brigadier General Mont- gomery Corse filled his pipe from an old oilskin pouch. Tobacco was one item of supply which this army never lacked. He was as impatient as his men for what was about to happen, and only half listened to the latest chapter of a long stand- ing conversation between two of his officers on the subject of raccoons and the stalking of raccoons. This debate had flourished for at least a year in all categories of weather and season.

Corse profoundly regretted the decision by higher authority which had left his regiments behind. The brigade resented the implied slight. He feared it would begin to affect their fighting spirit. Alone in his tent in the evenings, he contem- plated the map. By his reckoning, the division's center of mass would now be around Winchester. *It was far, but not yet too far.*

Standing there, Corse, for some reason, found himself thinking of Jackson's funeral. *The streets of Richmond had been packed with the silent crowd. A vast sea of black clad mourners clutched tiny flags. He had been one of the pallbearers. Pete Longstreet, Richard Garnett and Sandie Pendleton had been among the others. Jim Lewis led Little Sorrel, following close behind the ammunition wagon which bore the coffin.*

He realized that someone was speaking his name. Captain George Hulfish, the brigade Assistant Adjutant General, had upon his face the expectation of a reac- tion.

Corse shook his head, as if to clear the cobwebs. "I'm sorry, George. What did you say?"

"It's the train, sir. You can hear the train!"

He turned to face into the southwest. A lifetime of hunting and two wars had affected certain adjustments in his ability to hear distant sounds, but finally he began to hear the train. At first, it was more a tremor running through the air than a sound. Then, the whistle of the approaching engine sounded remotely tiny and shrill, shrieking feebly in the distance. The nearly imperceptible rattle of the cars continued to be submerged in the voices of the storytellers. He was compelled to listen.

"It's a hard thing," the brigade commissary declared, continuing a thought. "First you love the dogs, and hate the coons, then you love the coons and start to hate the dogs. Then you start to hatin' yourself for the whole thing, and how you ought to be home in bed with momma, listenin' to the wind in the chimbley instead of lookin' up through those wavin' pines at the moon and the sky."

"You're right in that, if in nothing else," Hulfish retorted. "The damned coons are too likable. I'd rather shoot whistlepigs myself, how 'bout you, General?"

Corse puffed in silence a moment before speaking. "No, no, I can't ever hunt them."

They waited on the rest of it.

He turned toward the engine sound for a second, then swung back to them, taking the blackened wreck of a pipe from his mouth. "My Aunt Nettie, some of you knew her. She and her husband, Edward Youngblood, lived out on the Washington Turnpike, near the Abingdon Plantation. Well, when I was a boy, I spent most of the time out there in the summer. One day I was sitting on a stump by one of the Abingdon fields. It was full of woodchucks. I had an old small bore rifle with me, something my grandfather gave me on my twelfth birthday. I had shot several of the little beasts. Unknown to me, Aunt Nettie walked up behind me just as I fired at another. I hit it badly, didn't kill it outright. It screamed and ran around the field bleeding everywhere. It sounded awfully human. Nettie wept and begged me to stop its suffering. I had a hell of a time catching that animal to kill it. She cried half the night. I promised her I would never hurt another whistlepig."

The train rolled into sight around a woodline. A battered engine preceded the long procession of passenger cars and freight wagons. Brakes squealed, steam hissed from safety valves in the engine. The train groaned to a halt, a suitable representative of the railroad network of the Confederate States.

Troops poured out of the cars. They began to unload their belongings from the freight wagons. Several officers descended the short iron stairs from the first car.

A tall, black headed man in immaculate grey approached. The double row of buttons and three stars on his tunic showed him to be a colonel. With a moderately casual salute he came to a halt before Corse. "Alexander Stewart, 27th North Carolina Regiment. You are relieved, sir. Good luck!"

They shook hands.

The commissary officer had positioned his wagons alongside the track to better transport the North Carolinians' gear to the brigade's camp. Butternut Negro teamsters stood in the wagon beds alongside some of Corse's other men. They packed the wagons with the loads handed up to them by the newcomers.

Montgomery Corse strode down the line of vehicles to the center of the line. He grabbed a wheel rim, putting a foot on the hub. Hands reached down to pull him up and over the side.

Captain Hulfish bellowed for attention from beside the wagon. "Corse's Brigade! Attention! Listen Up!"

Heads rotated up and down the line.

A radiant look of triumph filled Corse's face as he addressed his men. "Our friends from the Old North State are come to set us free! Pitch in to get them settled! This campaign will end the war! Marse Robert needs his best! No one can leave us behind! We march at first light!"

A roaring cheer set in. The men of the brigade yelled and waved their hats. The 27th North Carolina stood silent, and then began to shout as well, unable to withstand the moment. The railroad engineer gave three loud blasts of his whistle.

25 June
(Loudon County, Virginia)

Pickett's division came hiking up the road. The column of fours stretched away into the distant, hazy hills, wrapped around the western edges of the Blue Ridge as thought it were a monstrously long, implicitly menacing serpent.

Kemper's Brigade was last in the division's order of march. One interminable hot and footsore day blended into another in memory. The dust choked and fouled everyone in the column. Horses changed color magically as the miles passed. The streams they forded washed men and animals in strange patterns. Horses with black legs and grayish barrels gave rise to raucous amusement among infantrymen too tired and bored to miss any opportunity for laughter.

Sergeant Jepson Thacker believed that the best way to deal with really long marches, like these, was to be somewhere else in your head. He had worked out a program of reminiscences and fantasy which kept the thought of the tender spot on the top of his left foot from preying on his mind. He knew from hard experiences that to think about such things insured that they would worsen. His company commander was already more interested in that foot than Thacker would have wished. The last thing he wanted was a ride in the company mess wagon. His mess mates and the black teamsters would never let him forget it. Today was only about average hot. He settled his gear by shrugging it into more comfortable positions as he moved forward. *That damned foot!*

Claude Devereux would have been pleased to know that Thacker had been punished enough for his adventure in the 'stews' of Richmond to make him wish to avoid a repetition of the experience, but not enough to provoke him to desert. Thacker thought often of Devereux, wished in fact that luck had made Claude his commanding officer. There was something about the way the distinguished, gentlemanly figure in dark broadcloth and Panama hat had listened with such concern to his memories of Fredericksburg. Through the pain in his foot, he willed up a review of the talk in the steam launch during the ride to City Point.

"What are you thinking, Captain?" The skinny red headed major had asked.

"We passed Malvern Hill back there. We were in that whole business in front of Richmond."

"That's where you were made an officer as I recall."

Devereux appeared reluctant to speak of it, seemed to stand back inside himself even more than usual. "There were vacant positions that needed filling."

"My God," He remembered saying. "You might say that, Cap'n! Hell, there were so few of us left in the 7th Virginia that I had a time gettin' up a card game! Gaines' Mill was the worst."

"Frazier's farm was the bad one for us," Devereux had said. "We got mixed up with their infantry in a woods, at night. Of course, it always appears that you lost more men than you really did until casualties and stragglers start coming back." Devereux had seemed to watch to see if he would accept that.

In the cockpit of the big steam launch the three horses had whimpered and stamped their feet in blindfolded frustration.

Thacker had noticed that one of them had managed to kick manure all over another. "Lieutenant," he had said, addressing the youngest officer with a good deal of relish. "Your horse has soiled himself. That saddle and you are going to be an edifying spectacle."

The lieutenant had grimly commenced cleaning up his mount as best he could.

Devereux had questioned him while they had watched the Signal Corps officer work. "Tell me," he had asked. What has happened to Pickett's Division since last Fall. I've been away."

"Nothin' much," Thacker recalled saying. He had felt called upon to reflect the diffidence which was so much a part of Devereux's makeup. "We've been in a few little things, nothin' much. At Fredericksburg, we were to the south of the main fight and only got in it at the end. It was Cobb's Georgia brigade in front of the heights that had all the doin's. One of those boys told me later that they were standin' four deep in a sunken road with the back ranks loadin' and handin' up rifles as fast as they could to the ones in front. Them Yanks, they just kept coming on. Cobb's men were shootin' and yellin', 'Come on Yank, bring them shoes and rations up here! We don't want to walk that far for 'em!' It was Gawd awful! You know how the boys get when their blood is up, Cap'n!

Thacker knew a genuine fighter when he saw one. He would have rejected utterly the notion that he also recognized in Claude a member of the ruling class of his society, that his feelings for Devereux were not unlike those with which his ancestors had closed ranks behind a host of tribal leaders. Like his comrades, Thacker would have found such an idea demeaning and foolish.

Up ahead, he could see a group of mounted officers sitting their horses beside a 'T' shaped crossroads. "That's Snicker's Gap," ran through the ranks.

The head of the regiment's column came abreast of the mounted men. The regimental commander swiveled in his saddle. "7th Virginia! Attention! Pass in review!" The color sergeant rotated the staff of the battle flag so that he carried it past the reviewing party at a forty-five-degree angle to the ground.

"Ready, Eyes left!" the colonel cried.

In this position, Thacker saw that Johnson, in the 'four' in front of him was growing a nasty boil on the right side of the neck. Then he remembered to look at the mounted group. Pete Longstreet sat a big, ugly horse in the midst of a crowd of staff officers. To his left was the unmistakable face of George Pickett.

"Ready, Eyes front!

Thacker tried to remember the last time he had seen Longstreet. It was a while back. He began to think of Emma, and the farm. *Those hickory stumps in the new pasture should be getting rotten enough to be 'diggable'.*

The head of the 7th's column turned left into the main road, heading uphill, over the gap.

"I think I have never seen them in such fine condition. You are to be compli-
mented, George." Longstreet had the habit of talking to people without facing
them. He never took his eyes from the troops passing in the dirt road before him.

"Yes, they all somehow seem to have the right clothes on," Pickett said. "Must
be the fault of Major Moses back there. What do you say Rafe? Are you to blame
for this unwonted uniformity?"

Major Raphael Moses, chief commissary officer of Longstreet's corps, shared
most of the staff's view of George Pickett. They knew him to be charming, mer-
curial, competent, and brave to the edge of folly. He was everyone's friend. His
new found love affair with a sweet faced eighteen year old girl was something
which most of them found to be delightful. "No, General," Moses began, "I
think it must be piracy that is at the root."

Longstreet held up a hand. They all listened. You could hear it again, artillery,
off to the east, a low rumbling, threatening in the way that distant summer
storms threaten.

"Stuart?" Pickett suggested.

Longstreet nodded. "He has them stopped over there around Middleburg.
They must suspect where we are going, but they can't be sure, unless they can see.
You have to give Jeb credit. He is really good at this."

"What will he do as we keep moving north?" Pickett asked absentmindedly.

"Don't know, suppose he will move up alongside us. Let's move, gentlemen! I
want to camp near Berryville tonight. Care to join us for some five card stud this
evening, George. Fairfax there could use your money. By the way, George how
long do you think it will take Corse to catch up?"

"Not long, They will march day and night to reach us. You know him.."

26 June
(Duke Street, Alexandria)

The wagon stood in the street in front of the Italianate house. Everyone had a
hand in the loading of the wagon. Devereux's mother insisted on believing that
somehow she must be responsible for the final contents of the wagon which
would carry her son and Betsy White's into unforeseeable circumstances.

Devereux's father made an appearance around mid-day to share the latest
news of the city's gossip concerning Lee's invasion of the North.

No one knew where either army might be at the moment.

Charles left after a few moments of searching for words which he could not find and which Claude would not help him with.

George, Joseph and Bill White loaded the vehicle. Bill asked again what Claude thought would be needed.

Devereux refused to help him. "For God's sake, Bill! I don't need to tell you something like that! Take whatever you think we might need to survive. Don't forget some whiskey. We will be visiting Hooker again." With such minimal instruction, he left to find his wife.

Warren Biddle arrived at the Devereux residence in late afternoon with his aunt.

Claude and Hope came down from their rooms in the 'ell' to join his mother in her reception of these guests.

Biddle's field kit lay in the foyer where one of the White men had left it.

"You will stay the night, of course," Clotilde insisted. "Claude says you will depart so early.."

Biddle accepted the offer. He definitely had been expecting it.

Amy sat looking at Hope, inattentive to the talk around her.

Devereux glanced at his wife. Her cheeks, neck and ears displayed a slight flush which might have made him think her feverish if he had not known the cause. His eyes met Amy's.

She looked away.

"We'll be glad to have you with us, Warren," Claude said. "Judge Renfroe certainly speaks highly of you, and any kin of Amy is always welcome in our house, isn't that right, maman?"

Devereux's mother did not hear him. She rarely misunderstood the undercurrents in such scenes. She did not much care what the blue clothed boy might think, but the sight of Amy in distress, tortured by jealousy of her beloved daughter-in-law was more than she would allow. "I am sure you men have much to discuss," she declared. "Go, oversee what the Whites are doing, Claude! We ladies will be in the garden."

27 June
(Fairfax County, Virginia)

"You can't go west of here!" the sergeant insisted. "Secesh cavalry all over the place! "We got run out of Fairfax Court House around dawn. They're everywhere." The man had blind panic in his face.

"What regiment is this?" Devereux demanded with a peremptory command in his voice. He expected the soldier's fear to make him biddable.

"First D.C. Cavalry. You'd better go back, they'll be coming down the turnpike any minute! They were right behind us!"

Devereux and White looked at him.

He sat a foam covered horse beside their wagon. The tree lined, macadam road was quiet in the morning light. They shared the hard sprung front seat of the vehicle. Biddle and two Sanitary Commission men rode in the back. Their anxious features appeared, peering over Devereux's shoulder.

The sergeant reacted to Biddle's shoulder straps with a courteous "Good Morning, sir!"

"Did you lose anyone?" Devereux asked, seeking the dimensions of this supposed 'disaster'.

"We lost poor Captain Bradshaw. The murdering swine came right down the road headed for his billet. Mosby's cutthroats were with 'em. They wanted Bradshaw dead, dragged him out of his rooms. One of them shot him in the street, made him kneel there, gave him a piece of paper to look at and killed him with a sawed off scatter gun. We tried to get his body back, but there was too many of 'em."

Bradshaw! I remember the name. Isaac what have you been up to?

White heard a sound behind him.

The wagon shifted on its springs. The two young Sanitary Commission men were climbing over the tailgate.

"Leavin?" Bill asked. They made off down the road toward the Potomac.

"What did he look like, the man who killed Captain Bradshaw," Devereux asked softly.

"What do you mean? We were too far off to see that. Why would you ask me that?"

"Look behind you, sergeant." White said.

The cavalry squad spun as one man toward the roll of the terrain at which the road disappeared a quarter mile away.

Two brown horsemen with floppy hats had appeared over the crest.

With ringing curses, the sergeant's squad wheeled their horses.

"Don't leave me!" Biddle yelled.

The sergeant took him up behind. The blue troopers galloped down the turnpike, rapidly overtaking the escaping Sanitary men.

The two vedettes cantered forward, carbines held with butts against the saddle bow. A cavalry company breasted the rise behind them, the riders coming on in a neat column of fours.

Devereux and White sat mute by the road, motionless.

The scouts swept by. One turned in his seat to watch them. The lead company halted by the wagon. A shot rang out behind them.

White turned to see that one of the vedettes had dismounted to fire at the retreating figures. Two sets of fours left the head of the approaching force to help the scouts in their pursuit.

A very young captain arrived astride a tall buckskin horse. He considered them both. "This your slave?" he asked. There was neither friendliness nor courtesy in his tone.

"No. He's Virginia free born," Devereux answered. "He works for me, always has."

"Can you prove that," the officer asked.

"Yes, Cap'n. I have my papers with me," said Bill.

A gauntleted hand stretched out.

During the young man's perusal of these documents, another handful of horsemen clattered up the column to arrive at Devereux's wagon. A dusty, harried looking colonel reined up beside the youth who held White's identity documents. "What this, Dawson?" the officer questioned.

"Nothin' much, sir. Just these two. This is a genuine free born Virginia nigger sittin' there. God knows what the other might be."

The colonel walked his horse to one side so as to see the painted sign on its canvas. "Sanitary Commission, you can prove you're with them?"

Devereux said yes.

"You people have a reputation for compassion toward all, including our men. Is this a justified reputation?"

"Yes. Might I ask with whom I am speaking?"

"No. I'll tell you when you can ask questions. Who are you?

Devereux told him.

"My Lord! Will wonders never cease! A Devereux of Alexandria. What are you doing riding in that wagon, Devereux? You aren't really with these New England Bible thumpers, surely that can't be."

"Things are not always as they seem, sir," Claude responded without expression.

The other man laughed. "Thomas Munford," he said at last. Where are you going?"

"Edwards' Ferry."

Another laugh rang in the morning air. "A little out of your way aren't you? Give the man his papers, Dawson. We must be off." He held his horse alongside the wagon to speak once more to Devereux as his regiment lurched into motion. "I can summon spirits from the vasty deep," Munford whispered hoarsely.

"But will they come?" answered Devereux.

"I thought as much. A good thing they gave us a signal or two." The cavalry commander laughed yet again. He grew serious, half talking to Devereux, half watching his men go by. "I'm worried, Devereux," he said. "Stuart is changing this move north into something unforeseen. He refuses to listen to anyone, but his old cronies. Hampton and I can do nothing with him. I don't really know where we are going after we cross the Potomac. Try to tell someone."

"I'll try."

The sound of hooves announced the approach of several troopers. One of them had Warren Biddle trotting along in front of him on the ground.

Devereux leaned toward Colonel Munford. "Let the fool escape!" he said. "We need him where he is."

With a tilt of the chin, Munford was gone in a cloud of dust. His staff kicked their mounts into motion. A burly soldier took Biddle up behind him as the column departed.

The battle standard spread in the air as it passed. Second Virginia Cavalry was emblazoned upon its fabric.

32

Thespians

28 June
(Frederick, Maryland)

Hooker seemed about to spring at him from his place beside the fireplace. His blonde hair and whiskers contrasted spectacularly with the red of his cheeks. Hand written dispatches and colored maps littered the floor about his chair. "God damn it, Devereux!" he yelled. "Why should I put up with such discourtesy and interference? They act like this way toward me all the time. Did I ever show you the letter the president sent me when he gave me command of this army? No? Well, I assure you that it is one of the most remarkable bits of official correspondence you are apt to see! Old Sam Cooper was noted for his ability to write dispatches that cut without bruising, but that little note was beyond belief!"

Claude still held in one hand the "portefeuille" in which he had carried the letter of instruction and his other identification papers. Strangely, incongruously, his mind took note of the cracked, painted wood of the fireplace mantel.

The half dozen staff men and couriers in the living room of the big house stared from one to the other in anticipation of further heated words.

Hooker's face grew more suffused with blood. "He had the gall to suggest that I might be a danger to the Constitution! Him, of all people.." He remembered his surroundings and thought better of continuing. "They have sent you here as a spy! You are here to spy on me! Do you want that? I thought we were friends."

"Now, Joe. You don't mean that. You know Claude would not come here to do you an injury. Let him explain." The soothing voice of Hooker's chief of staff floated from a corner.

Devereux's eyes met those of Brigadier General Dan Butterfield.

Devereux sought Hooker's gaze. "General, I don't deny that I was sent to your headquarters to keep track of your doings. I could have told them that you would see through this nonsense about the Sanitary Commission. I point out to you that I have not tried to deceive you in this way."

Hooker shuffled the three sheets in his hand, looking at each in turn. "That's true," he finally said. "You told me right up front. Are they out to finish me, Claude? Is this the end?" Desperation showed through his normally sunny nature. He glanced about the room, seeming to vacillate between a desire to clear them all out and a despondent craving for company. He pivoted back to face his guest.

"I've got him, Claude! I've got Bobby Lee, that old fox. His cavalry is running loose somewhere for no good reason. George Sharpe is sure Lee has his three infantry corps spread all over central Pennsylvania to our west and north. I've got a lot more men than he has. I'm going to catch him spread out like that, and that will be all. That will be all! Do they know that in Washington? Does the president know that?"

Jesus, can things really be as bad as that? Devereux cleared his throat, and began to speak, choosing his words with care. "No, Joe, they don't know that. In fact, they think you won't close with him, that you will lose your nerve again, as they say you did last month.

Strangled sounds of angry protest formed a background.

Hooker examined Devereux with minute interest. He put a hand on the chair's wing back. "And, you, Claude, what do you think?" he asked.

I think you have to go if we are to have any chance at all. I think you are a grand man and a fine soldier. "I think you are a hell of a fighter, Joe. If you are left in command there will be a huge battle somewhere up here, but they don't think that. Do you know that Lincoln has offered your command to John Reynolds? Do you know that?"

Hooker's head bobbed rhythmically several times. "I had heard this. John is too polite to let on, but word gets out. I have tried to resign command of this army before, maybe I should again." He glanced at Devereux and then at Butterfield.

"They'll never take it," Butterfield retorted. "They'd be terrified of the thought of trying to change leaders in the middle of this. The army might disintegrate without you."

Hooker swiveled back to Devereux. "You've just been there."

Devereux shook his head. "I am not so sure they would keep you. Stanton talks against you all the time." *That's all you get my friend, no more.*

Outrage spread around the room.

General Butterfield snorted his anger. "To hell with them, Joe! You don't need this."

That's his money talking, Joe. Don't listen. You're a professional soldier. You have nothing to fall back on..

Hooker seemed to shrink into his inner self for a moment, contemplating something visible only to himself. He spoke to a lieutenant colonel who stood by the door. "Does Crenshaw have the telegraph to Washington working yet? Yes? Claude, you and Dan stay and help me write this. The rest of you, leave!"

An hour later, Devereux emerged from the building into warm afternoon sun. Frederick overflowed with Army of the Potomac troops, animals and wagons.

There were so many.

Little groups of headquarters clerks and officers crowded against him as he elbowed his way to the street.

The cavalry escort for the commanding general of the army lounged in the surrounding streets and alleys.

Devereux guessed the yellow legged horsemen to be several hundred in number. Red and white swallow tailed guidons were everywhere.

Puffy white clouds slid by above, making a pleasing kaleidoscope of the bright, yellow day.

Bill waited by the wagon with someone, someone familiar.

The young man wore a farmer's coarse work clothes. He was of medium height with curly black hair peeking out under a straw hat. Tied to a ring in a granite block at the curb was a refined little mare. She looked at Devereux, watching him with soft eyes.

"Alexander Hunter," Devereux said with his hand out. "I thought you were with Longstreet. Actually, I haven't seen you since you transferred from the 17th to the cavalry."

The quick intelligence of the man looked out at Devereux. "Bill and I have been visiting and looking at all this," Hunter replied. He waved a hand at the passing sea of blue. "Always nice to see a neighbor, Claude, always nice! I remember well your father's help when we were having that little problem at Abingdon ..."

Devereux was blank.

Hunter tried again. "My sister's difficulty with the Philadelphia bank.."

"Yes. of course, it was nothing. Banks are always losing these things, forget it."

"No. We seem to work for the same folks now, Claude. Harry Jenkins sends greetings."

Devereux and White smiled at the thought of the red headed major.

"What terribly serious message did he give you for us, Alexander? And, how did you find us? And how are you able to wander in here among these folks?"

"Your wife pointed us in the right direction." Hunter looked puzzled. "She wasn't always so keen on our side, if memory serves me."

"That's right, but she is now."

Hunter smiled. "Well, I was not thinking of her as an ally, so we sort of felt around the subject of where you might be until she lost patience with us, and straight out asked what we wanted with you, and did it have to do with Harry Jenkins' business with you. A beautiful, charming convert, what could be better.

As for your other question, I am a horse feed contractor for this lovely army, Mister Devereux. Would you like to see my papers? They are of the best. I assure you."

"You said us, Mister Hunter?" Bill injected into the conversation. "You said, Mrs. Devereux pointed us.."

"Yes," Hunter agreed. "I have a partner. He's the tall fellow with the mustache across the street. There are scouts out all across the army's front. Jenkins loaned us two to Longstreet for this expedition. We started in Washington, poking around, then I remembered that Harry had said we should check with you, and here we are! Do you think we should get off the street?"

Devereux was unconcerned. He shrugged. "Perhaps. Bill, have you seen anywhere we could get a drink? Good. Let's go, Alex. What's his name?" he asked, inclining his head toward the man across the street.

"Harrison, Jim Harrison. He's from Richmond, an actor in fact."

Across the street, an officer of artillery left a group standing beside a pair of wagons. He crossed the dusty road to stand before Devereux.

The Virginian did not really notice him until he sensed the tension in White and Hunter. He turned to look Wilson Ford in the face. "My, my, Captain. Are you still after me, or do the laws of chance govern this meeting?" *He must be an artillery liaison officer here with army headquarters..*

Ford struggled for an answer. He watched his enemy remove his Panama, pull a snowy handkerchief from a pocket and mop his brow. The desire to hit the man swept over him, flooding his face with blood.

"Feeling warm?" Devereux grinned at him. "Heard from your friend? What's his name? Ah! Johnston. *Mean, mean, you know his name.* Went to New York didn't he?"

"Why are you here?" Ford whispered.

"Well, I am here on the Commission's business. General Hooker asked me along on this chase after Bobby Lee. Miss Biddle insisted I should come."

The one armed soldier flinched.

Devereux looked at him closely. *You poor bastard. She's mine and will always be..* His expression changed. There was pity in it now. "Actually, my wife and mother also thought I should leave for the front. I don't seem to be doing very well with women lately.."

Ford turned on his heel and walked away.

The tap room of the Calvert Inn seemed completely full at first with soldiers. Its decrepit barman and elderly waiter were unaccustomed to so much trade.

Devereux's money got them a table by a window. The roaring noise of the place made it desirable for a talk. Devereux looked at Harrison while Alexander Hunter spoke to bridge the gap of strangeness between them. After a moment's thought, Claude produced several small, flat metal plates from his pockets. He examined them, selected one, and laid it on the table in front of Harrison.

The scout picked it up and looked at it for a second. "I told Jenkins this was not a good likeness of me," he said, putting the Daguerreotype in a pocket. "Thank you."

"You are an actor?"

"Yes."

"Do you know Booth?"

"Edwin?"

Devereux hesitated. "His brother, I believe."

"John Wilkes? He uses the name Wilkes alone at times, for what reason I know not."

"Yes, John. Is he a good actor?"

"Untrained, but he has natural ability. You know him?"

"Slightly. Is he with us?"

"Is Seward a weasel?" Harrison laughed aloud at his own joke. A number of soldiers turned.

Hunter waved at them, picked up the bottle and went to pour a few shots.

"In truth, it might be asked why he is not yet in uniform." Harrison was perplexed by his own question.

Hunter returned. "Good lads and true!" he called to the blue clad guests. "I think we should get on with this, Claude," he whispered.

"Yes. They do appear to be growing curious." Devereux smiled at the enemy. "I think one of you should go to Lee to tell him that Hooker will be replaced with George Meade tomorrow. Between us we should be able right now to figure out where their main forces are. The one who goes to Longstreet can carry that information."

They agreed.

"Whoever is left should try to find Stuart," Devereux continued. "The fool is somehow farther east and south than any sensible plan would require. He must be told that Lee is going to have to fight up here. It will be all or nothing.. Those damned Yanks are looking at us again. Let's give them the bottle and get out of here."

"You are from the cavalry, Alex. You should go to Stuart," Harrison said outside in the street. Where do you suppose Lee might be?"

"Greencastle, Chambersburg, somewhere in the Cumberland Valley," Devereux answered. "Can you find him? I'll give you what I know."

"Start talking."

33

The Crest

29 June
(Harrisburg, Pennsylvania)

The city began to empty early in the morning of the 29th.

A general sense of unease had pervaded the western and southern suburban outskirts since the previous afternoon. Fear hung in the air like the electricity and oppressiveness that precede a thunderstorm. In the heart of the city people stood in small groups on street corners reading emergency editions of the news while leaning closer to catch the views of anyone who might have recent information. Soldiers passing in the streets returned frowns, puzzled by the intensity with which their movements were scrutinized by the citizenry. An hour before sundown of the long summer day the first wagons appeared in the center of the city. The state government offices poured forth a cataract of boxes and chests. The wagons filled and departed to the east.

Patrick Devereux sat in a large, scroll backed wicker chair at one end of the veranda of the Commercial Hotel through most of the 29th. His rigid leg rested on a small hassock provided by a solicitous porter. From this post he watched the flow of business and political activity in Harrisburg come to a near halt just after noon. Deathlike quiet settled over the streets. Couriers appeared at intervals. Their mounts had suffered much in the summer heat and humidity. The Pennsylvania legislature began to load its papers and ancestral portraits into yet more wagons at three o'clock that afternoon.

A number of well-dressed men came to talk with Patrick in his post of observation. White jacketed waiters with European accents supplied them with cool drinks against the terrible, desiccating warmth.

About Five o'clock, a horse drawn streetcar appeared at a distant intersection. Patrick remembered that the street from which it had come led to one of the Susquehanna River bridges. The car made the turn, rolling steadily forward, approaching his point of observation. The small, blue figure of the conductor waved its arms and shouted to people in the street. Some of them began to trot alongside the streetcar to listen. The voice carried far down the oddly silent street. "They were a'waitin' for me! At the last stop in Camp Hill! They said they needed a ride into town! One of 'em tried to get his horse to climb into the car!"

A serious looking man in police uniform emerged from the hotel to stand before the oncoming streetcar with upraised hand. The conductor gaped at the figure of authority. Self control returned. "Secesh cavalry," he said, more calmly than an onlooker might have thought possible a moment before. "They are all over Camp Hill by now! The leader told me to come in and tell the Governor that they will be in to call on him tomorrow."

Frederick Kennedy made his way out of the crowd around the streetcar. He found Devereux, and took a chair beside him. A waiter brought Kennedy a large, cold glass of lager.

The tumult of the street scene around the streetcar ebbed. More policemen and other civilian officials arrived to interview the trolley man.

Patrick turned from this scene to his friend. "Well?" he asked. Kennedy put down his glass. "There's nothing in the town, nothing, a few militia companies." He laughed aloud. "Stuart's people will eat them for breakfast. Do your meetings go well?"

"There will be a surprisingly warm reception in some quarters if Lee succeeds in occupying this place," said Patrick. "If I were a Republican, I believe I would leave for a while."

Kennedy savored the thought. "Tonight, tonight we will find them," he whispered.

Crossing the river into the western environs of Harrisburg proved easy to do. The two Confederates rehearsed a story involving stranded children and a desperate widow needing rescue. It was not needed. A constant procession of vehicles flowed east across the river. The wagons carried to safety inhabitants of Camp Hill on the western bank and their most treasured possessions. A preoccupied Pennsylvania militia captain waved them forward onto the bridge at the eastern end, too distraught to listen closely.

The shadowy streets of Camp Hill were filled with the ghosts of a departed population. Someone had thought to light the gas street lamps before he went. They hissed and wavered with variations in pressure which threatened total darkness. Dogs barked from the pools of dimness provided by the depths of alleys. An occasional vehicle passed, the occupants squinting in the dark. All traffic appeared to be headed for the river.

Kennedy drove the hired buggy. Patrick's leg protruded on the right side. He writhed inwardly at the memory of the difficulty with which he had taken his place. A hotel porter had helped him onto the seat. The buggy rolled steadily toward the western outskirts of inhabited ground. Kennedy stopped the team at a fork in the road. They studied the possibilities. One branch curved gently around to the left, holding in its visible curve the suggestion that it might meander back to the riverbank. The other street ran straight into the southwest. The trolley track lay in its center. "That way," Kennedy said, pointing with his chin at the more westerly choice.

Large trees surrounded the macadamized paving of the street, seeming to press in against the surface across which their iron tires rumbled. They reached the end of the evenly spaced circles of light. Beyond the final circular spot of illumination, a pinpoint of yellow light could be seen. The buggy moved forward into the dark street. Patrick Devereux looked back at the street lights. The sight reminded him of the experience of standing alone out of doors in the night beside an unshuttered window. The rings of light seemed rooms contained within the darkened house of night. The point of yellow light grew and solidified. Devereux puzzled over its nature. The house surrounding the light slowly took shape. The window which framed the light could now be seen. The horses stopped abruptly. One looked at something to its right. The other tossed its head. Devereux watched a fist come out of the gloom to grasp the animal's halter. Rough hands grabbed at his stiff leg and coat. They dragged him from the seat. He fell heavily to the ground, and lay in the street, enclosed by a forest of legs. From the far side of the buggy, Kennedy protested loudly the manhandling.

"Get up!" The voice crackled with hostility. A foot prodded Devereux in the flank. He held on to the spokes of the right front wheel, pulling himself to the side of the wagon and rising to one knee. "Whut's wrong with you, boy!" a man beside him growled. Patrick continued to struggle with the problem of finding enough leverage to get the straight, stiff leg under him. He said nothing. Someone seized him beneath the arms, hauling him relentlessly upward until he rested on both feet, one hand on the wheel. "Damn it! I didn't ask you to touch me!" Patrick snarled. He turned with some difficulty toward the men around him. "Give me my crutches! They're under the seat."

Three dark figures encircled him. He could smell them in the night. They smelled of horse, tobacco, and the general reek that accompanies soldiers who have been in the field for weeks. All those smells combined to assure him that they had found the Army of Northern Virginia.

The form to his left made a sign.

The man closest to the wagon seat rummaged around until he found the crutches.

"Thank you," Devereux muttered, settling the crutches in his armpits. He heard Kennedy coming around the heads of the team. He did not seem to be alone.

"Who are you?" demanded the figure to his left.

"I am Patrick Henry Devereux of Alexandria, Virginia. That is Lieutenant Frederick Kennedy of the Confederate Army Signal Corps. We have reconnoitered the city, and have come to give you what we know."

"Scouts," the voice commented.

"Spies," said Devereux.

"This one knew the right signaling words, Major," offered one of Kennedy's guardians.

There was a short, but anxious pause. "You came 'round and got in front of us?" the major's voice inquired.

"Yes, sir. We did that," Kennedy answered.

Devereux felt his right arm gripped and his hand raised. Another hand fit into it. "Charles Felts," the major's voice proclaimed. "I'm with the 17th Virginia Cavalry. Jenkins is our brigade commander. Why don't we go in the house over there? He'll be back in half an hour." The kitchen of the shabby little house seemed a homely setting for such a meeting. The yellow flame of the single candle guttered on the table, throwing its reflection on the window glass.

Brigadier General Albert Gallatin Jenkins looked the lawyer that he was. There was about him an indifference to the require-ments of military propriety that seemed quite natural, and not in the least affected. A long, black beard rested evenly on his chest. Its curly tendrils made his hollow cheeks and pale complexion striking. Sunburn colored his ears. The collar of a red checked shirt peeked from within the half-open grey material of his uniform vest. Small brass buttons glinted in the wavering light. A fine boned, long fingered hand felt a burn mark in the old oak table at which he sat.

Fred Kennedy went on at length with details of militia dispositions in Harrisburg and the exact pattern of streets and squares.

Devereux examined General Jenkins as his friend spoke. The general did not appear to listen closely.

"You were in Congress, weren't you?" Patrick asked.

Jenkins looked at him, glad of the interruption. "Two terms. Do I know you?"

"No, we are a political family. You may know my father."

"Of course! How foolish of me! How is your lovely mother?"

"Well, quite well."

"I know your brother as well! He arranged the placement of an inheritance for my wife three, no! It was four years ago, splendid man! The securities are still paying well."

"They would be doing that." Patrick countered. "My brother is very good at that sort of thing." The edge in his tone stopped the conversation.

What the hell is this? Kennedy thought. *Are we going to act out the Devereux family feuds right here?* He cleared his throat. "Would you like us to take this intelligence to General Stuart, sir?"

Jenkins leaned forward.

Several of the cavalry officers around the room turned to the group at the table.

"You know where he is to be found?" asked Major Felts.

"You don't?" Kennedy questioned.

"No one on our side of the line of contact with the Yankee army has seen him in four or five days," said Felts.

Jenkins' intelligent, inoffensive face swung from one of his two guests to the other in evident mystification at this thought. "My brigade is not properly part of General Lee's army," he said by way of explanation of some circumstance as yet unrevealed. "We generally are employed in the southwest, Roanoke, Bristol, don't you know. We are accustomed to acting in defense of our home area. We do raids in what the Yankees call West Virginia mostly. We really are more in the line of mounted infantry. I'm no 'outpost officer,' not good at large sized cavalry operations at all. You need one of these fancy West Point or VMI educated fellows like Felts there for that kind of work. General Lee pulled us into his army for this 'soiree'. We have led the way for Ewell's Corps. He and Rodes are at Carlisle, back on the road a piece. Jube Early is down at York trying to cross the Susquehanna. Stuart fought the Yankee cavalry at several places down in Virginia. He was trying to keep them from seeing too soon where we were heading. Our Northern friends never quite got through him. That probably accounts for their perplexity with regard to our whereabouts this last week. When that was all done, General Stuart took three brigades of cavalry, the three he is most accustomed to, and moved north. He was supposed to hang on to Ewell's right flank, protect it from prying eyes, etcetera. I expected to have him catch up with me before this. No sign of him. Odd!"

All those present thought about that, thought about how dangerous that was.

"The newspapers say there was some sort of cavalry force tied up in the northern fringes of Washington a few days ago," said Patrick. "I assumed it was a diversion."

"Where did they go?"

"Last seen en route northeast into Maryland."

"Northeast? Why would he go northeast?" Jenkins scratched his bearded chin.

Kennedy returned to the business at hand. "No idea. Are you going into Harrisburg tomorrow?"

Albert Jenkins just looked at them. "Tell them, Felts," he ordered.

Major Felts took the fourth chair at the little square table. He found a sketch map in one of his pockets. "Courier from Second Corps came in before you showed up. Our original instructions to take the city and then go farther east are canceled. Lee has commanded the army to join him as quickly as possible. Rodes' Division has already marched south from Carlisle. We have officers on the road to find Early with the same news." Felts saw the obvious question in their faces. "We don't know why. The order doesn't say. We are going to assemble on this little town." He pointed to a tiny village on his map. It was situated at a spot where a good road came down from South Mountain.

Devereux read the name. Cashtown.

"Can't be more than ten houses," Kennedy commented. "What's this bigger place just to the east?" He indicated a larger village several miles east of Cashtown where roads ran together thickly.

"That's Gettysburg," Major Felts replied. "We went through there a week ago with Early."

The Confederate officers in the little room laughed at the thought. General Jenkins looked apologetic. "Jubal pretty well cleaned them out," he said. "I am going to pull back from here at three in the morning. I'll cover Ewell's back as he moves away. What will you do?"

They looked at each other. "I guess we'll go find the Yanks' main force, and see if we can do this again," Kennedy said.

"Do you want some help getting back into Harrisburg?" Jenkins asked.

Kennedy smiled. "No, General, we'll just tell them we've seen the devils themselves." He held up his glass, looking for the bottle that had somehow passed him by on the last round.

34

Armageddon

1 July

As the two armies entered Pennsylvania, each had been intent on its own goal.

The Confederate Army of Northern Virginia sought the final battle, a Napoleonic climax of the kind which Robert E. Lee had believed in all his professional life. He thought it to be the only satisfactory outcome of war.

The Northern Army of the Potomac marched to defend the heartland of the United States from a blow that sought to kill the possibility of reunion.

These two armies groped across the land as though they were sightless.

In truth, the Southern army was nearly blind. The strategic conception that Lee had brought to his campaign plan had been bright with the promise of a chance to prove the futility of coerced reunification but it had begun to go awry almost as soon as his soldiers had forded the Potomac. For some unknown reason, the cavalry division of Lee's army had disappeared. James Ewell Brown Stuart and his all-important horsemen were not to be found. They had last been seen heading northeast from Gaithersburg, Maryland, destination, unknown. Lee had told Stuart to cover the right flank of the army during the march north into Pennsylvania, and to that end, Stuart had kept personal control of most of the cavalry, including the regiments most skilled at reconnaissance. Without them, and Stuart himself, Lee could only guess at the enemy's whereabouts.

For this reason, both Longstreet and Lee himself were surprised and nearly unbelieving when Harrison, the scout, found them in Chambersburg. It was only after prolonged discussion and interrogation of Harrison that Lee ordered the army to assemble at Cashtown.

The Union government chose this moment of great peril to replace the commander of the Army of the Potomac. His successor, Major General George Gordon Meade, possessed an odd set of qualifications for the post. He had a reputation for fussy competence as an engineer officer of the regular army, a history of prosaic reliability in command of a division of infantry and renown for a temperament of such irascibility that many feared to approach him. He inherited from Hooker three important things, an army second to none, a well-thought out plan of action, and an effective staff. What he could make of these riches time and fortune would show. For now, Meade drove northwestward through the shimmering days of high summer, searching for an enemy whose depredations were widely, if inaccurately reported in the daily press. He led with a strong force of cavalry commanded by the best horse soldier in the Union Army, perhaps in either army, John Buford of Kentucky.

The Southern Army marched into Pennsylvania under severe strictures. Robert Edward Lee did not wish to participate in a campaign of barbarous devastation waged against a civilian population, however hostile. To this end, he issued what came to be called the "Christian Order." It demanded a standard of conduct which would threaten none but soldiers. It forbade looting and destruction of private property. It dealt with the respect due to women. There was some grumbling in the ranks. Men made reference to well-known events connected with the presence of Northern armies in the South. Nevertheless, nearly everyone supported the commanding general in this matter. There were several executions for crimes committed against citizens of the United States by Confederate soldiers. An unexpected by-product of this policy was the widespread printing in central Pennsylvania of the exact text of Lee's order. In the midst of the campaign, Confederates were surprised to be confronted by German farmers who lectured them in broken English as to their required conduct while brandishing a copy of the order in question. Such encounters are thought to have been the occasion for acts of violence, some of which may have gone unreported.

The two armies finally came together in a fashion which can be thought of figuratively as resembling what might happen if an arrow were to collide with the side of a large serpent, the snake being at that moment engaged in coiling inward toward itself, swinging its head back toward the point of collision. Buford's cavalry division was the arrowhead. Ambrose Powell Hill's Third Corps happened to be at the place of impact. The snake's flank surged at the arrow head. Hill's divisions beat and beat at Buford's dismounted troopers. The shaft of the arrow rushed forward in the form of John Reynold's Union infantry divisions coming fast at double time to the side of Buford's men. All the while the snake's head curled back toward its body. It was a knowing, cunning snake, and Jubal Early's division of infantrymen were the fangs. A. P. Hill had risen above the crushing pain of the disease which was killing him to think to send couriers dashing to Baldy Ewell's Second Corps when his men first ran into the Yankee army outside Gettysburg. Armed with this news, the snake's head moved forward, sliding down from the north, aimed at the shaft of the arrow..

Devereux and White arrived in Gettysburg about 11:00 A.M. They drove up the Taneytown Road from the south in the midst of Major General Oliver Otis Howard's 11th Corps staff.

Lincoln and Stanton had relieved Joe Hooker as Devereux had predicted. Devereux got up early to see Hooker off with due consideration. A small group of friends gathered in the street at Frederick to say farewell. Devereux intimated that if Hooker decided to leave the army, he should look him up. The look on Hooker's face had been indecipherable.

Major General Meade had accepted the validity of Devereux's documents and identity as an assistant to Secretary Stanton without comment. He made available the use of the army's telegraph. He said Devereux should go where he chose. For the moment, he had more important things to worry over than a War Department representative in the midst of his army. He was graceless enough to say this.

Devereux sent Stanton his first telegraphic report from Frederick, then joined Howard's Eleventh Corps Headquarters on the move north.

Howard was a West Pointer and a Maine man. He was among the most pious of Union Army generals. He was rivaled in either army only by Stonewall Jackson in intensity of religious feeling, but somehow he lacked the Presbyterian elder's battlefield luck. His mostly German troops had been beaten repeatedly by smaller Confederate forces and did not seem to have much taste for real combat in spite of the fact that they were all volunteers and had a large number of abolitionists among them. He had lost an arm in the first year of the war. This had not dimmed his personal enthusiasm for the war and he had returned to active service as soon as he could. It was his Army Corps which had crumbled before Stonewall's attack at Chancellorsville. His zeal for the Sanitary Commission was unbounded. He was immensely pleased that a Commission inspector would accompany his staff. He gladly made a place for Devereux's wagon in his official "family."

Devereux had a map of south-central Pennsylvania spread on his lap as they rode up the road to Gettysburg. It came from the box of 'necessities' which Bill had provided for them. He consulted it as they rolled along. Howard borrowed it once to measure distances. Several miles south of the crossroads town, the sound of battle began to roll down across them. Howard and his aides left the column. Jumping a fence into the adjoining pasture, they galloped cross country to the sound of the firing. The noise grew, and grew. Small arms fire could clearly be heard. The road ran gently uphill toward a crest, to the right of which there was a wrought iron gate opening into a cemetery. At the top of the hill, they came even with the cemetery gate. The town of Gettysburg lay before them. Devereux and Bill saw that if they remained in the column of march they would be swept through the town and into the line of battle which must be beyond. White pulled the team around to the right. They passed through the gate and into the cemetery. Across the cemetery, Bill saw a two-story brick arch which opened into another road. He drove to the arch, pulling up to one side inside the cemetery wall. The word "Evergreen" was laid out in the brick of the portal.

Howard's lead division went straight down the north side of the hill, into the town. There was a short open space at the foot of the hill, followed by the many frame and brick buildings of Gettysburg itself.

Devereux tried to remember if he had ever been in this part of Pennsylvania. The noise of an engagement to the west of the town interfered with his thinking.

They moved the wagon back to the northwest edge of the cemetery hill, seeking the best view. From this vantage point, a broad expanse of grassy meadows and fields in crop stretched diagonally away to the westward. A group of pretty brick school buildings stood on a low ridge beyond the fields. The fight was not on that ridge. It was somewhere beyond. Union army regiments could be seen crossing the ground occupied by the school. One of the buildings had a white cupola. There were several small, blue figures crowded together there. One of them had a brass telescope. The sun glinted wickedly from its barrel. An artillery battery rolled forward onto the ground between the school buildings. The six guns looked like toys at this distance. The artillerymen began the drill which would bring their weapons into battery, prepared to deliver their lethal fires to the west. Devereux watched as the horses were unhitched and lead down the reverse slope into shelter.

An immense cloud of dirty white smoke drifted back from the unseen ground west of the school buildings. The fight was there. As they watched, three shells burst in the open ground between the cemetery and the school buildings. One of them happened to detonate in the midst of an infantry regiment taking a 'short cut' across the cultivated land. Three or four men went down, A thin, howling shriek overcame the background sound of gunfire.

Wounded streamed back over the ridge, coming back past the brick school buildings, competing for the use of the two roads with advancing troops.

"We're going to sit right here and watch this," Devereux decided aloud. "We don't want to get closer. That crest is low enough that there are bound to be a lot more of our own shells coming over 'long'.

White had not been paying much attention to the scene. He could not take his attention from the Yankee soldiers still passing in the road by the cemetery gate. He nudged Devereux to make him look at them.

A general stopped his horse in the road in front of the gate. He was at the head of a long column of soldiers. He was met there by a courier who had come pelting up the road out of the town. The messenger's horse heaved and glistened with sweat in the heat.

"Which one is that?" Bill asked. He meant the general.

"Von Steinwehr," Claude said. "Yet another of these remarkable Germans who they have so many of. Most of them came from Europe in '49 and '50 after having lost their revolution against their kings. Now they think we will do as a substitute enemy."

The divisional column swayed into motion. The troops marched up to the gate and turned right in obedience to the outstretched arm of one of Von Steinwehr's officers. As they watched, the soldiers filled the cemetery. Wagons arrived. Shovels and pickaxes made the work of entrenchment more possible in the hard soil of the little hill. A staff officer approached to ask them to move the wagon. His brigade's main line of defense needed the space. The two spies asked if they could help in some way. He declined with thanks and said the major problem just now was that the soldiers did not like digging in a graveyard, but it could not be helped. They moved back to their original spot just inside the archway in a space no one seemed to want. Bill unhitched the team to let them graze. They sat and watched the Yankees dig for a while. Devereux finally walked away to talk to nearby officers. "Damn!" he said when he returned. "This is Howard's reserve force! Now he's in charge. Reynolds was shot this morning, killed instantly, apparently by a sharpshooter!"

White's instincts as an old soldier reacted to this news. "That means they will hold this hill no matter what."

"That's right! Even if they are defeated out there in front of that school. They will try desperately to hang onto this high ground. They say those people over there are Hill's. They think they have beaten him off."

In truth, firing had died away to an occasional flurry of shots.

About three in the afternoon, it started again. Artillery fire and musketry reached a new crescendo in the unseen battle west of town. At roughly the same time the clamor began to spread to the north and east, creeping along the extended, curving battle line which Howard's men had created by their arrival. Von Steinwehr's infantrymen did not appear able to decide which area was the more threatening. Little groups of soldiers drifted back and forth across the hill from their newly completed trenches. The roaring, rolling sound attracted them like a magnet. Unit commanders shooed them back to their own positions as fast as they could, but the soldiers returned as soon as the officers went to some other part of the cemetery. The torrent of noise rose to a peak in the northeast. Over the background racket of gunfire a new ingredient could be discerned. The shrill cacophony of the "rebel yell" was heard. Blue clad soldiers stared at each other, remembering, anticipating, each man alone with the echoing memory inside his head.

Away, in the same direction, Devereux could see the smoke of musketry growing nearer as fighting approached through the streets of the town. All at once, a mass of Union infantrymen broke from the edge of the line of buildings below, broke into the open, headed for the low hill on which Von Steinwehr's division waited for whatever might follow from the sreets of the town.

The Rebels came into the open. The grey-brown lines poured out of alleys, streets and the backyards of houses to scream their anger and hatred at the backs of their fleeing enemies. Men shook their fists at the sight of Von Steinwehr's lines. The Southern line of battle rolled forward toward the base of the hill.

Bill grabbed Claude's arm, pointing at scattered blue flags among the red. "Look! Pelicans!" he said. "It must be Ewell's Corps! They've come in on the flank!" It was true. Among the square red flags, a solid block of banners bearing the image of Louisiana's symbol of bloody sacrifice could be seen.

"Hitch the team!" Devereux yelled above the din. "We don't want to be here if they arrive suddenly!"

A tide of refugees from the units that had already been defeated flowed over the hill, headed for some as yet undetermined destination in the rear. Devereux watched with sardonic amusement. He presumed that the Provost Marshal's cordon of cavalry would halt the rout somewhere short of Baltimore. *Too bad,* he thought. *You boys could probably use the exercise..*

Von Steinwehr's men opened fire in a series of crashing volleys which staggered the oncoming grey lines. The Union soldiers fired in unison, on command, in the drill that made their massed muskets into one single, many barreled weapon. Officers stood in the open, just behind the trenches, shouting the commands which were the justification for their existence. Minie balls sang through the air across the hilltop. Bill climbed onto the wagon's seat, and pulled the frightened team's heads toward the opening in the cemetery's arch. He cursed the off lead horse which stood stupidly still, unable to move in its terror. He laid on the whip, raising a welt across the animal's back, and it stumbled forward through the gate where he turned them right toward the shelter to be found behind the hill. Devereux climbed over the seat into the bed of the wagon in order to see better. To left and right of the road, a white cloud of smoke eddied and swirled. Bullets from Southern rifle fire struck the trees and rocks around the departing wagon, whizzing in the air and flattening themselves against hard objects with an ugly sound.

Something hit the tailgate of the wagon, tearing an irregular, splintered hole in the wood. Devereux felt a stabbing pain which he knew must mean a splinter in his left leg.

Alongside the road, a Federal lieutenant colonel, standing sword in hand behind his regiment's line, threw up his hands, and grasped the wreckage of his face. The officer stumbled blindly toward the road, and the wildly swaying path of the wagon. The blinded man evaded the grip of a sergeant who reached for him. Devereux saw white bits of bone and brown beard between the fingers. He lunged across the side of the wagon, trying unsuccessfully to fend off the man's suicidal advance. The wagon lurched horribly as it ran across the colonel's back.

Bill pulled up at the bottom of the grade. They listened for a moment. A practiced ear told the story. "They've gone back.." White cried aloud. "Damn it! They've gone back.. They should come on, now!"

Devereux was not disheartened. "They'll rally, Bill! They'll be back shortly, just wait and see!"

But that was not to be. Southern commanders who had fought all day against this same enemy were now seized with anxiety at the sight of the low hill. They would not be back today.

The two spies waited an hour amid the passing Northern soldiers, waited for the renewal of an assault which must surely penetrate a defense maintained by nothing more than Von Steinwehr's small force.

The sun sank to the western horizon.

"I don't understand, this. Where are they?" Bill whispered.

Devereux shook his head. "Something is wrong. Let's move back down the road a bit." He pointed at a grassy track. "Here's a path in the direction of the road we came in on. I don't know where this road goes. Let's get back on the other one. My boot is full of blood.."

When they stopped, Bill cut open the seam along the inside of Devereux's trouser leg. The long, narrow piece of tailgate had gone in on the outside of his leg. Half an inch of yellow wood projected from the entrance wound. Most of the splinter could be seen under the skin. It was close to three inches in length, a quarter inch in diameter. The pointed end protruded from an exit wound on the back of his calf.

Devereux looked down at it for a minute. He leaned against the wagon, one hand on his friend's shoulder.

Bill looked up at him. "Claude, I believe the best thing is to pull it straight out."

"I know. Go ahead.."

They were far enough away to feel safe from the firefight that could still be heard around the cemetery. Perhaps this was an illusion, but it was a necessary one. A small, white house stood across the road. Civilian refugees huddled confused in the yard. Devereux reckoned that the earlier fighting had flushed them from the town. "Go ahead." he repeated. "I recommend you pull on the big end." *Might as well try to..*

White grasped the little piece of wood and tugged gently. The portion above the skin broke off in his hand. "God damn it! I hardly touched it!" he exclaimed.

One of the refugees detached himself from the group. It was James Harrison, their fellow spy. He crossed the dirt road, between passing army vehicles, picking his way through the stream of wounded making their way to the rear, leading a buckskin horse. "Hello, Devereux," he said in an offhand way. "I believe I can help with this," he said. "I actually studied medicine once, if briefly." He knelt next to White to look at the leg. "Ugly, but fortunately, just under the skin. I don't suppose a scalpel and tweezers are a possibility?"

"This is a Sanitary Commission wagon," Bill said after looking at Harrison for a moment. He rose to climb into the vehicle where they heard him searching among the boxes within. "Interestin' fellah," Harrison said to Claude. "Does he always look right at you like that?"

"Always."

"Interestin'.."

Bill returned with the instruments, a bottle of alcohol, and a shallow dish. He put them on the ground, and then poured an inch of alcohol into the dish on top of a knife and tweezers.

Harrison watched him. "What's your name?" he asked.

Bill looked at him suspiciously. "May I ask why, sir?"

Harrison laughed. "All right," he said. "If I need to have someone cut on me, I'd like to have you around my friend.. All right, why don't you hang on to Devereux. I have to lay open enough of this skin to get a good grip on that wood. If we don't get it out, it's blood poisoning for sure!"

"Bill White," Devereux replied. "That is his name." He set his hands on White's shoulders, to brace himself against the pain. When it came, the entire universe focused in his leg. Sweat began to run down his face, dripping off his nose into the dust. After a long thirty seconds, Harrison held up a narrow, bloody finger of wood. He threw it away. "This really should be sewn up," the scout mused to himself, while contemplating the long, jagged edged cut. "But, in the circumstances.." He shrugged. "You can let go now, Devereux." The subject of the impromptu surgery made a conscious effort to relax his grip.

Bill's face was set in grim lines which softened as Devereux began once again to breathe deeply, removing his white knuckled fingers from his friend's shoulders. "I'll find something to make a dressing," Bill said, disappearing once more into the wagon's interior.

"I presume you have come from, our side?" Claude rasped, trying to emerge from the narrow world created by the fire in his leg.

Harrison watched him curiously, conscious of how much he had hurt this man. "Yes," he said. "I found Longstreet the night of the day I left you. They were over near Chambersburg.. He took me to see Lee. I thought at first.."

"You thought what?" snapped Devereux, suddenly the superior officer.

"There appeared to be a certain reluctance to see me.."

Bill had reappeared with bandages. He set about the creation of the kind of field bandage which long practice had made familiar. He listened.

"Why would that be?" Devereux asked. Tension entered his voice.

"I don't know.. You don't think Lee finds such as we unpalatable, do you?"

"No. I don't believe that." *Christ, I'd better not believe that.*

"Well, Mister Claude," Bill. "You know Colonel Lee … He can be mighty starchy about some things. You remember the time Mister Jake and Mister Pat, they were shootin' partridge on Arlington out of season and Colonel Lee, he turned them over to the sheriff, and Mister Pat he was seein' the young Lee lady about then as I recall."

Well, I guess you don't trust him if you're talking like that, Devereux thought.

Harrison listened intently. "Bill, do you think General Lee would find what we are doin', dishonorable?"

Bill stopped work on Claude's dressing to look up at this strange white face. "He might, Mister Harrison. He might indeed."

"Well, we'll just have to take that into account, Mister Bill.. That's all there is to that." Harrison turned his attention back to Devereux. "Longstreet sent me in here yesterday, to see what I could …" Harrison turned his face up toward the whirring, whining sound of rifle bullets incoming across the cemetery hill. "I, don't believe I can get back through that.. There's just too much in between …"

Devereux looked at him. *No. I don't suppose you will,* he thought. The crowd of Union Army walking wounded coming back off the fighting front just beyond the hills made an arresting backdrop. "You'll have to decide for yourself," he finally said.

"Yes! Yes," Harrison mused. "I do conclude that it will not be possible for me to return.. See you in Richmond, Devereux!" With that, the scout swung up onto the buckskin. "Mister Bill," he said. "You keep the faith!" With that he cantered off down the road, scattering soldiers as he went.

The leg stiffened as the sun sank. A surprising chill set in. Firing died away with the light. They searched for some sheltered spot in which to spend the night, finally settling in across the road from the frame house with a wood behind them. The wood seemed infinite in its gloomy depths although an inspection of the map showed that a major road to Baltimore was back there a few hundred feet away. Through the dusk, they watched a growing stream of blue-black infantry and rumbling guns turn off the road from the south and make its way up the long grassy slope of the ridge behind the house. The crest of this gentle roll in the ground flowed south from the cemetery while tending lower and lower until it hardly could be called a ridge. Beyond its apparent end two improbably steep hills grew from the gentle farmland.

"They'll dig in on this," Bill said from his place in the wagon bed. "This is the best ground." He meant the whole sweep of relatively high ground from the cemetery south. The sound of shovels came to them in the clover scented air to confirm the accuracy of his opinion. Bill laughed at the clank of the tools on stones and the hoarse voices of exhausted young men committed to work in the darkness. "I am a prophet," he said.

Claude didn't reply. The rip in his leg hurt too much for small talk. He said, "Why don't you see if you can make us some kind of shelter on the ground with that tarp I saw in back of the wagon bed. I don't fancy sleeping on the boards in that wagon, but, it might rain." With that, he disappeared into the gloom, taking shape again in silhouette against the lamplight now glowing from the windows of the cottage.

He stood for a time listening alone in the darkness just outside the circle of light at the door of the house, listening to the voices. Soldiers coming and going jostled him in the shadows, apologizing for their clumsiness even as they felt his arms to outline the shape of this human obstacle. Their fatigue was a palpable thing in the air. It could be smelled on them compounded with the smell of horse and fear.

An argument began within the house. Voices rose. More than one person joined in a chorus of angry challenge. Words could be heard. "Open flank, damned Germans!" came through the walls clearly in one voice. Howard's unmistakable baritone replied in outrage. "We were let down by the cavalry once again! Buford! You should have prevented a surprise from the northeast! You say there were patrols there. Where were they? We would have seen them if they had fallen back before the Rebels!" A third, less distinct voice could be distinguished. It grew louder as the man speaking approached the door. An oblong of yellow light opened like a window into another world. Bearded, blue clad men sat about a wooden table in a room dim with cigar smoke. The dark form of one them blocked a clear view of the occupants even as he closed the door behind him and descended into the yard to stand beside two horses held in waiting by a cavalry corporal. The newcomer leaned against a rail.

Devereux listened to him breathe. The sound held the rasping irregularity that means weariness so deep that it may kill. In the moonlight Devereux could distinguish the single star insignia of a brigadier general on the shoulder.

The corporal's back swelled in heavy breathing, gathering volume as it filled with emotion. He looked at the other man in the dim light, leaning toward him, as if to see him more clearly. Words poured from him, unleashed by the injustice he had heard done to his leader. "We held back Hill's whole corps, General! Don't they know that? We lost half the outfit on those damn ridges!" Anger filled the soldier's voice. It rose in pitch and volume. "Anybody who thinks we didn't fight good today should come down and tell them that's left!" he shouted in a voice which would have carried much farther than the required distance.

There was a sudden silence inside the little building.

"Carpenter, that will do.." Buford said.

They moved off along the gentle slope, leading their mounts toward the south.

Devereux followed for fifty yards before speaking. "General Buford ..." He came up beside them in the night.

The corporal raised an arm as barrier and protection for his chief from this stranger.

They stood silent in the darkness, each man gauging the other's size and nearness. "Carpenter, some light," the general's voice commanded.

The soldier took hold of Devereux's arm with on hand, extracted a match with the other and lit it with a fingernail. The small yellow flame seemed immense. It made a ball of illumination which contained their three heads and those of the two horses.

"I know you," John Buford said at last. The small fire had extinguished itself. Its remains lay at their feet, a glow of red and orange, shrinking as they watched. "Where was it?"

"The White House. I met you there at an evening's smoker party."

"Of course, the banker fellow. Do you still work for Stanton?"

"Yes.. I am here representing him, actually.. What happened today?"

Buford sighed. "Ah, well." he said.

"We held the Johnnies 'till the infantry could come up!" the corporal said quickly. "General Buford picked the ground to defend. We stopped Heth's and Anderson's divisions. If it hadn't been for General Bu.."

"Carpenter, for God's sake, do you mean to sell me by the pound?" Buford asked. Claude could tell from his voice that he was happy that one of his men would defend him. *We all need a little human fellowship when the wolves circle,* Claude thought.

No one said anything for a minute.

Devereux tried to think through the veil of his weariness. The hypnotic, sawing sweetness of the insect noise of a summer night began to take effect. *I'll fall asleep standing here,* he thought. "What will Meade do," he asked?

Buford put one hand on his horse's neck. He rubbed the big animal slowly. The drooping head turned to him. "I have had this one two weeks, all of two weeks," he said. "Surely they will defend this ground, but, who can tell?"

Devereux picked his words with care. "I heard that business back there. I will speak to Stanton."

The weariness and resignation in the man showed in his voice. "As you see fit.. I will deal with my problems in my own way. I must find my troops. We left them some distance off. There is a problem with rations. Good night."

The sound of their going left him alone in the pasture. Scattered firing began somewhere beyond the ridge. It rose to a miniature crescendo, dying away as rapidly as it had come.

Bill's deep voice sounded from nearby. "Patrick is right, Claude.. You must not help such as Buford. Not ever!"

"Did you hear it all?"

"All."

"They made a wonderful fight, a wonderful fight. You know Anderson.. You know what his men can do! Two thousand dismounted cavalry stopped him and Heth. Astonishing!"

"They are our enemy, Claude. They are your enemy! I don't want them to fight well. Not ever.."

Devereux felt for his arm in the dark. "I know, my friend. I know.. You're right as usual, but My God it was a wonderful fight.." Hanging onto Bill in the dark for support, Devereux struggled to make his aching legs work well enough to carry him back to their camp.

Hoof noise on the road awakened them in the lean-to Bill constructed. There were just a few horses. Then there were many behind them. Devereux lit a match to look at his watch. It was four thirty. He listened a little longer, listened to the number of horses. "Meade," he whispered in the dark. "The army commander has arrived on the scene. It took him long enough." Without further words they rose to disassemble their shelter and make coffee.

After a few minutes, soldiers bivouacked nearby in the grass began to rouse themselves from the dew soaked ground as wood smoke and the aroma of the brewing coffee drifted away from the campsite to attract them. The spies made room around the crackling flame for them. Bill filled the tin mess cups as they emerged from haversacks. "Who are you all with?" he asked a soldier whose massive blue body stood before him.

"Headquarters escort. We come in last night with the Provost Marshal. This is mighty good.."

The next man held out his cup. "Hullo Bill," he said. "You don't make coffee as good as Snake, but it'll do."

Bill stood transfixed staring at the face in the early dawn light. "Johnny. It can't be you."

"But it is! And it's Corporal John Quick I am now. I always knew I had it in me to assume my proper role in life! Captain Devereux? It is good to see you, sir!"

Devereux stared at the Irishman. For a moment all he could see was the hulking figure in blue, then slowly he began to see the face of an old friend. *Kennedy said Quick changed sides after they were captured,* he thought. *He thought it was a trick John was playing on the Yankees. Are we in the bag, or does he just want to come back?* He looked at his coffee cup, then around the circle. "It's good to see you as well, John. I remember well the last time we met.. My brother was there."

"Ah, the lootenant! Cap'n, you'd have been so proud! A lovely boy. He brought us through the most Gawd awful business there at the end, most of us. A veritable Horatius at the bridge he was! I hope the Lord has looked over him."

"He was well, when last we had word."

"Yes, that is what Sergeant Kennedy said."

"Fred?"

"He and your brother Pat came in with us last night, from Emmitsburg. I saw them there, and we got reacquainted." *I should have known,* Claude thought. *This man's only loyalty is to his friends.*

Bill resumed his rounds with the gallon pot.

Dark figures swiveled their heads from Quick to Devereux and back, trying to follow the talk, trying to understand.

"And you?" Devereux asked.

"Ah! It's ready to go home I am. This has been an interestin' holiday. It was better than the other possibility. I was not lookin' for that, but, I want to see the old reg'ment. Sergeant Kennedy sent me to look for you."

"Lieutenant Kennedy."

"A lootenant he is now! My! My! We all rise in the world. He says I can come back. Is that true, Cap'n, is it?"

Devereux seemed somehow a smaller man, drawn in upon himself. *If I don't get this right, we're through,* Claude thought. He looked across the fire at Quick. "Can you come with us now?"

"Sir, my officer fell down in wonderment at the papers your brother is carryin' from General Halleck. The General-in-Chief no less," he said to the surrounding soldiery. "My officer, he says I should make sure you are well taken care of."

"Good. Go bring the others here."

Quick threw the remnants of his coffee in the fire. "Yes, sir," he said with an engaging grin.

A second later Devereux looked up to add a thought. Quick was gone.

The Second Day

Morning ripened into a fiery July day. From their sheltered position behind Cemetery Ridge the band of spies and deserters watched the comings and goings of Union batteries and regiments seemingly without number.

Devereux fretted. The noise of the fight sometimes reached them from beyond the higher ground. Whatever was going on beyond the cemetery ridge did not appear to be continuous. He walked to the house on the other side of the road twice. The first visit to army headquarters ended in a short interview with the army commander. Meade told him to go find a suitable hole in which to hide, that he did not want him killed in the immediate area of the headquarters.

Devereux replied that he could not do that, that he would be nearby throughout. Meade scowled and turned away. His second visit to the Army of the Potomac's makeshift command post came to a sudden halt as Colonel George Sharpe emerged from a building to find him in conversation with a courier still standing beside his winded horse. "What the devil are you doing here?" Sharpe asked angrily. "We are far too busy to fool with you now!"

"I, really can't leave, Colonel Sharpe," he said. "Stanton would not accept any explanation I could give."

"Stanton?"

"He sent me, I.."

"Don't bother explaining! I have grown accustomed to the distrust of our government!" His expression softened somewhat as a memory came to him. "We, some of us, appreciate the counsel you tried to give Joe in Frederick. Butterfield told us."

"I only wish he had listened. I was sure they would relieve him if he sent that telegram. *And I was terrified that he might not do it.* I presume that you are trying to judge the number of enemy troops present?"

"You know all sorts of things, don't you?" Sharpe said. "I suppose that it is inevitable that you know so much, given the circle you run in. Yes. I have three of my people in the loft of this hovel. We are piecing together information from every source we have, comparing it to the field records which travel with us in that wagon over there.."

Inspiration struck. "My brother is a notable student of military affairs" Claude said with enthusiasm. "He is with me at our camp across the way. If you need some additional help in what you are doing."

Sharpe contemplated the man before him. In his mind a prudent desire to reject the offer was strengthened by the suspicion and dislike he felt for Devereux. He knew well the story of the way in which this strange man had killed Lafayette Baker's investigations. He exulted in Baker's humiliation and expected that Baker's enmity and backbiting might for a time be inhibited by the experience. For that he felt that he should be grateful to Devereux. At the same time, he cringed at the apparent ease with which the security chief had been defeated. Among his other concerns was his rather exposed status as a former member of Hooker's staff, an intimate and close friend of the deposed chieftain. He weighed the factors, and finally decided to play it safe.. "I'd be glad to have him.." he said.

And so it was that Patrick laboriously climbed to the loft to join three junior officers struggling to know the truth of Lee's army. Their slips of paper and maps covered all vertical and horizontal surfaces. In the heat of the little building's upper room these young gentlemen were not disposed to question the availability of another brain to be applied to their task. Patrick's encyclopedic knowledge of military organization and quick grasp of the simple methods of their work soon made him a member of the group. Before an hour passed, he knew that he had found his metier. His leg counted for nothing in this. The mind that might have made a memorable commander could perform such feats of deduction in constructing order of battle from fragmentary information that all else faded into insignificance.

About two o'clock in the afternoon he made a sudden leap of reasoning based on cavalry reconnaissance and old prisoner examinations. "Kemper's Brigade," he said abruptly, breaking the concentration of those around him.

"What?"

"Kemper's Brigade.. They were around Chambersburg until late yesterday afternoon."

"Why do you say that?"

"A courier from Captain Dahlgren's cavalry raiding group says they took a prisoner near there at about 4:00 P.M.. The man said he belonged to a company called the Marion Rifles. Your files say that is another name for the Virginia Rifles. He claimed to be from Bristol.. That's not possible, unless he was a conscript. The Virginia Rifles are actually Company "B", 3rd Virginia Infantry.. A prisoner examination file you have from eight months ago clearly states that the 3rd was still in Kemper's Brigade."

"If that's true," one of them said.

"Pickett's Division could not be here yet!"

"That's right," George Sharpe answered. He had come up the stairs, having heard the first part of the exchange. "But, if I know the roads, they could be here soon!"

Patrick measured the distance on a map, using his hand as a protractor. "In about two hours," he said.

"I'll tell Meade," Sharpe told them, starting down the steep stairs.

"Well done!" commented one of the lieutenants.

"Thanks." Patrick answered. Pride filled him until he remembered one of his classmates from VMI who was now major of the 3rd Virginia Infantry.

That day, beyond the cemetery ridge and the mile long expanse of grassy field that separated the armies, the Rebel leaders sought to discover what might be done to bring about the final, mercifully complete destruction of Meade's great host. They tried to devise a plan which would give them the climactic victory their country desperately needed. Throughout that day Lee struggled to make his army function in it's customarily loose jointed, but deadly way.

There was something wrong, something missing. Perhaps it was Stonewall Jackson, gone forever to his rest "across the river." Perhaps it was the heat. Perhaps it was something oddly absent in Lee himself. An objective observer on the scene might well have asked why so skilled a soldier allowed a situation to occur in which his smaller force coiled itself around the outside of the enemy's long, strong, position. He might have questioned the decision reached by Lee this day to seek to coordinate in time two massive blows at opposite ends of the enemy's convex line of battle. The geometry of this effort might have raised eyebrows. Above all, he could have asked why Lee wished to continue attacking at all since such attacks would inevitably risk the destruction of what could not be lost, the troops themselves.

After arguing unsuccessfully against renewal of offensive action, Dutch Longstreet tried all day to bring his two available divisions to the south, to put them in place as one wing of Lee's intended double envelopment. Nothing worked very well. Guides became lost, generals lost their tempers, horses foundered in the heat. Nothing worked well, nothing. Late in the afternoon, a young staff officer suggested to Longstreet that it would be well to move faster. He remembered for a long time what the lieutenant general had said. "I have no intention of doing anything with one boot on.." Longstreet did not wish to continue to attack. The truth was that he did not want to make this attack. He had argued against further assaults that morning. The old man would not listen, could not seem to see anything but Meade's army spread before him as on a banquet table.

Between and around the armies, in the places where the first day's fighting had been, men and horses rotted in the sun. Their body cavities swelled and filled with the gaseous products of their decomposition. The sound of an obscene flatulence carried across the landscape. The lucky had been killed more or less instantly. The rest sank into darkness after an eternity of pain and loneliness. Across the field the endless process of killing wounded animals continued. This was the only anodyne available for their misery.

By late afternoon, Longstreet was ready. At last, John Bell Hood and Lafayette McClaws had their men in place at the south. Richard Anderson's troops of A.P. Hill's corps stood ready to their left to support the attempt.

It was 4:00 P.M.

Just then, Pickett's Division arrived on the field as unwilling spectators and bystanders to the coming attack. They had marched steadily and rapidly from their last bivouac near Chambersburg, thirty-odd miles away. George Pickett asked Lee to include his men in the afternoon's attack. The offer was declined, and they were forced to watch from the edge of the woods on Seminary Ridge as the rest of First Corps went forward without them.

At the northern end of the lines, beyond the town and Culp's

Hill, "Baldy" Ewell's Second Corps waited for the right moment in which to strike Meade's right, waited for a moment when that end of the Union position would have been weakened in moving men to stop Longstreet in the south and center.

It was time.

With the "Whup! Whup! Whup!" of the Rebel Yell building across the brown ranks, Evander Law's Alabama brigade trotted out of the woods along the Emmitsburg road. They were the southern end of the attacking Confederate force. Their commander pointed at the crest of the big, tree covered hill before him. No one in Law's Brigade knew the locals called it Big Round Top.

To Law's left, the Texas brigade loped forward across a small space of open ground. Colonel Jerome Robertson led them forward, moving fast to stay ahead of his band of human wolves. They all thought he kept up well for a man who had been a medical doctor.

Farther along the line were "Rock" Benning's Georgians and Barksdale's hellion Mississippians.

They all went in together, as Longstreet had demanded, all except Pickett's men.

Bill White heard it coming first, heard the yelling somewhere inside himself. To see better, he and Devereux and Kennedy walked up the back side of the ridge that ran down from the cemetery. They stood with the gunners and drivers of a battery, just next to a small patch of trees.

Off to the south, the screaming, demonic, banshee voices were tangible presences in the fields and woods in front of the Round Tops. The Union artillery was there in the woods. They fired at first in volleys, and then as rapidly as the individual guns could be loaded. At the same time, the volume of small arms fire grew and grew. Groups of cannons were heard to fall silent in the midst of firing. It was clear what the sudden cessation meant. They were gone, out of the game forever.

In the middle distance to the southwest a force of Confederate infantry swept across the fields toward what looked like an orchard.

Federal artillery and infantry waited there.

The brown line halted to deliver a volley. All the artillery horses went down at once. They seemed to have been struck by the gods. The gunners paid no attention and stood by their pieces, loading and firing until the banshees reached them..

Devereux sensed motion around him and looked to the right, across the open fields to the west. There were yet more Southern infantry coming out of the woods across the valley.

A restless, shifting, turning movement set in among the soldiers around them.

"Let's be gone," he told his men. They walked back down the slope to their little camp. John Quick and Bill took the horses farther back into the woods. Devereux found shovels and a pick axe in the wagon. He and Kennedy began to dig holes big enough for five men.

Beyond the ridge, the maniac sound of battle crept steadily to the north. Incoming Confederate artillery fire began to search the fields and woods around the campsite. The fire originated in the Southern held territory beyond the town. Time passed imperceptibly, twisted into a pattern particularly suited to the moment, to the incessant hammering of the big guns. The battery among whom they had stood on the cemetery ridge opened fire at targets to the southwest. Devereux remembered that there was a group of farm buildings and a red barn beside the road in front of the ridge in that direction. The range from the battery to those buildings would be only a few hundred yards. He stopped work on the hole, handing his shovel to Bill. "I'll go for Pat," he said while scrambling over the lip of the excavation.

As he climbed awkwardly out of the hole, he felt the cut from the splinter wound open and wetness spread inside his trouser leg. At the same time, action on the hill to the left of their former position with the battery caught his eye. The blue soldiers on the crest were moving back in a semicircle. They began to fire their rifles at something beyond the ridge.

A brown line surged over the crest. There were perhaps two dozen riflemen and a handful of officers. Among them was a big man with a long beard. He was conspicuous in grey. At his side was a soldier bearing the familiar, square red flag.

Union men closed in.

In an instant the ragamuffin infantry were gone. Nothing was left of their momentary presence but a number of inert forms scattered across the hill. The

Union troops on the scene continued to fire at the unseen backs of the retreating enemy.

Devereux looked down at Bill. "Did you recognize him?"

"No, he was none of ours. Not from our division."

Claude went to Meade's little headquarters, seeking his brother. He there met with a rebuff.

"They're busy," Sharpe said. "We will protect him."

Ewell's supporting attack began at sundown, two hours too late to do any real good. Early's division carried the top of the cemetery hill. Jubal led the assault himself. At the same hour, the old Stonewall Division fought its way into the Union Twelfth Corps' trenches on Culp's Hill just behind Devereux's camp.

Somehow, it all counted for nothing.

A Union infantry division streamed back from the cemetery ridge to stop the advance on Culp's Hill, and no one came to help Early hold the cemetery itself. After several savage Union counterattacks on his position, he knew it was hopeless. With yet more bitterness and sorrow in his warrior heart, he pulled his men back off the hill to save them from certain destruction.

The moon had set when Patrick arrived to join them.

Two army headquarters clerks came along to help if he had difficulty in the rough ground.

He took his place by their fire.

They watched the soldiers' backs disappear in the dark.

"What time is it?" Patrick asked.

"11:30," Kennedy responded.

"There was a council of war tonight," Patrick told them. "I could hear it from upstairs. They all voted to stay and fight. All the corps commanders. Meade accepted their opinion."

Bill's steady gaze held him from across the fire. "Is our regiment here?"

"Can't tell. They know Kemper and Garnett are present with their brigades, but there is no sign as yet of Armistead and Corse. You just can't tell. You don't know what you don't know. Just about all the rest of the army is here, just about all."

"Ours or theirs?" Quick asked.

The fire crackled, spat, and hissed.

"I should go to Richmond when this is over, Claude."

"Why?"

"I now understand exactly how they do it, how they figure out the strength and location of an army. It is really very simple, just a matter of keeping the right records and thinking the whole thing through logically." He laughed. "Maybe that's why we didn't come up with this ourselves. Too logical. It might make a big difference, Claude."

Devereux watched his brother across the fire.

Patrick was looking at him strangely, hopefully.

The older Devereux smiled. "Good. Excellent idea! I think you should leave tonight, you and Fred and Johnny."

"No! Not without you."

"Rubbish! The more people we have here.."

"The captain is right," Quick interjected. "Someone should leave. The more people, the more targets.."

Devereux looked around the circle of faces.

None would meet his eyes.

"Will no one go?" he pled.

Kennedy lit his pipe from the fire with a twig.

"Very well," Claude whispered. "Tomorrow we will spread out across the back of the line to see what can be learned that might be of use."

Patrick held up a forefinger. "I forgot something.. At the end of the council Meade said he believed that Lee would attack tomorrow in the center, there!" He pointed at the low mass of the ridge behind Meade's headquarters. The rough outline of the group of trees at the crest stood out clearly in silhouette.

"Did he have some reason to say that?" Kennedy asked. There was real anxiety in his voice. He could not have said why he was disturbed by this news, unless it was the intimation of real talent on Meade's part.

"No. No. I think he was just guessing.."

The Third Day

Sharpe's men came for Patrick at dawn.

Claude protested, and tried to persuade them that his brother was both exhausted and ill, but they took him anyway.

They watched the group disappear into the interior of the small house. Throughout the morning the remaining four men labored at the task of improving their shelters. The pits began to look like trenches.

There was a peculiar calm across the battlefield. Nothing seemed to be happening during much of the morning. Devereux thought of walking into the woods behind their position to climb a big tree to see exactly where the line between the armies might be. He seriously considered this several times, but decided against it. Bill changed the bandage on his leg.

At about 1:30 P.M., a Confederate artillery bombardment began. The thunder of a hundred guns preceded the rushing sound of incoming projectiles. Shells burst randomly throughout the shallow valley behind the ridge. The gentle roll of the crest must have been too much for the ranging ability of the Southern gunners. Most of the fire just cleared the top of the hill to beat the ground beyond. Solid shot streaked into view, zooming over the top to bound along the grassy hillside. The black iron spheres resembled nothing so much as the balls employed in lawn bowling. Several crossed the road, bouncing inches high at each impact with the earth. The cannon balls entered the wood line near the Sanitary Commission wagon. The nearest struck a three inch sapling, tearing it to bits and leaving the stump a mass of white splinters and shredded bark.

From his place in one of the trenches, Devereux anxiously studied Meade's headquarters. Men poured out of the building. It seemed impossible that so many men had found room to work inside. He watched as two soldiers helped his brother off the little porch. Patrick attempted to hobble along with them. They finally picked him up, carrying him toward a group of men lying on the ground halfway up the slope. At that spot the curvature of the hill caused there to be a terrain "shadow" that the Confederate fire passed harmlessly. Patrick and his companions took shelter in this ribbon of safe ground, prostrate while the shells struck below and behind them.

As was often the case, the army's animals paid a high price. The horses tied to fences around the headquarters house suffered terrible deaths. One solid shot killed three together. They lay in a row in front of the little white building.

It seemed endless. Devereux began to feel that all his life had been spent under a rain of explosives and metal balls. So great a weight of shot struck the earth near the two holes that he could not help but wonder if the bombardment was having any effect at all on the Union positions on the western side of the ridge. It went on for so long that he began to get used to it, began to accept it as a normal existence, his portion in life.

Federal artillery on the cemetery hill worked their guns under a steady pounding. The roar of their pieces served as counterpoint to the more distant reports of the Confederate cannon. As Devereux watched, a howitzer emplaced in the cemetery itself was struck. The barrel, wheels and axles of the piece flew wildly apart, uprooting headstones and throwing them wildly across the ground.

It stopped.

Devereux looked at his watch. The bombardment had lasted more than an hour. He looked at the ridge, and watched his brother and the men around him pick themselves up cautiously, slowly standing erect and turning toward the crest. They appeared to be listening to something. The Union infantry troops occupying the long hilltop must have heard the same sound. All heads more or less pointed westward. As he watched, Patrick got his crutches into action. He started uphill, toward the group of trees.

A mile away, across the grassy valley from the cemetery ridge, Pickett's Division lay waiting in the woods. They had come up to this position in the early morning hours. The officers occupied themselves with the usual business of placing the long lines of men in the order in which they would attack.

After that, the men lay down, pretended to sleep, or devoted themselves to the routine of preparation for a major action. They cleaned weapons, wrote letters, talked to their messmates and made final judgments on the comrades with whom they would go forward against the guns.

Jepson Thacker lay on his back looking up through the leaves and branches of a patriarchal and seasoned oak. He had the thick trunk of the tree between him and the Yankee guns. The smell of leaf mold and wood smoke hung in the air. He tried to keep his mind on the beauty of the forest scene through the long wait under fire. The 7th Virginia Infantry Regiment was all around him, stretching out to either side of his company. The company had stood the artillery fire well. Cannon balls had caromed through the trees for the last hour. From time to time one killed or maimed, but for the most part the soldiers simply stepped out of their path. The shrapnel from air bursts in the tree tops was a more serious matter. They had lost several men to shell fragments.

In the midst of it all, "Pete" Longstreet rode into view, going down the line, slowly passing them by on a tall black horse, looking at them with an odd, pale expression on his usually ruddy features. The black horse shied from the sounds of falling leaves and branches ripped off trees by passing solid shot. A sergeant in Thacker's regiment stood up to yell at Longstreet. "You damn fool! Do you think we need you to do this to make us fight? Get the hell out of here before you get killed!" Longstreet bowed his head to the man, and rode on.

When the barrage stopped, Thacker sat up and looked for his company commander. The captain stood fifty feet away talking to an officer from another company. Thacker just caught the end of their talk. "Oh! Here we go!" the other officer said. "Please do remember me to your cousin Sally! I haven't seen her since before the war.."

The captain walked back. "Get 'em up Jepson," he said. "I expect we'll be leavin' now.."

The regiment formed and dressed its ranks. Thacker saw General Kemper and his staff take their place in front of the center of the brigade line. This happened to be exactly in front of Thacker's company.

"Watch Morrison and Davidson," the captain said in a soft voice beside him. "I'm takin' everybody in today, everybody. If they drop out, kill 'em."

Thacker nodded. He checked his revolver to make sure none of the explosive metal priming caps had somehow been lost.

Claude came up the hill to stand beside his brother on the ridge just as the Rebel infantry began to emerge from the distant woods. He intended to remonstrate with Patrick against their presence, but the scene before them silenced him. "My God.. My God," was all he could manage. There was at least a mile of troops forming in front of the wood line across the valley. In the center of the line lay a triangular projection of forest. To left and right of this feature regiment upon regiment of the familiar motley brown figures moved into position, coming out of the trees and halting behind their leaders and flags. Somewhere, a band began to play.

From his post behind the company's two ranks, Sergeant Thacker looked up and saw the mile of open, gently rolling ground for the first time. He had been busy correcting the alignment when they first emerged into the sunshine. Now he saw it.. It looked like the surface of a dinner plate. The far lip of the plate was a low ridge with a small patch of trees in the middle. Union artillery and infantry covered the ridge line. A road with some farm buildings beside it ran across the plate about three quarters of the way to the trees.

Enemy artillery started again. The iron balls sailed through the air. One struck the ground in front of a neighboring company. It bounced into the ranks, tearing a hole in the formation. Men screamed in pain, screamed with the sound that came with the knowledge of irreversible mutilation.

In the ranks, the men began to talk to each other as they looked out across the landscape of their fate. "Gawd damn it!" one said loudly. "Who's got it in for us? I guess old Bobby Lee, he don't have no fu'ther use for us! Whut did we do to deserve this? Somebody's got it in fer us, fer sure."

A rabbit ran from cover in front of the regiment, streaking through the ranks into the woods behind the troops. A soldier in the front rank of Thacker's company sang out. "Run rabbit! I'd run too, if I's a rabbit!"

"Steady, boys! Steady!" the regimental commander called out.

With a crash of cymbals, the sweet song of fifes, and the barbaric rattle of its copper bottomed drums, a regimental band struck up a tune at the left of the division line.

Thacker could not at first see them. The forest of men was too dense. Heads turned toward the music, then swiveled back to watch for more incoming shells. The invisible band strode forward, turned to the right and marched down the division front toward Thacker's regiment.

He concentrated on the music.

> Stack arms men, pile on the rails,
> We'll build the campfires bright.
> No matter if the canteen fails,
> We'll make a roaring night.
> Here Shenandoah brawls along,
> There burly Blue Ridge echoes strong,
> To swell the Brigade's rousing song,
> Of Stonewall Jackson's way …

They passed before him. Their dress contained some elements of the finery of prewar militia elegance. Travel stained long white gauntlets, and a number of black frogged blue jackets were the most obvious relics, but in the main they wore the rough butternut of their army's true uniform. He tried to remember who had a band with them. He could not.

The drum major raised his mace. The band lengthened its stride, marching to its assigned place at the right of the line..

Thacker focused on a drummer in the rear rank. The mulatto bandsman played his instrument with great spirit, bringing the sticks up to a perfectly horizontal position at the level of his nose after each flourish. On his back was a red and black checked shirt. Across his back was slung a banjo.

The band moved away, out of sight. They played on.

> No matter if our shoes are worn,
> No matter if our feet are torn,
> Quick Step! We're with him ere the dawn …

Major General George E. Pickett rode out in front of his division. He brought the horse around to face them.

The band reached its proper place. The music stopped.

Pickett looked at his watch. He raised his head, filling his chest, and ordered the attack. "For your homes! For your honor! For Virginia! The division will advance. Forwaard! March!"

Four thousand, seven hundred officers and men stepped off on their left foot as the band struck up a new tune.

> There's a yellow rose in Texas,
> That I am going to see,
> No other darkey knows her,
> No darkey only me,
> She cried so when I left her,
> It like to broke my heart,
> And if I ever find her, we never more will part.

Thacker thought of his wife, thought of the fence he had not finished.

The men were singing. Pickett waited for the refrain.

> She's the sweetest rose of color
> This darkey ever knew.
> Her eyes are bright as diamonds,
> They sparkle like the dew.
> You may talk about your Dearest May,
> And sing of Rosa Lee,
> But the Yellow Rose of Texas
> Beats the belles of Tennessee..

The general turned in his saddle. "Left Obliique! March!"

The division pivoted on its right foot as one man.

They moved beyond some woods on the left. Thacker saw that there were more troops advancing there. The 45-degree turn would bring them together in one formation.

The Confederate spies stood among the Yankee army and watched the advance come on. The stand of trees was slightly to their right. Just to the front waited a battery of artillery. Fifty feet farther down the modest slope stood a stone pasture wall, three feet high. Union infantry stood elbow to elbow behind it, their regimental and national colors planted among them. More U.S. troops stood in solid lines along the crown of the ridge to either side of the Devereuxs. Claude knew his people should leave, that there was no good reason for personal participation in this tragedy. Nothing could have made him go.

"Why! Why!" Patrick sighed beside him. "There could not be a stronger position than this! Why!"

"What would you have them do?" Frederick Kennedy asked from beside him. The question reflected his confusion at the spectacle before him.

Patrick waved an arm. "This cries out for a night attack.. No one could lose his way here. Mon Dieu!"

Down among the infantry, behind the stone wall, the veteran riflemen stared at the oncoming line.

The distant band continued to play.

And here's to brave Virginia,
The Old Dominion State.
And here's to the bonnie blue flag
That bears a single star.

Hurrah! Hurrah!
For Southern rights, Hurrah!
And here's to the bonnie blue flag
That bears a single star..

A gunner in the battery before them shook his fist at the oncoming enemy, screaming "Remember Fredericksburg" at the Pennsylvania afternoon. *You're right,* Claude thought. *We shot you to pieces there, just like this. Now it's our turn, damn you!*

There were two major parts to the approaching column of attack. These corresponded to their original dispositions to either side of the triangular patch of trees. All the troops to the left carried the blue flag of the Old Dominion as well as the familiar red battle flag. Those to the right had only the red flags. As the Federal troops watched, the force with the blue flags made another 45-degree marching turn to bring it into perfect alignment with the rest of the column of attack. Artillery fire from the high ground at the southern end of the Federal position continued to tear holes in the alignment of the oncoming troops. These imperfections closed without interruption in the forward movement. The march across the plain before them had the perfection of a garrison review at West Point.

Among the blue riflemen behind the wall, admiration for what they were watching warred with murderous intent. A swarthy, mustachioed First Sergeant of the 69th Pennsylvania Infantry leapt to the top of the wall, waving his kepi at the sky. "Three cheers for the Johnnies!" he yelled at the sky. "Hip! Hip! Hurrah!, Hip! Hip! Hurrah!, Hip!...."

Thacker heard the cheering, wondered for a second if it meant anything. The brigade went down into another fold in the ground. In the bottom, they were out of sight of the fearsome position on the ridge before them. The guns to the right continued their terrible work, playing upon the straight lines as though their missiles were the balls in a grotesque game of billiards. They marched up out of the bottom, emerging from the depths as though they were new-made men sprung directly from the bowels of the earth itself. As they came up the slope, a collective sigh escaped them. The awful ridge seemed so close now.

The artillery forward gun line lay just ahead of the dip. Dead horses and men were scattered on the field. The cannoneers ceased fire as the infantry passed through the line, masking the fires of the batteries. Officers stood at the hand salute, their faces strained from the trial by fire they had just concluded. The gunners and drivers covered their hearts with their hats. "Good luck, boys!" they said. "We'll be with you as soon as we limber up! Don't stop for nuthin'!"

Thacker scrutinized his company commander. His stocky, farmer's body trudged steadily along. The man had not looked back since Pickett ordered the advance. It was blindingly clear that he would advance to the regiment's objective alone if they did not follow.

Thacker looked at the two "play-outs" he had been cautioned against.

One of them peered back at him.

Don't you do it! I don't much want to kill nobody today, 'specially you.

Small arms fire began to feel at them. The conical Minie balls whirred by in growing numbers. The infantry on the ridge fired at them by volleys. Men hit with the big lead slugs jerked backwards or spun crazily from the impact. Thacker stepped over a soldier named Herbert Jamison, a friend from home. He had gone down in the front rank and lay moaning, clutching his abdomen. *Too bad, too bad, a belly wound. Yer a goner fer sure..* "Close up! God damn it, Morrison! Close up!" Thacker bellowed at his company. *My Gawd, Herbert. Who will tend to your ma?*

Grasshoppers flew up in clouds from the standing grain as they pushed through it.

The band played on behind them.

The sun's low down the sky, Lorena.
The frost gleams where the flowers have been ...

They reached a split rail fence beside the road. There was another on the other side. The captain climbed through between the upper and lower rails. Standing in the dust of the road, he turned for the first time to look. A smile creased his homely face at the sight of them. A bullet hit him in the back, throwing his body forward into a fence post. It slid down the rough wood. The post pulled and tore the skin of his face. He lay motionless in the road, his feet pointed at the enemy.

Thacker dropped his rifle, kneeling to pick up the officer's sword.

The line climbed through the fence on the other side of the road. A group of farm buildings stood in the way. Thacker's company passed to the right of a red barn. The ridge was two or three hundred yards off now. The enemy infantry fired continuously. White smoke wrapped the hillside, drifting toward the attacking force. He looked left and right. As far as he could see, the troops still pressed forward. There were several thousand men left in the ranks. They now were all across the second fence. It looked like he still had thirty or so men on their feet in the company. The colonel commanding the regiment lay in the shadow of the barn, shot through the head. They halted just past the barn to straighten their alignment. A great, rumbling, growling began to swell from the ranks. Someone in the next company fired his weapon at the ridge. An officer yelled "No!", but his attempt to maintain the tight control needed in the assault was hopeless. The Southern infantry began to shoot at the ridge. Through the smoke, Thacker glimpsed the first rifle shot Union casualties. He watched some of the blue forms pitch back away from the wall.

The brigade started forward down a grassy slope. An officer raised his voice to be heard above the din. "Home, boys! Home! Home is just beyond that hill!" The men began to yell. The wavering shrillness of their battle cry was answered by the deeper sound of Union cheers.

The attack picked up speed through the smoke.

Thacker raised the sword, bellowing, "Come on, Come on!"

They trotted down into the bottom land at the foot of the ridge.

A battery behind the wall fired a volley of canister which ripped a hole in the regiment. Dead and wounded covered the ground to Thacker's left. Men dropped around him on all sides, kicking and clawing at the grass, victims of the point blank fire of the blue figures behind the wall.

He could now see the enemy despite the smoke. Their shoulders worked methodically in the familiar routine of loading and firing. A stand of colors dominated the section of wall in front of him. The national and regimental flags, stood there together. The regimental color shone a deep green. Upon it was embroidered a golden harp.

The line started uphill. They were taking fire from infantry farther south along the stone wall. Union regiments had crossed the barrier to turn and fire into their right flank.

Something hit him hard in the muscle of the left arm.

Some of the men around him were strangers. Things were getting mixed up. To his left, Thacker saw the Confederate assault roll up the slope. He reached the wall..

They all reached it.

The blue enemy started to draw back with the two flags in their midst.

One of Thacker's men lunged across the stony barrier to grasp the staff of the national color.

The red and white striped cloth writhed in the smoke and turmoil. A dark featured Yankee with the chevrons of a first—sergeant cried, "No, you don't, damn you!", and clubbed the Southerner in the face with his musket butt.

A soldier at Thacker's side bayoneted the sergeant.

The Rebel line of battle now stood behind the downhill side of the stone wall. Their riflemen loaded and fired with the skill and practice of long habit.

The Union infantry at the crest seemed shaken by the sight of so many of their enemy so close at hand, and protected by the solid stones of the wall. The blue troops began to look over their shoulders at the valley behind.

Thacker reckoned he had 15 men left.

Enemy soldiers began to appear on the hilltop in apparent flight from something happening to the left.

He looked in that direction. Blue and red flags surged across the wall in the area beyond the trees.

The battery firing steadily into the ground to Thacker's left was guarded by the remnants of the infantry pushed back from the wall. Small arms fire cut down gunners and infantrymen alike in the space around the guns. *Where's the Goddam' artillery?* Thacker wondered, looking behind him. There was no one at all behind the Rebel infantry at the wall.

A blonde young major from another regiment appeared at Thacker's side. He pointed at the battery.

Thacker suddenly saw the truth of it. The battery was the linchpin of the Union line. If it went, the whole center might fall apart.

The battery commander saw the major pointing at him. The man stood hatless in the sun, just behind his cannons. Blood ran down one hanging, useless arm. "1st Section! Action left! Double Canister!" he shouted. In response to his command, two of the guns began to spin on their wheels, manhandled around by brute force.

The blonde major hurdled the wall, sword in hand. "Take the guns! Take the guns!" he screamed at the men behind him.

Thacker stepped back far enough to get a start, and followed him over. What was left of the company went with him.

The two guns spun.

The day stood still as Thacker ran up the slope behind the blonde young man. The smoke seemed less dense. He watched the gun captain of the right-hand piece raise his arm as the men finished loading. Behind him, on the crest of the ridge, the Union infantry brought their weapons up in unison. Thacker's searching eyes found a little group of men in civilian dress. One of them leaned on crutches.

"Fire!"

Claude Devereux felt his heart stop. Through the smoke he saw the butcher's ground in front of the two Napoleons. The blonde officer's corpse lay broken on the grass. One of his hands very nearly touched an ironshod wheel. Behind him, the others were scattered, all the way down to the wall.

Farther up the ridge, beyond the trees, the Rebel attack surged almost to the crest. Human beings stood in ranks and fired at each other at ranges that did not exceed thirty yards. Men howled and rifle bullets whirred across the ground. It was clear that the moment of opportunity for Confederate success had nearly passed.

Devereux had his pocket pistol in hand. He looked about him for a worthwhile target. Major General George Gordon Meade sat his horse 100 yards away. He had just ridden onto the scene. The distance was too long, far too long. Devereux looked at Meade for a time. Glancing around, he spied a Springfield rifle on the ground a few yards away. He gathered himself up spiritually for the act that would surely be his last. He held his brother Patrick by the right arm. Kennedy had him by the left. Devereux thought of the aftermath of what he was about to do. He thought about the vengeance that might be sought. He thought of his youngest brother, and wondered if Jake lay on the field before them. He hesitated.

The shock of the strike of a bullet ran through the three of them. For an instant Claude thought himself hit. The sagging weight on his left drove a dagger of despair into his spirit. They laid Patrick out flat on the ground, a rolled up coat beneath his head.

The fight went on around the trees. It had become strangely unimportant. Bill ripped open the shirt. The wound was in the right breast. A bloody foam surrounded the hole. Pink bubbles formed and broke with each breath. The noise around them built to a crescendo. Abruptly, it was over. The men of Pickett's and Pettigrew's divisions drew back in a sudden, collective knowledge of failure. The broken fragments of the column of assault moved back across the field of death. For those farthest forward, there was no possibility of escape. They dropped weapons and raised their hands.

The victorious Federal infantry sat down in place to rejoice in their survival. Their captives sat with them, drained of life by their ordeal. There was much ostentatious sharing of canteens and tobacco with the defeated enemy. The prisoners had little to say. They mostly sat with their backs to their captors and watched the remnant of their comrades in their going. A Confederate colonel, taken prisoner inside the stone wall was brought at his request to the top of the ridge. He looked down into the nearly empty valley on the other side, and wept.

Patrick Henry Devereux died on Cemetery Ridge with so many of his countrymen. He lost consciousness almost immediately, sinking rapidly into a comatose state which ended in his final passage. Claude sat on the ground for a time with his brother's hand in his own, silent and withdrawn. Bill watched over him, guarding his own grief from those around him, afraid of what Claude might do. After a while, Devereux asked Bill to go for the wagon. As they waited for his return, a great cheering and huzzahing set in along the ridge. A cavalcade of officers rode south along the high ground. In the lead was a brigadier general, his red beard and hair flowing in the wind created by his passage. The general swept by, and as he passed, they saw that he and each of his staff dragged behind them in the dirt a Confederate regimental color. One of the riders passed so close to the four that the words "North Carolina," and "Sharpsburg" could be read embroidered on the flag.

Kennedy rose and found a rifle among the many on the ground.

"No." said Devereux.

Kennedy stared down the ridge at the departing horsemen. "Why not? I can hit the bastard between the shoulder blades from here! Why not, Captain?"

"Because you will die for nothing. He is one of many. His name is Hays.. He will pay. They will all pay. I promise you. I promise."

That night Devereux learned from Dan Butterfield that Meade would not attack, that the Army of the Potomac would rest on its arms in expectation of a renewal of Lee's offensive.

11:35 P.M., 3 July, 1864
(The Camp Behind Cemetery Ridge)

"Why do you think they will believe us?" Bill asked.

The question hung in the air between them. It probed the limits of their confidence in each other and those they served.

Devereux did not answer. He sat on the ground, cross legged, staring at the little fire on which they had set a can of water to boil for coffee. With one hand, he worked at arranging the burning pieces of wood to his satisfaction. The sticks hissed and popped as the heat drove out water. The other hand held the open silver case of his watch. "Tell them you come from me, from Hannibal." The two men studied each other in the unsteady, yellow light. They both knew how terrible was the risk.

Nearby, Fred Kennedy and John Quick sat with their backs to trees.

"Now, why would they take the word of a strange black man and an Irish deserter? Bill asked. "You know them, Claude. You know how bad this may be." White's eyes held no pleading, no expectation of a reprieve. In his heart he knew that Devereux would not relent, could not make a different choice.

"I must go home." Claude said as though the statement would explain everything. Patrick's body lay ten feet away, wrapped in a rubber army ground sheet. His boots protruded from one end of the covering. It was unacceptable that he was gone. Bill had caught himself making a mental note to tell the dead man that one of his heels was broken.

"I cannot cross the lines," Devereux continued. "The risk to our mission is too great. I probably could not get back."

"And Lieutenant Kennedy?"

"I have something for him to do in New York, something that will not wait." He looked at Kennedy. "Johnston Mitchell. His time is come. You will not forget?"

Kennedy shook his head.

Bill smiled for the first time this day. The expression held no joy. It reflected his relief that Devereux's mind still served him. Bill stood in one motion, stretching his arms toward the starlit sky. Squaring his shoulders, he looked down at his friend. "Remember his boys, and my children." With that he went to kneel beside the body to say goodbye. John Quick rose to join him, crossing himself as he took his place.

1:00 A.M., 4 July
(In Gettysburg)

"Halt! Who's there!"

The voice had no substance. It seemed to exist alone in a world of dimly seen buildings, a world filled with curbstones over which to trip.

John Quick prodded the man in front of him to his feet. The Union soldier had fallen in a clatter of mess gear and oaths.

Bill tried to make his voice carry to the Southern picket line ahead, but not to the Union outposts through which they had just come. "Don't shoot! Scouts returning with prisoners! Don't shoot!"

An ominous silence filled the space around them.

He leaned to the right, finding a clapboarded wall with his shoulder. *There must be a doorway somewhere along here.* He held his own prisoner tightly by the collar, pressing the muzzle of the revolver into the man's cheek. "Don't you make a sound, none!" he whispered in the ear. With that he flattened himself against the boards, waiting for a hurricane of bullets to sweep the narrow alley.

"You fellahs want to surrender?" the voice asked. "You had enough of this nasty old battle?" The voice was round with the warm, honeyed tones of the deep South.

"Nuthin' like that, Sor!" Quick cried out. "Two scouts with prisoners.. You've got to let us in! They hear! They'll be comin' behind us, for God's sake!"

The murmuring of several men could be heard..

"Come on in then," the voice instructed. "Single file.. Hold your weapons high above your heads. Don't do anything sudden!"

"Move!" White hissed, pushing his captive out into the middle of the narrow street with the muzzle of the gun. "Move your Yankee ass right down to that man, you hear me?"

The Union soldier groped cautiously ahead, feeling with his feet for obstacles. Bill looked back.

John Quick was just behind. He had the other prisoner by the scruff of the neck.

Nothing could be seen of the men with whom they had spoken.

Bill's prisoner came even with a crossing alley.

"In there, to the left," the familiar voice directed from somewhere nearby.

The Northern soldier hesitated.

"Go, damn you! He won't ask again!" White urged.

A new voice announced its presence from cover in a doorway just to Bill's left. "That's right, y'all move along now. I do believe your friends may be followin' you.."

Fifty feet into the alley, the unseen soldiers became tangible presences about them. Groping hands deprived them of the means of resistance. A hard grip just above an elbow guided Bill onward into the darkness. The man pulled him around a right-hand turn as they moved forward at a pace which displayed the familiarity of their captors with the town. The street seemed to widen slightly. The moon appeared for a second. It showed them to be surrounded by the wooden fences of the back yards of two streets of row houses. There were six men with rifles guarding them. The floppy hats had a terrible familiarity.

The moon slid into an envelope of cloud, but before it disappeared, the light showed them to be headed for a wooden stable standing behind the biggest house in the street. A yellow glow outlined the door and seeped between the rough boards from which it was made. One of their escorts pulled open this door to reveal stalls, a hayloft and a central space now occupied by several men grouped around a table on which stood the lamp. The guards herded the four into the straw-covered space before the table. Someone closed the door.

The aroma of horse filled Bill's head. Fear began to fill him as well, swelling in his chest like an India rubber balloon. He concentrated on the men at the table. There was a major, a sergeant-major, and, at the left, a brown bearded figure slouched in a kitchen chair. The three gold stars of a colonel glinted on the man's open collar. His hat, sword and pistol hung on a nail in a post.

The sergeant in charge of the prisoners stepped to the front, releasing Bill's arm in the process. He was a sandy blond, skinny man with a large Adam's

Apple. His pants were ripped, baring a hairy leg. He spoke in his soft voice. "Eve-nin', Colonel. Cap'n Brown passes these along to you with his compliments. They just come in down by the square. They's two scouts and two pris'ners.."

The colonel looked at the group. He held a steaming china cup in his hand. Gold rimmed spectacles were perched on the end of his nose. He had been read-ing something on the square table when they arrived.

Absurdly, Bill found that he recognized the pattern of the cup as one which could be found among the many in the Devereux pantry. The handle was miss-ing.

"Which are which?"

His regimental commander's question caught the sergeant by surprise. "Why, this fellah is the scout," he said, once again gripping Bill by the sleeve. "And the big Paddy is the other one." He trailed off in puzzlement, having now seen both White and John Quick in full light. He turned to look at the remaining two.

They stood quietly, dejectedly. Two dark men of medium height, they appeared resigned to their fate, taking little interest in the exchange. Like Quick, they were in the uniform of Union infantry. A first-sergeant's stripes marked one soldier's sleeve in white.

The Confederate sergeant leaned closer to examine Bill's face. His pale blue eyes searched the prisoner's features. Wonderment came over him. "I never saw a n—r so like a white man. We've got a lot of colored folks down home in Ala-bama, but I never saw nuthin' like you." He slowly released his grip, stepping back for a more distant look.

The colonel rose and approached, carrying with him the glass-based oil lamp. He stood in front of Quick, inspecting him carefully. "You claim to be in charge?"

John Quick's mouth opened and closed twice. His voice seemed to have failed in the presence of this unknown senior officer.

Bill suddenly grasped the situation from Quick's point of view. A slip which revealed him to be a Confederate Army deserter might result in summary execu-tion. "We both work for the Secret Service Bureau, Sir," he offered in the hope of diverting attention.

"Shut up!" rapped out the major from his seat at the table. "The colonel aint talkin' to you yet."

"Answer my question!" the man with the lamp insisted.

"No. No. I would not wish to deceive you, Colonel. Bill White, here, he is in charge.." Quick's face worked desperately. "Mister Dev.."

"John! No!" White exclaimed recklessly.

The major came up out of his chair, and around the table.

The colonel stopped him with a wave of the lamp. "You just stay where you are. Don't be so touchy, Henry. I believe I can do this all by myself."

The big, red headed man stood at one end of the table, leaning on it with one white knuckled fist. Fatigue and frustration showed in his face. He stared at Bill.

The colonel turned from them. "Jones. Bring the other two over here." He looked at the two Union prisoners in the golden light. "Turn around, all the way around." he said.

They rotated through 360 degrees.

"What in hell are you?" he asked.

"American soldiers!" the first sergeant proclaimed defiantly in a heavy German accent.

"We're all American soldiers, my Teutonic friend," the Alabama colonel replied. "Specifically, who do you belong to?"

There was no answer.

The sergeant-major had watched silently, but now offered a thought. "You don't have to put up with this crap, Colonel. Let Corporal Jones take 'em outside for five minutes. God damn foreigners! They got no business mixin' into this."

The second prisoner spoke up. "We are uff de 108th Ohio Infantry, Herr Oberst. Company "C," spezifically."

The German first-sergeant said something short and guttural.

The Alabama colonel looked inquiringly at the man who had addressed him.

The soldier shook his head. "You vud not be interested. Meine nahme iss Sigmund Rosenfeld. The sergeant iss, upset. He feels hiss duty, ztrongly, in dis."

"And you do not?"

"I tink I must try to live to be egschanged. Dere vill be more chanzes to fight you. I do not vant a private talk mit dat man!" He pointed at the major.

The colonel laughed aloud. The lamp threw kaleidoscopic shadows on the walls.

The stable door opened behind them.

A major general walked through the crowd into the circle of light thrown by the lamp. All those present stood in recognition of his presence. A tall, slender young man of elegant bearing, he peered at the group of four, leaning forward slightly to do so. Having seen them all, he took the colonel by the arm to lead him away.

"This is twice tonight, Sir," the colonel remarked. "I am beginning to believe you think we may have some difficulty here before morning."

"Not at all, Buck, not at all. I'm just restless, after all that happened. God knows what tomorrow will bring."

"General Rodes," White said softly.

Robert E. Rodes turned back to look at him again. He stared for what seemed a long time. "I know you," he said finally.

"Yes Sir, you do. I met you in Lexington. Mister Claude Devereux was there at Washington College. I was his, valet."

"Pat Devereux's brother?"

"The same! You and Patrick were classmates at the VMI. The two of you would come by Mister Claude's rooms on Jefferson Street to have a drink of a Saturday night."

"How have you been, Bill?" Rodes asked.

Ten minutes later John Quick and White left the stable en route to Lee's headquarters. The Alabama sergeant who had brought them in as prisoners now served as escort. As the three strode forward through the darkness, he wondered aloud. "Now, Bill. This scoutin' bidness has a good sound to it. How does a man get into that line of work?"

35

Judah

Monday, 21 September
(City Point, Virginia)

Moving slowly in the sluggish stream, the grey side wheel steamer picked its way among the moored river craft, creeping along toward the single pier. Tall stacks spewed black smoke from boilers buried in her vitals. A swallow tailed white flag of truce hung from the jackstaff, a U.S. Navy ensign trailed limp over the stern. The river lay flat and oily in the humid day. Across the wide James, scattered farms were visible amid the forests and fields. In the pilot house, the ship's officers squinted at the water, absorbed by their perpetual search for snags and submerged logs.

Exchanged Rebel prisoners crowded the rail, eager for the land, eager for their freedom. Their malnourished bodies had profited from a period of forced residence in the North. Space on the surface of the main deck was reserved for a group of canvas and wood litters. Union army medical corpsmen and a surgeon sat on hatch covers and the deck itself alongside their patients. The majority of the litter cases were missing legs. Most of the men missing an arm or hand stood looking at the land with their comrades.

A Union Army colonel emerged from the pilot house. He stopped in the doorway for a moment to thank the ship's captain for his hospitality, then took a place among the Federal military men at the hurricane deck rail where he gazed down in silence at the prisoners. A thoughtful expression spread across his features. He watched with interest their growing rowdiness as the ship approached the quay. Behind the river bank ahead, the familiar outlines of scattered farm buildings could be seen. There seemed to be more public buildings now than he could remember.

Solemn faced officials waited on the shore. Two middle-aged men in frock coats and high crowned hats stood in front, with two soldiers behind.

When the navy crew had finished the job of securing the steamer, the colonel walked down the gangplank behind a civilian colleague. The stern, clean shaven man in the lead wore black.

The prisoners waited impatiently on board, watching from the rail.

The two emissaries of the government of the United States halted in front of the Confederate group waiting at the end of the pier.

One of the Southerners stepped forward. "Welcome to the Confederate States.."

The civilian visitor held up a hand in protest. "Mister Colston, I have told you on the occasion of previous meetings that we will take no action nor make any statements which imply recognition of the existence of your supposed government, constitution or, president. Is that clear?"

Colston shrugged impassively. "Yes, I know. Shall we proceed as is customary? Good. Who will act for your side?"

The U.S. government delegate turned slightly, indicating with a gesture the army officer behind him. "Colonel Devereux is here today as military commissioner of exchange. He will make whatever arrangements are necessary."

"Very well, Davenport," Colston said while redirecting his attention to the blue figure. "Colonel, may we get on with the landing of our men?"

Devereux nodded impatiently, more interested in Harry Jenkins' presence in the reception party than in anything else in the scene. "Certainly, why not? Are ours ready?"

An unfriendly looking brigadier general told him that the Union Army men awaiting release would be at the pier in half an hour.

"Hmm! You are customarily more prompt," said Davenport, frowning.

Colston smiled widely. "Could we offer you some refreshment? The day is warm … We could repair to the parlor of this house.." He pointed to a rambling farm house a short distance away. The building had not seen the business end of a paint brush for some time. "I know the owner."

"This is not a social gathering. I believe I will wait on our vessel. Colonel Devereux, make the required arrangements. Do not enter into any agreements without consulting me!" He turned abruptly away, walking briskly back up the gangplank to the ship.

The Confederate prisoners watched him uneasily, afraid that some whimsical disagreement might delay their release.

The remaining commissioners of exchange watched him go, waiting for his disappearance into a cabin on board.

"Shall we get on with this?" Colston asked, taking Devereux by the elbow, and gesturing toward the path which led to the white frame house.

The Confederate general following behind asked if the trip from Fortress Monroe had been pleasant.

"Yes, a lovely day," Claude said. "Do you know the place well?"

The grey haired man attempted a smile, a process limited somewhat by the adhesions of a massive white scar involving one side of his mouth. "I was posted there for some years, in the Old Army."

They climbed three rather fragile wooden steps to enter the central hallway of the house. An open door to the left led them into a dining room. On the oval table lay a variety of papers covered with the careful script of clerks. Devereux looked down at them. He opened the satchel he had carried from the ship to produce similar documents. He looked at the general. "Are yours correct? So are mine. Let's sign."

The scarred man was momentarily taken aback, but responded with a lopsided grin of relief. An adjutant produced pens and ink for completion of legal transfer of custody of the groups of prisoners.

"Well, that's that!" Colston said brightly, as they finished the last of the papers. "General Oates, why don't you see to the details of this? Major Jenkins and I will entertain our guest."

Claude held out his hand as Oates started for the door.

The grey figure stopped to stare at him. The three stars and wreath on the collar dominated the room. "No," He said. "Courtesy does not require this of me. If you were a genuine Yankee, perhaps, but I will not shake the hand of a renegade Virginian." He bowed slightly, then disappeared through a door held for him by his aide. The door closed behind them.

The silence in the room was oppressive. "I am terribly sorry, Devereux," Colston murmured.

"No. No. It was my fault," Claude said. "I should have thought." He lowered his hand, and blinked, surprised that Oates' refusal had hurt so much. "What would you have done if Davenport had not gone back into the ship?"

"We did not know, but it seemed likely, given his calculated nastiness."

"In any case, it worked," Jenkins interrupted. "Come, Claude, he is waiting."

They crossed the hallway to dark, wooden double doors. These opened into a large room furnished as a parlor and study. Heavy drapes obstructed the view of the river. They billowed with the breeze from the water. Judah Benjamin sat in a swivel chair at a roll-top desk. His angelic countenance brightened as they entered. Rising to greet them with a broad smile, he took the spy by the hand. "Good to see you, Devereux, good to see you. I have so looked forward to this meeting. The president asks me to give you his thanks for your brilliant accomplishments in the public service, few have managed so much, and as well for the tragic sacrifice your family has borne."

Devereux bowed his head in acknowledgment, then took the indicated chair, holding the scabbard of his sword across his lap. "We have only a few minutes," he said. "I won't waste time. We want to know something, Mister Secretary, all of us."

Benjamin was attentive.

"Is it worthwhile what we are doing?" Claude asked. "My family, my men, we are all engaged in an enterprise of, some obscurity, some vagueness of purpose. We know our efforts have been of help to the army in the field, but I sense, we sense that you intend more."

"Devereux, we are all acutely aware of the risks you run, every day." Benjamin smiled.

The blue uniformed officer eyed him coldly.

Benjamin seemed discomfited by the intensity of the other man's attention. "The army is deeply grateful for your information," he said. "General Lee says that at Gettysburg your help was of great importance."

"Yes. Yes. We know that. I want to know what it is that you now think about the task you gave me. Gettysburg was another defeat. Vicksburg is lost. The Republicans have gotten through the Draft Revolt in New York. What do you think we should do, can do to help stop this rot?"

"I think you should stop seeking information of direct use to our military forces," Benjamin told him.

Sitting to one side, Jenkins opened his mouth to speak, then thought better of it.

"Why?"

"You are an instrument of our history. Your success leads me inevitably to the belief that we should employ your talents by attempting to directly change that history through your actions. You should not continue to risk everything by seeking information which cannot change the essence of things."

"That's a bit much, sir," Jenkins protested.

Benjamin bent slightly at the waist. "You do not deny that such activities are a great hazard, do you, Harry?"

"I take your point," Devereux said quietly. "I have been thinking much the same thing myself. We will end much of that, although I reserve the right.."

"Of course, of course.."

"What is it then that I should try to do?"

Benjamin leaned forward in the characteristic gesture that showed the approach of a turning point in his conversation. "Your reports read very well. Yale leaves its mark. Among their strengths, you would say that their economy cannot be stopped, and that their resources in men are endless ..."

The blue man agreed.

"This leaves the world of politics. Have I left something out?"

"Start enlisting blacks!"

"Yes! Yes! I am working on that. Unfortunately, this matter lies within the realm of our world of politics, but General Lee agrees as does the president. I have hope in this, but it will take more time."

Jenkins spoke, impatient with the civilian. "The Democracy, Claude, I believe it must be them. The general election of next year will be our greatest remaining chance."

Devereux considered that. "It is possible that we could do something with that. Many, many people are against the war. If there is more heavy fighting, with great casualties, and no real gain for the losses, if there is yet more interference with the civil and political rights of the citizenry, it is possible. It is especially possible in the Middle West."

Benjamin beamed. "We thought as much. Very good! Very good indeed! There you have it, a blueprint for action!"

"And then there is Lincoln, himself.."

"Yes, as head of his party, he must be discredited with the rest. That should be possible, given the man's reputation for buffoonery and extreme measures."

Jenkins held up a hand. "He doesn't mean that.. What do you mean Claude?"

"He is the glue that holds them together against us," Devereux answered. "They are such a disparate lot, our Republican and War Democrat enemies, that without him, and his relentless determination, they would have come apart as a coalition of groups long before this.."

Benjamin frowned, leaned back into the shadow. "What do you suggest? There are limits.."

"Are there?" Devereux asked, and then shrugged. "I suggest nothing. I merely make the observation. Keep it in mind."

"Your commission in their army was something of a surprise, Claude," Jenkins offered.

Devereux smiled unpleasantly. "Not to me! They have offered several times. There are certain advantages. I am assigned to the Secretary of War's personal staff.. The only difficulty has been in preventing medical examinations by their doctors, but we have managed thus far."

"You are a symbol of their hope for the restitution of the Union.." Benjamin breathed.

A knock on the door took Jenkins out to speak in low tones in the hallway.

"I presume that I am not your sole reliance in these political matters," Devereux asked.

"No, there are others and you will be told of them, as it becomes necessary. Do you have, friends who can be called into service to help in this undertaking?"

Devereux thought about that. "I do indeed. There are some intriguing people in Indiana, and there is an actor I am looking at. There is also much that still can be done with the immigrant workers of New Jersey and New York."

Jenkins returned. "They are almost finished. You should go now. The Secretary has something to show you."

"Ah yes!" said Benjamin. "I was saving this for last." He found a sheet of paper on the desk.

Devereux took it and read. "Harry," he said. "You know what this is?"

"I drafted the order. You are promoted to the grade of major and commissioned in the regular army of the Confederate States, and assigned to duty in my office."

"Congratulations, Major Devereux!" Benjamin intoned.

Devereux folded the order in half, then in half again.

"We will need that back, Claude!" Jenkins warned.

"No. No, I think not," he said with a shake of the head. "This will lie somewhere in the bottom of the deepest vault available to my family. Someday, someone will know to whom I was, in truth, a traitor."

He walked back down the path with Jenkins. The bright day spoke to him of life, of the promise that his life held.

The last Rebel prisoners were forming into ranks at the foot of the pier. They looked at him with hostility that need no longer disguise itself.

Beyond them were the blue coated warriors the ship had come to fetch. They stood in line to board the vessel. A captain called the men to attention and saluted. "George Myers, 14th Ohio," he reported. This is all of us. We sure are grateful.."

Devereux waved him off. "Let's go home!" he called out. "You boys want to go home, don't you?" The veterans raised their voices to the heavens.

The racket caused General Oates to come out of the house onto the rickety porch.

Devereux looked at him for a moment, then raised his kepi in salute.

Oates bowed stiffly across the distance.

Devereux pushed his way through the cheering soldiers.

They sought to touch him as he went, thanking him for their deliverance.

He went aboard to report the completion of the day's business to Davenport.

The End

Epilogue

The Adjutant and Inspector General of the Confederate States Army sat patiently, in dignified silence, to hear their report. The grandeur of his presence filled the room with an aura of civic virtue and hard work. The monastic simplicity of the setting was perfect. The Mechanics Building held all the War Department offices. This one was no different from the others. There were flimsy, temporary walls, a black pot bellied stove, an engraving of the president on the wall.

General Samuel Cooper was the most senior of all the officers of his country's armed forces. A member of an early class at West Point, he was old enough to have fathered almost every officer of that army. Born in New York, he had served for decades in the offices of the Secretary of War at Washington. When Lincoln was elected, Cooper was Adjutant General of the United States Army, a position which made him responsible for the careers of all serving officers. He knew them all intimately, and was held in awe bordering on terror by those who dealt with him. When he resigned and went South, many went with him.

He had an impressive face. A high, broad, forehead showed blue veins beneath the ruddy skin. White hair framed features that were both strong and refined. "You say he kept the order, the paper itself?" he asked after hearing the report. Exasperation warred with amusement in the old man's face. In the end, the bold-faced defiance of the deed triumphed. The multitude of smile lines on the map of his face came into use. "Well.. What can you expect from these gentlemen volunteers? I should have learned to anticipate such foolishness by now, and not have allowed you to persuade me to sign the damned thing!" He waved a hand expressively in dismissal of the whole business. The grey eyes fixed on a red-haired officer among the men now in his office. "Jenkins.."

"Sir?" the man replied a little warily.

The regal grey figure had the power to command absolutely undivided attention. Jenkins was at a place in his life where few men had much call on his respect. The old man behind the table was one of those remaining.

"How is he?" the general asked.

"Claude?"

"Of course." The elegant white head tipped slightly forward. One hand tugged at a wing of his collar.

Jenkins looked tired, or maybe desperate would have been a better word. "He looks older every time I see him," he said. "This business of ours with him is killing him a little at a time.. His brother's death sits heavily on his conscience, and now, now he wears their uniform, their wretched rags ..." He stopped himself, suddenly seized with an image of the man across the table as he had looked when dressed in blue.

Cooper looked up. "Claude wanted to be a soldier. I remember him when he was a little boy. He would come to the house with his grandfather, who was the most capable man I ever knew. We were great friends. Claude would have been a good soldier, is a good soldier," he corrected himself. There was a moment of awkward stillness in the room. The old man never showed emotion of this kind. He was always the same; polite, attentive, demanding, immaculately dressed. The only signs of human weakness he had ever shown were his embarrassed attempts to advance his son's army career. It was disturbing, and unwelcome that he should visibly waver in thinking of what Claude Devereux must do, and be.

"Well, what did Benjamin say to him?" he asked. There was a sharp edge to the question. It spoke eloquently of interdepartmental difficulties.

Jenkins answered. "He gave him to believe that his task from now on was to seek some direct political action with which to change our, destiny."

Cooper brooded on this for an interminable minute. He pulled, and pulled at a collar wing. With a snort of disdain he looked at Jenkins again. "Damned fool!"

Jenkins, and everyone else in the room knew exactly who was meant. "Winder caught two of Baker's men here in Richmond last week, did you know that?" Cooper asked. The old general stared at him to make sure he knew.

Jenkins said that he had known.

"And did you also know that both of them had only one goal here, to find proof of Devereux's guilt!"

A hollow feeling filled Jenkins, expanding outwards from the small, cold place in which his deepest fears now lived. Benjamin had succeeded in convincing him that the meeting at City Point was not the War Department's Business, not something that Cooper should be told in advance. "What do you think we should be doing, sir?" he asked.

"We should get him out!" Cooper exploded. "He knows they are hunting him. He must know! It will make him desperate. He will.." The sound of the old man's voice trailed off. He seemed to see something off in the far corner of the room.

Heads turned, trying to see it for themselves.

The general sighed at last. "Go away, all of you. He is yours now, yours and Benjamin's." He shrugged. "Perhaps he is our best hope. God knows he will stop at nothing."

"Nothing?"

"He will take you where you fear to go. He is their greatest danger, and maybe ours as well. Good night. I have work to do."

Jenkins rose, dismissed.

The great, grey head was once more bent over the heap of papers.

At the door, Jenkins paused, unable to leave without a sign.

"And what will he do?" he asked

Grey eyes focused on him from behind round spectacles. "I remember now that he killed one of his childhood friends in a duel," he said. "1853, I think it was. An insult had been spoken, a great wrong shouted out to the world. There was no way out of it, and so the man died. Have you left him a way out?"

"No, we closed them all."

"Good night, Major."

Jenkins shut the door softly, and walked away down the echoing corridor into the night.

Some of the People of the Book in Alphabetical Order

Anderson, Major General Richard Herron, CSA. Commanding General of an infantry division of Lee's army.

Babcock, John. Colonel George Sharpe's civilian deputy.

Baker, Colonel Lafayette, USV. Chief of the National Detective Bureau and colonel of the 1st D.C. Cavalry Regiment.

Benjamin, Judah Philip. Secretary of State of the Confederate States of America.

Biddle, Lieutenant Warren Knowlton, USV. Amy' Biddle's nephew.

Biddle, Amy. An official of the U.S. Sanitary Commission Lodge at Alexandria, Virginia. A native of New Hampshire.

Booth, John Wilkes. Actor.

Bowie, Lieutenant Franklin, CSA. An officer of the Confederate Army Signal Corps.

Bradshaw, Lieutenant Forbes, USV. An officer of the 1st District of Columbia Cavalry Regiment serving as Provost Marshal of Fairfax, Virginia.

Braithwaite, Commander Richard, US Navy. Brother of Frederick.

Braithwaite, Elizabeth. Wife of Lieutenant Colonel Frederick Braithwaite, United States Volunteers (USV).

Browning, Major Charles, USV. The Provost Marshal of Alexandria, Virginia.

Buford, Brigadier General John, USA. Commander of a cavalry division. He chose the ground and set the agenda at Gettysburg.

Butler, Major General Benjamin, USV. The Federal commander at Fortress Monroe on the Virginia coast.

Butterfield, Brigadier General Daniel (Dan), USV. Chief of staff of the Army of the Potomac. The composer of "Taps."

Cline, Sergeant Thomas, USV. A federal cavalry scout and intelligence courier.

Cooper, General Samuel, CSA. The Adjutant and Inspector General of the Confederate States Army. The most senior officer by rank of that army.

Corse, Brigadier General Montgomery, CSA. Commanding a brigade made up of the 15th, 17th, 29th and 30th Virginia Infantry Regiments. Another banker.

Corse's Brigade, CSA. Confederate Army brigades were usually named for the officer who had first commanded them. An exception was the "Stonewall Brigade" which was named by act of the Confederate Congress and who claimed that the general had been named for them. He agreed. Corse's Brigade included the; 15th, 17th, 29th, and 30th Virginia Volunteer Infantry Regiments.

Davenport, William. An Assistant Secretary of War.

Davis, Jefferson. President of the Confederate States of America.

Davis, Varina Howell. His wife.

Devereux, Charles Francis. Banker and father of Claude, Patrick and Jake,

Devereux, Captain Claude Crozet, Confederate States Army (CSA). In civilian life a banker at Alexandria, Virginia. (Hannibal)

Devereux, Hope Prescott. Wife of Claude. A native of Boston, Massachusetts

Devereux, Lieutenant Joachim Murat (Jake), CSA. Brother to Claude and Patrick. In civil life a classics scholar at the University of Virginia, currently serving with the 17th Virginia Infantry Regiment.

Devereux, Patrick Henry. Claude's brother, also a banker of Alexandria, Virginia

Devereux, Marie Clotilde. Wife of Charles and mother of his sons.

Devereux, Victoria. Patrick's wife.

Early, Major General Jubal Anderson, CSA. Commanding General of an infantry division in Longstreet's Corps. Lee's "Bad Old Man," and one of the most underrated men in either army.

Ellis, Jefferson. A clerk in Major Browning's office.

Farinelli, Captain Marco Aurelio, USV. A foreign volunteer officer. A professional soldier.

Ford, Captain Wilson, Artillery, USA. A Regular Army officer assigned because of a disabling wound to the National Detective Bureau.

Fowle, Captain William H., Jr. CSA. Yet another banker from Alexandria, commanding Company "H" (the gypsies) in the 17th Virginia Infantry Regiment.

Galbraith, Lewis. Mayor of Alexandria under Union Army occupation.

Green, Thomas. Lawyer and Confederate political agent at Washington. (Sophocles).

Halleck, Major General Henry Wager, USA. General in Chief of the United States. A noted intellect.

Hampton, Brigadier General Wade, CSA. Commanding General of one of Stuart's brigades (1,500 sabers.) One of the richest planters in the South.

Hare, Philip. An agent of British Intelligence.

Harrison, Lieutenant James, Signal Corps, CSA. An actor and also a scout.

Hennessey, Terence. A civilian clerk at the National Detective Bureau.

Herbert, Lieutenant Colonel Arthur, CSA. Commanding the 17th Virginia Infantry Regiment. A banker.

Hood, Major General John B., CSA. Commanding General of another infantry division in Longstreet's Corps.

Hooker, Major General Joseph, United States Army (USA). The commander of the Federal Army of the Potomac.

Hunter, Sergeant Alexander, CSA. 4th Virginia Cavalry Regiment. The master of Abingdon Plantation near Alexandria, and a cavalry scout.

Jackson, Lieutenant General Thomas Jonathan, CSA. (Stonewall) Commander of the Second Army Corps of Lee's army.

Jenkins, Brigadier General Albert Gallatin, CSA. The commander of a cavalry brigade that did not normally operate with Jeb Stuart's division.

Jenkins, Major Harry, CSA. A staff officer of the Confederate War Department Secret Service Bureau in Richmond, Virginia.

Jourdain, Colonel Edouard, French Army.. The French military attache at Washington, D.C.

Kennedy, Sergeant Frederick, CSA. A Non-Commissioned Officer of the 17th Virginia Infantry Regiment.

Kruger, Father Willem, S.J. The pastor of St. Mary's Catholic church in Alexandria and Claude Devereux's confessor. A native of the Netherlands.

Lee, General Robert E., CSA. Commander of the Confederate Army's District of Northern Virginia and the army of the same name.

Lewis, Jim, CSA. A free man of color of Lexington, Virginia. Stonewall's camp cook.

Lincoln, Abraham. Sixteenth President of the United States.

Longstreet, Lieutenant General James, CSA. Commanding General of the First Army Corps of The Army of Northern Virginia. (Lee's army). An Army Corps was made up of three or more infantry divisions.

Marshall, Major Charles, CSA. An officer of Lee's staff

Mayo, Joseph. Mayor of Richmond, Virginia.

Meade, Major General George Gordon, USA. Commander of the Army of the Potomac at Gettysburg.

Mitchell, Major Johnston, USV. A volunteer officer assigned to Baker's National Detective Bureau where he is chief of counter-espionage operations. A newspaper man in civilian life.

Morgan, Lieutenant Thomas Cabell, CSA. Currently serving with the 43rd Virginia Cavalry Battalion (Mosby's Rangers).

Mosby, Major John Singleton, CSA. Partisan Commander of the 43rd.

Munford, Colonel Thomas T., CSA. Commanding officer of the Second Virginia Cavalry Regiment.

Neville, Major Robert, 60th Rifles. Assistant military Attache in the British Legation at Washington and an officer of British Intelligence.

Pickett, Major General George E., CSA. Commanding General of an infantry division (about 5,000 men) in Longstreet's First Corps.

Quick, Private John. (Johnny), CSA. Company "H", 17th Virginia Infantry.

Renfroe, Judge Caleb. An assistant Secretary of War in Washington.

Roberts, Sergeant Major Pierce, CSA. 43rd Virginia Cavalry Battalion, (Mosby's Rangers).

Rocklin, Henry. Hare's colleague.

Ruth, Samuel. Superintendent of the Richmond, Fredericksburg and Potomac Railroad..

Seddon, James A. Secretary of War of the Confederate States of America.

Seventeenth Virginia Infantry Regiment, CSA. This is the "Alexandria Regiment", an unusual Confederate army unit in that most of its members were urban people from the City of Alexandria, the District of Columbia or nearby Maryland. At full strength it would have had more than nine hundred riflemen formed into nine companies. The companies came from the pre-war Virginia militia or were created for the war. They included two companies raised from among the Irish immigrant parishioners of St. Mary's in Alexandria. Their priest blessed their flags at the altar there.

Sharpe, Colonel George, USV. Chief intelligence officer, Federal Army of the Potomac.

Simpson, Major Robert, CSA. Second in Command of the 17th Virginia Infantry Regiment.

Slough, Brigadier General John P., USV. The Federal military governor of occupied Alexandria.

Smoot, Sergeant Isaac, CSA. A soldier of Mosby's Rangers.

Stanton, Edwin. Secretary of War of the United States.

Stuart, Major General J.E.B., CSA. Commanding General of the Cavalry Division of Lee's army. Stuart's men usually numbered about 4,000 sabers.

Thacker, Private Jepson, CSA. A rifleman of the 7th Virginia Infantry Regiment.

Venable, Major Charles, CSA. An officer of Lee's staff.

Wheatley, Harrison. Partner in the firm of "Devereux and Wheatley Bank and Trust Company."

White, Bill, CSA. A member of the Devereux household now serving as lead teamster of the 17th Virginia Infantry Regiment.

White, Betsy. Cook in the Devereux household and wife and mother to all the Whites.

White, Private George, Jr., United States Colored Troops (USCT). Bill White's older brother.

White, George. Butler of the Devereux household, and father of the White brothers.

Wood, John. Manager of a hotel at Ashland, Virginia.

"Snake" Davis, CSA. An Alexandria man serving as head cook of Company "H", 17th Virginia Infantry Regiment.

978-0-595-47476
0-595-47476-4

Printed in the United States
153733LV00004B/163/A

9 780595 474769